St Kilda Dreaming

by

Paul Sharman

The Conrad Press

St Kilda Dreaming
Published by The Conrad Press in the United Kingdom
2025
Tel: +44(0)1227 472 874
www.theconradpress.com
info@theconradpress.com
ISBN 978-1-917673-08-2
Copyright ©Paul Sharman 2025
All rights reserved.
Typesetting and Cover Design by: Levellers
The Conrad Press logo was designed by Maria Priestley.
Printed and bound in Great Britain by Clays Ltd, Elcograf
S.p.A.

Prologue

Expecting to find Ossian, the surprised Victorian tourists found a community living in harmony with nature and each other. There was a good life here; each had their role to play. Young supported the old and work was shared according to ability. The homes evolved with the elements and after a particularly violent storm, could be repaired or rebuilt from island resources. We were not the supposed heathens, but our native reticence prevented us from telling them otherwise. Anyway, we spoke Gaelic, and the Englishmen would not have understood if we tried.

With the best of intentions, the wealthy visitors, from the south of England, started a trust fund to finance a street of modern cottages for us. We weren't so sure, but the first phase of the building project improved our traditional blackhouses. They were at least built end on to the winds sent to try our strength and resolve. As I said, we were not heathens and followed the ways of the Lord where we could, but the Church of Scotland still sent out missionaries to guide us, and our beliefs.

Reverend McKenzie led the building work; he wasn't a bad man though his God let him down in the end. His children died of tetanus as much as ours did, his wife tried a softer approach which enraged him, and he left us as a broken man. No wonder, he worked himself into the ground with only his Bible for comfort, but his walls still stand as a legacy to shared hardship. McKenzie did have enough respect for our culture and environment to build with the elements, not against them like his successor, Reverend Mackay. His only success was the new well dug at the end of the village. Our lives would never be the same again.

That Mackay, he just wanted to dominate us, filled our hearts with guilt and never lifted a finger to help on the land or repair a blackhouse.

During his time, we had new modern homes built. He liked to see the neat line of bungalows with their front doors and windows facing the sea, standing firm against winds that blew across the bay. Builders brought in from the mainland had no idea what or who they were dealing with; even disrespected their own God, ripping up our gravestones for building material.

Mackay's so called Christian religion broke us. Like fools, we abandoned our earthly delights in favour of paradise in the next life. Stories, music, poetry so important to us were thrown away in favour of his scriptures and unaccompanied plainsong.

Why did we fall for this madness? We even turned against nature, slaughtering birds on an industrial scale and poisoned our fields with their offal. We knew better, but it was hard to resist new ways imposed on us for fear of God's wrath, and that Mackay hadn't a clue about farming. Our run-rig system had never failed us, before we enclosed the fields around the village and its new well.

The new cottages were poor compared to our thatched blackhouses. Damp and hard to heat, we burnt peat, fetched from the top of the hill, just trying to keep warm and dry. We even had to buy coal from passing steamers when we could afford it. Condensation ran down the walls and when the winds blew, many a tin roof ended up in the burn.

It seemed personal, the more we modernised the more the wind undermined our lives at St Kilda. It became a nightmare and no wonder the young folk began to drift away.

4

War came in 1919, when we were shot up by a German submarine. Not much damage done to the village but once again men from outside tried to spoil our way of life. The skipper at least had the good manners to warn us of his intentions so we could stand clear, unlike the U.S. Navy missile that nearly brought the twenty-first century resettlement to an abrupt end.

By 1930, there were hardly any adults of childbearing age left on the island; when that young woman died of appendicitis, because she couldn't get medical treatment in time, it was the final straw.

We evacuated on twenty-ninth August that year, leaving only cats behind to fend for themselves as best they could. We loved our dogs but couldn't bear the thought of their having to adapt to mainland ways and regulations. Reluctantly we drowned them in the bay before leaving. Most of the livestock was sold to pay for our passage but out at Boreray and Soay, there simply wasn't enough time to collect the sheep before the boat sailed. Their feral descendants live on to this day.

Our island home became a private nature reserve before the government became interested and banned a way of life shared for generations. No birds or eggs were to be taken, not one field to be cultivated and not one ruined cottage to be rebuilt and, they forcibly insisted, not one family to return.

Then the military came. Male resettlement taking over where the ministers left off. Their buildings stood for everything wrong at St Kilda. Concrete blocks standing square against the elements; materials brought in from outside, even bricks all the way from England. They needed stone for the road they built and had the audacity to blast out a quarry on the slopes of Conachair, our sacred hill. Golf ball shaped radomes and tall masts were erected on the skyline, as if to provoke the wind and, like the tin roofs before them, many ended up blown into the burn. The terrorist attack demolished much of the remainder.

When the military finally left, defeated by the island, it was thought that Mothan in the water supply had caused their depression and anxiety. It was part of it, but alcohol abuse didn't help either. Away from the checks of family life, if not healthy, it was understandable. St Kilda had been an important tracking station for the Hebrides Missile Range, but the men couldn't get their act together. They tried to evacuate in an orderly manner but after the accident during the airlift, so much useful kit was left behind. We will make good use of that.

Mothan has grown in profusion since the climate began to change. Growing where the ground is wettest and most depleted of nutrients, the plant thrives on trapping unwary insects. Like the insects, the men would have been unaware of what was happening to them. Slowly becoming absorbed into the fabric of the island. As were we all, after we stopped drinking from the running burn and used the new well.

My family came out to St Kilda from Edinburgh, to be custodians for the Western Isles Trust. Due to the recession, they couldn't afford to employ another Warden.

There was an air-crash on the day we arrived, the pilot made the same stupid mistake as had other flyers before him.

We tried to make the best of it, but things just went from bad to worse, or so those from off-island like to think; those with no understanding of what it's really like here, living in a failed landscape. When will they learn that it shouldn't be like this.

It was a shame my father died like that. He thought he was joining the Angels; I hope he found them. Like Lot's wife, my mother turned back so it was only natural I took her place; the Bible justified what I did, though my sister wouldn't join me in his bed.

6

I did slit the throat of that stalker; it was a kindness. The Great Skuas, the Bonxies, would have torn his eyes out before disembowelling him alive. As for the police sniper, she asked for it, aiming at my sister when she was trying to protect us after the missile strike. The other policewoman was lucky to have only lost an eye.

I am going to try again; I owe it to my father and, when his child is born, together we will rebuild this island community.

Paul Sharman December 2024

1

Sabotage

The explosions at Mullach Mór were barely noticeable over the relentless dance video blasting from the 60-inch plasma TV screen in the bar. The only sign that something was wrong was the temporary dip in electricity supply as the secondary back-up generator inside the 1970s diesel power station burst into life.

On top of the hill, the main communication mast toppled across the newly refurbished radomes risen like mushrooms from the exhausted nineteenth century peat workings. A few seconds later a second explosion brought down the elevated radome at nearby Mullach Sgar.

Having heard the blasts, the Base Supervisor raced from his room. He leapt into the dark blue Land Rover parked outside the loading bay and roared along the sea front road toward the series of hairpin bends leading to the island summit and origin of the explosions. Skidding and almost losing control on the algae covered bend by the fire pond, he crashed the Land Rover down into low ratio before grinding at maximum possible speed up the series of 1:4 bends toward TOTH.

Top of the hill, a military acronym still used by the civilian contractors running the radar tracking station at the summit. Their main remit was to track Surface to air missiles test-fired on the Hebrides Range, their performance assessed against target drones of a type increasingly deployed in Mediterranean conflict zones.

With Stornoway Coastguard closed there was no need for suicide. The bomb team could execute their attack, destroy island communications and make their getaway before any alarm could be transmitted to the nearest responders on South Uist.

Suicide attack, they had been advised, would be better saved when attacking a crowded city rather than an isolated Atlantic island that, for most of the infidel nation, existed only in its imagination. The military complex on South Uist was well protected but out at St Kilda, 50 miles down range, the terrorists had taken advantage of an all too obvious security weakness.

The attack had been devastatingly simple. A series of small charges had been detonated to cut the steel cables guying the north-east side of the mast while further synchronised charges cut the steelwork at the base of the tower. The remaining cables steered the falling steelwork onto nearby radomes. Using a similar tactic, the broader tower on nearby Mullach Sgar had been blown down using the top-heavy weight of the radar installation as an effective lever. It would be a while before the tracking station would be operational again.

The small fishing boat had anchored unseen in Glen Bay, on the north side of the island. Using the sheltered anchorage, away from gale-force south-easterly winds common around St Kilda, the boat would not have seemed out of the ordinary sheltering in stormy conditions. But on this night the moon was full and the sea calm, ideal conditions to land unseen from a small dingy and quietly trudge up Glen Mór to the top of the hill.

With the island staff either in their rooms or drinking at the bar, the saboteurs from the mainland made their way virtually unchallenged on the thousand-foot ascent up the glen. Just the regular rush of wind as defensive Great Skuas dived at the moonlit heads of unwelcome intruders to their nesting territory.

No muffled middle eastern curses as the Bonxies struck at unprotected heads of the terrorists from mainland Scotland.

Urban disaffection in Edinburgh and Glasgow had ripened young men for indoctrination into a perversion of Islam that promised martyrdom in return for acts of political violence.

Jihadists, they called themselves. Inflammatory words from on-line Mullahs in the mountains of Pakistan inspired under-employed young men from the Central Belt to start secretive paramilitary training in the mountain landscapes of their own imagined nation.

Finding island communications wrecked, Derek began to shake. Like many working on the island, duty free alcohol had made him dependent. Reaching through the open passenger window he took out the quarter whisky bottle in the glove compartment to steady his hands with a dram before getting back into the Land Rover to drive back to the Base for help.

Without thinking he selected high gear ratio and covered the flat road between Mullach Mór and the T-junction at Mullach Geal in good time. Turning down hill and nearly rolling the vehicle at the first hairpin he realised his mistake and tried to push the small yellow gearshift back into low ratio on the move. Cursing at the protesting gearbox, the reduction gears slipped into neutral.

Before he could fully take in the speed of the freewheeling Land Rover it accelerated into the next and sharper bend. Fear took hold as he flung himself across the front seat and tried to get head and shoulders into the passenger footwell. Uncontrolled, the Land Rover bounced along the crash barrier until, at the end of the rails, it careered across the moor before dropping eighty feet to the quarry floor below.

The Base Supervisor died unnoticed in the broken remains of his vehicle while his team were buying yet another cheap round at the bar. Only in the sober light of morning would the full horror and implication of the previous night's events become clear.

After breakfast, a small team of technicians waited outside the loading bay for the long wheelbase Land Rover to transport them to the top of the hill. The mist on the hill shrouded the fallen masts from view as they joked and shared cigarettes. Aware that communications were down, sorting the problem would have to have priority that morning. Maybe just a fuse or two; at worst a damaged connection somewhere on the moor. Whatever the problem, they were experts, and it shouldn't take them long to fix it.

By nine o'clock the six men had been waiting thirty minutes and still no sign of Derek. Keith, one of the older hands suggested he checked Derek's room as they hadn't seen him in the Mess at breakfast either. He came back after a few minutes.

'Strange... he is not in his room, and it doesn't look like his bed's been slept in either. Well, we had better get up to TOTH and fix things without him. I'll go and get the old Land Rover from the garage.'

'Hang on a minute, I'll go and check the medical wing. He might be in there for some reason.'

Niall had a feeling that all might not be right, and Sally, the duty nurse ought to know. He returned with her looking somewhat perplexed. Apparently Derek had been noticeably reclusive of late, and she had been concerned considering his history of depression.

'I think we ought to treat this as a missing person incident,' Sally suggested. The men looked surprised but agreed that finding Derek should be the morning's priority. Comms could wait for an hour or two.

'OK,' she said. 'I need you to go to the top of the hill. One to stay in the vehicle and three of you spread out and check the Cambir and Glen Mór. The other two work your way back across Conachair and across to Oiseval.'

She sincerely hoped he had not taken his depression to the Gap, the scene of a fatal fall not many years previously

11

when a day-tripper had deliberately jumped off the three-hundred-foot cliff.

The search party needed one man to stay in the vehicle and relay radio messages back to Sally. Due to the mountain topography, battery powered VHF handsets could not transmit from one side of the island to the other. Sally was to stay at the Base and be ready to receive Derek as a casualty should it be necessary. She did not consider it necessary to call for Coastguard assistance just yet, especially since the closure of Stornoway meant they would have to fly from Aberdeen. If it turned out to be a false alarm the bill wouldn't be worth thinking about.

It was a squeeze getting all six of them into the old short-wheelbase Land Rover. The side facing bench seats had never been popular, especially when descending the 1:4 hill when the two foremost passengers felt the rest would end up on their laps. The rust-streaked vehicle sprung to life readily enough though. Like all vehicles on St Kilda, it was well maintained. For some of the shift mechanics, their work became a way of life. Certainly a few of the older men found unpaid overtime a more absorbing pastime than watching raunchy pop videos in the Puff-Inn.

The cloud-base on Conachair was just above the quarry. As the small four-wheel drive vehicle negotiated the first hairpin bend the mist became patchy. Passing the historic libation stone on the right of the road, an adjoining track entered the quarry giving a view to the foot of the rock face.

The libation stone at the entrance had historically been used for good luck by St Kildan women returning from milking in Glen Mór. Being mischievous spirits, Brownies were supposedly associated with this glacial boulder and failure to make a deferential gesture was inviting trouble.

Maybe the cattle would pick up mastitis or similar ill should they omit to poor a little fresh, creamy milk on the rock. Should the worst happen, the sick beast could be cured by application of a poultice prepared from the small mauve flowered herb they called Mothan.

The antibiotic poultice would be rubbed on the udder and good luck was said to come to anyone who drank the milk from a cow that had eaten Mothan. Climate change had brought mild, wetter winters to St Kilda and now the plant was flourishing as heavy rains washed out nutrients from the soil.

Mothan, known elsewhere as Butterwort or *Pinguicula vulgaris* is a carnivorous plant and survives poor growing conditions by trapping and digesting insects incautious enough to land on its sticky leaves.

A feeling of being similarly trapped and assimilated into the landscape had led to several military personnel being removed from St Kilda on mental health grounds.

Recently, a party of visiting geologists had been trying to ascertain the limits of ice age glaciation and had chipped off a sample of the libation stone for analysis back at the University of Edinburgh. Disregarding superstitious respect, their research had proved inconclusive. The island kept its secrets hidden and their research project proved an expensive failure.

Derek's vehicle was spotted lying on its driver's side. Keith drove the old short-wheelbase vehicle along the bumpy track to where Derek's Land Rover lay wrecked. Diesel fuel and spilled battery acid had given the surrounding wet ground a toxic, rainbow tinted hue. The anti-roll bar rested on a large stone giving a view of the bloodied side window, smeared with dried blood from the wound to the Derek's right temple.

A few flies were hovering around the sunroof, which had been burst open by the impact. Derek's left arm was curled over his head fixed in rigor mortis. There was no need to go to the top of the hill.

Keith radioed back to Sally who heard clearly what they had found. She asked them to return to the Base and collect her, along with a stretcher from the medical wing.

The subdued party returned downhill past the slippery bend at the fire pond. No one had noticed the Great Skua, the Bonxie, alight on the wreckage of the Land Rover as they drove away.

Sally shortly returned with Keith and Niall to the quarry. They would have to upright the Land Rover before she could remove Derek's body. Aidan volunteered to drive the articulated four-wheel drive loader up to the quarry and very carefully placed the forks underneath the Land Rover.

Assisted by its position lying against the large boulder, the twisted vehicle rocked over onto four wheels. Derek's body, frozen in a semi-foetal position, fell back across the front seats. The hand bent over to protect his head before he died was swollen and bruised from the blood that had drained into it overnight. It was not going to be easy to place his contorted body on the stretcher.

'There is going to be no easy way to do this', Sally said.

They should place him as he was in the back of the Land Rover. With the two men in front, she would sit in the back to try and prevent his stiffened body from toppling and further injury. She would call the Coastguard for help when they returned to the medical wing.

They had all been shocked by what they had found and were halfway back to the Base when Niall remembered all communications on the island were down for a yet unascertained reason.

Sally knew that the island's topography had in the past prevented VHF transmission to the Coastguard when they were based at Stornoway. She had always managed to telephone for help in the past. Now the microwave telephone link was down their only chance was the hope that a VHF handset might be able to transmit their call for assistance along line of sight from the top of the hill.

Turning round at the helipad they briefly called the others waiting by the loading bay. The radio message advised they would be going to the top of the hill to try and transmit a message to the Coastguard for assistance. Sally wasn't sure whether this would work but it was worth a try.

Keith drove the rusting Land Rover and its grim passenger up through the hairpin bends into the low cloud. It was the strange silence up there that alerted him to the fact something was wrong.

The wind always blew on top of the hill and the whistle from the mast anchor cables could be heard yards before reaching the radar station. Today even with a fresh wind rising to force six, through the mist they could hear nothing. Approaching the office building, he had to break hard to avoid the tangled mast and cables lying across the road.

'What? Oh, shit!'

The reason for comms failure became at once apparent. Keith leapt out of the Land Rover and ran to the fallen mast. He was a specialist radar technician and was so appalled he almost forgot about Derek's body still curled in the back of the vehicle.

Sally pulled the collar up on her light nurses' jacket and walked over to him.

'OK, Keith. Now we know what happened but not how. Presumably, Derek came up here to investigate last night, before he crashed on the way down. She placed her hand gently on Keith's arm. For now, let's see if we can get the Coastguard out to help us before even thinking about repairing this mess.'

She picked up the VHF handset from its cradle on the dashboard and selected channel 16 for emergency use only. Out of habit she called '*Stornoway Coastguard, Stornoway Coastguard...this is Kilda Base. We have an emergency... please respond...over?*' She repeated the message several times before remembering Stornoway Coastguard had been decommissioned.

It was when she called 'Mayday, Mayday' that the call was picked up by the retreating fishing boat and relayed to Aberdeen. By this time, the small fishing boat hired by the terrorists was nearly back to Stornoway.

Their pretence of an overnight fishing trip had to look realistic, so they had returned slowly to arrive back mid-morning. It was with grim satisfaction they heard the emergency call on channel sixteen. Omar, his name recently adopted, replied at once and giving his precise location using the boat's far more powerful transmitter to alert the Coastguard to the fatality at St Kilda. Smiling, he realised that in relaying the alert he had acquired a good alibi, should the need arise.

The Sikorsky S-92 lifted off from Aberdeen Heliport at 10.30 that morning crossing the Grampians before heading out over the Minches and onward to St Kilda. The pilot acidly remarked that since moving the operation to the east coast it took at least forty-five minutes longer to respond to emergencies in the Western Isles.

Arriving nearly an hour later, the Coastguard Helicopter touched down at St Kilda's tiny heliport.

Sally and the team of technicians were waiting in the glibly termed international airport lounge, the small concrete hut at the head of the landing craft slipway. Derek's body remained stiffly curled in the back of the Land Rover. His limbs had begun to soften which made it easier for the Coastguard paramedics to place him in the strong canvas body-bag. The body was examined, and an initial report form filled out. Obvious injuries were noted including his missing left eye and scratched face.

Sally was surprised she had not noticed this before. Neither had Keith or Niall when they found him battered and dead earlier that morning.

'Bloody Bonxies,' she muttered under her breath.

The Great Skua had entered the wrecked Land Rover through the open sunroof. Sally's swift return had prevented any further carrion feeding.

The large brown predatory seabirds had returned to the island thirty years after the 1930 evacuation. Hated by the men of St Kilda as egg thieves stealing their living, the ground nesting Skuas had been persecuted and driven from the island in the nineteenth century. As if remembering their historic persecution, Bonxies attacked all, especially male human intruders to their nesting grounds. Year on year, the Soay Sheep on the island sustained the rising population of these aggressive birds.

The Bonxies hunted like wolves, lambs were easy prey. They always took out the eyes first leaving the blinded victim to stumble around defenceless before ham-stringing the lamb and ripping out its living stomach. Had he not been found in time, Derek, lying dead in his wrecked vehicle, would have been just more carrion to be recycled into the island ecosystem.

17

2

Decisions

The Minister for Defence Equipment, Support and Technology was incandescent. He had not long approved another multi-million-pound budget to maintain the Hebrides Range.

The South Uist complex was the only site in the UK where the MOD could safely test tactical missiles and was by far the largest employer on the Western Isles. Time and time again he had received reports of alcohol abuse but always passed the problem back down for local management to deal with.

The current situation was a legacy of military culture when given the opportunity to cheaply drink yourself to oblivion, you weren't considered a man if you didn't do so. Duty free drinks had remained even though regular servicemen were rarely seen now at St Kilda. Crown tax exemption was still a perk confirming the island's reputation as a place to get cheaply plastered but they had really done it this time. A drink related fatality and a terrorist attack to boot. Ironically, it seemed the deceased base supervisor, an acknowledged alcoholic, had been the only one sober enough to respond that night.

Initial investigation confirmed most of the men were drinking in the bar while organised security at the remote tracking station had long been forgotten. Recent defence reviews recommended St Kilda's tracking capability should be transferred to the Aberporth Range, hundreds of miles to the south.

With the Watchkeeper programme successfully up and running the Aberporth team had admirably proved their worth. If they could remotely operate unmanned high altitude and long endurance aerial vehicles anywhere in the world, the Minister was struggling to find a convincing reason to continue funding St Kilda with its all too obvious psychological problems.

Isolating a small male community and providing them with cheap alcohol made no sense at all and was a health and safety liability for the MOD. If Aberporth were clever enough to detect dolphins playing with floating targets many miles out to sea and avoid blowing them out of the water, how could he justify penning up valuable human resources at the remote and outdated Cold War tracking station at St Kilda.

The men had seen it coming. Three months after the attack the news came almost as a relief. At least they now knew their periods of isolation on Britain's remotest habitable island were coming to an end. The Puff-Inn had been the first thing to close. With serial histories of alcohol related incidents, it had come as no surprise. This time with ministerial condemnation, the closure wasn't going to be the usual fortnight's restriction. This was going to be permanent.

Each time the bar had been temporarily closed there were assertions that the Base would lose valued employees with a catch all measure that punished the innocent majority for the irresponsible behaviour of a guilty minority.

This time, the terrorists had highlighted systemic rather personal failings and if they were to be honest the demolition of the tracking station offered an honourable way out of the trap many of the men found themselves in. The island had become a human pressure cooker. A couple of dozen men without female company on an orbiting space station would have fared little worse than the radar operators at St Kilda. They would be going home to locations as far flung as the Channel Islands even Malta.

A few of the older men reacted to the closure with sadness. Away from strained relationships and increasing chaotic mainland lives, St Kilda had become as much their island home as it had been for the thirty-six elderly evacuees departing aboard HMS *Harebell* on August 29th 1930. It seemed the military re-occupation in 1957 was coming to a similar demographic end. The military presence had become outdated along with its ageing staff.

In 1930, the St Kildans evacuated at their own request. The community had become too elderly to cope with the hardships of remote island existence. The Base employees were similarly ageing. The average age was around forty-eight and with many approaching retirement, St Kilda had become a very unattractive place for younger employees.

Not simply the age difference of an unbalanced team but coming from the mainland a lot of the young men and the occasional young woman were appalled to find regular heavy drinking despite repeated drug and alcohol awareness programs from their formative education. The Scottish Government had given priority to cutting down alcohol and drug related social problems but, on arriving at St Kilda, it seemed nothing had changed. Peer pressure to drink ensnared young and old alike.

For the younger men, Cold War fears of their older colleagues were hard to comprehend. The young men simply had no need to journey into a psychological wilderness to escape the sum of all fears, nuclear apocalypse.

Theirs was an imminent world and threats to be feared were more from terrorist attack or climate change. Suicide bombings killing or maiming hundreds in Edinburgh or Glasgow were tangible concerns.

Mutually assured destruction should nuclear armed nations of east and west square up to each other was considered history. For the young, the sum of all fears was to go through the educational system to find themselves unwanted by an economic system favouring unmanned production whenever possible.

Technicians were always going to be in demand but, due to what they saw as the irresponsibility of the middle-aged, highly educated young men and women feared already uncertain employment paths were closing to them, especially in the Western Isles. The likely departure of MOD personnel presented the St Kilda Trust with more than one conundrum.

The tracking station infrastructure could be repaired, updated and remain on Mullach Mór and Mullach Sgar but operated remotely.

For the MOD, the savings had to be considered against the cost of demolition and removal of demolition material from St Kilda. The rent would still have to be paid until the Base complex had been demolished and the ground restored, as far as possible, to its original condition.

In recent years, The Trust had insisted on the military infrastructure being painted olive green to minimise the visual impact. For modern visitors the buildings were a sensitive issue. Like the Victorians before, tourists came to have their pre-conceptions confirmed. Visitor information excluded any reference to the 1970s army base, but the first sight on landing had been the dilapidated accommodation block and diesel power station.

Campers spent their nights in Britain's most remote camp site listening to the throb of heavy diesel engines, their tents illuminated by the glare of sodium lights. A far call from the remote Utopia promised by the tourist industry.

Since the Land Reform Act of 2003, many overnight visitors took their tents over the ridge and wild-camped on the far side of the island. The slog over the top of the hill worth it for a peaceful night's sleep and away from the noise of drunken men and heavy machinery.

Recent modernisation of the base facilities included the sinking of a new borehole at An Lag. Crystal clear water now overflowed into the already boggy ground near the old well creating a botanical haven for insectivorous Sundew and Butterwort, the psychotropic Mothan.

The service agreement between MOD and the Trust provided the island Wardens with electricity and potable water supplies. They also had access to medical assistance should it be required.

On the odd occasion a visitor injured themselves, first aid was always to hand. The twice weekly helicopter flight from Benbecula brought mail and groceries from Balivanich and contact with the outside world. On days when bad weather prevented the helicopter flight, isolation seeped into the consciousness of all on the island. Since the destruction of the communication mast, internet access had ceased completely although the telephone link had been restored to pre-digital standards.

Without MOD facilities the Trust staff would find island life difficult. Not impossible, but with supplies coming in by tourist boat in summer and Coastguard assistance a telephone call away, the situation did not look too bad.

There had rarely been any Trust staff on St Kilda during winter months, it being deemed unnecessary to maintain a presence during the time of few visitors. However, as a responsible employer, the Trust was obliged to follow national health and safety at work regulations.

While the MOD was on the island, access to medical facilities, clean water, electricity and regular supplies were possible. Once the military had left this could not be guaranteed and the Trust human resources manager was beginning to have qualms about keeping staff on the island. Mental health problems were becoming apparent for its isolated staff, as well as for the military.

Concerns over dilapidated military buildings and staff facilities at St Kilda were not the only items on the agenda for the meeting in Edinburgh. At the Extra-ordinary General Meeting the Regional Factor had another big issue to juggle with.

The elephant in the room was reform to the Common Agricultural Policy. Since 2004 much emphasis had been placed on environmental cross compliance in return for agricultural subsidy. The Europe wide policy of supporting small farmers to stay on the land had been much abused but since Irishman Ray MacSharry held the post of European Commissioner for Agriculture there had been targeted funding for environmental conservation within the EC.

This had been particularly aimed at economically disadvantaged areas of western Europe and the Hebrides became a prime candidate for financial assistance for agriculture, nature conservation and community development.

The EU Habitats Directive had made funding available for co-financing of conservation projects. St Kilda attracted funding for its Wardens, administered by Scottish Natural Heritage, but since the global recession the situation was changing. The six-yearly review was rapidly approaching and SNH had been advised that co-funding of conservation through joint operation with the Trust on St Kilda was likely to cease due to changing social needs, Europe-wide.

The needs of Europe's remnant small agricultural communities had never been quite forgotten. They were the hidden and disadvantaged sector of rural society the Common Agricultural Policy had been set up to protect back in 1958.

Due to the current chaotic economic climate, the time seemed ripe to get back to basics. Funding of nature conservation, seemingly so important in the late 20th century now seemed an outdated luxury.

Brussels was arguing that European social funds should be used for supporting human society rather than nature which was considered quite able to look after itself. After all were not Europe's most precious habitats a result of past human management.

Greater emphasis was going to be placed on supporting small farmers to manage their lands in a sustainable manner. Gone were the days of unlimited inputs of tractor diesel and artificial fertiliser. There was a brave new reality ahead, an almost back to the future mindset was coming where everyone would have to live within their means and natural resources.

The Western Isles Trust was, for all practical intents and purposes bankrupt. That was the unavoidable conclusion to be drawn from the Extraordinary General Meeting.

For all the work of the marketing consultants, the letting of holiday cottages plus income from membership and investments were not going to make the books balance.

The Trust Director made his point to the stunned St Kilda manager.

'With Common Agricultural Policy reformed yet again, that fund is simply not going to be available to us. CAP once again insists European money is used to support the agricultural community to keep them on the land. Nature conservation must take second place; cross-compliance will shortly be a thing of the past.'

'To be honest we will need a small farmer to support on St Kilda. We certainly have enough sheep there to qualify but we must turn away from viewing the island as an open-air museum to becoming an agricultural holding once more.'

The St Kilda Manager rose to her feet. Josephine Miller had been juggling funding from Scottish Natural Heritage, Historic Scotland and rents from the MOD to finance conservation at the St Kilda World Heritage Site. Now the rug was being pulled out from under her feet.

CAP reforms meant funding would be targeted at social, not wildlife projects. Historic Scotland had been struggling for years since the 2008 banking crisis had shelved the Heritage Bill. This left archaeologists at St Kilda struggling for their share from the common pot.

If funding was only going to be available to support a viable agricultural community, she asked, what was going to happen about the Trust's obligations toward maintenance of World Heritage status on the island?

The Director continued his speech.

'As you are no doubt aware, World Heritage status is simply an accolade for the Trust. It does not bring any funding and adds to our financial burden. I, for one, would be happy to see St Kilda returned to a viable human community following the remit of regenerative agriculture. We may have a World Heritage Site on our hands but unless that brings in cash we might as well forget it.'

He paused and allowed Josephine to speak.

'If the future management aim for St Kilda is to support a viable agricultural community, where does that leave me? I am an archaeologist not a farmer. I also employ Wardens and archaeologists to protect the wildlife and cultural heritage, what about that small community?'

The Director continued, but to Josephine it felt like the decision to stop funding her work had already been taken.

'We must follow the funding trail and adapt our management accordingly. Otherwise, we won't be able to run a teashop, let alone a World Heritage Site. We have gone into this quite thoroughly and decided on a new set of objectives for managing St Kilda.

'But where does that leave me?'

Josephine was becoming visibly stressed.

'As you are already aware, your post is up for review this December, so we ask you to be flexible and possibly consider other opportunities. You have done a great job handling the logistical nightmare that is St Kilda. An agricultural tenant on the island will make management so much easier. However, we will still need someone to monitor integrity of our archaeological resource.'

He continued.

'To be honest, it's not really my area. I feel there is no imminent threat to the natural resources of the island that we can realistically manage; climate change is beyond our control now so, like other organisations, we will adopt an approach of managed retreat. We will just have to wait and see what happens. However, what we are proposing today is to employ a custodian family. They will effectively resettle St Kilda and, at least on paper, try and make a living from the sheep flocks already there. Yes, I know it's hardly likely to be an economic flyer considering the distance to market, etc. but the enterprise, unlikely as it might appear, will bring in much needed European funding until the economic climate picks up. The custodian will be given a strict tenancy condition to protect the island's archaeology and you, as our consultant, will be contracted to make sure that happens. It remains essential that, like everyone else involved with St Kilda, protecting our natural and archaeological heritage remains high priority. There will still be a policy of minimum intervention in the natural processes on the island archipelago. As before, the Trust's impact on the internationally precious island fabric must be kept to an absolute minimum.'

Josephine seemed preoccupied.

'So, you are telling me that my post is effectively to be made redundant in December?'

The strain was beginning to show around her eyes. She had already been suffering ill health brought on by conscious denial of the emotional attachment she felt for St Kilda. The personal attachment had always made delegation difficult. It sank home that she was now being asked to hand over completely.

'In so many words,' he replied. 'Yes.'

The meeting closed with a return to the usual friendliness between colleagues, but her eyes betrayed the intense stress Josephine was experiencing. Management of *her* St Kilda was being taken out of her hands.

The Director came over and with a sympathetic and genuinely friendly smile quietly asked her to give priority to placing an appropriate advertisement in the Scottish national press. Now that it seemed more than likely the MOD would pull out of their lease, the Trust had to pander to Holyrood's nationalism or risk further alienation from an increasingly impoverished Scottish population. Quite bluntly, unless the Trust moved their goalposts in line with the nation, there would be no more funding for any of their jobs.

3

Utopia

The village always looked bleak at this time of the year. The grass growing along Main Street cropped short by hungry sheep. Now, several weeks after the autumn equinox, brown tinged moorland framed the still green fields between the cottages and the sea.

The late greenness a legacy of excessive manuring with seabird offal and domestic waste in the late nineteenth century. Nothing had been wasted, human waste and kitchen scrapings valued as much as the cattle dung collected from the byres each winter. As the population aged, peat ash contributed less to the nutritious compost spread over the fields. The nitrogenous waste from the byres began to lose its potash balance as fewer villagers had the necessary strength or inclination to collect peats for their hearth fires in the final years of occupancy. Climbing fourteen hundred feet to the nearest peat on Mullach Mór had become beyond the physical abilities of most.

In the latter years of the nineteenth century, fit young adults began to drift away in search of an easier life. Following the First World War arrival of the military on the island the few young men still on St Kilda were tempted away by soldiers' tales from the outside. Young women too, left with more worldly new partners. It had been a genuinely sad day when on the twenty-ninth of August 1930, the villagers finally left for good. The final straw had been the death of young woman dying from appendicitis. The community had simply been unable to get medical help in time.

Under Trust management, family names are commemorated on discretely placed roofing slates inside the remains of their former homes, devastated by winter storms following the evacuation.

By the early twenty-first century, six of the cottages had been sympathetically restored to accommodate conservation volunteers, building contractors and the occasional tourist party. Sheep researchers, on island for around nine months of the year considered the rented cottages their homes. A long running research project brought a steady stream of students to St Kilda to study the ecology of the feral sheep flock abandoned by the departed villagers.

The six habitable cottages required ever increasing protection from the elements; winter storms strengthened with the changing climate, increasing in intensity year on year. The weather was becoming less predictable as the phenomenon of North Atlantic Oscillation meant that, sooner or later, the atmospheric jet stream would move, and weather patterns change for better or for worse.

Resistance to the elements at St Kilda always ended badly. The Warden had to consider the worst-case scenario when closing the cottages down for the winter.

As well as a thorough cleaning, felt roofs had to be re-proofed and the wire ties holding them down repaired. Inside anything perishable had to be removed and furniture either removed from contact with the floor or protected by placing wooden legs inside cut off plastic bottles. Tables wore waterproof boots to protect their wooden legs from water trickling through the walls and settling on the concrete floors. Just one of the problems inherent to the modernised nineteenth century cottages still battling against, rather than existing with the environment.

Another problem for the Victorian builders had been and still was the wind. With idyllic summer views across the bay, in winter the cottages stood four-square against south-easterly gales.

By the end of September, the Warden boarded the windows against elemental forces rarely experienced on the mainland. Chipped and eroded paint on these boards bears witness to the ferocity of winter at St Kilda. In between the boarded up 'white' houses with pitched roofs, chimneys and clean rooms stand 1830s 'black' houses. For the St Kildans, the timeless thatched Hebridean blackhouses evolved with the landscape to become capable of withstanding almost everything the North Atlantic weather systems could throw at them.

Oval in shape, these timeless homes had been built with double faced dry-stone walls filled with rammed earth, the roofs were thatched and orientated end on to the prevailing winds. The irregular surfaces of the walls helped to break the force of gales and in the living space a central hearth sent smoke up to preserve the thatch. Due to the smoky atmosphere, the interiors of these vernacular dwellings did indeed become black.

With the house cow over-wintering on the lower side of the cottage, Victorian tourists often reported having to clamber over a dung heap, also used by the human occupants, when invited inside. Each year thatch was repaired or replaced; the discarded material removed and added to the village compost system.

By the twenty-first century, very little remained of the old village, a nucleated clachan, visited by the English philanthropist arriving in 1812.

Avoiding the Mediterranean warzone, his romantic cruise brought Thomas Dyke Acland to discover a superstitious British community living in what he imagined to be illiterate squalor and poverty. The cash free community also come to the attention of the Church of Scotland.

Not long after Acland's visit, Dr John MacDonald landed in Glen Bay on a missionary visit to the community. He was to report back to the Church of Scotland in

Edinburgh and concurred with Acland that the lives of the inhabitants were much in need of improvement; not just physically and agriculturally but also spiritually.

Through his evangelism, Dr John MacDonald came to be known as the Apostle of the North. At St Kilda he found what he considered a semi-pagan community ripe for conversion.

With Acland's assistance, MacDonald raised money to build a kirk and Manse and appointed Reverend Neil Mackenzie as its resident minister. Enabled by outside money and Mackenzie's missionary zeal the St Kildans were persuaded to abandon their sustainable way of life in favour of a fundamental and puritan vision of the world around them. Architectural design, written scripture and a cash economy were readily adopted by the easily converted, some would say gullible, St Kildans.

Led by Reverend Mackenzie, the re-housing project sustained his vision of industrious manly virtue without desire for physical gain or female sympathy. The social tension and confusion brought by his nineteenth century restructuring of egalitarian village life sowed seeds leading to the voluntary evacuation in 1930.

In 1843, the Free Church chose to break away from the secular Church of Scotland. The event took place in the neo-classical church of St. Andrew in Edinburgh New Town. In challenging the secular Enlightenment, the Free Church was ridiculed and so sought to build religious congregations away from scientific contradiction.

At first resisted by the island's landlord, Macleod of Dunvegan, it took the unexpected departure of eight tenant families on thirteenth November 1852 for Macleod to allow the Free Church a foothold on the island.

Taking advantage of Macleod's assisted passage scheme to leave his Hebridean estate, they were not victims of Highland Clearance. Rather the eight families sought sanctuary in Australia where they believed they could follow their religious beliefs without secular persecution.

The ill-fated attempt to escape St Kilda led to almost all thirty-six voyagers dying from diseases which their isolated lives had afforded them no immunity and without the island's medicinal herbs, particularly Mothan, they had no way to treat even simple ailments as they headed toward a new life away from the unhappiness of their island home.

There would be no more escape attempts. The Macleod estate could ill afford to lose any more of its tenants, so the Free Church was allowed a foothold at St Kilda.

The Free Church patriarchal management of the island continued into the twentieth century when the loss of young adults to the mainland made the community unviable. The mainly elderly community evacuated their village in 1930 for what they thought would be an easier life on the mainland.

With the villagers gone, the island became first a private, then a designated National Nature Reserve. Like the Free Church ministers before them, twentieth century scientists could now work without interruption or fear of contradiction from inconvenient villagers.

Film maker Michael Powell was discouraged from filming on St Kilda for fear of encouraging emigrant villagers to return to seek employment in return for local knowledge.

Free thinking St Kildans were henceforth to be confined to postcard and myth. Julian Huxley, a naturalist arriving with the military advance party in 1957, encountered a returned native and recorded one *Homo sapiens* on his species list. Such was the detachment from human life that preceded scientific and military occupation of the island.

The enlightened and supposedly objective neo-colonialists were now detaching themselves from fear of contradiction on St Kilda as had the Free Church elders half a century before them.

Operation Hardrock, an appropriate name for the Cold War invasion, saw St Kilda as just that, a hard rock 50 miles out from South Uist. A place for manly virtues without softer distractions.

Hardrock came just five years before the Cuban Missile Crisis when any thinking person in the United Kingdom feared being caught in east-west nuclear crossfire. St Kilda provided both a listening station in the north Atlantic and a down range monitoring post for tactical missiles test fired from South Uist.

In the nineteenth century, St Kilda was considered *Ultima Thule,* Utopia at the edge of the British world. In a nation under threat of nuclear Armageddon, the late twentieth century saw the vision return.

Visitors arrived at the jetty after an arduous three hour crossing from Harris considered themselves secular pilgrims to an island reverberating with echoes of lost Utopia. Free Church members saw themselves as true pilgrims to the still consecrated village Kirk, even conducting the occasional service to reconnect with a purer Christianity.

It is said that tourists see only that which confirms their preconceptions, while the traveller explores the reality of their destination.

The Royal Airforce came as travellers in 1957. Their personnel arriving by helicopter shuttle and landing craft from Benbecula. It was considered important that staff did not stay on the island long enough to become new natives. Stay too long and the magic wears off. The illusion fades and the reality of St Kilda creeps in like the winter damp trickling through the thin walls of its Victorian cottages.

St Kilda gained the reputation of an almost holiday posting for the national servicemen sent out over the summer months. Few men over-wintered on the island due to difficulties of keeping them supplied.

Without challenge from women or children, St Kilda did provide a bastion of manly virtue sought by Mackenzie a century earlier.

Military planning created its own landscape. Arriving to have their preconceptions confirmed, tourists complained or consciously ignored the infrastructure. They had come to find Utopia, but the world-famous abandoned village was dominated by a Cold War military Base, equally devoid of family life.

4

Evacuation

Operation Hardrock spawned a culture sustainable for a few months at most in the emptied landscape. Only made bearable through duty free alcohol and in later years multi-channel satellite television.

The other side of this false Utopia was alcoholism. Lack of female company led to tension, sometimes physical confrontation, when women conservation volunteers first appeared. In response the transitory females formed distrustful cliques or became promiscuous. Towards the end, an easier option for the aging men was to drink in the bar and watch scantily clad dance divas gyrate across the large plasma television screen in the Puff-Inn.

The plan had been to evacuate the Base by the end of September, before the weather broke and winter sea conditions made landing craft crossings impossible.

The world had been a very different place in 1957 when the military launched their occupation. In the second decade of the twenty-first century the United Kingdom found itself in a subordinate position compared to the successful new economies of Asia.

Even the once powerful United States had managed to adapt and work with rather than stand against a world they had previously sought to dominate. In Britain, without political impact or effective military power, the ongoing economic crisis led to newly commissioned naval assets being sold off to defray sovereign debt. The scrapping of newly completed Nimrod surveillance aircraft had been just the beginning of the second phase of the scale-down of UK armed forces.

It was the last week of October when the RFA *Mounts Bay* anchored inside the shelter of Village Bay. Her sister ship the *Largs Bay* had already been sold for service in the Australian Navy.

That had been an outcome of the Defence Review of 2010. The only other available transport had been the *MV Randaberg*, successor to the red and white liveried *MV Elektron* lost in a North Sea storm a couple of years before. The commercial owners of the brand new *MV Ranadberg* had declined to send their flagship to St Kilda given the inglorious history of *MV Elektron* running aground there in 2000.

The *Elektron* had subsequently and mysteriously lost power and been towed back to port in inexplicable hurricane conditions. Salvage costs had come close to making the owners insolvent. All commercial shipping operators knew to disregard the sea and wind conditions around St Kilda at their peril.

The RAF Chinook had arrived the day before and managed to land at St Kilda's small heliport with some difficulty. Even such a large helicopter had been severely buffeted by turbulent down drafts spinning down from Conachair.

The theory was that the topology of Village Bay and the narrow island of Dun reflected northerly downdrafts back toward the base of the hill in the vicinity of the heliport. Only a sudden reversal of the windsock prepared the pilot for the unexpected blast from the south.

On the morning of the evacuation, the pilot was prepared unlike the previous afternoon when a blast of turbulent air had nearly slammed the large machine into the steep slope of Mullach Sgar.

Bill and Archie were watching the aircraft take off, its cargo net loaded with military equipment, and land it on the heaving deck of the *Mounts Bay*.

'I never thought I would see this day, Archie. This place had its ups and downs, but I'm going to miss the old place.'

'Not me,' he replied. 'My missus will be glad to see me home a bit more.'

Archie had only worked there month on, month off for a couple of years while Bill had been there since 1989. Some men had adapted but for many, posting to St Kilda had led to breakdowns either mental or marital, sometimes both.

The Chinook had begun to lift the island vehicles across to the *Mounts Bay*. The two small vans and three Land Rovers had been all in a day's work for the pilot from RAF Odiham.

The big Case 821E wheeled loader was a different matter. Having pushed many stranded landing-craft off the beach it was now itself in need of assistance from the Chinook and its capable crew. After some deliberation, the decision had been taken to drive the Case onto doubled up steel sand ladders that had lain unused since 1957.

By now, the Caterpillar D10 brought over at the start of Operation Hardrock was several tons of salt rusted scrap metal and would be left behind. Equally vintage steel chains, fitted with five-ton hooks were locked onto the four corners of the impromptu cradle.

The weight of the chains meant that four men were needed to stand on the cab roof to attach their chains to cargo hooks on the cables lowered from the hovering Chinook. With the chains attached, the men jumped down and watched from the concrete cabin, the International Airport Lounge.

The men gasped and swore as the Chinook tried to lift off with the familiar Case twisting and swinging beneath. Even with two five-thousand horsepower Honeywell engines the CH-47F heavy lift helicopter was at its operational limit with this jury-rigged payload and in gusting winds the rusting chains creaked ominously. At full power the Chinook staggered across the waves toward the

37

Mounts Bay. Despite the load being spread across four corners of the wheeled loader, the pilot had severe misgivings about this job.

Just managing to lift the Case up to landing deck level the pilot hadn't seen the large water devil spinning across the bay toward the ship. The spinning column of spray raced toward the Chinook and its unwieldy load.

For the rusting nineteen-fifties chains the sudden twist of the Case proved too much and a welded link near the front nearside of the sand ladders gave way. The Case tilted and, on three chains, swung violently into the raised accommodation decks forward of the loading cranes. Several cabins on levels 3 and 4 were badly damaged and the Case fell onto the landing deck and narrowly avoided demolishing one of the cranes.

For the Chinook pilot this was going to a bad day. For the Captain of the *Mounts Bay,* he had begun to wish he had never sailed for St Kilda.

The chains and sand ladders attached to the Chinook had become entangled with the ship's cranes and the pilot decided to jettison the hoist and leave the *Mounts Bay* crew to sort out the mess.

Radio traffic between the bridge and the Chinook had been clearly heard in the Base. It had not been pleasant listening even if confined to precise military phraseology. Recriminations flew between officers of the three services involved.

The Case was a write-off but, apart from loss of heavy-duty steel cables, the Chinook was unscathed. The Captain of Royal Fleet Auxiliary *Mounts Bay* was going to have to write an embarrassing report concerning around a million pounds worth of damage to the ship already earmarked to join the *Largs Bay* in Australia the following Spring.

'Well, that's fucked it Archie.'

As acting Base Supervisor, Bill had seen many minor disasters and near misses on St Kilda in his thirty-year service. The previous Supervisor's fatal Land Rover crash had been the worst but at least no one had witnessed the accident apart from the Bonxies.

The wreck of the Case, thanks to the RAF's cocked-up Chinook airlift had been the most dramatic and in full view of the few remaining employees on the island.

Hovering safely beyond Levenish, away from turbulent winds, the Chinook pilot radioed that after lifting the Case he had to return to Benbecula to refuel. He would then be flying back to Hampshire for repairs, giving him time to think how to explain the loss of the hoist cables and cargo hooks, one CASE forward loader and a million pounds worth of damage to the RFA *Mounts Bay*.

The accident with the Case had been the last straw for the Ministry of Defence evacuation and it was decided to cut their losses and abandon the remaining equipment at St Kilda. After all it wasn't going anywhere.

The Trust would no doubt complain but considering their practical need for military logistics, there wasn't much they could do about it. No organisation could afford to stand on principle, ignoring economic realities anymore. At the end of the day the Trust were owners at St Kilda and the MOD only tenants and in doing a flit, at the end of the day, it was going to be the landlord's problem.

Bill and Archie were joined by Sally the duty nurse for that month. Scratching her head, she commented it was a pity the end had to be marked by such a fiasco.

The logistics team had always prided themselves on handling their equipment professionally. Forwarding turntable trailers onto rolling landing craft had been no mean feat, nor had driving the old Case down from TOTH, negotiating the hairpin bends without so much as a scratch. Not long before the decision to leave St Kilda, a mobile crane had had a scary moment up there, operated by a civilian driver. A sudden blast of wind had nearly blown it off the road to rest precariously on three wheels against the safety barrier. The Case had come to the rescue and connected with a heavy tow chain the military driver had put the loader into low gear ratio and functioned as a brake engine while the ungainly crane made its unsteady way down the steep mountain road.

Sally had heard of so many feats of men and machines since Operation Hardrock. As one of the paramedics she had also treated many accidents when men and machines had not always worked in harmony.

One accident she remembered well was the time a drunken airman, on her watch, fell off the top of the sea defence wall twenty feet onto the rocks below. A young woman conservation volunteer had been skinny-dipping on a warm midsummer night and the word had got around. Drunken men poured out of the Puff-Inn to the cliff edge like lemmings and one of them fell onto the beach below. That was the story going round Harris anyway. It was yet another believable St Kilda story.

'You coming to the bar tonight, Sal?' Bill asked. 'It's going to be your last chance before we close down the power station.'

Sally had rarely been seen in the bar. A disproportionate amount of her time had been taken up with alcohol relate accidents. She found the male bar room banter depressing and the perpetual dancing girls on the TV pathetic. She preferred to spend her evenings in her own quarters socialising with the occasional female Warden.

'OK, just for once I will, Bill. Can't see me coming to much harm with you and Archie there!'

'Rodger and Roz will be there too, and I reckon Keith and John will turn up. It's the last night for all of us.'

The cook, Rodger, and his assistant, Roz had been working at St Kilda for years. He had previously worked in the Army Catering Corps stationed across Europe and the Middle East. Roz had come to work on St Kilda following break-up of her marriage in Glasgow. She preferred her month on St Kilda to the month spent in a lonely bed-sit back in town.

Keith was the senior radar technician on the island and had been busy supervising the packing of sensitive tracking equipment for Chinook transport to the *Mounts Bay*. John turned his hand to many jobs on island from simple plumbing to cleaning and decorating. He had been responsible for ordering supplies and receiving deliveries arriving on the weekly supply helicopter service.

There had been no landing craft since August due to strong winds driving heavy seas from the north. Now the Warden had been made redundant it would have been John's responsibility to set the traps and watch out for rats when the landing craft dropped its ramp on the beach.

Rats had never been known on the island but there was always a first time. The large St Kilda Field Mouse confused a few of the visitors but unlike rats they posed little threat to ground nesting seabirds. There were enough sheep remains on the island to satisfy the hungriest of mice.

Anyone who spent more than a few hours on the island knew Bonxies were the real problem, slaughtering Puffins and other smaller seabirds. They took lambs too but with the birds' statutory protection there was little that could be done. John despised these large brown predators and would have given almost anything for a 20-gauge shotgun and an endless supply of cartridges. It was rumoured he had taken his Sunday walks into Glen Mór to 'accidentally' tread on ground nesting Bonxie eggs. John loved birds but not Great Skuas.

The last remaining staff met in the Puff-Inn around 8.30 that evening. There hadn't been much clearing up after the evening meal in the canteen. Not like the heady days a few summers before when there had been around fifty men to cater for.

Roz made a special effort to make the bar homely. It wasn't often a woman's touch was seen in this male bastion. The pool tables hadn't been used much since they had been told the Base was being closed. At her request the large plasma screen TV was turned off and she had brought her own CD player and gentler music to play that evening.

She had placed small tea-lights on each table. The effect was almost magical. Multitudes of model Puffins, Puffin murals and all manner of Puffin related artefacts came to life in the flickering candlelight. It had felt good to be able to express her creative side instead of consistently having to weather the storms of male banter that usually dominated conversation in the Puff-Inn.

Sally was the first to arrive. Roz heard her footsteps coming down the corridor from the nurse's quarter before she hesitatingly opened the door into the bar. 'Oh, my... Roz. You have made this lovely. How many are coming tonight?'

'Well, there's me and you,' she laughed. 'Bill and Archie, Keith, John and, of course, Rodger. Roz and Rodger had got on like brother and sister since he arrived to replace Janet, the previous head cook. Janet had retired the previous year and had originally accepted the post at St Kilda following an acrimonious divorce. In her spare time, Janet became a successful artist inspired by the land and seascapes around her. She had retired to South Uist to concentrate on her painting and be closer to her children.

Rodger came in next. Collapsing into a deep armchair and staring at the blank screen. 'Sorry Rodge, no TV tonight; not even football,' Roz teased. He was known for dressing up in Celtic football strip whenever his team's matches were televised. He jokingly protested but, on this their last night on the island, there was no need for bravado. It was going to be an emotional evening for all of them.

The other four came in together and Roz assumed her usual position behind the bar. Catering staff took it in turns to do a stint behind the bar in addition to kitchen and canteen work. With such small numbers they had decided to share the cleaning duties between them rather than leave it to Roz and Rodger.

'Here we are then, the Last of the St Kildans......'

Bill was being ironic as usual but this time he meant it. Everyone had a drink, even Sally, as they sat round the table under the picture window looking out on the bay. It had seemed a strange juxtaposition with the large television screen blank as dusk settled on the world famous view of Village Bay outside. Roz put on one of her CDs and with drinks in hand the small group began to relax and, for once, opened up to each other.

The lights of the *Mounts Bay* looked like a small industrial complex shining across the water. They could see the wrecked loader had been put back on its wheels and somehow manoeuvred away from the damaged accommodation decks. Not a good ending for their Case, thought Archie, but he had to concede the guys on the ship must have worked hard to get it upright even with the help of the cranes.

Without the sound of the television set, the rumbling diesel power station a hundred and fifty yards away could be faintly heard. For the occupants of the Base, it was the beating heart of St Kilda. Landing craft had shuttled back and forth over the years bringing diesel fuel to keep the island's life blood flowing. Bill had often wondered why it hadn't been replaced with wind turbines. After all St Kilda had limitless wind energy to draw on rather than rely on fossil fuel.

Apparently, it was something to do with the island's world heritage status. The seascape would be affected as visitors approached from Harris. St Kilda wouldn't look so wild and remote for the tourists with wind-turbines on the summit, but then the diesel power station came as a shock anyway when they landed. Campers regularly complained of the continuous rumble of engines through the night, not to mention the bright lights around the building.

The lights were no problem this time of the year but in late summer, the Warden was always asking for them to be turned off. The steady rumble and bright lights attracted young sea birds leaving their burrows at night. The fledglings left at night to avoid predation but after weeks in dark underground nests, they were drawn to lights around the Base.

The Warden would go out at first light to pick them up and keep them in cardboard boxes before release from the jetty in the late evening. The generator engines were being shut down for the final time the following morning so the next season's Pufflings would head out to sea without human distraction.

There would be some good equipment left behind now the Chinook airlift had been abandoned. They would be leaving on a *Mounts Bay* RIB, the rigid hulled inflatable boat used to ferry personnel to and from shore. The Base had its own RIB but that had already been airlifted aboard.

'Hey Bill!' where've you gone?' Rodger snatched him back from his thoughts.

Roz passed round a bowl of mixed nuts. Sally was looking a bit uncomfortable. She was happier in her professional role and, mixing in an intimate group, she felt out of her comfort zone. She took a deep drink from her glass and found herself speaking from the heart for maybe the first time on the island.

'This place, it could have been so good here.... '

Roz noticed the changed tone of her voice and moistening eyes.

'Those cottages, all empty where there should have been families, could have been some life in this village. There would have been enough work on the Base or TOTH

44

for a couple of families. Instead, what do we have? St Kilda might as well be an oilrig rather than a place where people have, and still could, live, love and grow old together. They could be real homes again.'

'Hold on, Sal. That's a bit hard, isn't it? We have had a good time here, though sometimes I have gone near stir crazy when the helicopter's been late. Then when I am home and the wife's getting at me, I'm glad to be back.'

Rodger was never shy of discussion when he felt criticised. Despite his bluster, he had a sensitive side.

'That's just it, Rodger. No one ever stays here long enough to make it their home. We do a month on and a month off. No-one is allowed to stay here; this place should be resettled and given some life again.'

Sally's argument had been raised before. Archaeologists working on the island often commented that they found it hard to contextualise what they were doing when the clock had been deliberately stopped at 1930. Sally had thought about that too, perceiving an island frustrated by consciously blocked opportunity.

A lot of the men suffering from alcohol induced depression had passed through her consulting room. They thought St Kilda a place of doom. She had seen several of the guys come to her in tears saying they could stand it no longer and she had arranged quick evacuation for their psychological wellbeing.

Sally hadn't mixed much on an informal basis. She was known well enough as the woman to see for a cut finger or a bad back. Occasional tea and sympathy but she had kept her personal side well hidden, only Roz had noticed she never honestly opened up. Now with a drink in her hand, she was ready to explode.

'Just look at this place, it's completely unsustainable! It's only the alcohol that keeps you men sane, if that's not a contradiction in terms. The drink is so cheap here; if it was at mainland prices it wouldn't be quite so bad. The place is killing you all and you just don't see it! There's so much free energy here, wind and wave power unmatched anywhere else in the UK but what do we do? Preserve this, conserve that and all the time bring in ship loads of diesel; it's completely mad. The birds are dying because of climate change and still we burn diesel day and night. We live in a bubble, drinking ourselves stupid in this open-air museum, an open-air laboratory where we are not allowed to touch anything. Too tell you the truth I am fucking glad the Base is closing. Until there's some real life here, I for one will never be coming back.'

The rest of the room were astounded as Sally threw down her glass and ran out of the bar in tears.

'Fuck me!' said Rodger. 'She must have been bottling that up for years.'

Roz gave him a knowing look.

'Just leave it, Rodge. Let her go and cry it out. I'm sure she'll be OK in the morning.'

'Aye, but she has a point though.'

Bill was the oldest employee on the island. In his late fifties he wasn't going to do anything but take retirement when he left the island. The younger men returned to their glasses and suggested they switched the television set back on. Roz conceded defeat but left her tea-light candles on the table. The younger men relaxed without the need for much thought or conversation. The beat of the dancing girls smothered the rumble of the power station and any other disquieting thought.

'You boys won't be seeing them again after we shut down tomorrow,'

Bill remarked, stating the obvious.

They had never been one for MTV or the many copy-cat channels, so Bill and Archie left early returning to their respective rooms. Roz asked the other two to turn the set off when they left and returned to her own room also. As was the time-honoured custom in the Puff-Inn she sold a couple of last rounds, albeit small ones, before bringing down the shutters for the final time.

After breakfast Bill and Archie walked across the sheep-grazed lawn toward the power station. It could have been designed as an icon of modernism when oil was cheap and seemingly inexhaustible. A couple of years previous it had been shut down for major servicing and the temporary generator brought out by landing craft. It was just a quarter of the size of the original equipment. In the previous year, most visitors had arrived onboard cruise ships heading to or from Arctic destinations. In the northern winter they headed south to the Antarctic; the crews commenting on the similarity of St Kilda's monolithic power station to those on Greenland and South Georgia.

The power-station emitted its comforting rumble twenty-four hours a day, seven days a week and it was now about to fall silent, maybe for ever.

The Soay sheep began their daily grazing round at the power-station. The warmth and comforting vibration somehow encouraged a good night's sleep for them, unlike the humans at the campsite. The turf on the south side of the building was cropped bare and, until the alpha females gave the subtle signal to move, the sheep lay down contentedly, chewing cud in the morning sunshine. Only when the weather turned wet and windy did they take shelter on the north side of the building, joining a mix of tired seabirds, drawn to walkway lights the night before.

'They're going to miss us, Bill.'

Archie had a soft spot for the sheep.

'Aye, they won't know what to do without you, Archie,' Bill joked.

Bill was nothing if not pragmatic. He was resigned to the ending of his employment and getting home to South Uist. At his age there would be no more work but Archie, having come from a farming background, would most likely find work with the RSPB project for regenerative agriculture conserving wild birds on the Hebrides.

The Ministry of Defence still favoured human life over birds and the Rangehead Base was staying open as a source of employment for the younger men and their families. The future of the Balivanich camp, directly linked to the St Kilda operation looked more precarious.

In the morning, Bill and Archie began their shut-down preparations and silence fell surprisingly quickly. Rodger started up a small portable generator to operate a minimum service for the canteen. The guys would still need lunch before they left.

The plan had been to drain down the fuel lines and ensure all remaining diesel was stored in tanks near the helipad. Fire risk with diesel fuel was considered minimal but always a possibility. In the limited time available they simply turned off the fuel valves where the pipes entered the building. They didn't even have time to drain down the water-cooling system. Through heat exchangers waste heat was piped around the base. One small token toward sustainability, Bill thought ruefully. A pity the wind turbines he had dreamed of maintaining had never been built.

As a final gesture Bill and Archie made a thorough job of topping up the lubricating fluids, greasing whatever still had to be greased in a digital age. They swept the generator hall floor and tidied the small office and tool store. When they left around 11.30 the closedown had begun to feel like a normal maintenance event but locking the doors behind them, the unaccustomed silence indicated finality. There was no need to turn off already extinguished lights.

The two men walked over to the quadrant housing the KGB offices. Kilda Generating Board, the name had been thought up long before Bill came to the workshop and garage area known as Red Square. Fire assembly notices put up in the restored cottages told occupants to gather at

48

Red Square. Not the best of instructions, Bill had thought, but everyone working on the island knew what it meant.

The intention had been to take all the tools away with them, but it wasn't going to happen now. The vehicles had now gone, apart from the rusty bulldozer which was permanently staying.

The large Nissen hut that passed for a sports hall had collapsed earlier that year. The wind had made short work of the corrugated iron structure and this winter's storms would certainly see the curved sheets blown away to join remains of galvanised roof sheets blown into burns and gullies from cottages abandoned years before.

Twelve-thirty and time for lunch. Bill and Angus walked over to the canteen to join the others for their last meal at St Kilda. It seemed somewhat odd that despite their small company, lunch appeared just as usual. They walked along the counter helping themselves from the hot buffet. The small generator outside the back door could be heard working hard and then suddenly spluttered to a halt.

'Sodding Hell!'

Rodger had had to cope with the machines insatiable demand for fuel since Bill and Angus had closed the power-station. He went outside and topped up the small tank on top of the small Honda engine. Thankfully, he thought, he wouldn't be doing it again that evening. In fact, they would hardly have time to clear up before donning their protective immersion suits ready for the short RIB crossing to the *Mounts Bay*. With the heating system shut down it was already beginning to feel cold. The heat from the one functioning cooker barely touching the gathering chill of the autumn afternoon.

Rodger had prepared one vegetarian meal for Sally. He was glad she wasn't Vegan too, he thought. That would have been really problematic. Sally had appeared for lunch, though had been noticeably missing at breakfast. Preempting further embarrassment, she apologised for her previous night's outburst.

'I really am sorry for my behaviour last night. Think I really should have joined in with the rest of you more often and not bottled things up so much.'

Inwardly, Roz agreed. The men nodded but let the issue pass without comment.

'Don't let it get you down, Sal. It's this island, we all blow up sometimes. Real storm in a tea-cup kind of place.'

'Thanks, Roz.'

Sally was genuinely grateful for Roz's tactful acknowledgement of what it was like, frustrated at male indifference to the family opportunities women perceived.

With lunch finished and no more essential work to complete, Rodger and Roz went to pack their personal belongings and get ready for departure. The remaining men had their own personal immersion suits so no need to struggle into outfits too large or too small which was the usual case with newer employees.

Rodger and Roz quickly managed to wash the crockery by hand, there being neither time nor power for the dishwasher. Plates and cups were stacked to dry, and the floor given a cursory mop. That was as far as it went that afternoon. Roz thought that whoever followed them would find a *Mary Celeste* of a kitchen when they arrived. She couldn't quite believe no one would be taking over when they finished their final shift.

Rodger was still struggling to zip-up his extra-large immersion suit when the RIB left the *Mounts Bay*. Bouncing across the choppy swell it soon reached relative calm in the lee of the jetty. The skipper checked his watch before jumping ashore to tie the craft to the mooring bollards.

The small group of six remaining Base employees had brought their luggage to the top of the steep stone slipway. One of the best in the Hebrides, once, or so they had been told. Seal pups certainly liked to sunbathe on it in the Spring but now just the occasional sheep trotted down to nibble at the seaweed washed up by the high tide. Sheep that adapted to eating seaweed managed to thrive in winter when more conventional grazing was exhausted.

There were no vehicles to transport their belongings down the steep flagstone slipway. It was never easy at the best of times and a sudden squall had brought a shower of rain making the slope particularly treacherous. Carrying their rucksacks and suitcases down to the jetty steps and the waiting RIB, Bill was reminded of an old archive film he had seen of the first evacuation in 1930.

Here they were again carrying their belongings down the self-same slipway to a waiting small boat. There was no chance of getting the *Mounts Bay* anywhere near the jetty of course. It was the RIB or nothing. Passing their bags down to the skipper, he stacked them between the seats. The craft was designed to carry twelve so there was plenty of space. The steps had always been tricky and with the Warden gone, untreated algae had made them very slippery. Bill slipped and hit the back of his head on the concrete edge. He picked himself up seemingly unhurt but quickly became aware of slight double vision. Sally had been right behind him, her hands full with her own luggage and unable to save his fall.

'Shit! Oh, fucking shit!' Sally's second public outburst in twenty-four hours betrayed her obvious tension. She couldn't get off St Kilda quick enough and it seemed here was yet another casualty for her to deal with.

It was lucky he hadn't fallen into the sea; the red life rings had long been put into store. For some reason the Warden had seemed more concerned they were not going to be washed away in bad weather than be available in case of emergency; but still, that was Trust business. A remote manager had given the instruction, but it made no sense to her to put away lifesaving equipment at precisely the time it was most likely to be needed. On top of swearing, she wanted to scream with frustration.

Bill had mild concussion and would soon be alright. She told him he had hurt his dignity more than anything else and the small party took their seats in the RIB. The skipper pulled away from the jetty, heading back to the *Mounts Bay,* sheltering from the swell beside the promontory of Dun. This turf covered finger of rock had been attached to the main island of Hirta three hundred years previously, but the sea had broken through one stormy February night creating the most recent island in the St Kildan archipelago.

The fast RIB bounced across the swell slowing only as it approached the rear of *Mounts Bay.* The pontoon deck guided the small boat and its passengers into a different world and, once inside the warren of warm corridors, apart from the movement of the swell, it was barely distinguishable from any another military accommodation.

The officer who met the departing St Kilda team informed them the ship would be sailing at 18.00 and directed them to the spacious Mess to relax and wait for their evening meal. Wiping condensation from the windows, Bill looked back across Village Bay, toward the jetty they had left only a few minutes before.

The end had come swiftly; St Kilda was once again evacuated, and that night would lie empty for the first time since 1957. The squalls seemed to have blown over, and in the evening light the grey concrete power-station stood silent against the darkening slopes of Conachair. The remaining olive-green Base buildings were less distinguishable now, and only the Factor's House and the refurbished Manse stood out as evening fell; their empty authority emphasised by whitewash.

The younger members of the group seemed happy to be leaving and were already up and exploring the mess deck. Bill sat by the window and pondered on this the second evacuation in a hundred years. The island really was empty now, just a few Fulmars still swirling around the cliff tops, other seabirds left during August. Even the Bonxies had left, with their young well fed on smaller birds and carrion. There would be no easy pickings until spring lambs played among the Mothan flowers in An Lag.

Bill smiled at the effect the new borehole had on the flora there. Mothan flourished where the water overflowed. As a diabetic he rarely touched alcohol, and the sweetly tainted tap water had had no effect on him. He had been unaware of the subtle perceptual changes in the minds of his drinking colleagues. The Base had finally been abandoned in a hurry, not just because of the Chinook and Case loader fiasco but because of an approaching deep Atlantic depression forecast for sea areas Rockall and Malin. This was likely to bring Force Nine south easterly gales to sea area Hebrides within the next forty-eight hours. Even for a large ship, like the RFA *Mounts Bay*, Village Bay was no place to be caught in a strong south-easterly. Sheltered on all sides except from the south-east, Village Bay had seen many wrecks in such conditions.

At 18.00 sharp, the large ship raised its anchor and with a parting blast from its horn began the night sailing to Loch Carnon. As the ship pulled away in the calm evening light, a sudden blast of wind came out of nowhere and a water-devil raced across their bows before dissipating in Village Bay. The captain scratched his head at the inexplicable phenomenon before the ship entered the rising swell beyond Levenish, the small island at the mouth of the bay.

Bill pondered on the end of another era for St Kilda. Cradling her coffee, Sally considered how it might have been, how her life might have panned out on the island had women been allowed their full role in the community.

The others were simply glad to be going home. Queuing at the buffet counter, Rodger was glad to be on the customer side for once, joking with Roz, who was unusually subdued, about what they would be getting up to back in Glasgow. Rodger assumed that their matey-ness would continue back on the mainland. As for Archie, it looked like a return to farm-work on the crofts of South Uist. He had an interview with the RSPB the following week. Sally would join the bank nursing team in the Western Isles Health Board and the rest of the St Kilda staff were to be absorbed into the Rangehead workforce.

There seemed little likelihood of funding for another Warden on the island in the foreseeable future and the Western Isles Trust had already placed their advert in the Scottish national press for a custodian family to take up residence at St Kilda as soon as possible.

5

Shooting Party

Snow had been falling heavily in the Cairngorm mountains. The cold had come early, and the mountain hares had no time to complete their seasonal transition from brown to white, making them easy prey for Golden Eagles circling above.

The eagles were a success story in an area ecologically degraded by two centuries of field sports. The native Caledonian forest had been dying due to the high deer population. Scotland's mountain landscape had been carefully managed to sustain high numbers of deer and Red Grouse for the autumn shooting season.

Scottish Natural Heritage had previously been able to pull in European funding under the EC Habitats Directive to regenerate native forest ecosystems based on Scots Pine. However, away from managed regeneration areas, ancient trees fell to die alone among grass and bracken that should have been full of vigorous young seedlings. Red Squirrels took a fair number of pine seeds, but intensive deer grazing was the prime cause of regeneration failure of the once widespread Caledonian Forest.

European money paid for deer proof fencing to protect river valleys from excessive grazing and inside the fences the ecosystem was recovering. High fences proved an obstacle to hill walkers and a death trap for Black Grouse blindly flying into the high tensile steel strands.

They also looked very ugly and with a mission to re-wild their Cairngorm estate, one enlightened landowner had taken the controversial decision to remove fences and discourage deer by other methods.

To ecologists, re-introduction of the wolf, absent for four hundred years, would have been the obvious answer. They knew that idea would be a non-starter due to opposition from the farming community and commercial deer stalking interests. Tourism, too, had begun to suffer from declining deer numbers in the Cairngorms.

This particular estate had taken a zero-tolerance approach to deer in the unfenced regeneration zones; they were simply shot on sight. They were considered vermin, with no closed season. Scottish Natural Heritage had licensed year-round culling while, to the locals, natural science experimentation took priority over livelihoods dependent on field sports, or so the Press was reporting.

It was obvious to the Scottish Game Keepers Association that with intensive culling a vacuum would be created drawing in deer from surrounding estates, in turn reducing deer numbers available for their own stalking clients. There would be a considerable reduction in income as wealthy shooters began to seek sport elsewhere.

The experiment proved a failure as deer were drawn in from open moorland to shelter in the empty forest and numbers on the Estate actually increased. SNH funding to the Estate was conditional on deer numbers being reduced to a level sustainable within the forest ecosystem.

The corporate group from Canary Wharf had chartered their small plane from East London Airport, looking forward to catching the Red hind shooting season in November. Stag shooting had closed in Scotland but continued for a few weeks longer down on Exmoor where milder conditions prevailed. Even on south-west England's moors, snows had come unusually early. The Cairngorms were experiencing arctic conditions rarely experienced before mid-January.

Estate stalkers were in position, their white overalls improvised camouflage for the snowy conditions. The small team of marksmen lay in wait, watching for the deer to break cover. Their rifles were fitted with sound moderators to minimise disturbance to both winter walkers and protected wildlife.

On the other side of the plantation estate workers stood in line, clearly visible on the snow-covered hill side. The nominated leader of the group waited until he received the VHF radio message that the stalkers were in position. Raising his arm, he waved silently to the rest of the team strung across the hill side.

The group entered the forest, as far as possible keeping to line, minimising the chance of sheltering deer running back past them. It proved hard work crossing snow filled ditches and clambering over fallen timber; the plantation had been allowed, in forestry terms, to deteriorate to a semi-natural condition.

Nervous deer bolted in front of the line of beaters struggling through deep snow among the trees. Calling and shouting added to the fear of deer running forward into the designated killing zone. The thuds of shots hitting their targets were barely audible in the wintry landscape as, one after another, the fleeing deer were silently gunned down.

When the killing was over, carcasses were loaded onto a soft-tracked cross-country vehicle and taken for processing in the estate deer larder. Income from the sale of carcasses to game dealers helped offset the reduction in estate funding from SNH. For weekend walkers and cross-country skiers from Aberdeen, the only signs of conservation managed slaughter were blood stains in the snow and the odd cartridge case missed by the stalkers clearing up before returning to their vehicles.

The employed stalkers resented having to take part in the slaughter. The Head Stalker resigned, and the Estate Manager protested against a culling policy that contradicted game management wisdom acquired over generations. Protest cost him his job and a younger more ecologically focussed manager was appointed to continue the regeneration work.

Accessible to centres of population, the Scottish government planned to re-wild the Cairngorms as an icon of national virtue. For hill walking politicians, inspired by John Muir and Yellowstone, re-wilding was long overdue. For the indigenous human community, it felt like ethnic cleansing. The Monarch of the Glen was now considered vermin.

The shooting party had had a less than satisfactory corporate break. The Braemar hotel had been first class and, unexpected in the heart of the highlands, they found Lithuanian staff providing exemplary service.

The problem had been the lack of deer. Long days out on the hill with an allocated stalker had proved fruitless. A few deer had been seen but since the culling policy on the neighbouring Estate, they had become alert and stayed beyond range of their hunting rifles. One shooter, frustrated at the lack of result, wanted to chance a long shot but was dissuaded by stalkers whose professional ethics demanded certainty of a clean kill before any shot was taken.

The City group were used to achieving results and were no strangers to hard work, but days on the wintry hillside with nothing to show for it was beginning to feel like failure. Back at the hotel they drafted a complaint to the sporting tour company which had organised the trip.

After several heated telephone calls, it was agreed that the group would be offered a complimentary sightseeing flight. After an unproductive week on snowy hillsides, the flight would show them a different aspect of what Scotland had to offer.

The tour company contacted the charter plane operator they had used to fly the group to Aberdeen. The pilot suggested a trip out over the Hebrides and over to the St Kilda islands. The frustrated shooters accepted the compromise of a flying out to the World Heritage Site before turning south for London. Time was going to be tight, but they could refuel at Benbecula and then make it back to London in one stretch.

Early on Monday morning, a large taxi picked up the considerably hung-over party from their hotel in Braemar and dropped them off an hour later at Aberdeen airport. Suitcases, rucksacks and rifle cases were loaded into the twin engine Piper Chieftain. The aircraft could accommodate all nine of the group and their luggage and, with large passenger windows, should prove ideal for a sightseeing flight that morning.

The aircraft took off easily and turned west toward the Cairngorm Mountains. They approached mountains soon after leaving Aberdeen. Following Royal Deeside, the pilot pointed out Balmoral Castle the Royal Scottish holiday home.

Looking down the frustrated shooting party could see groups of stags and hinds on the slopes of Lochnagar. It seemed the Royal estate had managed to keep its herds at home away from managed slaughter to the west of Braemar. The Piper continued along Glen Dee and the visible absence of deer was remarked upon compared with Balmoral.

Glen Dee turned northward into the snowy heart of the mountains, but the light aircraft continued on a westward course, passing over remote and deserted hunting lodges before the land dropped toward Aviemore. The wintry scene below was mesmerised the group before they were snapped out of their reverie by unexpected clear air turbulence. The Piper dropped three hundred feet before levelling out and climbing back to its intended flight path.

'Sorry about that, folks,' the pilot apologised. 'We are on the edge of localised high pressure over the cold Cairngorms and the pressure will be dropping as we head into the milder west. Just to let you know it will also be

59

getting windier as we approach the Atlantic. Probably a good idea to make sure your seatbelts are fastened. The north-westerlies can get pretty gusty over the hills.'

The landscape changed beneath them as the Piper headed toward Mallaig. Passing over Loch Lochy and Loch Arkaig conversation turned to possible summer fishing holidays. Passing to the south of Skye the pilot pointed out the islands of Eigg, Rum and Canna. He was in his favourite flying area, the mix of sea and islands a welcome change from executive commuter flights to London or across the North Sea to Norway.

'Canna's an interesting place. They were advertising for new families to move there. They wanted to re-kindle the human community rather than the usual story of just funding nature conservation.'

His comment brought murmurs of agreement from the party deprived of their sport by nature conservation in the Cairngorms.

'I did hear they are going to try something similar at St Kilda. As you will shortly see, that really is some remote place. Good luck to them is all I can say!'

Looking down they could see the Caledonian MacBraine car ferry crossing from Oban to Lochboisdale on South Uist. It was a signal for the pilot to turn the aircraft north-west toward Benbecula.

The small aircraft was already being tracked by radar operators at the Hebrides Missile Range. The bored operators often broke their tedium by tracking small low flying planes as if they were actual targets for their missile testing programme. After the embarrassing terrorist incident at St Kilda an airborne suicide attack had to be considered a possibility. The pilot assumed they had already locked onto his aircraft and jokingly called them on VHF.

'OK guys, I've got my hands up! – over.'

'Bang, bang, you're dead, man!' came the Hebridean accented reply.

'Where are you heading? - over.'

'St Kilda. Just for a ride around the island. What are the conditions like out there today? – over.'

The ranges provided a very detailed weather forecast, ostensibly for missile testing. The last thing anyone wanted was a Sea Viper getting blown off course and scaring the living daylights out of a passing fishing boat or worse still hitting St Kilda. It had happened once before in the early days of military occupation when a small missile had hit the Base kitchens. Although the incident had occurred way back in the 1960s the Hebrides Range had never been able to live it down.

'Wind 335 degrees, 25 knots, gusting to 45 on the cliff tops, no significant cloud base to worry about – over.'

'Thanks guys, catch you later when I call in at Benbecula – Piper out.'

The MOD meteorologists predicted fresh north-west winds gusting over the cliff edges. At least there would be no low cloud to worry about. St Kilda often generated long plumes of cloud when moist warm air lifted over the peaks of Conachair and Boreray. Under such conditions, helicopter flights to the island were suspended until visibility improved. Even over the normally mild Western Isles the unusually cold weather and northerly winds were keeping the air clear.

The St Kilda archipelago could be clearly seen on the horizon. Beneath them the Monach islands lay deserted; no one bothered putting sheep there nowadays. The lighthouse keeper's cottage stood empty since automation made human presence redundant.

As the plane approached St Kilda from the south-east the enormity of the rocky islands awed the party to silence. To the right the Stacs of Boreray were white with guano from the largest Gannet colony in the north Atlantic. The birds had left in October, but the prevailing high pressure weather system had prevented autumnal storms from washing away faecal evidence of their occupancy.

Three hundred or so white sheep grazed the green south facing slope, descendants of a flock of Highland Blackface abandoned in 1930 after their elderly owners evacuated their island home. For the sight-seeing party from southern England, it seemed incredible that generations of St Kildans had farmed such a precipitous landscape.

Approaching Levenish, the small island marking the entrance to Village Bay, the pilot turned south to begin a clockwise circuit of the main island of Hirta.

'Afraid the rules say we must keep two miles away from the island, so we don't disturb the birds. There's none nesting here this time of year, but I don't want a blot on my license.'

The pilot added, 'But as the island is empty now the military left, we can get in a bit closer. We're not supposed to go below two thousand feet either. The guys on the Ranges will be tracking us but they won't mind. It's only the Western Isles Trust who would kick up a fuss and they've laid off their last Warden. Don't think there is anyone back on the island yet.'

The Piper followed the cliffs of Dun about a thousand yards out from sea caverns running under the headland. Skimming the waves, the party could see the light from Village Bay reflecting through the caves. The motion of the swell clearly visible rising and falling against the pink algae encrusted rock walls.

With the wind coming from the north-west the Piper could maintain lift at lower speeds. Looking up, the passengers saw the ruins of the radar installation on Mullach Sgar, the incredible scree slopes of Carn Mor and the towering cliffs of Mullach Bi in near perfect conditions.

Ahead lay the island of Soay, the island of sheep, named by Norse Viking settlers twelve hundred years earlier Between Hirta and Soay lay a narrow strait blocked by sea stacks capped with Guillemot droppings. The aircraft passed caves, homes to countless Atlantic Grey seals and safe refuges from Orca hunting packs.

Killer whale pods were known to occasionally hunt around St Kilda, but the departing Base staff had reported seeing them frequently that autumn, following shoals of fish following colder waters flowing down from the north.

One of the sightseers spotted the wreckage of a second world-war fighter plane lying shattered across the scree slope facing Hirta. He thought it inappropriate to mention what he had spotted as the pilot was already struggling with strong wind gusts as the aircraft flew toward the gap between the islands. The pilot opened the throttles and turned the Piper westwards to circuit Soay rather than risk flying through unpredictable turbulence in the canyon.

Out to the north of Soay flying conditions became more predictable and the north-westerly wind lifted the plane as they turned eastward to fly between Boreray and Hirta. They were going to fly past the highest sea cliff in Europe, so the pilot said.

The shooter who spotted the wrecked Bristol Beaufighter on Soay told the others what he had seen. The pilot had thought not to mention this aspect of St Kilda's history but now it had been brought up he would explain the wreckage.

'There were a spate of air-wrecks here during the Second World War. No one really knows why but for a while the island came under an air exclusion zone. Probably the most famous wreck is that of a Sunderland Flying Boat that came down in the valley you can see on your right.'

The Piper was passing Glen Bay, the northerly landing point used by the terrorists earlier that year. They could see

63

the long valley of Glen Mór leading up to the damaged masts and radomes on the spine of the island. Now, seventy years after the event, large pieces of aluminium fuselage and other wreckage could still be seen strewn across the glen.

'It's a war grave,' said the pilot. 'Strangely, no one really knows what happened. As you can see, there should be no real problem flying up that glen and over the top into Village Bay. Should be a piece of cake, the military tried to bury the remains of the plane so no one else would fly up there sight-seeing and come to a similar fate. No one can explain that crash, it's quite a mystery.'

The aircraft continued past the eastern cliffs of Hirta, hardly a bird to be seen at that time of year. As the pilot said, they were looking at the highest sea-cliffs in Europe rising almost sheer to nearly fifteen hundred feet above sea level.

The lonely trig point at the summit of Conachair marked the last point in the UK cartographic triangulation survey, obsolete since the advent of satellite Global Positioning Systems. Hard to imagine, the pilot explained, that Ordnance Surveyors carried bags of concrete all the way up there just so they had a fixed point on the planet to work from. They climbed up at night with a car battery and spotlight to point at the next trig point on the Uists, that way they could plot survey lines without heat haze causing refraction problems.

'You are a mine of information, aren't you?'

Jim Wilson one of the London bankers voiced his frustration to the pilot.

'We came up here for a shooting holiday, for a bit of excitement, not a guided walk, and I suppose that's it now.'

The aircraft was approaching Levenish again and the pilot was turning to follow a bearing of 120 degrees for Benbecula airport where he would refuel for the journey south. Jim's words stung the pilot, after all it wasn't his fault the Estate had slaughtered most of the deer in the southern Cairngorms.

'OK, point taken. I'll take you around the island of Boreray before we head back.'

The group murmured assent, but Jim had a further idea.

'We came to Scotland for a bit of excitement, and it looks like we have a chance out here. How about you fly us up the Glen, the one where the Sunderland crashed. That lumbering great thing never made it over the top but in this light and faster plane it should be a doddle. It would be really cool if you'd fly as fast and low as you can up the valley and then rocket over the ridge into Village Bay. Better than a ride at Alton Towers, I reckon? Come on pilot what do think.'

'What I think is I would stand a good chance of losing my job. I also think, given the reputation this island has for flyers it would be a very foolish manoeuvre.'

'Oh, come on, man. Be the hero just for once, eh?'

'Well, I suppose it could be done. We'd have a strong tailwind with the north-westerly funnelling up the glen today. It's just the last few hundred metres, I have heard, that can be so unpredictable. A mate of mine used to fly helicopters out here and he said if anyone asked you to fly out here, you should run as fast as possible in the opposite direction. Even landing at the helipad required nerves of steel as the wind can turn through all points of the compass in the last moments of approach. Supposedly, sudden turbulence is created by this mountain jutting out of the sea into Atlantic airstreams.'

'Yeah, right,' said Jim. 'Tell you what, why don't we have a whip round for you? Say we put in a tenner each for the ride of a lifetime. Then we can go back to Benbecula and fuel up for the trip home.'

The rest of the group had mixed feelings about flying up the glen but not wanting to appear less than macho in the face of Jim's challenge they all agreed.

'OK, ninety quid says you can do it! That's straight in your pocket, mate. As you said earlier there's no on the island to report you, so come on, go for it!'

The pilot was beginning to get caught up in the bravado and he could certainly use the extra cash. Even as a well-paid charter pilot his work was drying up as the recession worsened and it would pay for a good meal out with his wife. They had been having difficulties lately and he felt she would appreciate the gesture, if nothing else.

'Well alright but be prepared for turbulence as we pass over the top. It's a clear day and I won't be able to see anything before it hits us. I am going to have to insist you all wear your seatbelts or I may be scraping you off the cabin ceiling after we drop. So, first a circuit of Boreray then I'll open her up and give you the low-level ride of your lives. Don't say I didn't warn you, though.'

The pilot pocketed the ninety pounds and banked the aircraft to the left for the short crossing and anticlockwise circuit of St Kilda's second biggest island. This stunt was going to take a lot of fuel, and they would absolutely be going straight back to Benbecula afterwards. It did feel good though, just to let go of the reins for once.

God knows what the Range radar operators would think as they tracked him from South Uist. Probably wouldn't see him again until he came over the top anyway. That's if they were watching St Kilda at all. They rarely bothered unless the Range was live and compared with computer simulation, the expense of firing real missiles was prohibitive unless the military client insisted and paid-up front.

Passing round the north side of Boreray, the shooting party showed little interest in the spectacular scenery passing to their left. Not one of them mentioned the white sheep that had somehow survived for a hundred years since their last shepherd abandoned them. The aircraft turned at the guano whitened Stacs and dropped height to begin its approach to Glen Bay.

'Bit like starting an attack run, lads?' The ex-Royal Air Force pilot was getting into this and dropped the aircraft as low as he dared, skimming the waves would have been out of the question at any other time of the year as a million seabirds would have risen in protest making bird-strike inevitable. As it was, only curious seals turned to watch as the twin engine Piper flew toward them with throttles wide open.

The engine notes in the cabin changed from a gentle purr to a full-throated snarl. Outside, had there been anyone to hear, they would have assumed the scream of the fast-approaching plane to be part of a military exercise. That it was a civilian charter plane breaking every flying regulation in the St Kilda management plan, the flight path was not only irresponsible, but had they made it back to Benbecula, quite unbelievable.

'OK folks, here we go! Don't say I didn't warn you.'

The shooting party were glued to the windows of the Piper as the ground-rush brought home just how low and fast they were flying. A first sudden warning gust lifted the plane over the low cliff at the foot of the glen. Hurtling over the small lochan, now deserted of Skuas, the aircraft roared past ruined homesteads of the Amazon's House, built by a forgotten community thousands of years earlier. The pilot had accepted the challenge and was now simply concerned with flying as fast and low as his nerves, and the aircraft, would permit. He put the sudden gust down to local conditions and nothing to worry about. The weather was clear, and he could see the concave slope ahead rising in front of them toward the ridge they would cross before dropping into Village Bay. At this speed and low altitude, the aircraft was committed.

'Look! fucking deer, boys!'

Jim spotted the flock of brown Soay sheep scattering in front of them. Wreckage from the Sunderland lay all around as the Piper followed a line of cleits guiding the aircraft up the rising hillside.

These small stone storehouses were found across the island and were uniquely built to take advantage of local wind conditions, not fight against them. Air blew through gaps in the dry-stone walls and capped with turf roofs these simple but effective stores dehydrated hay, peat, and other heavy island products, even in rainy conditions, before being carried down to the village.

Too late, the pilot was hit by the implication of these structures. He had read avidly about St Kilda and remembered how the villagers took full advantage of the wind to dry their produce. They were heading at full speed into an aviator's death trap.

'Brace, brace!' he screamed to the passengers, all bar one out of their seats to look out of the panoramic windows.

The brown sheep had stopped running and looked back impassively as the Piper rose toward the ridge where generations of cleit builders had taken advantage of winds that could predictably blow from any direction. Pulling back hard on the joystick the pilot managed to lift the aircraft above the certain but unseen turbulence beneath them. Such was the forward speed of the plane that the Piper made a near vertical climb approaching the ridge before its underside was hit by a gale-force north westerly air current.

With the underside of the fuselage and wings hit by the wind blast, the near vertical aircraft was picked up and thrown across the ridge like a dry leaf. The Piper hit the ground, cart-wheeled and came to rest smashed against a group of cleits in the wind gap below Mullach Bi.

The propellers had hit the ground at maximum revolution, ripping the starboard engine from the airframe.

Lying almost upside down, there had been no fire or explosion. Safety features in the fuel tanks had prevented spillage. The dying aircraft shifted against a supporting cleit; machined alloy panels scraped along hand-built granite walls. The gust subsided, and the remaining breeze soughed gently through rough moor grass to cool the remaining engine until the metallic chinking finally subsided.

At the back of the plane there was just one survivor. Phil Brown had been the only one to have heeded the pilot's advice to remain strapped in his seat. Blood and other body fluids were splattered against the remaining cracked windows. Several panes had been knocked out as the aircraft flexed on impact and male bodies lay broken across the inverted cabin interior.

The luggage hold under the tail had burst open leaving rucksacks and suitcases scattered along the earth dyke built by island women to mark the limit of safe grazing for long departed cattle that once supported St Kildan life. Many of the cases had burst open on impact, their contents swirling around the cleits before rising to be picked up and blown over the cliff edge by the gusts.

Phil Brown had managed to uncomfortably extricate himself from his four-strap harness, falling to the padded ceiling without further injury. The wind blew through glassless windows as he crawled out on to the moor. Trying to stand, the urge to vomit brought him back to his knees. It was an instinctive response to the overwhelming shock of the situation and after a few minutes retching he stood up. Only when he turned around and looked back did he realise he was the only member of the party to survive the crash.

The Piper's panels scraped against granite as it slid down the cleit. The sound made him turn again just in time to see the plane slip and tumble over the cliff edge before another sudden gust blew him to the ground. The plane bounced off rocks below the Lover's Stone, before disappearing into the Atlantic swell. The small aircraft sank under the waves, breaking up in the bio-diverse submarine caverns, one of the reasons for St Kilda's world heritage status. The battered machine and its broken occupants slid gently down to decompose in chasms below the island leaving hardly a trace of its passing. The small oil slick would be dispersed in minutes by the natural energy of the north Atlantic.

Phil picked himself up confused by the sudden calm that had returned. The blast of wind that had nearly sent him, maybe even tried to send him, over the edge to follow the lifeless shooting party had dropped as quickly as it came.

Looking up to Mullach Mor a thin plume of mist was beginning to stretch out from the ridge dividing the island into its two distinct halves. He thought he heard dogs howling hundreds of feet below but put it down to imagination playing tricks on him. Seals, disturbed by the falling wreckage of the Piper, had temporarily ceased their mournful song but were now resuming their eerie calls.

Phil instinctively followed the path along the ridge until he looked down on the village a thousand feet below. In his state of shock, he had failed to notice the rusting rotary engine from the wrecked Sunderland Flying Boat close to the starboard engine of the Piper where it had been ripped off in a similar air-crash years before.

The line of abandoned cottages and allotted plots appeared peaceful, conserved in a state of arrested decline. At the end of the street six cottages looked habitable with tarred roofs but not a wisp of smoke from any chimney hinted at occupancy. Beyond the whiteness of the larger Factor's House the military buildings lay silent. Not a sound other than wind and sea.

Phil saw no sign of life other than brown sheep grazing the rich south-facing pastures of the field allotments. It was a long way down to the deserted Base where help could have been found just a few weeks before. The island felt totally empty of human life; layer upon layer of history evident in the landscape but not a living soul to be seen.

Out in the Atlantic, at least fifty miles from the nearest working telephone, Phil sat down dejected in his isolation. As awful as it had been, the wreckage of the Piper would have provided some small comfort, the broken aircraft a connection with familiar reality.

The chill wind decided matters and he began to head down toward the village. He noted with surprise that on the ridge road was written in white paint *Welcome to St Kilda* – an improvised landing strip where the wind was consistently from the north-west. The military had obviously learned a trick from their island forebears.

He entered the radome buildings left unlocked by the departing technicians. No light came on as he flicked the wall switch inside the door and all phones were dead. Coming outside again the wind was singing in the wires that guyed the few remaining masts to the island.

A few yards down the track toward the village, the wind blew strongly again but from the south this time. Five minutes later he came to a collection of cleits protected by a circular dry-stone wall. The winds were swirling again, the vortex drawing particles of dried grasses upwards until they caught the prevailing current and disappeared. He stood puzzled at the anomaly then caught sight of the helipad a few hundred feet beneath him. No wonder pilots had trouble here, he thought.

It was then he saw the wake of a small boat moving fast across the swell from the east. He could just make it out to be a large red and white cabin cruiser and now that the wind was blowing up from the bay, he could hear the approach of powerful diesel engines. His exhausted mind wondered how rescue could be coming before he had even called for help. Anyway, how could he have called for help from this abandoned place.

The thought reminded him to check his mobile phone. There was no signal, it being at least fifty-five miles to the nearest cell phone mast. Even with a modern smart phone he quickly realised there was no chance. The GPS function told him where he was, but it couldn't let anyone else know. So how did this fast-moving boat know he was here?

As quickly as he could, he ran down the hill until the pain in his knees slowed him to a walk. A large rock on the left of the track caught his attention. It looked freshly damaged as if hit by a vehicle. He had a bad feeling about this place and hurried on downhill to where a beaten path extended from the street of abandoned cottages toward the track. He could clearly hear the engine note of the powerful launch now as it approached the jetty.

For some reason the boat made a sweep past the beach before turning back to the jetty. The skipper must have been checking something in the bay before deciding to tie up alongside the sea-weed encrusted steps against the seawall. Phil was later to learn that the Western Isles Trust had forbidden compartment boats to tie up at the jetty for fear of rats or other alien species coming ashore. Now, with no Warden, there was no-one to enforce the rules.

Following the path past derelict cottages, the buildings became potentially habitable as he came nearer to the empty Base. The white painted two-storey house looked as if it had been lived in recently. If he was to be a modern-day Robinson Crusoe, at least he would have a good roof over his head, and with all these sheep, no shortage of mutton.

The end of the path brought him to a second white house beside an early nineteenth century church building. Compared to the villagers, the ministers who lived in the Manse must have thought their residence palatial indeed.

The well-built Manse was compensation for those on a mission to save Britain's remotest community from their home-grown religious expression. Now Phil Brown needed saving himself and he made his way down the steep slope to the jetty to find a small group of people landing from a blue and white hydrofoil launch. He had seen and heard the Beluga roaring into the bay. Boxes were being passed from the launch onto the concrete jetty and looking up the group seemed as surprised to see him as he was to find them arriving that afternoon to resettle Britain's remotest community.

6

Arrival

The confirmation letter arrived on Monday morning. It listed their itinerary and essential things to take and asked that the family be ready to leave for St Kilda as soon as possible. Erica was the only one required to give any formal notice to her employer. David Williams' associate lectureship had not been renewed that term so he would only have to let the Job Centre know he would be unable to sign every fortnight. Deborah, though theoretically required to give a term's notice was effectively firing herself.

A brief note to the Principal would suffice as she had no intention of returning to what she saw as a thankless teaching profession. Agatha would soon be leaving high school, post-16, so no serious problem there. Going to St Kilda would be the opportunity of a lifetime and, with good grades already, she could pick up on higher education when they came back to the mainland. Erica, their older daughter was pretty bomb-proof and could make herself at home anywhere. Her part-time position in the wholefood café wouldn't hold her back from a new adventure.

That same afternoon Deborah went to see a local estate agent and arranged to let the house, fully furnished, on a short-hold tenancy. With the current recession letting would be no problem, she was assured. There was the matter of the cat of course; she would have to go with them so on the way home Deborah visited a hardware store and bought a travelling basket for her pet.

The car was going to pose a problem, but Erica suggested her friend Dan meet them at Leverburgh and let him drive the estate car back to Edinburgh. In return he could have free loan of the vehicle while they were away. At first neither Dave nor Deborah were keen on the idea. They didn't know Dan that well, but Erica obviously thought well of him, so it was arranged.

He would make his way to Leverburgh on Harris by bus, staying the night in Stornoway. When they left for St Kilda, he could take the car back on the condition it was looked after and serviced regularly.

The list of essentials was pretty obvious; warm, waterproof outdoor clothing, stout boots, rucksacks, personal medicines and so on. Absolutely no firearms were to be taken and no alien species to be introduced on the island whatsoever.

Even then no thought was given to the cat; after all she was simply another member of the family. Rod and line fishing would be allowed if kept away from areas frequented by seals. There was no need to take fishing equipment as there would be plenty stored in the boathouse adjacent the jetty. Dave was quite looking forward to fishing, he had only ever dallied with the sport in the past.

The main thing to remember was that they had volunteered as Custodians, which meant they had been accepted as volunteers to represent and support the Western Isles Trust interest on the islands. It would be a responsible role and, as with paid positions, subject to regular appraisal.

Josephine added that she required certificates of health from their doctor to keep on file in Edinburgh along with any other personal information they thought relevant. As they were to be with their next of kin, they could ignore that part of the medical form, but a friend's contact details would be useful in case of emergency. Sally would keep a file with copies of their medical details to aid her in case of problems while they were out there.

Despite her outburst on leaving St Kilda, Sally had seen the advert and offered her services as volunteer nurse. Finally, she thought, life was returning to the abandoned village, and she would be proud to play her part in the resettlement.

They were to report to Don Macintyre on Leverburgh Pier at 0800 the following Monday. He would load their belongings into his fast launch and take them out to St Kilda. The winter crossing would take about three hours and likely to be rough going; anti-seasickness medication was advised.

Josephine's letter reminded them there was no mobile phone signal on the island, but they would find satellite phone handsets and spare batteries in the former Warden's office in the Manse. The satellite phones would be their lifeline and were to be well looked after. There was a solar panel battery charger they could use to keep the batteries fully charged should there be problems with the generator.

The list went into minor detail, but the lack of mobile phone signal and poor radio and TV reception sounded a positive bonus after their busy lives in Edinburgh. Erica had her doubts about lack of mobile phone signal, but apart from that all arrangements seemed fine. They were to ring Josephine as soon as they had settled in.

Packing, unpacking and repacking became the norm for the Williams family. It was a bitterly cold, but the dominant high pressure kept moist snow laden winds away. As they completed their preparations the cat was restless sensing change coming.

The Friday before the rendezvous at Leverburgh Pier saw them load their final essential belongings into Dave's Peugeot estate. The cat was in her basket intermittently protesting at the unaccustomed turn of events.

Setting off, leaving suburban Edinburgh for the west coast came almost as an anti-climax. The only one to see them off was Dan, giving Erica a final and appreciated hug. He promised to be at Leverburgh first thing on Monday morning to collect their car.

Leaving Edinburgh, they travelled west along the M8 toward Glasgow. They were to pick up Sally on-route, finding her tenement proved the first challenge of the day.

Feline protest became more vocal as human tension rose as they drove around housing blocks of central Glasgow looking for her address. Although now well into the twenty-first century, neither Dave nor Deborah had thought to equip the Peugeot with sat-nav. Deborah's Toyota had been written off by her insurance company after being stolen and joy-ridden by boys from Castlemount High School. That had been the last straw before she took sick leave on grounds of depression and anxiety.

Eventually Sally's apartment was found, and they loaded her surprisingly minimal belongings into the car. Dave had thoughtfully fitted a roof rack to accommodate her luggage, but it turned out to be unnecessary. Sally, he reminded himself, was an old St Kilda hand. She knew just to take the minimum needed from regular experience travelling on the small charter helicopter from Benbecula.

Past the turning for Glasgow Airport, they crossed the Erskine Bridge bidding the Central belt goodbye and headed north-west toward Crianlarich. Following the A82 and A87 the Peugeot reached Uig ferry terminal on Skye mid-afternoon, just over five hours after collecting Sally. They were only just in time for the CalMac ferry loading vehicles to Tarbert on Harris.

For Dave, who had driven his passengers all the way, the one and three-quarter hour crossing felt like a well-earned break. He settled down in the café area of the boat with enthusiasm and ordered a full all-day breakfast to the dismay of Deborah who, for the moment, thought better than challenge the cholesterol intake. Agatha, surprisingly, joined him in bacon and eggs while the other three women chose their allegedly healthier options. Whatever the outcome of the potentially rough crossing to St Kilda, they would at least start the voyage well fed.

The ferry sailed into a gentle north-west breeze blowing across the Minches. The motion of the sturdy ferry proved not to be a problem and Dave was spared the indignity of seasickness for the time being. The catering staff in the café remarked how calm it was compared to conditions a year earlier when many winter sailings had been cancelled.

'Pretty good sailor, I am!' Dave quipped to his female co-travellers.

'We'll see,' provoked Erica. 'Just wait till we set off from Leverburgh.'

Sally was silent, feeling that seasickness was not a suitable topic just as they were eating. Agatha was transfixed, gazing out of the windows spotting the occasional Gannet dropping like a stone to catch fish spotted just beneath the surface. Swallowed whole, the Gannets then took off into the wind to gain the extra lift needed on a full stomach.

Docking at Tarbert a handful of cars, three refrigerated vans and their occupants disembarked the ferry. The Williams party pulled into the car park in the centre of town to get their bearings.

It was late afternoon and already getting dark as the last bus arrived from Stornoway. There would be no onward connection to Leverburgh due to no passengers requesting the destination. Financial cutbacks had curtailed the connecting service for the winter.

Their sailing to St Kilda would be a special charter, Donald Macintyre having brought his boat out especially for them. Even his regular summer sailings were weather dependent, and passengers often waited several days before sea conditions were suitable for the crossing.

Delayed sailing meant extra business for local bed and breakfast establishments and Don was canny enough not to deprive guest houses of business for the sake of a rough crossing. Keep everyone happy was his motto when it came to St Kilda.

Turning right at the red telephone box on the edge of Leverburgh, Dave slowed the Peugeot as they approached the Pier with its cluster of fish sheds, workshops and pub adjacent the empty car park. Lights were on in the pub and a couple of regulars were already sat at the bar.

Deborah was keen to find their accommodation before anything else, so Dave turned the car round and drove back up the short hill from the Pier. The hostel stood on an area of raised ground to their right, a hundred yards or so in front of the freshly whitewashed Free Church Kirk. They had missed it driving past from the other direction, but the hostel looked welcoming. It had been freshly decorated in bright and cheery colours.

No problem with parking outside the door at this time of year. There were no other occupants that week and the owner, Euan invited them in with genuine enthusiasm. He had opened the hostel especially for the group. They would be out of luck with the restaurant, but he assured them that bar meals would still be available in the pub.

Euan's partner Liz was working away as journalist assigned to report on long term effects of continuing riots in England. Edinburgh's recent riot seemed to have been a one-off, but Deborah was particularly keen on avoiding getting caught up in anymore.

They were shown to their pine clad rooms; Dave and Deborah shared one room and next-door Erica and Agatha settled in for the night. Sally was pleased to have a double room to herself. She preferred her own company at night, spending her days mentoring others was fine but out of hours personal space meant a lot to her. The Williams' cat was not allowed indoors but was accommodated in the kennel at the back of the hostel reserved for summer visitors' dogs.

They all agreed to meet outside in half an hour and walk down to the Moorings for their last meal out and social occasion for the foreseeable future.

Walking down they could see the three refrigerated vans parked up with small auxiliary engines running to cool their loads. It had become necessary to run the chillers in winter since climate change had warmed the once frosty nights. They would be collecting frozen fish from the trawlers before returning to the Skye and onwards to supermarkets on the mainland.

The last of the daylight was rapidly disappearing as they entered the warmth of the pub. Erica had already remarked that it seemed less cold here than it would have been in Edinburgh that night.

Dave was about to enlighten her on the effect of the Gulf Stream on the Western Isles but thought better of it. He had had a long day; in fact it felt like considerably more than a day since they set out on the M8 motorway that morning. It seemed time ran slower in the west. Sunset was certainly thirty minutes later than Edinburgh, he thought to himself.

Gathering at the bar they studied the menu. There were no specials out of season, so it was going to be micro-waved meals or nothing. Fresh salad was a surprise though.

The pub had links with the organic grower's co-operative for Harris and Lewis. Idealistic incomers had arrived in the late twentieth century and had now become established members of the community. Initially expected to fail, their endeavours had brought a new energy to the economically dying area south of Stornoway.

Polytunnels could supply fresh produce at any time of the year, even January. The polythene clad greenhouses were commonplace and should winter gales destroy the coverings they were easy and cheap to replace.

With the price of sheep fluctuating year on year, many landowners had also embraced wind-turbines to supplement their income. The big development on Harris had been controversial but for a while local builders found a reliable source of employment. The controversy was soon forgotten when the returns started to role in. Wind was predictable, free and available all year round to all in the Hebrides prepared to harness its natural energy.

Dave bought a round of dark local beer. He was hard up since losing his job, but the occasion demanded the gesture. Agatha asked for a soft drink and was satisfied with a cola. The others gratefully accepted the Hebridean beers.

The food came within a few minutes; nothing that special but at the end of a long day the Moorings supplied a good meal in the small dining room adjacent the bar. The five travellers were hungry and ate virtually in silence.

As they finished their meal, Erica commented she had just seen a middle-aged man enter the bar with a guitar case. A few minutes later, a similar aged woman carrying a fiddle came in followed by a younger man with a banjo. It seemed to Dave that the Moorings was hosting a music session. A final bonus before they set off for an unknown life in the morning.

The session proved to be a quieter affair than he had expected. It seemed the three musicians from Leverburgh simply came to the Moorings to practice in the warm atmosphere of the pub. It also seemed a bit odd to Dave that the trio were playing country and western classics rather than so called Celtic music he had expected to hear in the Hebrides. The locals liked country and western, so the band kept atmospheric ballads, jigs and reels for tourists during the summer months.

This time Deborah got up to buy the round. Dave felt uncomfortable about it, but too tired to protest. With a sigh he sat back against the bench and turned to his daughters.

'So, here we are. What do you expect the next few months are going to be like?'

Erica smiled and shrugged. 'Don't really know, Dad. It is going to be interesting though. We will just have to wait and see what happens.'

'Agatha?'

She looked up from studying a tourist brochure on Hebridean wildlife.

'Sorry, Dad. What was that?'

'I was wondering how you expect to find life at St Kilda?'

'Oh, that's easy. I'll be studying the birds and any other wildlife. I am looking forward to being recorder for the Trust. My long-term aim is to work for them out there, it would be just perfect. Realistically though, I doubt anyone will get employed solely as an ecologist in this recession. Yes, I am really looking forward to walking out each day with my binoculars and camera. It's a dream come true!'

Sally, though not directly involved in the conversation thought to comment.

'What you will find is an end to social life as you know it. The island is effectively dead. It was problematic before, when the MOD guys were there, but we will be starting from an almost clean sheet. I know the place, but you are going to have to make your own social lives out there.'

Erica remained silent but Agatha was adamant.

'I don't need a social life! I'd be quite happy without anyone out there. Anyway, people just ruin things for me.'

Returning with a tray of drinks, Deborah frowned as she caught Agatha's last comment. Agatha's self-isolation was the one thing that worried her about her younger daughter.

As a young teenager she rarely joined in with the girlish escapades of her peers. She seemed alright on the surface, but it was hard to know what made her tick, how she really felt growing up in an uncertain world. Sometimes Deborah thought Agatha was old beyond her teenage years, so unlike Erica who had blundered into just about every pitfall waiting for a growing young woman. At least Erica had survived, and her newfound worldly wisdom might prove an asset for them all yet.

Deborah passed the drinks around; Dave accepted his beer, noticing she gave him an inquiring glance. There were odd occasions during their marriage when she had wondered about Dave too.

With all his professed academic equality and diversity, from time to time she had caught glimpses of another side to him; a patriarchal yet fragile side to his character, an inflated ego that was easily offended.

Not a totally bad trait, it was nice to think that when it came to the crunch he might rise and slay any dragon threatening her family. Completely unrealistic of course and where they were going, she felt, though had yet to openly mention, they would need a strong maternal presence to hold the family together.

If she was completely honest, she would have preferred not to have had Sally with them. Again, that was an unrealistic, Sally's skills would be needed should any medical emergency arise, but she was another mature woman. Could she turn out to be a potential rival?

'Mum! Where have you gone?'

Erica had noticed Deborah's thoughts drifting away and perceived a passing shadow.

'Sorry, Erica; I was miles away.'

Her daughter's astute perception felt uncanny at times, but Deborah returned to the present as the trio of musicians struck up across the other side of the bar. The middle-aged guitarist was singing the Eagles classic 'Take it Easy' and the lyrics struck a chord with her.

'I'm a running down the road trying to loosen my load. I got seven women on my mind.'

Poor Dave, she thought. He's got all four of us women to keep in order out there.

'Four that wanna own me, two that wanna stone me, one says she's just a friend of mine – take it easy, take it easy.'

'Hey Dave, this must be our song, eh?'

He pretended not to notice his wife's tease. Bit too astute perhaps?

'When are the other three arriving then? I'll have quite a harem by the sounds of it!'

Erica laughed, 'In your dreams old man!'

'We'll see what we can do for you when we get to St Kilda – old man!'

Deborah was back into the family jokes. Sally, although feeling slightly excluded, managed a smile.

The musicians stopped their song abruptly to take their drinks and chatted amongst themselves. Clapping didn't seem appropriate as the performance had seemed more of a rehearsal than anything else.

The evening in the pub continued. Dave got up to chat with the musicians, now seated at the bar, while the women chatted and laughed together around the table.

Sally's yawn reminded them all that they had an early start, needing to be back at the pier for 07.30 to get their stuff loaded and hand the car over to Dan, who had arranged to meet them there.

They got up to go, somewhat reluctantly in Dave's case. He was beginning to feel at home in the bar chatting with the locals. Leverburgh was more sociable than he had expected, and he would have been happy to have ended their westward trek there if he had the choice. Agatha would have never forgiven him of course.

Cheery goodbyes from the bar staff and late drinkers sent them out into the blustery but dry darkness. The sparse street lighting made their route back to the hostel only just possible without resorting to a flashlight. Agatha rummaged in her fleece pocket and produced a small head-torch. After city life the darkness came as a surprise. Goodness knows what it would be like on St Kilda with no outside light at all, thought Deborah. But still, there would be nobody else there to worry about and precious little need to go out after dark anyway.

'Fuck, shit!' Dave, slightly drunk had walked into an iron bollard just at the right height to hit him where it hurt most.

'Excuse my French, ladies. I hadn't expected it to be this dark. There'll be no rioting in Leverburgh, that's for sure. You can't see enough to do anything out here!'

None of them noticed the *Beluga* had tied up to the jetty before they left the pub. Donald Macintyre would be in the Moorings shortly when the real music session started and would be finishing in the small hours of the morning, when in summer it would already be light.

'Come on, Dad. Let's get you home.' Erica put her arm through his and the group wound their way back up the hill to the hostel and waiting beds.

Euan was still up when they got back. He wanted to know what they would like for breakfast. Options ranged from a full fried breakfast to fruit and yoghurt. Coffee, tea or fruit juice for drinks. Dave, in his bruised and slightly drunken condition opted again for the full fried breakfast with coffee while Deborah, Erica and Agatha chose from muesli and fruit options. Sally asked for filled rolls to take with her. She didn't want to eat anything before the sea crossing to St Kilda.

Lying in bed next to Deborah, who by that time was fast asleep, Dave tried to think what it would be like. He imagined pioneer families led by their knowledgeable patriarch making their way into unknown territory. Yes, it was his manifold destiny to be doing this. With his family he would be resettling St Kilda.

After the rebuff from the Head of Geography, he could regain his self-esteem in a man's world. Looking at his wife snoring gently beside him, he felt aroused by the warmth of her body. It felt reassuring that she had opted to come with them. He hadn't expected this adventure to have come about so easily. Perhaps, if he ever got the chance, he should thank the young car thieves who made all this possible.

The grey and windy dawn came all too soon. The north-westerly was driving the swell onto the pier. Donald Macintyre was fuelling the boat as the Williams sat down for their hostel breakfast. Sally had picked up her filled rolls and taken a walk down to the pier to chat with Don.

Don and his young assistant Lachie were busy checking that all first aid supplies and other requirements for the journey were in place. The *Beluga* hadn't been out of Tarbert since the end of last season, and this was not going to be an easy crossing. It rarely was, even in the summer months.

Dave enthusiastically tucked into his fried breakfast. The black pudding, eggs and bacon were complimented by mushrooms, tomatoes and fried bread. He washed it all down with a pot of strong black coffee.

'It doesn't get much better than this, does it?'

The women looked somewhat appalled at his indulgence that morning. Erica and Agatha picked at their own light breakfasts. Deborah kept to tea and toast noting that Sally had kept to her planned abstinence that morning.

Euan came over to them, looking at his watch, and suggested they had better get down to the pier promptly as Donald would be ready for them by now. Taking the hint, they all got up and fetched their overnight bags to load the car for the three-hundred-yard journey to their new life.

The cat was retrieved from her night in the kennel, and it took only a few moments to get her, protesting loudly, back into the basket. After paying Euan they piled in and drove the car down the hill to where Donald and Lachie were waiting for them. They unloaded the baggage into the gently rocking red and white launch that would be their lifeline between Harris and St Kilda.

There was no sign that Dan had arrived to collect the car. It turned out he had missed the first bus from Stornoway, so Donald recommended that Dave leave the car in the Moorings car park.

Lachie would drop the keys off at the hostel later and Euan would sort things out when Dan turned up, there being no other accommodation open at that time of the year.

Dave was taken aback by the informality of the arrangement, but it seemed to be the way things worked in Leverburgh. Everyone knew each other and most of each other's business in the small resident community.

The boat was loaded by 08.15 and the group safely on board. Despite the informality, Donald and Lachie were professional operators and insisted on giving a short health and safety presentation. They were surprised to see the cat basket and it was left to Sally to explain.

'I did warn them about the no alien species rule, but there will be no-one there to complain. It might be nice to have a pet around anyway.'

'On all accounts, never, ever take off your life jackets on the crossing. We will be sailing west across a north-westerly wind today – so it's not going to a comfortable crossing, I am afraid. I strongly recommend that you always stay in the cabin and Lachie will do his best to keep you comfortable.'

Don's euphemism implied that seasickness was going to be inevitable, thought Deborah.

'In the unlikely event of emergency, the life-rafts are stowed on deck. We have the latest communication technology so if the worst came to the worst we wouldn't be bobbing about for long – I hope!'

Don rarely wore his own lifejacket; it was a local joke that if you saw him wearing one you knew the crossing was going to be bad. He was wearing it that Tuesday morning and underneath, a warm fleece and on his head, a matching woollen hat.

Lachie, as was his norm, dressed casually in jeans, trainers and a nylon bomber jacket. Lachie threw his cigarette into the water and untied the mooring ropes. Donald gently pushed the throttle levers forward, deftly controlling the burbling diesel engines and the *Beluga* pulled away.

Only when they were safely past the moored fishing boats did he open up the powerful twin diesel engines. Surging forward, the *Beluga* mounted each swell before twisting to the left and rising again. The group sat grim and silent in the cabin. Sally felt vindicated by her abstinence regarding breakfast. She had made this trip several times before when the helicopter had been cancelled due to poor visibility..

Soon regretting the fried breakfast, Dave went to get up and go aft. Lachie gently but firmly placed a hand on his shoulder, implicitly recommending that he stay seated as the boat rose, twisted and fell across the rising swell. He handed Dave a plastic pint glass to catch his regurgitating breakfast.

With grim fascination, Agatha began to think of several species of seabirds which regurgitated oily food to feed their young. The thought made her feel queasy too and Lachie noticed the signs and passed her a pint glass as well.

Dave filled three plastic pints over the next few minutes and Agatha just one. Deborah lasted a few minutes longer and Erica just managed to keep her breakfast down, though her ashen face betrayed how she was feeling. Only Sally remained virtually untouched by the gastric protest around her. For her, the unhealthy smell of cat diarrhoea was more likely to upset her composure.

By the time the boat passed the Monach lighthouse, on the island of Shillay, the swell had risen considerably. White horses were breaking over the bow of the *Beluga*. The relentless corkscrew motion allowed only intermittent views of one of the most isolated lighthouses in Europe.

Dave was by this time past caring about anything other than getting this crossing over with. Shortly afterwards Agatha caught sight of the island of Boreray away to the right. The iconic image of the second largest St Kildan island appeared and disappeared as the boat lurched towards their destination. With minds concentrated on surviving the crossing with stomachs intact, the unexpected arrival into calmer waters of Village Bay came as a complete surprise.

Passing rocky Levenish, the island at the entrance to the bay, the roar of *Beluga*'s engines changed to a steady drone as the boat slowed into the final approach to St Kilda's jetty four hours after leaving Leverburgh. The trip could take an hour less in optimum conditions.

Donald perceptibly relaxed and Lachie went aft to light a cigarette, looking around him at the island he had not expected to see until next Easter at the earliest. For him the most noticeable thing that morning was the almost total silence. Apart from the drone of their engines and the slapping waves, the island was to all intents and purposes dead.

There were no signs of life anywhere. No rumble from the power-station floated across the bay. No beep from the reversing Case loader greeted them, as it used to. The sounds of St Kilda had changed, and it wasn't just the seasonal absence of seabirds. The village seemed really dead this time. The only movement was the slowly moving flock of brown Soay sheep grazing the village fields.

Taking a last drag on his cigarette, Lachie spotted a solitary figure walking past the front of the power-station toward the jetty. The figure stopped briefly, looking out toward them as they slowed toward the jetty.

The tide was high and there would be no problem tying up the *Beluga* for a couple of hours. There would be no Warden to complain about it either. The idea that rats might come ashore from the *Beluga* had always seemed ridiculous to Don, but he had to abide by the rules if he was to keep his business.

Lachie went back to the helm and spoke quietly to him, saying that he had seen someone walking toward the jetty and it might be prudent to moor to the orange buoy they used in summer months.

Don rightly sensed his passengers had had enough that morning and decided to tie up at the jetty anyway. Transfer by small open dingy was always risky for the passengers and the Williams party looked done in. The figure now walking down the old slipway toward them was a surprise though.

Phil Brown was feeling sick again after the shock of all that had happened to him that morning.

They had left Aberdeen in high spirits for the trip of a lifetime and now he was the only survivor of a foolish, very foolish plane wreck. He had heeded all received advice about air travel. He had sat at the back of the plane, kept himself strapped in his seat and survived while the other eight now lay dead, somewhere under the waters of north Atlantic.

Whether they were dead or alive when the Piper went over the cliff, he would have no way of knowing but they were certain to be dead by now. He hoped that they were dead before the aircraft slipped under the waves into whatever watery grave awaited them.

The thought of his companions trying to claw their way out as the water rose around them proved too much and he staggered and fell retching on the slippery descent to the jetty. He picked himself up as the *Beluga* came alongside.

Don Macintyre looked at Lachie, 'Who on earth could that be?'

As far as everyone knew, the island was empty. By now the Williams party noticed the man walking, painfully by appearances, toward them. While the others began unloading their belongings and equipment, Sally briskly walked over to him. She didn't have a chance to ask her first question. Phil Brown broke down as he tried to explain what had happened on the far side of the island.

'We crashed, we bloody crashed. They've gone over the cliff, they're all gone.'

He was sobbing as Sally placed a comforting arm around him and led him to sit down on the stepped jetty wall.

'OK, can you tell me your name?' she asked.

'It's Phil, Phil Brown and I am from Banstead in Surrey.'

'So, Phil, can you tell me if you think you're hurt beyond the scratches I see?'

Sally assumed there couldn't be too much physically wrong with him if he had, as he claimed, walked from the top of the hill.

'I was in the back of the plane, and I thought that low flying run pretty stupid, so I stayed strapped into my seat just in case. Even the pilot advised it but no-one else seemed to listen. It saved my life, but I think the rest are all dead. I tried to ring for help, but all the phones are down.'

Sally asked further, 'Where is the wreck, Phil. We'll have to go up there and see if there is anyone else left alive.'

Phil explained that just after he managed to get out of the plane, a strong gust of wind had blown him to the ground and sent the crashed plane sliding over the cliff.

Sally walked back to the others. 'Seems we have a serious incident to deal with, just what we didn't need!'

Previously, the Base Supervisor would have taken charge in such a situation. Now it would be up to her. She explained the situation as related by Phil.

Don shook his head, 'They never learn; this is no place for aerobatics. However, we'd better do something; I'll go out to the mouth of the bay and try calling on VHF. Somebody ought to pick it up when I am past Oiseval and Dun.'

VHF radio transmission had always been problematic in the Bay due to signals being blocked by the topography of the islands. As the youngest and fittest member of the party, Agatha volunteered to walk up the hill to check if there were any survivors up there. Sally suggested she went with her knowing the terrain like the back of her hand.

The *Beluga* surged out beyond the entrance to the Bay. Donald switched his VHF radio to Channel 16 and made an emergency call. He tried several times before he got a crackly reply. Not from the closed down coastguard station at Stornoway but from the Rangehead Offices on South Uist.

'Hi, Don – what's up?-over.'

The operator sounded quite jocular at first, but her tone became serious as he described what he believed to have happened to a small sight-seeing aircraft.

'OK, I'll pass the message to the Range Supervisor, and I expect we'll get a chopper out there shortly. I'll notify the Coastguard in Aberdeen as well, but I am sure we will get there first-out.'

Agatha and Sally made their way slowly up the twisting track to the top of the hill. Agatha's lungs and legs were soon complaining with the relentless climb from sea-level to fourteen hundred feet in less than a mile.

They got their breath back at the T-junction where the track separated to service the radar installations at Mullach

Mor and Mullach Sgar. Walking along the earth dyke at the top of Glen Mór they soon saw the ripped turf where the Piper had come down.

Various personal items lay scattered at the top of the glen but of the aircraft itself there was no sign. They walked over to the cleits near the Lover's Stone and saw that Phil's account had been correct.

One cleit showed damage from the plane's impact and there was a clear gouge in the turf where the inverted tail had dragged the ground before the plane slid over the cliff and into the sea hundreds of feet below. Apart from gouged turf, a few oily smears on the granite were the only evidence the Piper had ever been there. Other rusting aircraft parts in the vicinity had been there since the Second World War.

It had taken them forty-five minutes to walk up from the jetty. Donald had obviously got through to someone as a small helicopter could be seen approaching from the south-east.

After slowly circuiting the area, so the pilot could check the direction of the wind from the movement of ground vegetation, the helicopter finally settled on flat ground near the Mullach Sgar radome. Strong winds deflected from the cliff edge passed over the top of the helicopter after it landed. The pilot and paramedic walked over slowly. From above, they had seen no sign of the Piper and in their heavy immersion flying suits were not going to rush.

'Doesn't look like there's much we can do here. Just one survivor, Sally?'

'Yes, he's down at the jetty. Probably best if you take him back with you. It's been a real nightmare of a day for him by all accounts.'

'Righto, Sal. We'll flip down to the helipad and collect him. Is he hurt?'

'Don't think so. But he was in shock when he came down. I'll leave him to you. Can you contact the Coastguard and explain they might as well stand down for the time being. Nothing further anyone can do here for now. They might send a salvage vessel out later, but I doubt they'll bother.'

The small helicopter was buffeted by winds from all directions before settling again several hundred feet below at the helipad. The crew walked along the road to the jetty, past the deserted Base.

In the past they would have been invited in for a mug of tea, maybe a dram, but not today. Phil Brown was still in shock but managed to walk along the seafront to the helipad unaided.

He was seated and strapped in the back seat of the helicopter after assuring the crew he would be alright. The chopper was buffeted once again as it took off and followed the sheltering slope of Oiseval before turning into the following tail wind back to South Uist. As the small helicopter disappeared over the horizon emptiness returned to St Kilda.

Don Macintyre had stacked all the boxes, cases and rucksacks at the landward end of the jetty, waiting for the short transit up the slope to the Manse. It was an old habit from when the military obliged with Land Rover transport to carry baggage up to the cottages.

'Well, that was an unexpected introduction for you out here. To be honest, just about anything can happen out here,' Don remarked.

'So that must be us just about done. Remember you can ring me when you get your phones up and running and I am generally available on VHF Channel 12, but of course you'll have to go up to the top of the hill if you want to transmit beyond the bay. I'll be coming out regularly after Easter but for the next few months you should have enough tinned stuff in the Base stores to be getting on with. I know I shouldn't say this, but this island used to grow the best barley in the Hebrides. It's a shame these fields have been left untended after all the hard work the St Kildans put into them. Josephine would hate me for this but if I was living here, I'd be turning the ground right now. Sod the archaeology, it's the present that matters not the mess of the past.'

Dave looked shocked at the archaeological heresy he was hearing. The women simply nodded their agreement, apart from Agatha whose mind seemed to be elsewhere, gazing across the bay toward the cliffs of Dun. She was the only one to notice a spinning column of spray, a sea-devil, disappear into one of the sea caverns running under the thin, peak ridged island.

'Come on, let's get our stuff up to the Manse.'

Group activity would get them all focussed, thought Dave. It hadn't been too good so far with a plane crash and local advice that the heritage organisations had been getting it all wrong.

The last fifty yards up the flagstone slipway proved harder than he had expected. The former Warden used to clean weed and algae off the stone path but now it was slippery as grease. They had all slipped and fallen a couple of times before the luggage was stacked up outside the Manse porch.

The stone wall at the front of the house had been quickly thrown up after the Manse had been renovated and the work of unskilled volunteers was already beginning to fall. Soay lambs thought nothing better than running along the wall bleating to their dams. Ovine traffic was not what the wall had been intended for and instead of enhancing first impressions of the island the crumbling wall hinted at decay and impermanence.

Even Dave had to admit that Josephine's instruction that they were not to change anything, not even make minor repairs to damaged walls was a bit ridiculous. Funding for the resettlement project could be withdrawn if they tried any such thing.

Deborah had the keys, and she walked around the Manse opening front and back doors. She found the diesel generator left for them in the small store on the end of the building. The boat house was a few yards away on the sea front.

It struck her that in an all-electric home they would have to start this generator every time they wanted to make a cup of tea. This was not going to be easy but at least the machine had a battery powered starter motor. They went inside to find the Manse dry and clean if noticeably unaired. The building contractors had made a good job of the house unlike the wall outside.

Draught proofing around doorways and double glazing was excellent and she would soon have the house cosy for the rest of the family. Sally walked around with her, marvelling at the standard of the accommodation inside the Manse.

The Warden's office was well equipped with modern computers and high-tech communication equipment, just a pity there was such a limited electrical supply.

The shop held a good stock of books on the Island, so no shortage of background information there. Don had mentioned he liked the shop to be open for his passengers before they left the island.

It did smell a little musty in the shop, probably a legacy of so many, often damp, human bodies crammed in there during the summer tourist season. At the end of the corridor from the front porch was a living room complete with new looking three-piece suite, and to cap it all, mounted on the wall beside the window, an enormous plasma television screen. That small generator was going to have its work cut out, Deborah thought.

Past the small bedrooms they came to the all-electric kitchen. It was spotless, whoever had been here last had been obsessive about cleaning. Sally made the comment that obsessive cleaning was often to compensate for deep seated unhappiness. Whoever had used this kitchen before them had not been happy, even with panoramic views across the bay to the now darkening rocks of Dun.

They moved on down the corridor to the shower rooms and toilets. The new fittings were already beginning to rust and blue green copper stains in the wash basins indicated acidic water was eating away at the copper pipes.

Likely to be a few stomach upsets before they get used to this water supply, Sally thought. They had been assured the water was potable and the high acidity would no doubt help nullify the effect of bacteria from the frequent sheep corpses lying in the water catchment beneath Conachair.

They were not supposed to dispose of them but to leave them to rot so as not to affect the island ecology. The sheep population was to be left to rise and fall as nature dictated, according to the strict brief from the Trust.

In the back porch area, there was a laundry room and additional toilet for visitor use. There was also a large upright freezer, clean and emptied, as there was no mains electricity supply. The tour around the house brought home to Erica just how unsustainable life on St Kilda had become.

'Not just unsustainable regarding energy,' Sally added, 'but how could the community have sustained itself without family life. There were just not enough women here and those that were here generally beyond childbearing age. No wonder a few of the female conservation volunteers went home pregnant. The communal urge for procreation is a strong one, stronger still where there is so little outlet for its expression.'

Outside, cleits stood timeless, scattered across the hill side like so many enormous barnacles. Sally pointed them out to Dave and Deborah.

'Just look at those cleits, the St Kildans had it right. You could store anything in those. The wind blows in through the dry-stone walls and the turf capped roof keeps the rain

97

out. They used to store everything in there from Puffin meat to peat for their fires.'

'Don't think I'd fancy going up and over the hill to get milk for my tea though.'

Agatha made her first comment since they started the tour of the Manse.

'Ah, but youngsters like you held the community together. That's how it worked, Agatha. The young supported the old and when they became too infirm to go up the hill a new generation of youngsters would support them. The change came at the end of the nineteenth century and beginning of the twentieth when the youngsters left for a better life on the mainland. As for the latter years of the twentieth century it was just ridiculous. No matter how pally the men got, there was no way they were going to produce kids to keep the place going.'

The women had to laugh at Sally's wry observation. Meanwhile Dave was exploring too. He had found the office and shop and realising everything was dependent on electricity decided that he would assume responsibility for getting the generator going.

He left the women to their exploration of the domestic domain not realising Deborah had already found the generator and fathomed how to use it. As Josephine had written down in the general instruction folder, there was a key cabinet in the office and he quickly found the brass key marked 'Flare Store,' the small dry extension room which now housed the generator they would all depend on.

He had to stoop slightly to get in there and brushing cobwebs aside found the machine and control panel mounted on the wall. There was a laminated instruction card hanging on the back of the door but as he couldn't flick on the light until the generator was running, he took it outside to read. It looked easy enough; make sure the fuel tank was topped up – it was. Make sure no heavy use appliance was switched on before starting up.

He was sure the cooker and heaters in the Manse were all turned off. He checked the oil; it looked fresh and golden. This engine didn't look like it had ever been used. The key was in the ignition switch, and it was just a simple matter of turning the key and off she'd go. That's what the instruction sheet implied but when he turned the key all he heard was a grating noise as the ratchet of the starter motor failed to engage with the gear ring on the main engine.

The battery was exhausted. He unscrewed the caps on the battery and peered into the cells which were grey and sulphated. Even with his limited mechanical knowledge he could tell this battery was scrap. Oh, well there was probably another battery in the Base somewhere and there was a manual method to start the engine with a cranking handle.

Rust was beginning to show through the galvanised coating on the starting handle clipped to the side of the generator. He inserted the handle onto the end of the engine crankshaft and turned it as hard as he could. As the engine came up to compression the handle stopped dead. There must be a knack to this, he thought.

The same thing happened a second time, he was getting nowhere. Male pride was at stake, and he wanted to get the generator running to impress the women if nothing else. He stepped back from the small engine and invoked, half seriously, whoever or whatever was the patron saint of small engines. Trying a third time he put all his effort into turning the handle. It stopped dead again but this time the handle slipped on the crankshaft and came off in his hand.

Having put so much energy into swinging the handle his head came down hard on top of the generator air intake casing causing a deep cut and heavy bruising to his right eyebrow. Roaring with pain and frustration he rushed out of the Flare Store dripping blood onto the cropped turf outside.

The blood flow quickly stemmed but the bruise had swelled impressively by the time Deborah ran round to see what on earth had happened. They had heard him bellow and Sally was fast behind her.

Without asking for his agreement, she turned his head and felt the injury. Dave winced but before he could say anything was told he would live but should be more careful in future. The resettlement wasn't going to work if there was going to be a run of avoidable accidents. Sally went to the First Aid box in the office and came back with antiseptic wipes and an adhesive plaster.

'This really ought to have a stitch in it, Dave; but you'll have to live without for now until I find out how to get things sterilised with no electricity.'

Dave's bellowing had snapped Agatha out of her reverie and, while his cut was being dealt with, she went into the shed and brought the instruction card out into the daylight.

'So, for manual start, it says - first ensure the de-compressor lever is lifted - whatever that means?'

Dave reached for the laminated card and scrutinised the instructions again.

'Hmm! I think I'll try again.' His eyebrow was stinging badly, and the swelling felt like wobbling jelly as he turned the handle easily with the de-compressor lever lifted. Agatha read out further instructions to him.

'First, lift the decompression lever. Rotate the starting handle and when a vigorous momentum has been reached lower the de-compressor lever and the engine should start. Repeat procedure if engine does not start at once.'

Dave swung the handle as fast as he could with his right arm and lowered the de-compressor lever on top of the engine with his left. Immediately the small engine puttered into life. A brief puff of black smoke issued from the exhaust pipe coming out of the side wall of the stone shed. The generator was running.

'Well, Dad – when all else fails, read the instructions, eh?'

Agatha could be merciless, and Deborah and Sally simply grinned, they were enjoying his humiliation. Feeling doubly foolish, Dave noticed that Erica was nowhere in sight.

'Has anyone seen Erica lately?'

Agatha called for her sister several times before the nearby kirk door opened and Erica came back out into the daylight.

'It's dark in there with the shutters up but I managed to see enough. God, this is a sad place!'

The group walked over to the Free Church building with its high Georgian window frames, the only hint of ornamentation apart from an impressive wooden lectern. Unused for years, damp and mould were taking their toll inside. Dry rot was appearing on wooden panels at floor level and iron gratings supposed to allow adequate ventilation were rusting unpainted in the salt laden atmosphere.

Through the gloom, they entered the rear annex which housed a simple school room where, according to the display boards, scholars from age four to forty would receive education in the sight of the Lord. Some early photographs had been reproduced showing groups of children scowling at the camera while their teacher kept strict control of what should have been a happy school group.

'You know, I couldn't help thinking that the photographer froze the life out of those children when he took the picture. No wonder they wanted to leave when they grew up.'

'That's a bit hard, Erica. They must have had some fun out here.' Deborah commented.

'Yes but looking at such photos perpetuates the misconception. It must have kind of fed on itself. You know, in a way a bit like us coming here expecting to just find cottages and there's a bloody old army base here. They don't show that in any tourist brochures, do they, and the photographer here didn't show any happiness in the children either. God, it makes me mad!'

'Erica, I don't think you should be blaspheming in here.' Dave was being half-serious. 'We don't want any more bad luck, do we?'

The diesel generator had settled down to a steady putter and Sally, sensing the subject ought to be changed suggested they went into the kitchen and made their first cup of tea at St Kilda. There was plenty of tea and sugar left for them in tins and plastic boxes in the cupboards, only dried milk of course. Switching the electric kettle on raised the exhaust note of the generator from a gentle putter to a deeper pop, pop, pop sound reminiscent of an approaching fishing boat, thought Sally.

'Well, I'm glad I won't be sleeping beside this racket,' she joked. Sally had yet to take her stuff up the path to the Factor's House. It wouldn't have changed much since her previous contract ended. Just a few mouse droppings to clear up she assumed. The large St Kilda mice seemed to love that house.

She suddenly remembered the Williams cat was still in its basket in the Manse hallway.

'Hey, what about the cat?' Sally was genuinely concerned.

'Flipping heck, I'd forgotten about her with everything else going on. I'll go and get her.'

Deborah returned with the now purring cat in her arms. Its fur somewhat greasy after the crossing but happy to be in human habitation and familiar company again.

'You know we never gave her a proper name, did we?' This time Agatha spoke for the cat. 'She can't just be called 'cat' now she's come out here with us. I'd like to call her something special.'

'Like what?' queried her mother already pouring the tea into immaculately clean cups.

'Cailly! That would be brilliant, really cool in fact.'

'Cailly? You mean like Kylie, Kylie Minogue?' her mother was puzzled.

'No Mum, Cailly after Cailleach the Gaelic word for wise woman.'

'Shouldn't that be more like Kaya?' interrupted Dave. He had already done some background reading on the area and thought Cailly too much of an Anglicisation, even diminutive.

'Cailly sounds sweet though. I agree with Agatha for once; let's call her that; the sweet little wise cat of St Kilda.'

Deborah's maternal authority settled the matter.

'Anyway, now we have found out the hard way to get electricity into this house I propose that, when we have finished our tea, we have a look round the rest of the village. We have enough food for tonight so we can leave checking the Base till the morning.'

A few minutes later the family, led by Sally, set out to explore the village. Turning left out of the front door the first building they encountered was the boat house.

Opening the sliding door, a quick peek inside revealed a dated RIB on its rusty trailer. The old rigid hulled inflatable boat had been used to store various related bits of clutter. Several lifejackets had been stowed but were showing signs of mouse damage. Somehow the rodents had managed to climb up and into the boat. Several fishing rods were stacked in a corner and a couple of crab pots lay to the right of the door. There was an old metal cupboard in there and when opened revealed a collection of rusty tools and boxes of fishing accessories, hooks, line and various lures.

'We'll be alright for some fish then,' commented Dave. The women ignored him and turned around to go outside.

The next building was a two story late eighteenth-century stone-built house perched right at the sea's edge.

Cliff erosion had eaten the ground away almost to its foundations.

'This,' said Sally, 'is the Feather Store. It was the best building on St Kilda and used to store the island produce before it was shipped away by the Factor to pay rent in kind. It's only recently been in use as accommodation.

There's a very basic flat upstairs, though downstairs is still storage space. It's full of ladders and building materials. It must be a wild place to stay when there's a storm raging. Don't know if I'd fancy it myself, though.

Erica was quietly thinking that the Feather Store flat might be just the place she could fancy living in, away from the sterility of the refurbished Manse. Already, she wasn't intending to stay in the Manse for any longer than was necessary. One of the shutters on an upstairs window had come loose and was swinging in the breeze.

Dave went up the stone steps into the flat to secure it from inside. The rest of the group followed, including Cailly who was by now showing a keen interest in the smell of mice in the flat. Dave secured the shutter, and they found themselves in semi-darkness and stumbling slightly they made their way back to the door. The mouse smell was strongest near the kitchen area and had they opened the low cupboards they would have seen crockery and cutlery stained with fresh droppings and mouse urine.

Out in the fresh air again, Sally led them to the straight path that ran gently uphill through the village. The first structure they found was a well, protected by dry-stone walls and turf capped roof. Erica asked why the water looked stagnant and undrinkable in this supposedly pristine environment. Dave suggested it was because the well hadn't been used in years, not since the 1930 evacuation, probably. Small purple flowers grew in profusion around the small, corbelled building.

'Yes, it's a common problem with old wells. If you don't keep drawing water from them, they stagnate and become breeding grounds for all sorts of unpleasantries,' Sally informed them. Erica walked over to the lip of the well and began scraping with her boot to release the stagnant water.

'Erica! What are you doing?'

Dave was aghast. After all they had been told about not touching the archaeology, his daughter was altering it within hours of arrival on St Kilda.

'This water needs to flow! As Sally just said, the well will be no good unless we use it. It is as good as poison as it is.'

Sally protested, 'Erica, I would strongly recommend against drinking any well water here. There are many rotting sheep beyond the head-dyke, and you could catch just about anything drinking from wells. The water supply for the Base is connected to the Manse. It is by no means perfect, but at least drawn from a relatively uncontaminated underground source. Two years ago, the chlorination plant was closed due to associated health risks and a new borehole was dug in An Lag. Let's just drink tap-water, OK?'

The Williams were surprised to hear Sally being so forceful but accepted that on matters of health, she was to be respected. That is apart from Erica who had been stung by the unexpected rebuke at her effort to improve the well.

Moving up the path they passed between large, almost monumental, dry-stone walls. Entrances in the walls marked storage areas of a similar style to the cleits on the hillside above. Copious sheep droppings showed their adoption as shelters by the village sheep flock.

As soon as it rained, Sally said, the well-fed village sheep made a beeline for the nineteenth- century shelters leaving their lush grazing until the downpour ceased. It was the same with strong sunshine and high winds. They really had it made in the village, unlike the flocks away on the hill and far side of the island which had to fend for themselves in all weathers.

'Down in the village, they are a bit wimpy,' Sally added.

Cailly's tail went up as a brown Soay ewe and her yearling lamb came along the muddy path toward them. The lamb seemed fearless, and the group watched with some amusement as the lamb went up to Cailly and touched noses with her. The lamb was much bigger than the cat and after a moment's hesitation, Cailly rubbed herself on the lamb's shoulder.

Introductions having been made; the lamb jumped up effortlessly onto the remains of a fallen cleit while its mother eyed Cailly with some suspicion. The sheep were virtually fearless of humans who for years had studied them as part of, a long-running Edinburgh University research project. Cats were an unknown quantity but finally assuming Cailly to be harmless the ewe joined its lamb on the ruined cleit, knocking a few more stones down as it climbed up.

'Look at that,' pointed out Erica, still smarting from her rebuke. It's OK for sheep to knock everything down but we must just stand here and watch them do it!'

'Fraid so, Erica. It's part of the deal being here,' said Sally. The sheep get everywhere, and we must just let them do what they want. They've considerably altered the ground flora, cropping the turf much closer than it used to be when villagers controlled their livestock.'

'Come on, I'll show you where I'm staying.'

To Sally, Erica was showing signs of becoming trying. She hoped Erica would be able to cope with living here. If her behaviour became too much, Josephine had advised that, as Nurse, she could recommend removal of anyone she considered psychologically unsuited to custodianship at St Kilda.

A few yards further they came to the first and largest house in the village. Compared with the single-story granite cottages further along the 'street,' the white painted and rendered two floored Factor's House was impressive.

It had been the home of nurses in the past and was now being returned to its former function. Sally led them in through the front porch to show them around. Immediately in front of them was the island's one proper bathroom. Sally was to have exclusive use of the one and only village bathtub.

Deborah was envious. Candle-wax marks were clear either side of the taps showing someone had luxuriated here just a few months earlier, presumably Sally. The house had been the privilege of the University sheep project leader when on island. Like so many of her colleagues she had been made redundant when funding for her research had been withdrawn.

The sheep project had run almost uninterrupted since the first evacuation and, the now middle-aged project leader had worked with the Soays since her graduation in the late nineteen-seventies. A collection of eco-philosophy magazines stacked in the porch attested to the earlier occupant's green sentiments.

Erica perked up at the sight of these magazines. Her sulk lifted as she thumbed the top copy.

'Well, this is better. A kindred spirit at last; what a pity she's not here anymore.'

'Yeah, overall, the women here did get on well as a small, outnumbered group. We used to meet at the first cottage up the street to get away from the male enclave. We had some good times in there, I'll show you in a minute.'

Sally was coming to life revisiting better memories from past employment on the island.

The Williams were shown the two rooms downstairs housing the basic kitchen and living room which doubled as an office. Going out the back they were shown external stairs leading to the upper floor housing two bedrooms and toilet.

It was all basic, functional and tidy but although not as strong as in the Feather Store, here too there was a smell of

107

mouse urine. Cailly had gone into the storage area behind the toilet following the enticing scent. A sudden commotion attracted their attention and a moment later the cat appeared proudly carrying a St Kilda field mouse in her jaws.

'What, with Erica and now the cat I don't know why I bother!'

Dave's frustration was becoming clear.

'We've only been here a few hours, and the archaeology and wildlife are getting damaged. Can I remind you we are supposed to be looking after this place!'

Sally gave him an exasperated look and moved on.

'OK, let's go and look at House One where we all used to meet after work – and Dave, please lighten up.'

She led them around the back of the Factor's House and back onto the grassy street, reinforced with granite sets. 'Mind your footing here; the tourists were always slipping over on this section.'

They followed the path over a small clapper bridge of granite slabs. The water of the 'dry burn' rushed beneath them. Cailly was a bit hesitant, still carrying her mouse.

Sally continued, 'This stream used to supply the village and Base water before the borehole was drilled. It sometimes ran dry in the summer as the flow was diverted into those holding tanks over there.'

A short way up the hillside to their right stood three large and rusting water tanks. They had been painted green to lessen their visual impact but now rusting and holed were an eyesore.

The more recent concrete platform above the new borehole was already weathering to a dull grey, matching granite walls nearby. It often overflowed and around the wellhead the saturated ground supported prolific growth of Butterwort, the 'Mothan' plant known throughout the Hebrides for its allegedly beneficial yet psychotropic properties. The sheep had grazed everything else to the ground but wisely left the Mothan untouched.

'There's a local myth that drinking the milk of the cow that ate the Mothan brings unnatural good fortune to the drinker.'

Sally added that was a bit unlikely considering sheep would not touch it but there was an anecdote about an island priest exiled for lascivious behaviour on the island. He had been taken for trial at Dunvegan Castle to explain his unholy communion with the good wives of St Kilda but got off with nothing more than a ticking off due to effects of eating Mothan before the hearing.

'Dan told me a tale like that about Fly Agaric mushrooms, Sally.'

Erica was interested in this subject.

'Apparently Lapland Reindeer herders used to drink the urine of their animals to get high. If they ingested the mushrooms direct, they could go mad or even die. Hope Mothan isn't as powerful as that?'

'Don't worry, Erica. The new well is covered with a concrete cap so no Mothan is going to fall in and even if it does, it will bring us unnatural good luck and maybe, along with the good luck, a bit of lascivious communion too,' she laughed.

Approaching the first cottage, Cailly dropped her mouse and showed interest in the faint food smells coming from a drainpipe below the first window. Behind them, in a flash of brown feathers a small hawk pounced on the dead mouse and flew away with it.

Agatha spotted the small fast flying bird.

'Hey that was a Merlin! They must be here all year round. They're going to like you Cailly.'

Cailly was less than impressed and made a resentful chattering miaow as the bird flew off with her precious mouse.

Entering the basic looking cottage, the Williams were surprised to see another large and well-equipped electric kitchen on one side and dining room tables and benches on the other; in the fireplace stood a Scandinavian wood-burning stove.

Above it, on the mantelpiece, various postcards had been placed having been sent from all over the world by past conservation volunteers, particularly those who had collaborated with the sheep project. There was a well-stocked bookshelf and boxes of board games and a loft hatch, behind which Sally told them, 'Sheepie' stuff was stored. Another inviolate area beyond the prying eyes of men, she added without offering to explain further.

Deborah asked the obvious question.

'St Kilda is treeless, right; we are not allowed to dig peat so what gets burned in that stove, Sally?'

'Thought you'd ask that. The Base used a hell of a lot of packing crates and pallets. Everything came containerised in some way or other so it could be handled by the mechanical loader; the one I remember nearly getting dropped in the sea when we left. The wood is stored in the open shed just over there.'

She pointed to the military workshop area about a hundred yards away from the picturesque cottages.

'We can go and get firewood anytime we like though I suppose it will run out eventually now the Base is closed.'

Dave felt a slight pang of concern. He hadn't reckoned on a women's meeting place like this. He could sense they were looking forward to private get-togethers organised by Sally, to which he would feel, if not actually be, excluded.

Back on the street Sally pointed out House Two, the female dormitory conveniently next door to their meeting place.

They stopped and entered House Three, the museum. It was difficult to read the display panels in the winter light, but they obviously told a balanced story of past island life.

Erica commented that they should go back there later when there was more daylight.

House Four, the bleak male dormitory stood empty, its ex-army single beds pulled away from the wall to protect the mattresses from damp.

Sally led them into House Five, a well-equipped workshop and paint store. Deborah tripped on the step inside the front door and only just saved herself by grabbing hold of the work bench vice. Seeing her sucking a bruised finger, Sally was reminded of the island's primary health hazard.

'That reminds me; tomorrow I am going to have to double check your anti-tetanus status. You will have read that this island had a big tetanus problem in the past. Tetanus is the last thing we want to catch while we are out here.'

The last habitable cottage, House Six had been faithfully restored by the Western Isles Trust to its original design. Entering the small wood panelled lobby, doors to the left and right opened into the two rooms of the St Kildan 'White House.' Windows looked out across fields leading to the sea. Open fireplaces allowed for adequate ventilation, but the rooms smelled of damp and it appeared water had been oozing between the single skin stone walls and concrete floor.

'In spite of these being the most modern houses in the Hebrides when they were built, they soon became undesirable. Thin walls couldn't keep the occupants warm. The tin roofs led to condensation problems and the open fireplaces were terribly inefficient compared with the central hearths of the Blackhouses.'

Sally was obviously very knowledgeable on St Kildan community health issues, thought Erica. Leaving House Six, it was noticeably gloomy outside. Wet flakes of sleet were beginning to fall, and apart from Erica, the group were eager to get back to the Manse.

111

They had left the generator running and anticipated warmth and light ahead for a cosy first evening. Erica noticed an especially large cleit just off the street. Standing alone in a nearby enclosure, the circular stone building had the usual turf capped roof but also a wooden door with rudimentary lock.

'Hey, Sally; what's that place over there?'

'That's Lady Grange's House, or where it used to be. Lady Grange was exiled here during the Jacobite Rebellion in the eighteenth century.'

'Why?' asked Agatha.

'Apparently, she questioned her husband's politics, and his Jacobite pals considered her a security risk. She was sent to Skye first but, still questioning her husband's authority, she was eventually sent out here where she wouldn't be heard by anyone with political influence.' Sally laughed, 'I read somewhere that she practically drove the St Kildans mad with her bossiness!'

'Fucking hell!' Erica was shocked that Sally thought this funny.

'You know, I heard that this place was considered Utopia, a land of equality, an island republic. It seems to me it's worse than the mainland ever was.'

'That's just it, Erica. In its isolation, away from moderating cultural influences, the St Kildan community exhibited extreme versions of cultural trends prevailing on the mainland. It was a case of cultural inbreeding and became just as unhealthy for the community as genetic inbreeding, which incidentally isn't recorded much here. Sorry, I am going off on one of my pet subjects. Let's go back now.'

There seemed to be something Sally had almost touched on but thought better of it, noticed Deborah. She connected this to Josephine's aside that their experience was likely to prove interesting. A shiver ran down her spine not altogether as a result of the squall of sleet that hurried them back down the path toward the Manse.

Though neither had voiced it, Deborah was joining her husband in having doubts about this venture, even before their first day was over.

Electric space heaters had warmed the living room and kitchen area. The bedrooms, though chilly were at least dry compared with the cottages. They gathered in the kitchen.

Sally had decided to stay at the Factor's House to reclaim her home after her short absence from the island. Deborah offered to prepare their first evening meal, suggesting it might be a good idea if they took turns in future, but somehow feeling this role could be hers for the taking.

Dave unpacked their bags in the double bedroom before wandering into the living room followed by Cailly who settled down to sleep on the settee, sated from two more St Kilda mice caught and eaten while the Williams explored the cottages. They had been easy prey compared with their sharper counterparts back in Edinburgh, and twice the size too.

Erica helped her mother, and Agatha followed her father's example by unpacking her bags in the front bedroom. Erica would leave her bags until later.

The generator suddenly increased its revs. Deborah also noticed the electric rings on the cooker dim slightly.

'Dave!' she shouted down the hall. 'Something's going on with the generator, can you check it out?'

There was no answer but instead she heard the familiar voice of a BBC newsreader.

'Dave? You are not doing what I think you are doing, are you?'

She marched into the living room to find Dave on the settee with Cailly settled on his lap. He was watching the early evening television news on the large television set dominating the room.

'Dave, we came here to get away from television and the mindless clutter we had to tolerate back in Edinburgh. Now you have brought it here to us.'

She frowned and added, 'on a practical note, I am trying to cook dinner, and you are hogging the power supply with that thing. Come on, husband dear, play fair if you want feeding tonight.'

Disgruntled, Dave shifted Cailly back onto the cushions and turned the set off. Immediately the generator settled down to chug away steadily outside.

'There's a battery radio in my suitcase, give that a go if you want to hear the news.'

Reluctantly Dave followed Deborah's advice and returned with the small portable radio. Turning it on, all he could hear was hissing where his favourite BBC station should have been. The radio could pick up, to him, unintelligible north Atlantic stations. Faeroese or Icelandic, he thought, and a popular music station from the Irish Republic many miles to the south.

'Typical!,' he shouted to Deborah. 'If we can't get Radio 4, we really are going to be disconnected out here.'

'Don't worry, Dave. Just let me finish cooking, OK?'

The meal was soon prepared, but before Erica went to call her sister and father, she mentioned they ought to check out what had been left for them in the base kitchen.

Don wouldn't be coming out regularly until Easter and the fresh stuff they had brought with them would only last for a few days. The fridge would warm up with the generator turned off. It wouldn't use a lot of power so they should leave the generator running in the background.

Erica had always preferred whole foods back in town and she didn't fancy living off tinned food for months on end. She fetched Agatha and Dave, and the family sat down to their first meal together at St Kilda.

'Just one thing missing, Debs.'

Dave's observation raised her hackles a little. 'Wouldn't it be great if we had a bottle of wine or two right now to celebrate our freedom from Edinburgh?'

With the meal finished the washing up was left till the morning and they retired to their rooms for an early night.

The Trust had certainly splashed out on refurbishment thought Deborah. There were small television sets in each bedroom and intermittent surges from the generator indicated when these smaller sets were in use. Erica remembered to switch off the room heaters. The small diesel engine surged again when Agatha had a hot shower before turning in. Finally, the generator settled down to a gentle tick-over supplying only the kitchen refrigerator and a low energy lightbulb in the corridor.

Sometime in the small hours Erica woke up to a dark and silent house. The generator had stopped running, having exhausted its fuel tank sometime in the night.

She reached for the small head-torch she had placed on her bedside cabinet, slipped on jeans, jumper, and heavy fleece jacket, and walked outside to sit down on the wall overlooking the jetty. The sea was swelling gently beneath her; it was high tide. No light could be seen anywhere on the island or in the bay. Reaching up to her forehead she switched off the torch and let her eyes become accustomed to the starlight.

It was the time of the new moon; the dark moon as she preferred to call the intuitive days when the moon lay in the Earth's shadow and unseen gravitational energy moved all waters below.

Deep in thought, Erica suddenly realised her period was starting. Good job she had thought to bring tampons. Bit unlikely there'd be many in the Base stores she thought, realising the irony of the situation. Not to worry, it was a good sign, and she supposed that living with the elements rather than forever trying to escape them would be bound to affect her. Relaxing, she pulled a woollen hat from her jacket pocket and pulled it over her short hair.

It was cold out in the St Kildan night. She reached into her other pocket and pulled out a battered tobacco tin and rolled a cigarette, she had mixed herbal cannabis with the light tobacco before they left Leverburgh. It had been a surprise to have been offered a deal in the Moorings carpark when she went out for a smoke. Some things never change, even in the Hebrides.

Dragging deeply, she took in just how many stars there were. Feeling alternately insignificant and empowered by the darkness, she could see starlight reflecting off the waters framing the dark silhouette of Dun across the bay.. She could just make out more starlight through the gap between Dun and the headland of Hirta. This resettlement was going to be a challenge, but it was going to be good, she decided. She barely noticed Agatha sit down beside her, woken too by the unaccustomed silence around them.

'It would never have been like this when the Base was occupied.'

Agatha, as usual, was straight to the point. She knew about Erica's soft-drug habit. With astute powers of observation, she had learned almost every secret in the Williams family. She knew about Deborah's brief affair with one of her school colleagues and had calculated, for the time being, not to divulge she knew. Her memory held a library of secrets, knowledge to be revealed only when necessary, necessary to furthering her own plans.

The two sisters sat together looking out over the starlit bay. In the clean air she couldn't help noticing the faint menstrual odour from her sister. The smell of cannabis quickly dispersed in the light breeze blowing offshore, but the subtle smell of her sister's period spurred her ambition for a fresh start, a new beginning for womanhood at St Kilda.

7

Practicalities

Dave woke before Deborah. He didn't take in the significance of the silence at first. It was beginning to feel chilly as the electric heaters had been turned off when they went to bed. Early morning sunshine from the kitchen window illuminated his way along the corridor to the bathroom. It was only after several minutes of waiting for the warm water to appear from the showerhead that he realised the generator had stopped sometime in the night.

'Shit! Now I'll have to fix that, I suppose.'

Dave also thought it would be good to get the generator up and running away from the critical gaze of women. He could retrieve his dignity after the previous afternoon's embarrassment with the machine.

Realizing the silence was probably due to no more than a lack of fuel he went back to his room and studied Josephine's brief. Diesel fuel was to be drawn from the tap on the wall of the power station, facing the sea. Jerry cans were to be found in the workshop area and were to be stood in the concrete bund to prevent spillage escaping.

Getting himself dressed, Dave went to the front porch and put on his heavy-duty fleece jacket and rubber boots over thick socks. Latent warmth from the sea had prevented a hard frost during the night but high on the hill close cropped heather was crisp and white away from the warmth of the bay. He imagined what it must have been like to have smelled peat smoke from their chimney on a crisp morning like this.

Walking over to the workshop area to find a jerry can, he was glad of his rubber boots. The grass was littered with sheep droppings and at the front of the south facing wall, the turf was heavily eroded where generations of sheep had rested close to the comforting sound and warmth of the power-station. They had moved elsewhere now the great engines were silent.

Just a couple of months before, there would have been several men walking with Dave to begin their day in the workshops. He felt slightly spooked at the thought. He was entering a place of ghosts to borrow tools from men who had occupied the island for almost ninety years before abandoning it in as many days.

Five-gallon metal jerry cans were stacked neatly at the back of one of the vehicle garages. He took one and also an orange plastic funnel hanging up nearby. Crossing the yard, he could see the empty office where the supervisor would have been organising the day's work.

At the bottom of the concrete slope from the yard, Dave turned the corner and placed the can beneath the tap on the power station wall. Opening the filler cap, he placed the nozzle of a short black rubber hose into the neck of the can. He opened the valve to let five gallons of diesel fuel fill the can. Filling the can took less time than he had expected, and it was overflowing by the time he managed to turn the tap off.

The bund was black with the evidence of countless similar spillages and Dave was, again, glad of his rubber boots when he stepped over the low concrete wall to retrieve the, by now, heavy fuel can. Stepping back, his oily rubber boots lost their grip on the dew wet concrete, and he fell heavily. Diesel fuel slopped from the can as it lay on its side. He had fallen heavily, and his hip felt bruised when he picked himself up. Cursing he up righted the can and secured the locking filler cap. A sizeable pool of fuel had settled on the concrete standing. He knew this would have to be cleaned up and went to look for something suitable.

Outside the office door he found a fire-bucket full of wet sand. Algae was beginning to grow over cigarette butts stubbed out in the sand weeks earlier.

He returned to the spilled diesel noticing a large blue beetle struggling through the toxic liquid. He quickly trod on the insect to spare it a lingering oil-soaked death and emptied the sand and cigarette butts on the spillage. He would return with a shovel to clear it up later and, hopefully, before his sharp-eyed young daughter spotted the sand and asked awkward questions.

Approaching the door of the Flare Store with the jerry can he had to kick away fresh sheep droppings in front of the entrance. A nearby Soay yearling watched with interest as he opened the door and went inside. Instinctively he flicked on the light switch. Naturally nothing happened. Not wanting further embarrassment, he decided to read the instruction card, outside, before attempting to refill the fuel tank.

A flow chart indicated that in the event of non-start due to lack of fuel the tank was to be replenished and then the engine had to be bled. There was a diagram with arrows pointing to two screws on the fuel filter housing and injector pump.

He could feel a sick tension building up, realising he hadn't a clue about this sort of thing. He was an academic, not a mechanic but the job was obviously going to need a large screwdriver. He could manage that at least. Retracing his steps, he returned to the workshop and took a large plastic handled screwdriver from the tool rack above the long workbench under the window.

Erica was waiting by the Flare Store when he got back. She too had wakened to find the generator dead and had gone to investigate. At least it wasn't Agatha, Dave thought. He had a better rapport with his eldest daughter, and they could sort out this problem in an adult way.

'It's run out of fuel. Trouble is the instructions say we have to 'bleed' the engine and I haven't got a clue.'

He was always honest with Erica; a quality she appreciated after the insincerity of most men she knew back in Edinburgh.

'Let me see, Dad. I've done this once before when Dan's van ran out of fuel. I turned the ignition key and kept the engine cranking while he undid the bleed screws.'

Scrutinizing the print beside the diagram on the instruction card, she read out, 'Slacken bleed-screw (A). When fuel flows from around bleed-screw (A) without bubbles, close the screw tightly. Repeat procedure with the bleed-screw (B) on the injector pump housing. I think we can manage this, don't you? If the engine fails to restart, repeat as necessary.'

Dave acquiesced to Erica's knowledge on the matter and offered to turn the starter handle while she conducted the technical part with the bleed-screws.

This time he remembered to lift the decompression lever, and the engine turned easily. He filled the fuel tank beside the generator. It would have been easier had the tank been on top of the engine and the fuel run through by gravity.

Dave's mind was beginning to take a practical turn, but such layouts had long been considered a fire risk and the engine had to be cranked to raise fuel from floor level. He turned the handle slowly watching with interest as Erica undid the first screw until fuel spurted out following the rhythm of his arm movement.

With Erica half bent over the engine, he couldn't but help notice how his daughter had grown into a shapely young woman. Quickly dismissing further thoughts of that nature, he watched her undo and then close up the second screw. She reached into her jacket pocket and produced a tissue to wipe up the small spillage on the side of the engine.

'Think that will do it, let's give it a go then.'

Dave swung the handle faster this time and Erica reached over and lowered the decompression lever. The engine started straight away, and the handle automatically slid off the end of the crankshaft. Dave clipped it back in place on the side of the generator casing. On Erica's advice, the fuel can, funnel and screwdriver were left in the shed for future use.

'Time for a coffee after that, I reckon, Dad?'

He agreed and they went back into the Manse. Dave left his diesel-stained rubber boots in the porch and followed Erica to the kitchen. She attempted to wash the diesel off her hands but instead found she had effectively waterproofed her skin. Her fingers were beginning to itch, and she held her fingers under running hot water for as long as she could bear to counteract the irritation.

'I'm going to have to see Sally for some hand cream. She wants us for Tetanus jabs today, so I'll get some later.'

'Ah, yes,' Dave remembered. 'She said she was going to come down around ten this morning, if I remember rightly. Give us all a chance to wake up before we have our shots, she said last night,'

Sally appeared in the kitchen doorway around nine-thirty and joined Dave and Erica for coffee. There was no sign of Deborah or Agatha yet, though movement from the bathroom suggested one of them was already up, Agatha probably if it involved showering.

At times Dave had been concerned about Agatha's obsessive showering, but Deborah had assured him it was simply a teenage girl thing and nothing to worry about. Good job they had got the generator going, he thought.

Deborah had been wide awake since Dave got up. She had lain in their bed in the back bedroom taking stock of the new and unfamiliar situation she now found herself in.

Her job had quickly been filled at the high school. With so many highly qualified young applicants there had been no problem filling the vacancy. She was on St Kilda now so there was little point in labouring the doubts that kept her awake for much of the night.

The failure of the electric supply had occurred after she had finally managed to drop off to sleep so when she joined the others in the kitchen, all seemed normal. There was just a faint odour of diesel fuel competing with the enticing aroma of the bacon Dave was frying for them.

Erica had brought several weeks supply of muesli and was already tucking into her breakfast. Deborah noticed with annoyance how she put her spoon down to scratch her fingers from time to time.

Having shared breakfast with them, Sally asked if she could use their shower. The Factor's House had no electricity supply since the power station had been closed down. Cooking was going to be a problem, but she had managed to light the woodstove next door in House One and boiled a kettle. It wasn't going to be too bad once she got herself organised.

Sally showered and returned to the kitchen to discuss her plan for the vaccinations.

'Seeing as it's going to be dark and cold in the Base medical room, I'll go and fetch the Tetanus vaccine from the medical room and treat you in here, much nicer.'

Sally had been issued with a universal key to the Base and leaving the Manse, she turned right and entered the deserted loading bay. It seemed strange yet also familiar walking the quiet corridor past empty offices and up the steps to the medical wing. She turned right and with her own separate key opened the locked door into the consulting room.

She had discussed vaccine storage without electricity with her senior medical officer back on South Uist. Sally had been assured that as long as the vials were stored below 8.0C they would be fine for the duration of their shelf life. It had been thought highly unlikely that the temperature in the unheated buildings would rise above that figure. All seemed uncannily in order, just as she had left it.

She returned to the Manse with two vials of tetanus vaccine, a 5ml plastic syringe and a packet of disposable hypodermic needles. She also brought a packet of individually wrapped anti-septic wipes.

With the family gathered in the kitchen, the good natural light made vaccination easy. Given St Kilda's history of tetanus deaths, Sally wanted to make sure the Williams were protected.

She noticed the redness of Erica's fingers and the way she rubbed them together to relieve a skin irritation. Erica explained about bleeding the generator earlier that morning.

Dave had hoped to have kept that secret between the two of them but now it was common knowledge. Deborah made the practical suggestion that they should keep two jerry cans full of fuel outside the Flare Store at all times and top up at least once a day.

Agatha was less sympathetic and was more concerned about localised effects of spillage on the island ecology.

'Come on, it's our first full day here and we must have better things to worry about. First of all, I am going to ring Josephine.'

Dave went to the office and connected up the satellite phone. It took a few moments to connect to the national telephone network but the call to Inverness connected surprisingly easily.

Josephine was pleased they had arrived safely but, other than wishing them well, she sounded preoccupied and cut the call short, saying she had a meeting to attend and needed to prepare for it. They were to contact her if they needed administrative back up, but Donald Macintyre should be able to deal with grocery supplies, etc.. She would be in touch again to advise when the first tourists were likely to arrive.

Dave returned to the kitchen.

'That was short and sweet. She doesn't sound too bothered. We are to consult with Don for supplies and such like. She'll let us know when the tourists are going to arrive.'

'Hopefully never!'

Agatha made no bones about wanting to be left alone in their new island home.

'I'm looking forward to Dan coming over.'

Erica was more positive about visitors.

'It will be good to have another man here too,' Dave chipped in.

'I could second that!' Deborah teased.

'Now, now, people!' Sally suggested they explored the Base and then she would take anyone who felt like some exercise for a walk round the island.

Sally led them to the loading bay next door and into the long corridor she had entered earlier that morning.

'On the right is the corridor to the kitchens, canteen, gym and VIP lounge. Just up here, on the left, are the logistics offices where transport on and off the island used to be organised.'

She led the group along the corridor to the foot of a short flight of steps.

'This is the Base Supervisor's Office. Poor devil was killed in a Land Rover crash last October, same time as the terrorist attack you probably heard about.'

They climbed the short flight of steps.

'On the right is my area, the medical wing. I keep the door locked but there are First Aid boxes in all the offices, just let me know if you take anything out of them. I used to keep a record when I worked here but it's still well to keep them topped up. We've plenty of plasters and bandages.'

'Now here's the root of much past evil.'

Sally was only half jesting about the bar, quirkily named the 'Puff-Inn.'

'It was never a pub in the true sense of the word, but a recreational facility for the teams working here.'

Dave looked around in amazement. Flags from passing boats and signed T-shirts from transient servicemen decorated the walls. Mementos of everything from Special Services to Greenpeace brought home the many cherished memories embedded in the room.

There was a dark side too, Sally pointed out. Alcohol dependency had become endemic and was one of the reasons the MOD decided to pull their civilian contractors out and close the Base. The regular military contingent had been removed several years earlier but the hard drinking culture remained.

'Let's have a look in here,' she took a key from her bunch and opened the door marked 'Cellar.'

'Bloody hell!' Erica was genuinely surprised to see boxes and boxes of canned beer stacked from floor to ceiling. Well stacked wine racks occupied one wall and on the other, dozens of bottles of whisky and rum waited to be served to customers unlikely to ever return.

'Wish I'd known about this last night, Sal.'

Deborah had missed being able to serve wine with their evening meal.

'Technically, this stuff doesn't belong to us, but I suppose if we keep a tally and offer to pay later, we could have some of this, Sally?'

'Nothing to do with me, Dave. You know my feelings on the drink history out here. Be it on your own head, but I'd advise caution. Booze has done enough damage to lives here already.'

'Oh, Sally. You're being a bit hard, aren't you? This must have been a fun place, too.'

Erica thought about her social life back in Edinburgh.

'It couldn't have been that different from Friday nights back home,' she quipped.

'It was different,. there have been some awful incidents involving drink here. I hope you never have to find out for yourself, just believe me.'

Sally suggested they move on. Further up the corridor she pointed out the private quarters of the men who used to work there. Agatha crinkled up her nose at the smell of male occupation still lingering in the empty rooms.

'They weren't always too particular about where they dried their trainers,' Sally joked. She lightened up when they came to the exit door and led the group outside.

'Dave, I know you poked around here earlier, for the rest of you this is what remains of the sports hall.'

The corrugated iron Nissen hut had all but collapsed from the battering of years of damp, salt laden winds blowing up from the bay. She then turned around and pointed to the quiet power station building.

'There you see the once beating heart of the island. That place used to provide all the heat and power for the Base and the restored cottages in the village.'

The rest of the Base buildings looked tired. The temporary, sprayed concrete buildings were beginning to crumble but the power station stood proud; an icon of 1970s design. A sublime man-made edifice set against the slopes of Conachair, it almost looked appropriate. There was something surreal about the great structure and he could imagine great engines keeping the wilderness at bay.

'Now we have Red Square and the KGB offices.'

The Williams' looked puzzled.

'OK, I'll explain. This yard and workshop area was occupied by the maintenance crew whose primary purpose was to operate the power station. They called themselves the Kilda Generating Board and with initials like that where better to be located than Red Square.' She chuckled. 'Appropriate, for this place was set up at the height of the Cold War.'

'And cold it is too,' shivered Deborah.

'Think I've seen enough; I'd like to get back in the warm now.'

'We can go back along the sea front so you can get your bearings. Then I'll take, anyone who wants to, for a walk round the island. It's a crisp day and the walk will certainly do me some good after yesterday and that rough crossing. I'd like to check out the crash site too, just in case there's anything left lying around up there. There'll doubtless be an air-crash investigation team here soon and I'd like to see if there's anything worth salvaging before they get there.'

Dave was surprised at Sally's wrecker attitude to the crash but on thinking about it, knew she was right.

'We might as well make use of what's left up there, if anything is, of course.'

They made their way back to the Manse and after making sure they were adequately dressed, Sally took Erica and Agatha back outside, Dave and Deborah having declined another guided walk for the time being.

'We'll walk back along the front to the helipad then head out toward the Mistress Stone at Ruiaval. We can have a good look at the old blackhouses later.'

The three women set off along the sea-front pausing briefly to look down on the jetty below. They stood on top of the stacked gabion sea defence wall. The wire baskets were rusting, and a few had begun to sag and lose their stones to the waves.

Sally explained that in trying to protect the Base, all the engineers had managed to do was deflect the sea's energy a few yards along the shore where it was now undermining the Feather Store which had stood safely for two hundred years until now.

'This is where the drunken idiots fell off the wall after rushing out from the bar to see the student skinny-dipping.'

Sally recounted the story of the attractive young researcher who had allegedly 'enticed' men to the edge of the cliff. The Coastguard had been less than impressed with the explanation, but the siren tale from St Kilda had already reached mythical proportion in the Hebrides..

Sally went on to point out the jetty was one of the few places where rod and line fishing was feasible as the structure reached out beyond the kelp forest that surrounded all but the sandy beach two hundred yards further along the shore.

'It was pretty daft really; the guys went fishing but they had no way of cooking their catch. They were all fed in the canteen. Even when fishing boats came in and offered fresh herring the cooks turned them away because they were not allowed to take anything that had not come through official supply channels. It was like a basic human instinct to provide for yourself being played out, yet never coming to fruition. That's been the story of this island since it became a World Heritage Site rather than the sustainable community it once was.'

Further along the road, Erica enquired about the massive stone walls crossing the pasture that seemed to serve no logical purpose. The Soay sheep sunning themselves against it were in good condition and the ewes obviously in lamb.

'Those are the consumption walls, built simply to 'consume' the vast amount of stone removed to create this field system in the nineteenth century. Led by Minister McKenzie, villagers cleared stone from the land and, with their copious applications of compost, produced rich and fertile fields. I think I mentioned that these fields are reputed to have grown the best barley in the Hebrides. Looking at these sheep I'd say the ground was still pretty rich, wouldn't you?'

A few yards further they came to a series of green fuel tanks to the left of the road, half hidden behind a man-made bank and standing inside a concrete bund.

'This is the fuel store for the power station,' Sally explained.

She pointed out large steel plates thrown up on rocks nearby.

'They extended the slipway across the sand, but the sea was always lifting the steel roadway. It was an endless task keeping the landing-craft slipway operational. Being all electric we needed a hell of a lot of fuel to keep the power station running, a thousand pounds a day, I believe it cost, and us being in the windiest place in the UK too. Why they didn't bring in wind turbines, I'll never know.

Sally continued to explain the landing-craft procedure.

'The landing craft used to bring diesel fuel and when it beached the Warden had to stand and watch like a hawk to ensure no rat or other alien species came ashore. No cats, eh? The fuel landings were the weak point that could have burst the bubble of our island biosphere.'

Walking past the diesel tanks they came to a small helipad with its handwritten sign *International Airport Lounge*. Weeds were starting to grow in cracks in the concrete and the drains had long blocked up.

This tiny airport had a distinctly run down third world feel to it. The shredded orange windsock moved gently in the breeze. It had never been put away after the last evacuation flight left. The chopper pilot from South Uist had been glad of it when he picked up the survivor of the Piper crash on the hill above.

Hard to believe that had been only the morning before, it felt like weeks thought Erica, still struggling to take in everything that she was being shown.

'Here's the fire-pond. It supplies water to the hydrants around the Base. There's a big pump in that shed over there.'

Turning to Agatha, Sally pointed out, 'You see some great birds washing here in the summer. It's the only fresh water pond this side of the island. There's one in Glen Mór but when it's full of Bonxies no other bird dares go near it.'

'Ever heard of Saint Columba?'

Erica certainly knew the connection with Iona but according to Sally the Irish missionary had also landed at St Kilda. The remains of his early Christian chapel could just be made out beyond the twentieth century helipad. Sally led the group up a steep track not much more than a sheep path. After five minutes they stopped to get their breath back beneath the scree slope of Mullach Sgar. Apart from the considerable numbers of cleits using the ready supply of stone, she pointed out what looked like military trenches dug out in front of them.

'Those are the 'hidey-holes',' Sally continued. 'The villagers used to hide up here and keep a watch whenever pirates entered the bay. It was a regular occurrence in the Middle Ages, so I read. Barbary pirates from North Africa raided all up the west of the British Isles and took slaves back with them. The St Kildans wouldn't have stood a chance without somewhere to hide out and wait till they had gone. The hidey-holes are ideal places where you can keep a watch on the bay yet not be seen by anyone looking up. They can only be seen by looking down from above.'

Having got their breath back, following the cliff path they shortly came to another small settlement and some rusting remains of what, Agatha said, looked like harbour lights.

'What are these, Sally?'

'These are, as you rightly suspected, navigation lights. Any large ship, of which there were many, would sail slowly into the bay and when the captain saw these two lights align, he knew he had reached the safe anchorage point. A simple but clever idea, Agatha.'

Agatha thought the explanation a bit too simple but wasn't going to let Sally see it.

'Now we are at another ecclesiastical settlement. This is Saint Brendan's Chapel, another Irish missionary who came here to save the St Kildans. They must have been a bad lot in the Dark Ages!'

Sally laughed at her own joke.

'The reality would most likely have been a party of Celtic monks coming to settle closer to their God who could be found in wild and lonely places away from softer distractions on the mainland.'

'Away from distracting womankind too,' Erica was beginning to see a thread connecting male occupation at St Kilda.

'You've got something there, Erica. Victorians used to flock here to experience the Sublime. They'd imagine the wild bard Ossian playing his harp for them as they entered Village Bay. Most would look in awe from their cruise boats and wax lyrically on the divine works of nature without engaging with anything, least of all the island inhabitants who lived and worked here.

The Church was just as bad, flogging male fundamentalism out here without any one to challenge them. Nearer my God to thee, pah! Nearer their sad male egos, more like. I bet it's no coincidence the Cailleach's Cave is just below here. Brendan probably deliberately chose this place so he could build on top of her.'

This time both Erica and Agatha looked a little puzzled.

'Wait a minute; we've named our cat Cailly, short for Cailleach, the wise woman. Do you mean a wise woman, a witch actually lived here?'

'Not a witch, Agatha. You are just repeating male prejudice against a woman strong enough to have her own mind. Legend suggests there was a female deity resident on this island. She is reported from all over the Western Isles but out here on the horizon, the edge of the world to medieval Hebrideans, she made her home.

Later, I'll show you the Amazon's House in Glen Mór, a later interpretation of the Morrigan legend. The cave below us is named after her and from inside it, you are supposed to be able to keep a secret watch over the village, before sea-level rise of course.

There's a story of sea-borne raiders locking the chapel door after everyone had gone inside to hide and then burning the place down. Just one woman decided against ineffective sanctuary in God's chapel and hid in the Cailleach's Cave to survive and tell the story.'

Sally stopped abruptly.

'Oh, wow, just look at that! I've never seen so many here before.'

Agatha was equally impressed at the abundance of Mothan plants flourishing in the damp ground around the pool of St Brendan's Well.

She hadn't expected it, but Erica was really warming to Sally. Agatha was not so sure but listened intently to the legend of Morrigan, St Kilda's Amazon.

'Enough of my ranting about male injustice on this island; come on I'll show you where we women had the upper hand. Let's go see the Mistress Stone.'

The three women made their way across the grassy slope toward the rocky point of Ruiaval. Agatha noticed a subtle change in the springy turf. As they crossed the saddle of the headland, the grass beneath their feet changed to close cropped Thrift a plant she knew tolerated salt spray in a way few other vascular plants could.

Agatha realised this meant that, at certain times, sea spray from the Atlantic must wash over this pasture hundreds of feet above the calmer waters of Village Bay. The power of elemental forces waiting to be unleashed both thrilled and disturbed her.

Sally led her companions along a narrow path beneath a natural arch where a slab of granite had slipped from the Tor to form a bridge over the path. They climbed underneath and then up onto the slab above, looking down on the exposed Atlantic surging hundreds of feet below.

'Yep, this place is ours, girls!'

Sally explained how men wanting to impress their sweethearts would walk to the edge of this slab, stand on one leg and then reach down to touch their big toe clinging to the edge. If they overbalanced that would be it.

'No woman would marry a man until he had performed this feat for her; cool or what?'

Sally continued the history lesson.

'The fact was that a man had to have a good head for heights if he was going to provide for his family by collecting seabird eggs from the cliffs. This ritual ensured survival of the fittest. You were no good if you got scared on the cliff face. If you look further along you can see cleits built in the most ridiculous places. I reckon that was a test too. Extreme cleit building to prove you knew how to build a stone house on this inhospitable ground, as well as having a good head for heights. Just imagine coming out of your bothy first thing in the morning to find a five-hundred-foot drop right in front of you.'

She led them down from the Mistress Stone to follow the cliff path on the Atlantic side of the headland toward the first of the twentieth century golf-ball shaped radomes.

Fully exposed to the Atlantic, the prevailing wind from the north-west was relentless. The women pulled back from the cliff path and opted for the crumbling metalled track servicing the radome and ancillary buildings. A heavy door was banging open and closed in the wind.

'This must have been where that bloke tried to ring for help after the plane crash,' suggested Agatha.

'I never came down this far yesterday. Hey look at that!'

They could just make out the words *Welcome to St Kilda* painted on the crumbling road surface where it levelled out toward the flat-topped ridge of Mullach Sgar.

'Oh, yeah. Before the regular supply helicopter service, small planes would line up their approach here to drop mail and lightweight supplies. They used to drop a teddy bear by parachute to assess the wind at ground level and retrieve him later but one day he got blown over the cliff, it was a mystery as according to the pilot there wasn't a breath of wind that day. If you look further along, you'll see a zebra crossing and, so I have been told, there used to be red telephone box at the T-junction. That is just so bizarre but at least the guys did have a sense of humour when they first came here. I think I would have liked to have worked here then, but it was all alcoholism and depression by the time I arrived.'

Agatha recognised the T-junction where she and Sally had got their breath back the previous afternoon. The steep road back to the village dropped rapidly through a series of hair-pin bends. The grey granite cottages and blackhouses were catching the sunlight contrasting against the unnaturally green fields around them. They walked the few hundred yards or so over to the crash site and examined the damaged cleit where the light plane had gone over the edge.

'I just hope they were all dead before it went over,' said Sally.

The rusting remains of a Sunderland flying boat engine lay close by as further testimony to the perils of aviation in Glen Mór.

'I do hope this is the last accident here but somehow I doubt it.'

There was nothing to be seen lying on the ground around the cleit. The wind had already dispersed whatever could be blown away. The oil-stained granite would soon be blasted clean by the elements and the gouge in the turf would eventually grow over. Maybe an interesting summer season as new plants colonise the bare soil, thought Agatha.

The wind was beginning to gust around the cleits, and Sally suggested they kept moving before they got cold. Only

Agatha noticed the long green Cordura bag lying inside the damaged cleit, partially concealed by dislodged stones and turf.

Sally led them on past the Sunderland engine, following the low boundary earth dyke, the bank that marked the limit of safe grazing in Glen Mór.

'Curious isn't it, how the cattle knew never to cross this barrier? Bit like a modern electric fence; cattle could easily push past but had been trained to experience pain if they tried. It must have been a similar thing, the St Kildans must have trained their cattle to fear crossing this barrier, I wonder why?'

She left the question open for the sisters to ponder on as they walked toward the first steep climb for a while. The earth dyke terminated at a steep rocky incline just beyond a collection of cleits overlooking a steep grass slope to the sea.

The slope covered several acres and once sliding there would be no stopping anyone foolish enough to venture there in wet conditions. Experienced mountaineers had suggested taking an ice axe when she wanted to go there in the past. There was another relatively safe way down to Carn Mor if the men had listened to her.

The boulder field beneath the peak of Mullach Bi was home to breeding Puffins between April and August, safely nesting beneath the rocks in their thousands. There were stories of some kind of tunnel down there; maybe an aborted mining attempt had taken place in an age of eighteenth-century entrepreneurship.

Who knew? There were no records from an island without literacy, almost into living memory. Sally had never thoroughly explored Carn Mor so couldn't enlighten them further.

With aching knees, they reached the top of Mullach Bi where the path levelled out. The cliff on the seaward side dropped sheer for over a thousand feet and as the available flat land narrowed the path took them through a small pass where, below them, the precipitous slope into Glen Mór was accessible by only the most agile of island sheep.

'Good for the soul and bad for the knees is what I say about this path,' joked Sally.

Having held aspirations for small holding in the past, Erica was concerned to see the poor condition of the sheep in this area and asked Sally about it.

'The answer lies in the soil, Erica. Back in the village, the fields have had years and years of intense fertilising. The St Kildans made compost from whatever was to hand, from seabird offal to their own bodily waste mixed with soot from the peat fires. They even composted thatch when they re-roofed the blackhouses. Out here at the back of the island the land is much poorer though you'll see in a minute that any available flat area was cultivated at some time or other. We'll come to the Cambir shortly and flat areas there have obviously been farmed in the past.'

The Cambir peninsular reached out toward Soay, less than a mile north-west of the main island, Hirta.

From here, arguably the most dramatic views of the St Kilda archipelago could be seen, though few tourists had the fitness needed to venture so far from the village. Some would have been physically up to it but psychologically, it proved too much of a challenge.

Sally made a salient point about crossing to the far side of the island.

'Men in particular have to run the gauntlet of Bonxie attack during summer months. The local name for the Great Skua comes from the Norse for grumpy old woman. Morrigan the Cailleach, eh?'

It wouldn't be true to say there were no signs of human habitation on the Cambir, just no recent signs of it. The ruins at the foot of Glen Mór were ancient, from a time neither the archaeologists nor modern visitors could connect with.

'Psychologically, Glen Mór is an uneasy place for any man to be. Not so bad for women as we will be finding out.'

The women came to the 'neck' of the Cambir where the sea was eroding from both sides. At this narrow point the St Kildans had built another low barrier to deter livestock from entering cultivated areas.

More substantial than the earth barrier at the top of the glen, stones were crumbling into the sea at both ends of the wall. A few hundred yards further the women climbed to the end point of the peninsular and looked in awe at the strait below them and the slopes of Soay. Seals could be heard calling from caves beneath them.

Agatha asked the question, 'Soay Sheep, is that where they come from, then?'

'Yes,' Sally replied. 'Soay is Old Norse for sheep. Vikings named the island, apparently. After the 1930 evacuation a flock of one hundred was brought over to 'maintain the grazing.' In other words, they were brought over as four-legged lawnmowers. If you look around the island they are doing a pretty good job. Although I doubt you could find anything long enough to thatch a blackhouse roof today.'

'If you look over there,' she pointed to the island of Boreray four miles away to the north-east.

'With binoculars you can see descendants of sheep abandoned in 1930. Regular white Highland blackface but in 1930 there was no-one able enough to go and get them. Their descendants live on as Borerays, the most isolated flock in Britain.'

'Hey, look at that, another plane wreck?'

Erica had spotted metal wreckage across the strait on Soay. Near the top of the scree slope opposite lay the weathered remains of an aircraft.

'Yep, some other silly sods tried to fly through the gap only to find themselves picked up by the wind and slammed into the side of the island. That was during World War Two when this island was a flight training area. There's a small memorial plaque to them in the village Kirk.'

'This place is like a graveyard,' said Agatha, out loud this time.

'You'd be surprised Agatha. Over there on top of the island is an altar erected by the St Kildans in the nineteenth century. The Free Church insisted they worship every day and when they went off bird nesting or shearing sheep, they always took a lay minister with them; even on the Stacs out there.'

She pointed to the towering needle like rocks looming from the waters at the western end of Boreray.

'There's been some weird shit out here to put it mildly. Ever heard of the Great Auk?'

The sisters shook their heads.

'That's because it's fucking extinct! The Church really screwed up minds on this island. A party of men went out there and got marooned in bad weather. They came across a very large bird, a Great Auk. With all the stories of fornication and sin they'd been hearing, those sad bastards got it into their heads that they had found a witch who was conjuring up a storm just to spite them. They stoned the poor bird to death. Great Auks were the northern penguin, and this one was maybe the last one on the planet. It was stoned to death right here because local earth-based religion conflicted with patriarchal Christianity bringing about a medieval mind-fuck right here at St Kilda, and you wonder why I'm called an eco-feminist. I love the natural world, but those Church elders came here and screwed the place along with everything else. Their sad legacy is really embedded here, as you're bound to find out sooner or later.'

Erica and Agatha stood stunned into silence by Sally's outburst. It felt slightly uncomfortable to find themselves in this isolated spot with their guide in such a volatile psychological state. Agatha switched off from it all and concentrated on spanning the far side of Glen Bay. Erica reached out and squeezed Sally's hand in a gesture of support.

'Sorry, I've gone and done it again, but that tale of the last Great Auk really gets to me.'

'Oh, Sally; this island must be an awful place for you?'

'No, Erica. I see St Kilda as a place of opportunity. There's a chance here for us to put things right. Rebuild a real community where everyone's effort is valued, not just male efforts to dominate everything. Just look over there.'

Erica pointed at the radomes and fallen mast clearly visible in the distance on Mullach Mor.

'There could have been regular work here for several families. They could have continued small scale farming and had a resident nurse cum teacher, just like in the old days when this island still worked. Now look at it, a place where men attack other men over their precious ideologies. When we go back, have a look in the museum. You see old photographs of the women who lived here; I just don't understand why they accepted Church domination. Do we ask to be dominated like that?'

Agatha had been listening intently to the conversation and, though the youngest woman present, made a pertinent comment.

'I think that in accepting male values, we are not being dominated. In their pathetic attempt to dominate, lies our source of power. In their attempts to control, men demean themselves and that should actually empower us.'

Erica added, 'I expect it was more a matter of being worn down by unremitting hard work trying to keep a community going here. I did a little reading before we came and by the time of the evacuation the community consisted mainly of elderly women. There was only so much they could do after the men and young adults left, rather than stay and support them. Maybe it's no wonder women turned to the minister, a male figure strong enough to actually stay on the island to try and help, even if he was seriously misguided?'

The discussion helped Sally regained her composure and she led the party down the steep slope to the ruins at the foot of Glen Mór.

'Mind your step here, it's very slippery,' she warned.

The women slithered down the rock-strewn grassy slope to find substantial stone rows and outline of a megalithic stone circle.

'This area is a mystery. It's so old even the archaeologists can't agree on an age for it, but the consensus says it's the remains of a settlement begun four thousand years ago. It's easy walking now we are down here, and I'll try not to rant anymore. I shouldn't unburden myself on you like this.'

'That's OK,' said Erica.

'Continue with the tour, Leader!'

With the mood lightened, the women quickly crossed the bottom of the glen taking care to avoid the slippery rock slope leading to the sea.

'This, believe it or not is an alternative landing place and boats do occasionally anchor in Glen Bay to shelter from south-easterly gales. It must have been where the terrorists landed last year; the glen is full of Bonxies at that time, and I doubt they'd have managed their attack in daylight. There's a supposedly holy well here too.'

Sally led the group to a small well covered with a dry-stone shelter similar to the one Erica attempted to clear the previous evening back in the village.

'Around the time Church influence began, the 'Apostle of the North,' Dr John MacDonald landed here and blessed this well. It is lovely clean water and was probably a blessed well long before he came. We are only a few yards from the Amazon's House here.'

She led them up a sloping path past the lochan where, come the Spring, the islands Great Skua population would congregate. The Bonxies had a special attraction for this place though, she added, no-one had so far ascertained why.

'A research project for you, Agatha?' Sally quipped to the sisters.

Another stone settlement was now clearly visible but unlike anything they had seen before. Erica had travelled in West Africa during her student days and thought they reminded her of family compounds.

There were around a dozen compounds referred to by archaeologists as 'horned structures.' Three domed cells linked by a stone wall at the back of a horseshoe shaped corral, presumably for penning livestock.

'Indeed,' continued Sally. 'St Kildans made use of these structures as lambing sheds or as shielings when they had to spend the night away from home. It's a bit odd that they would spend the night here when home is just over the hill.

So much history has happened here that we simply have no idea about. The St Kildans didn't know what these buildings were for, but visitors named the biggest one the Amazon's House, connecting it with the Cailleach legend. Pretty well every nook and cranny on this island is connected to some mysterious anecdote or other, I just love it!'

The women began the long climb up the glen following the line the doomed Piper had taken the day before.

'Save your energy, folks. It gets steeper as we go. I always say it's easy getting down into this glen but not so easy getting out again. Bit like life - ha, ha!'

The climb proved harder than Erica or Agatha had expected and even more unexpected was the sudden blast of wind that hit them as they reached the line of cleits leading to the ridge. The three of them struggled to keep their feet and Erica's woollen hat spun away, snatched by an unseen vortex.

'Bloody hell! Where did that come from?'

141

Erica was annoyed at the loss of her hat and absolutely amazed that a wind like that came out of nowhere on such a calm day.

'That,' said Sally, 'is probably what caused the plane crash yesterday and also what downed the Sunderland all those years ago. The two-thousand-foot flying rule wasn't put in place just to stop birds getting scared.'

The women struggled up to the ridge and found themselves on the military road above the T-junction. Here they could see faint paint marks where the zebra crossing had been painted shortly after the army engineers finished Operation Hardrock.

'We'll turn left here and walk up past the terrorist damage and then onto Conachair before we go back down. Are you all up for another climb?'

Agatha looked at Erica who had just found her woolly hat lying beside the road.

'Go for it! We have survived so far.'

They followed the metalled road uphill through a double hairpin bend and soon came to the fallen communication mast. It had simply been pushed to one side of the road by the Case loader and abandoned. It was if the men had simply given up. No attempt had been made to dismantle or salvage the structure and the damaged buildings stood as reminder of the night that brought military occupation of St Kilda to an end. The women made their way around the fallen mast and onto the flat moorland beyond.

The moor was eroded to bedrock in places; this area had been the prime source of peat for St Kilda, informed Sally. They looked down a thousand feet to the sea on one side and saw an equal, though slightly less precipitous, drop back to the village.

'By the end of the nineteenth century, there were no pack animals. The landlord had prohibited them as they cost too much to feed and young adults were leaving the

142

island. Can you imagine getting on in years and having to struggle up here to dig peat and carry it back down again on your back? Yes, it would have been dried in cleits first but what an effort to warm your cottage and cook food down there. The old people had begun digging and drying pasture turf nearer home in the years before the end. Keeping warm had taken priority over grazing by the time the evacuation came.'

The ground started to rise steeply in front of them again and they followed the short cliff path to the summit of Conachair. A few minutes later they reached a stone cairn erected at the peak.

Sally informed them they were now atop the highest sea cliff in western Europe. The view across to Boreray and the stacks was breathtaking. On top of Stac Armin the white gannet guano dazzled like snow against the dark rock and sea beneath.

'That, she pointed out, 'is probably the biggest gannet colony in the world.'

She looked at Agatha who nodded her head in confirmation. The women had been out for several hours and, up here in the wind, they quickly began to feel cold.

'Come on, time to go down out of the wind, I think.'

Sally was eager to get back, though the sisters were fascinated by the new world revealing itself to them. Not simply the land and seascapes but fascinated by a landscape embedded with past failure and future hope.

'That's odd,' pointed out Erica. 'Why isn't that trig point on top of the hill instead of below the summit?'

She had spotted the Ordnance Survey triangulation point fifty feet or so below the hilltop. These cartographic survey points, obsolete since the advent of GPS technology were found on summits across the British Isles. It was imperative one could be seen from the other to facilitate survey using optical equipment.

'I've wondered about that, Erica. I reckon it must be that we are at the edge of the map here, the last trig point in the British Isles. Makes sense really as there's no more land to survey beyond here, is there?'

Satisfied with the explanation the group began their descent to the corrie at the foot of the short valley known as the Gap.

Between the two hills, the Gap or An Lag, its Gaelic name, held the remains of many stone structures. Lines of cleits on the slopes terminated at a nineteenth century stone walled field system.

These enclosures had been used for the annual sheep gathering and, so Sally explained, for growing crops in the one south facing level area away from strong winds and salt spray.

The first Church minister had had his head screwed on when it came to agriculture. Closer to the village, cleits were numerous and other stone structures became evident. Sally pointed out what the archaeologists termed 'boat shaped settings.' They weren't sure, but it was considered feasible these were Viking graves. With no timber on the island and the impossibility of dragging a boat up there, the Norse settlers had built stone boats in which to sail their fallen dignitaries to Nirvana. There was evidence of Viking burial practice on the island, also Victorian gravestones, but nothing from the Iron Age which, Sally emphasised, continued well into the medieval period.

'They really were culturally isolated out here, 'she added.

'Bet they had sky-burials,' quipped Agatha.

'That would account for the lack of funerary evidence from the Iron Age. The Bonxies would have liked that!'

From the head of the Gap, the women walked down what the Wardens had jokingly named the Valley of Death, there being so many Skuas nesting there in the spring and summer months.

Great Skuas nested on the flatter areas of Oiseval and the faster and meaner Arctic Skuas attacked anyone foolish enough to venture into their nesting ground beneath Conachair.

The trick was to walk strictly up the centre of the valley, between the two Skua territories, keeping the stone walled enclosures on your left. When the Bonxies swooped on human intruders, Arctic Skuas scrambled to ferociously defended their nests from the encroaching neighbours. The walker could then continue on their way unmolested.

The women walked down past the stone enclosures and found themselves at the head of the supposedly dry burn and old water tanks. The sisters were disconcerted to see so many sheep carcasses in the water catchment area.

'You can see why we had that borehole dug, can't you. Before, we had to heavily chlorinate all the drinking water out here. It wasn't reliable either; in summer we sometimes had to go without showers and drink bottled water brought in on the landing craft.'

The new borehole stood out in the marshy ground newly colonised by Mothan. The winter had been mild but, even so, there was an accumulation of dead brown leaves lying around the concrete well head.

Cloud was forming over Dun and behind them the summit of Conachair was now hidden. Moist winds lifted up over the cooling summits condensed into the long plumes of cloud. The phenomenon was famous, adding to the sublime effect beloved by artists and photographers and detested by helicopter pilots. A flash of brown feathers diving behind a nearby cleit indicated the Merlin was hunting and time was getting on. A few steps more and the women came out on the street beside the Factor's House.

'One thing puzzles me Sally, I know you cook on the woodstove in House One but what do you use for light in there?'

The Factor's House already looked gloomy in the lowering evening light.

'I thought of that one; I brought some oil lamps over with me just before my contract ended and left them in the Sheepie store. They work a treat with diesel oil. They'd have used Fulmar oil in the past so, in principal, not that different really.'

Agatha was eager to get back to the Manse; Erica said she would just walk back up the street and look at the old blackhouses before coming in.

Beyond House Six, the roofless cottages and empty windows were a poignant reminder of everything Sally had been talking about on their walk. The abandonment of this planned settlement must have been down to more than simply male intransigence.

Blackhouses stood between the shells of bleak Victorian cottages facing the sea. It looked like there had been two distinct phases in the development of the village. Two mindsets at work?

The wind suddenly gusted from the bay blowing off her hat for the second time that day. Odd, she thought the wind was from the north up on top of the hill, now it's gusting from the south.

The blackhouses were end on to the gust and low doors and windows faced each other across narrow alleyways set ninety degrees to the linear street, or Sea-View Terrace, she was thinking to herself. She went up one of the alleys and entered a roofless, yet still cosy blackhouse. The penny dropped; it must have been the wind that conspired against inappropriate Victorian planning to ruin this community, just as much patriarchal dogma.

The first phase in the development must have accepted indigenous wisdom and worked with the elements rather than stand against them, unlike the second phase.

Erica was slightly puzzled; the Manse was OK though. Facing the bay, it had stood firm since the very beginning of the nineteenth century. Designed by the lighthouse engineer Robert Stevenson, both the Manse and Kirk had been well located, to the side of the prevailing winds. Likewise, the eighteenth-century Feather Store was protected by the great bulk of Oiseval. Further up in the village, away from the Kirk and on the edge of the wilderness, winds gusted unpredictably and with far greater ferocity.

The ultimate folly had been to build the helipad in the worst possible position for safe landing. No wonder the pilots treated St Kilda with the greatest of respect, as Sally had mentioned earlier.

Slowly walking back, deep in thought, Erica imagined what it would be like to restore one of those eminently practical blackhouses. She had visited the Earthship houses near Brighton and could see distinct similarities in the way these structures worked with the elements and landscape around them.

She dreamed of a Hebridean Blackhouse with efficient wood stove and solar panels. Maybe a small wind generator would be a better idea, given the wind out here, even a micro-hydro system making use of burns running down from Conachair.

The prospect was exiting, obvious really but according to her father, the Western Isles Trust wouldn't entertain the idea of them changing anything. Well, she'd make plans to restore one of those black houses anyway.

Knocking on the door, she called into House One where Sally had lit the woodstove and was boiling a Kettle. A reproduction Victorian oil lamp was burning brightly on the long wooden table contrasting with the darkness in the stainless-steel kitchen opposite.

'Hi Sally, would you mind if I had another look at your books?'

'They're not mine; they've been left behind by volunteers over the years. Go ahead, borrow what you like.'

Erica studied the bookshelves and settled on a volume by Andrew Fleming *St Kilda and the Wider World.*

'I'll take this one and bring it back later, if that's okay?'

Sally said she could keep it as long as she liked. It was one of the more popular books on St Kilda and there were plenty more in the shop. Erica felt slightly uncomfortable in House One. Sally was using it as her personal space and Erica could sense she needed time to herself after her physically and emotionally draining tour of the island.

Evening was drawing in and Dave had topped up the generator fuel tank by the time she got back to the Manse. The diesel engine was beginning to sound comforting rather than irritating to her, a sign that there would be light and warmth inside.

Blackhouses could be made light and warm again too, she thought, and without the need for importing fossil fuel. She was fired up by her idea and longed to have someone to share plans with.

Erica shared her thoughts over their evening meal in the brightly lit kitchen. Dave was enthusiastic in principle. There would be nothing he would like better than restore a blackhouse and really live off grid using the plentiful natural energy around them.

There was just one problem and that was they were on St Kilda as custodians for the Trust and had to keep things exactly as they were when they arrived. Yes, it also felt nonsensical to him to keep a generator running on imported diesel just to be able to function in this house. It was alright for Sally; she had a wood stove handy and was used to the place. Deborah poured cold water on the whole prospect of restoring a blackhouse. She wanted home comforts and that included being able to flick a switch for light and warmth, especially as they didn't have to pay the bill for it.

'As long as I keep the generator topped up,' added Dave.

He was somewhat irritated by his wife's seeming lack of adventurous spirit he admired in Erica.

'Dave, I do actually have to stay on this God forsaken island with you, or had you forgotten that fact?'

Agatha looked up from her bird identification book and added that as far as she was concerned, she wanted electricity from whatever source as long as it kept her room warm and powered her laptop. Erica threw her hands up in resignation and continued her meal barely disguising her underlying tension.

Dave broke the ice forming around the dinner table by saying he had had a brief phone message from Dan. Due to the cost of ringing a satellite connection, he had just let him know the car was safely back in Edinburgh and that he was looking forward to visiting at Easter. Erica looked up, showing interest at the prospect of his company.

'At least he might be supportive of my sustainability ideas,' she commented.

Deborah was looking out of the kitchen window and in the front porch light she could see snowflakes beginning to fall.

'Brr! Now it's beginning to snow. Speaking for myself I am very glad we have got this generator and a free supply of diesel.'

Erica stood up abruptly and picking up her hooded coat by the door, put it on and walked down to the jetty for a smoke. The Atlantic Grey seal that popped up to watch her gave her fresh hope that her dream for living on St Kilda would be supported when Dan turned up.

He had promised as much, when they sat up late into the small hours at his flat, talking about the adventure she was about to undertake. He admitted that though 'obviously intelligent,' he was no academic and doubted he would finish his course.

If he had the opportunity she now had to live a sustainable life, away from the chaos of the city, he would do exactly the same. His words hadn't quite rung true, but they were good enough for her to feel very close to him and after they made love that night, she lay awake imagining how it would be with him on the island.

The Williams family established a routine around fuelling the generator that sustained winter life for them on the island.

Sally busied herself with looking after their welfare. She not only administered first aid as necessary but kept notes on their psychological state, effectively she kept a diary on the mental health of her co-residents.

Not one of the Williams family thought to keep a watch on her, apart from Agatha who made it her business to miss nothing.

Without electricity the bath in the Factor's House remained unused and Sally became a regular, if brief visitor, in the Manse to take her evening shower. Once washed, Sally kept to herself preferring to spend her evenings beside the woodstove in House One. It didn't take Cailly long to adopt the rug in front of Sally's stove as her favourite place and with the ready supply of St Kilda mice, the large sack of dried cat food brought from the mainland was little used.

Some birds wintered on the island; Redwings, Pied Wagtails, Meadow Pipits, Wrens and Starlings, plus the occasional vagrant blown in from the north Atlantic.

Cailly sensed there were no others of her kind on the island, the last cats having been shot as vermin in the 1930s. Cailly kept to the abandoned cottages and hunted mice along the stone walls rarely bothering the birds which would have involved leaving her cover.

The flash of brown as the Merlin pounced on yet another Pipit unsettled her and there were days when she refused to leave House One and made use of the sand tray placed inside for her by Sally, who understood her predicament.

The sheep that had previously gathered around the comforting rumble of the power station now spent their nights at the east end of the Manse drawn to the similar sounds and smells from the small generator maintained by the Williams family. They would gather to rest within the derelict walls of the old vegetable garden.

Winter passed on St Kilda with more quiet frosty days than in previous years. The prolonged cold brought little snow. It seemed to Dave, with his geographers' understanding, that the north Atlantic must be cooling with less moisture than usual evaporating from waters that should have been warmed by the Gulf Stream.

Caribbean warmth was failing to reach the north-east Atlantic and unusual cold was also being experienced in the west of Ireland, Norway and other western areas of the British Isles. The climate was changing and as soon as early March the first yacht arrived in Village Bay.

The sailor had taken advantage of the cold but calm sea conditions in early March, when in previous years, storms would have precluded any small boat from venturing out from the Hebrides.

An iceberg had been reported floating off the Faeroes according to the skipper who landed to make his acquaintance. He had heard that global warming was melting the Greenland icecap, and icebergs were being calved into the north Atlantic at an unprecedented rate.

The other side of the coin was that with less temperature differential between the tropics and the arctic the Gulf Stream was meandering, its erratic current slowing down the flow of warm water to the Western Isles that had kept them, several degrees warmer than the Scottish mainland. As if to compensate, in 2010 and 2011 Icelandic volcanoes had belched out thousands of tons of cooling ash into the upper atmosphere. There could no longer be any argument about it; the climate of the Northeast Atlantic was changing.

8

Realities

Beluga roared into Village bay bringing the first tourists to St Kilda just before Easter. The calm conditions created by high pressure over pack ice drifting south from Greenland had enabled an early start to the visitor season.

The Williams were caught on the hop with House Three, the museum, still mothballed for winter. Erica and Agatha quickly placed the exhibits back on display and opened up for the public.

Sally and Deborah got the shop ready for business while Dave went down to the jetty to greet the fare paying arrivals.

Don apologised for not notifying them beforehand, but he was taking advantage of the unexpectedly calm conditions. The weather was strange for the time of year, and he didn't want to lose out if autumn storms brought an early end to the season.

The visitors came ashore in good spirits. Don always reckoned on one or two cases of seasickness on the best of crossings. With the sea this calm, there were none. The arrival and departure of seabirds coincided with the Spring and Autumn equinoxes, likewise the human visitors.

Fulmars whirled around the cliffs greeting their mates and reclaiming their nesting places.

Puffins had yet to arrive from wintering out in the Atlantic. Similarly, the Shearwaters and Petrels were yet to return or the Great Skuas that predated on them.

Breeding success for the seabirds had been poor in recent years with changing sea currents taking sand eels and other small fish out of range of Puffins and Kittiwakes, reliant on them to feed their young.

Few visitors realised that seabirds could do everything but build a nest out on the ocean. If the small fish on which they relied to feed their young were carried beyond flying range the population was bound to crash.

Fulmars and other far-ranging birds converted their stomach contents to oil before returning to their young. A stomach full of oil contained far more calories than a beak full of small fish and Fulmars survived where Puffins failed. It was no wonder the Fulmar was a mainstay of the former St Kilda economy.

The exception was the Great Skua which, through size and aggression, managed to feed its young by intimidating other birds into giving up their catch or simply predating them. Screams of outrage, even from Greater Black-backed Gulls, announced the Spring arrival of Skuas on the island.

Away from safe confines of the village fields, new-born Soay lambs were taken by the large brown seabirds. This year, with fewer humans to contend with, Skuas began to predate closer to the abandoned village than ever before.

'Back on the jetty for three-thirty, folks!'

Don's cheery instruction to the visitors gave them about four and a half hours in which to explore the island. Not many made the long slog up the track to the island summit and those that did were increasingly bothered by Skua attack; the Bonxies he warned were getting worse.

While working for the Base, Sally often had had to apply dressings where heavy beaks and claws had torn at bald heads. Tall men were the most likely to be attacked.

The trick, she always advised, was to hold a walking stick up over your shoulder like an aerial and the birds would attack the highest point. It worked for Great Skuas, but not Arctic Skuas which would fly straight for your eyes.

With advice from Don Macintyre, the Williams soon managed procedures with the museum and souvenir shop.

Cruise ships were no longer coming to the island since Base facilities had been closed down.

After the Mediterranean sinking of the *Costa Concordia* in 2012, cruise ship operators steered well clear of rocky islands with few facilities.

Daily visits from *Beluga* brought with it new energy for the Williams family and, after several days of waiting, Erica was delighted to see Dan come up the jetty steps carrying a heavy rucksack and guitar case. Slipping on algal growth, his first comment had been to request a stiff broom, and he'd scrub the weed off the steps before anyone else came a cropper.

Erica thought this a good sign of practical sense and, putting her arm through his, led him up the slipway to the Manse. She took him inside past the shop and down the corridor to the kitchen.

He left his luggage in the hallway and sat down at the kitchen table as Erica made them both coffees. Since the *Beluga* was now making regular trips out, there was no problem with fresh supplies. Don bought vegetables from the Harris Cooperative and anything else could be arranged at a days' notice. Life was certainly going to get easier as Spring advanced into early Summer. Dan rolled a cigarette and struck a match to light it.

'Sorry, Dan; we'll have to go outside for that.'

Noticing an empty lager can on the counter near the sink he asked, 'Where does one get a drink round here?'

'Ah, you'd be surprised. The Base guys left a cellar full of booze here when they evacuated, the cause of their downfall I understand. We'd be doing well to get through that lot!'

'This is sounding good already, Erica,' and lowering his voice Dan added, 'I've brought you a fresh supply of weed, thinking you must be pretty low by now.'

The truth was she had barely touched it since their first night on St Kilda. The reality of being there had fully occupied her and there had been no need to induce relaxation after days spent hill-walking on the island.

'Well, thank you, Dan. Actually, I hardly touch the stuff now but since you're here I'll make an exception! Dad's not bothered but I'd rather keep the stuff away from Mum. We can have a smoke later. Now, when you've finished your coffee, I'll show you around. You can leave your rucksack in the living room where you'll be sleeping for now.'

Agatha was out looking for migratory bird arrivals and Dave and Deborah had gone out to the *Beluga* for a natter with Don and Lachie. Sally had her feet up, reading, in House One. The thin plume of wood smoke from the chimney indicated she was in.

Once the visitors had landed there was not a lot to do until the time came to open the souvenir shop, just before they re-embarked. The toilet block near the Factor's House was Sally's responsibility but usually only needed a quick clean after they had left.

It wasn't a bad deal in return for free accommodation, she thought. A whole house to herself was far better the single room in the Base she had used before.

Erica thought Dan looked as good as ever. Tall with a muscular body and long dark hair tied back in a ponytail, he looked the part in her eyes. If he shaved his short beard off, he'd be perfect, she thought. Maybe she'd have to give up on that for, as Dave had remarked on more than one occasion, shaving was not a priority for the men of St Kilda.

Whether it was the weeks away from normal social contact, she wasn't sure, but she felt very warm toward Dan as she led him along the street. Showing him the main points of the village, they passed the Factor's House and saw smoke from the House One chimney indicating Sally was in residence.

Erica had the inexplicable urge to show off 'her man' to her friend and possible rival when it came to Dan's affections.

155

Having only just landed, Dan's primary concern was simply taking in everything that was unfolding around him. He found himself in a deserted village on a remote island with his old friend, Erica and who knew what lay ahead. He had decided to be open about possibilities St Kilda might offer now that the recession had made regular employment on the mainland unlikely.

Erica knocked on the door of House One. Sally was particular about that, valuing her private space, even on the almost deserted island. She opened the door and was surprised to see Erica with Dan.

'Come in, won't you,' she said hesitatingly taking in the new arrival.

'Dan will be staying with us for a few days. He's an old mate from Edinburgh. It will be good to have another man here, won't it Sally?'

Sally gave Erica a questioning look, not quite sure what she was implying. She thought he looked a good catch whatever his reason for being here. Strong as well by the look of it, she thought.

Erica looked around the cottage pointing out the good supply of books to Dan and the only wood stove on the island. She had expected to find Cailly curled up asleep on the rug in front of it, but she was out.

'You've just missed Cailly, she went out a few minutes ago. She'll be back later, with a mouse no doubt,' Sally laughed.

Erica and Dan shared a pot of tea with Sally before continuing their tour round the village. Erica talked about the ruined blackhouses and how she would love to restore one. She longed to get away from the pristine confines of the Manse and live in a sustainable way, making full use of the natural resources the island had to offer. She looked to Dan whose nodded agreement didn't seem entirely convincing.

Erica opened the wooden lattice gate into the graveyard, and they looked at the gravestones surrounded by new growth of flag irises. The older stones showed no inscription, placed there by an oral culture having no need for the written word.

The later nineteenth century monuments did bear inscriptions commemorating wealthier members of the community, including the children of the first nineteenth century Minister. So many children had died of tetanus, and it reminded Erica to ask Dan if his vaccinations were up to date. Sally would sort him out if not.

There was an early twenty-first century gravestone marking a burial of ashes brought over from the mainland. A relative, no doubt. The graveyard rose several feet above the surrounding pasture, an indication of just how many St Kildans had been interred there.

Leaving the graveyard, the pair walked a few yards uphill to the souterrain known by St Kildans as the Fairies' House. Virtually every feature of the island landscape was associated with a human, natural or supernatural story.

The St Kildans could not explain this underground passage and named it the Fairies House to account for the doorway and ceiling being just four feet high. With his tall stature, Dan had trouble shuffling inside and returning to the day light complained of a stiff back.

'OK, I'll show you an even smaller house then, big man!' Erica joked.

She led him over to a nearby hummock known as Calum Mor's House.

'I've been doing some reading up on this and archaeologists suggest it is an Iron Age dwelling. According to St Kildan myth, it was erected in a day by Calum Mor, that's Big Calum by the way. He wanted to prove his worth after being told he wasn't man enough to go bird nesting on the cliffs. St Kilda is full of myths concerning male

157

challenge. There's nothing new under the Sun, is there? You'd certainly have a bad back shifting stone like those.'

She pointed at the stone lintel over the entrance just three-foot above ground level. It looked full of water, so Dan decided against crawling in there.

As they walked toward the village boundary wall, the Head Dyke as it was usually referred to, from amongst a nearby patch of Mothan two large brown Skuas lifted off and flew away lazily to perch and watch them from a nearby cleit.

'Those are Bonxies, Dan.'

'Bonxies?' he was puzzled by the name. 'Great Skuas, mean bastards so I've read, and they go for just about anything when they are defending their nests. That's what it said in the bird book lying on Sally's table when we were in her cottage.'

Dan was walking over to the spot the large birds had just vacated. There was something furry and obviously half devoured lying there. Erica followed him to see what it was they had left.

'Oh, God! It's Cailly, those bastards have got her.' Erica began to sob.

'This fucking place, Dan. If it's not one thing, it's another. Poor Cailly, she seemed so happy out here. Look her eyes have gone, they must have pecked them out so she couldn't see to get away before they killed her. She would have had no idea of the danger she was in until it was too late.'

Dan disengaged from the cruel reality he was seeing in front of his eyes. He had expected a light-hearted time, visiting an old girlfriend. He could now see himself getting drawn into a far darker world than he had expected.

The Bonxies watched from the cleit roof fifty yards away, waiting for the humans to leave so they could resume their meal.

'Hadn't we better pick her up? Those birds look like they will come back as soon as we are round the corner.'

'Your right, Dan, they will for sure.'

Dan pulled a plastic carrier bag from his jacket pocket normally reserved for wild foraging expeditions. Erica picked up Cailly by her eyeless head. Her rear legs were missing, and dark entrails spilled from her ripped stomach as she placed the small body in the bag Dan held open. He involuntarily heaved at the sight of the feline remains deposited in his plant hunting bag.

'We'd better tell Mum and Dad; they would want to see her before we bury her.'

Erica and Dan carried the bag and its gruesome contents to the jetty and called to the *Beluga* for Dave or Deborah to come over.

Deborah heard the concern in Erica's voice and got up from the cabin bench.

'I'll go over, Dave. It's almost time for the shop anyway. I wonder what's so urgent that she wants us. Hey, it's Dan by the looks of it. You've got a mate here now, Dave,' she joked.

It was Erica who spoke first. 'Mum, it's Cailly. She's been killed.'

'What do you mean killed? There's nothing here other than mice and sheep, is there?'

'Bonxies, Mum. They must have arrived in Glen Mór last night and come hunting around the village now there's hardly anyone here.'

'Dave! Dave! You'd better come over here.'

'Christ! Poor Cailly. She wouldn't have known what hit her. Hell, we can't even bury her in the village area. I suppose we will just have to put her in the sea.'

For fuck's sake, Dad. She's our pet! Why can't we bury her?'

'Erica, remember what we are supposed to be about here. We can't just go burying things willy-nilly and

159

confusing future archaeologists. Look the tide is flowing out; just slip her remains discretely into the sea and let the crabs dispose of her. It doesn't sound too bad an end, does it?'

It was Dan who eventually took the plastic bag and emptied Cailly's remains from the end of the jetty. The small, mutilated body floated, drifting out a couple of hundred yards before being spotted by more high circling Skuas. Screaming in excitement the birds dived and within seconds half a dozen Bonxies were paddling around her, squabbling over the meaty remains. Their brown heads bobbed up and down rhythmically, ripping further chunks from the cat's body. The gruesome spectacle was over in a few minutes before the birds flapped lazily away catching a thermal to lift them high over the bay before settling on Mullach Mor.

'Sorry, that wasn't the best of introductions to our island, Dan.'

Dave was genuinely pleased to have another man there.

'We've just need to get rid of this lot,' he gestured to the dozen passengers making their way along the jetty toward the *Beluga* which had come alongside from its mooring a few yards out in the bay.

'When they've gone, we'll have a beer. Has Erica shown you to the spare bed in the living room?'

'Yes, thanks, it's all sorted,' or soon would be when he found where Erica was sleeping, he thought. The unpleasant business with the cat still seemed too unreal to have actually registered with him, if it ever would.

Beluga roared out of the bay. Rising on its hydrofoils, the powerful launch headed for the Stacs and Boreray before turning toward Leverburgh, fifty miles away to the east, across the still unnaturally calm sea.

'That's some engine he's got in there, man,' commented Dan.

Dave nodded but thought it better to show empathy with his elder daughter and wife over the loss of Cailly than enthuse over marine horsepower.

Dan, sensing the sensitivity of the situation, walked over to Erica and squeezed her hand. Her lack of response surprised him. She seemed to have withdrawn from her pain inside a psychological shell. Deborah, having seen the tourists off, was cleaning the shop ready for the next day's influx. She would grieve for the cat later.

Agatha came back from her walk around the island to find Erica sitting smoking on the jetty wall. This was unlike her, and Agatha recognised the unhappiness in her hunched posture.

Seeing Agatha walking down toward her, Erica stood up and threw her roll-up into the water. She didn't normally smoke during the day and it surprised Agatha who realised something must be wrong.

'The Bonxies are back, Erica. The tourists will get a run for their money up there now!'

Agatha was usually sensitive to her sister's moods, but Erica's sob came unexpectedly. Tears ran down her cheeks as she explained what had happened to Cailly.

Out on the bay all was calm with no trace to indicate where the Skuas had devoured her bloody remains. Agatha reached out and took her sister's hand and this time Erica softened toward her.

'You know this island was full of cats and dogs, before the evacuation. There was an awful ending for them too. Rather than let government vets put them down, according to what I read, the St Kildans hung stones around their dog's necks and drowned them in the bay. The cats were abandoned and managed to live on for a couple of years before being finally shot out by visiting naturalists.

I suppose the Bonxies just saw Cailly as food; at least no one was trying to kill her simply for being there. They couldn't have known she was one of us.'

161

Erica was surprised at her sister's comment but felt better after crying and walked with Agatha back up to the Manse.

Dave and Dan were sitting at the kitchen table and had already consumed several cans of lager judging by the empties piling up. Deborah had finished making the shop ready for the following day's visitors and came in to join them.

'Really sorry about the cat, Erica.'

Dan repeated his concern over what he had witnessed. Erica was still numbed but managed a curt thanks before disappearing into her room to lie down. Agatha rarely drank alcohol but helped herself to an orange juice from the kitchen cupboard and joined her father and Dan round the table.

'I know it's a shame what happened but according to Sally we shouldn't have brought her here anyway. Josephine did say we were to ensure not to bring any alien species with us, alien to the island as it is now.'

'I don't know how you can say that Agatha. She was your pet as much as anyone's.'

Deborah was angry at Agatha's matter of fact approach to Cailly's death.

'You even named her! Christ, you girls are two complete opposites. One who couldn't keep her legs closed for longer than five minutes and you, hard as nails just to suit your own ends!'

Deborah ran from the kitchen and down the corridor to the bathroom.

Dave looked up when Deborah mentioned his elder daughter's past. He had to admit it would have been better had Erica behaved a little more responsibly when it came to her love life.

The abortion, insisted on by her mother, should have drummed some sense into her when it came to men, he thought. For him it was all in the past but obviously still a sore point with Deborah. Thankfully Agatha had been too young to really grasp what the family tension had been about at the time, or so he hoped.

Deborah could be heard vomiting in the bathroom, the tension over Cailly's death finally expressed itself.

For her it felt as if the protected predators had just taken from her the one comfort she had on the island. It had felt good to have a family to look after but staring out at the same view day after day was beginning to get to her.

She had hoped the women would have more of a meeting place in House One, but Sally seemed reluctant to share the space with anyone but Erica, who shared her feminist outlook on life.

Who was she to impose herself in their private space, a mere mother who had successfully raised two troublesome girls and supported a dreamer of a husband? What would these intellectual and child-free young women know about life anyway?

Dave was like a pig in shit out here, she thought. Cock of his roost after the put downs at the University, and now he had Dan to side with him too. They were both arrogant and weak, their enthusiasm propped up by the endless supply of booze left behind by the Base. To stop her thoughts from spiralling down further, Deborah took herself outside for a walk along the front.

There seemed to be more life out in the bay that evening. Apart from the usual Fulmars patrolling the cliff edges she could see other white birds briefly landing on ledges and taking off to pick something from the sea before returning. She had binoculars with her and could make out newly arrived Kittiwakes building seaweed nests for the new season.

The onomatopoeic 'Kitt-i-wake' calls echoed around the bay as they squabbled for nesting space on the limited ledges. One would sometimes knock another off its ledge to fall fluttering to the sea during squabbles over limited space.

Near them, she could see Razorbills and Guillemots similarly intent on claiming space to rear the coming year's chicks. Greater Black-backed Gulls were already on the lookout for unattended eggs and would predate chicks whenever they had the opportunity.

Skuas patrolled the skies overhead on the lookout for whatever feeding opportunity presented itself. From eggs to lambs, no nest left unattended would be safe now the Bonxies had returned.

Deborah walked to the helipad and followed the slipway down to the beach. Standing on the shore she noticed a small group of black specks floating out in the bay.

Focussing her binoculars, she saw the first Puffins had arrived gathering in rafts beneath the grassy slopes where they would reclaim the previous year's burrows.

There had been much concern over poor breeding success in Puffin population. They had to fly too far out to catch food for their chicks since global warming shifted the north Atlantic currents. Sand eels and other small fish followed plankton carried on the now unpredictable currents.

Puffins could only carry a full beak of sand eels so far before, ecologically, the effort became counterproductive. An exhausted parent bird would have to consume the catch itself to have enough energy to fly home.

Deborah often took a walk along the beach as it was getting dark, and that evening noticed phosphorescence in the waves. Her footsteps left brief glowing imprints in the sand.

Though she was not aware of the significance, the luminescence was the result of a spring plankton bloom and this year the small fish had returned to Village Bay to feed in their thousands, following a bounteous microscopic food source.

The seabirds of St Kilda would benefit from the recent cold winter which had switched the surface sea currents yet again. The cold, calm conditions had brought plankton rich currents closer to the islands than for many years. It was going to be a fertile year at St Kilda.

Cailly's death, though not forgotten, became less significant as the season progressed. Many smaller birds would have suffered from her predation had she lived long enough to see their arrival. Fledgling Wrens struggled in the wind as they emerged from the security of their moss lined nests, hidden inside stone walls around the village. Small, animated balls of grey-brown fluff would have been tempting prey for the most docile of felines.

The Easter vacation came and went and with Dave's agreement Dan decided to remain on the island.

His geography degree could wait, for he reckoned time spent at St Kilda would be the opportunity of a lifetime. They discussed accommodation and it was agreed that he could move, with his few possessions, into the Feather Store and occupy the small basic apartment on the upper floor.

Deborah had insisted he would have to vacate their living room if he was going to stay on the island. The Manse was accommodation for her family, and she wanted to keep it that way.

Although a relationship appeared to be developing between Dan and Erica, he certainly wasn't family yet and, if things developed between them, she didn't want another couple under her roof.

There was no power supply to the Feather Store so the small electric cooker in there was useless. He had to fetch water from the tap outside the Manse so for all intents and purposes the Feather Store served merely as his sleeping quarters, and a place where he and Erica could spend time together in private.

Erica spent more and more time in the Feather Store or sitting on the flat rocks outside as the summer evenings lengthened.

The light evenings saw Dave and Deborah take walks around the island at a more leisurely pace, often taking time out to watch the sunset over Soay, listening to the drumming of Snipe and seals calling from caves below.

Agatha was busy with bird recording and to all outward intents and purposes was perfectly content on the island. Spending most of her daylight hours outside, she had become particularly drawn to the foot of Glen Mór.

The natural rock arch, known as 'The Tunnel', was a particular favourite of hers. The wild sounds of nesting Guillemots and the singing of seals echoing through the cavern expressed the soul of St Kilda. Agatha's felt more and more connected with the Amazon's House and Morrigan, the mythical female warrior said to reside in the glen. While her elder sister dreamed of restoring village blackhouses, Agatha dreamed of resettling Morrigan's compound with a family of her own.

Dave's dream was to be head of his family of pioneers, following their manifest destiny to leave the chaos of Edinburgh and mainland Britain behind them.

Deborah just needed a recuperative break away from the pressures of trying to teach young people too distracted to achieve without professional help she felt too exhausted to give anymore.

As for Dan, he didn't have any more than transient dreams to guide him. Living rent free, with few responsibilities and good friends was enough. The facilities were a bit basic and lack of mobile signal tedious but all in all not a bad way to spend the summer, he considered.

From what he had been reading, Mothan would help all their dreams.

Dan would wait until the Williams had finished, before he went into the Manse kitchen to cook and take his own meal back to the Feather Store. Erica started to take meals over to Dan to save him having to cross over to the Manse to cook.

On windy days his food was often cold by the time he got to eat it. Like her mother, in spite of feminist leanings, out at St Kilda she found herself performing a supporting role for her man.

Nights in the Feather Store became the norm for Erica. Sleeping in two ex-Army single beds pushed together in the small bedroom overlooking the sea felt a magical experience.

Snuggled up on stormy nights, Erica felt at peace in a way she had not felt since childhood, before hormonal change and emotional trials of adolescence re-arranged her life.

Having Dan on the island, it seemed only natural to include him in her dreams for the future.

She would spend hours discussing restoration of a blackhouse; poring over archaeological plans she found in the Manse office. One thing she was enthusiastic to try was installing a modern wood-burning stove, like the one in House One.

The idea of sitting around an open hearth and coming out kippered in the morning didn't appeal much. If ever she realised the dream, her blackhouse would be an evolution on past tradition.

Dan was enthusiastic about living in a traditional Hebridean blackhouse, more for reasons of self-image as it subsequently turned out.

He could imagine himself sitting at an open cottage-door on a sunny day, playing his guitar and maybe singing a song or two. The hard work of climbing the hill to fetch peat and continuously repair against the elements never occurred to him. Life in the Feather Store with Erica was good and allowed him time for his own dreams.

Dan built a good friendship with Lachie and had arranged with him to bring the occasional bag of grass over on the *Beluga* from Leverburgh.

He had also asked for some seeds so he could grow his own in a window box in the Feather Store away from the critical eye of Deborah. He rightly assumed Dave wouldn't object but he didn't want Deborah giving him a hard time over it, seeing how reliant he was on using her kitchen facilities.

There was good fertile soil inside the cleits where generations of sheep had sheltered from bad weather.

He quickly found a suitable plastic box and punched drainage holes in the bottom. The box was filled with rich compost, the seeds sown, and placed on the inside of the south facing windowsill overlooking the bay. Lachie had brought him enough seeds for several sowings.

Growing cannabis plants had become quite a cottage industry in the Uists, now the MOD was cutting back. Virtually every holding had a geodesic dome or poly-tunnel greenhouse.

There was no shortage of seeds selected to thrive in the local conditions. No different to any other agriculture, Dan had explained to a slightly dubious Erica when she questioned the plants' ability to grow in the salt laden atmosphere of St Kilda.

What neither of them had considered was the predilection of the mice for sprouting cannabis. It seemed that no matter how they tried to prevent them, the resourceful Feather Store mice always managed to get inside the growing containers to dig up and consume the germinating seeds.

Eventually Dan conceded defeat and the two of them constrained their consumption of intoxicants to those retrieved from the Puff-Inn cellar room.

Over bottles of red wine, Erica explained to Dan how, in keeping with tradition, she would love to keep a house-cow in the lower side of her blackhouse. Dan felt that making his way over a dung heap to the living area extremely off-putting but kept the thought to himself.

One summer evening, as Erica quietly read one of the many histories of the island, she called Dan over as he played guitar on the Feather Store steps.

'Hey, Dan! This is interesting; the St Kildans used to rub a Mothan ointment on the cows' udders to produce good milk. And there was also a belief that anyone who drank milk from the cow that ate the Mothan would be endowed with good fortune. Also, any girl who placed Mothan under her pillow would have her future husband revealed in a dream; sounds a pretty cool plant!'

Dan would not have normally listened to Erica on the subject of St Kildan history but reference to a magical plant found on the island focussed his attention.

'I wonder what the Mothan is, Erica? Is there a picture of it in that book?'

'No, I don't see one, but it must be a local plant name. I'll go back to the Manse and fetch the Gaelic dictionary from the office.' She came back a few minutes later 'Here it is – Mothan; it's the Butterwort. So, it's an insectivorous plant able to survive in a nutrient poor environment by absorbing insects trapped on its thick leaves.'

She continued to read out loud.

'Oh, yes; that makes sense. The plant exudes a compound that both attracts and stupefies small insects. Oh, apparently any girl who chewed the plant before kissing her man caught him for life. Better watch out there, Dan!' she joked.

'That makes more sense than you think. Last autumn your Dad gave me such a bollocking, I thought I'd be asked to leave my geography degree at the University.

I had made a hooch out of vodka and Fly Agaric mushroom. One of the students was sick after trying it. I wasn't doing anything illegal either, just wanted to share the power of the mushroom as a shamanic tool.

We were on Calton Hill in Edinburgh. I had read it is one of the mythical hollow hills where fairies are supposed to live. Who knows, we might have seen one after drinking that brew.

What I am getting to is that Fly Agaric, associated with the Birch tree, contains a compound that attracts and stupefies insects too, hence its name. God, it was cold that day; one way or another we all had strange experiences doing our fieldwork. One girl even went into the back of St. Cuthbert's churchyard after dark and got herself raped.'

'That's enough of that, Dan.'

Erica didn't want to hear about another young woman's misfortune.

'There's no Birch here or any other tree for that matter, so get any ideas like that out of your head.'

'I hadn't given her any of the brew. She was just headstrong and determined to get to the bottom of the spirit of place there. She simply found out there's more to landscape than initially meets the eye. There can be so much hidden beneath the surface; things our society doesn't want us to find out about.'

Erica was looking doubtful as Dan continued.

'Who would have expected to find World Heritage Site St Kilda dominated by a run-down military base? Apart from those who used to work here, this is an imagined place. Every nook and cranny has some supernatural association. We just don't know about real connections here as the St Kildans wrote nothing down, simply passed oral tales down the generations before the Church of Scotland landed and changed the story. Then, Poof! Everything was lost as their Scriptures determined another way of being, equally imaginary.'

'You could have something there, Dan. The story changed and now we've lost connection to place. I look out beyond the village and see bleak moorland, void of any story. Even the military had stories about their life here. Echoes of their landscape are still strong, and we depend on them for so much. Will anyone remember us through our landscape, I wonder?'

Dan commented, 'We'll have to set about writing our own story first, our own landscape if we are ever allowed to.'

'Well, I want to make a start by restoring a blackhouse and bringing it into the 21st century, not taking it back into the nineteenth. I know Dad dreams of crofting here though I haven't a clue about Mum.'

'What about Agatha?'

'Ah, who knows what goes on in the head of that sister of mine? I really don't know; she hides behind everything being ecological and I don't think she includes emotion in the equations she is so fond of telling me about. One day she will learn that there are consequences to her energy flows.'

Dan was beginning to feel out of his depth and wanted to change the subject.

'There haven't been many tourists this week, have there? It's been good weather too. Lachie was telling me Don is getting quite worried after investing so much in that new boat.'

'Tourists, Dan. Sometimes I feel we are just tourists in our own lives. We never really get there; just see the bits we want to see. Never mind about looking under the skin of St. Cuthbert's dodgy churchyard, as that girl did, we rarely look beneath our own skins.'

'Not sure I know what you mean there,' Dan was puzzled.

'Do you know who you are, Dan? Who you really are? I see the happy go lucky boy, sometimes the big man. Yes, you are fit and strong, have a great body,' she smiled. 'But what really makes you tick? All I see is you being dependent on borrowed dreams; especially for your self-image, to quote a cliché you are adorned with dreams just like my Dad.'

'Christ, Erica. You are getting heavy!'

'There you go again, Dan. Invoking Christ; why can't you just be yourself and relate with me now rather than an imagined figure that you guys have kept alive for the last two thousand years. You men demean his mother, only wanting to acknowledge her as a virgin. What complete and utter male nonsense! Oh, fuck this I'm going to see if Sally's in. See you later, Dan.'

'Don't forget your torch, Erica. It's new moon tonight.'

'Dark moon, Dan; it's the dark moon so stop your guitar twiddling and listen to what you feel for once rather than rehashing someone else's second-hand emotions.'

Erica walked up the street at a brisk pace. A glance at the closed porch door told her Sally was not in the Factor's House, she rarely was until she felt it was time to sleep. Marching over the stone clapper bridge spanning the dry burn she slipped on the damp granite, worn smooth by years of tourist footfall and cursed out loud.

She was not in the best of moods when she opened the door to House One. It was warm and inviting in there, the music from Sally's small battery powered stereo system should have soothed her bad mood, but Sally's rebuke shocked her.

'Bloody hell, Erica! Can't you first knock before barging in like this?'

Stung by the unexpected reprimand, Erica found her own raging emotion too much and burst into tears in front of her friend.

'Sally, I am so sorry. I really didn't mean to upset you. I just feel so tense and screwed up. I just fell out with Dan and felt the need to get away and came to find you. I never thought about whether you'd want to see me, and in this state, sorry I am so selfish.'

'It's alright, Erica, sit yourself down and we can talk about it. I'll make us a cuppa.'

Sally filled the kettle and put it to heat on top of the wood stove. It was soon singing, and she poured the boiling water into two mugs of instant coffee. Erica took the mug offered and both women sipped at their hot drinks for a moment before Sally spoke.'

'You know, Erica; I am a paramedic and that makes me a Jack, or should I say Jill, of all medical trades out here. One thing I have noticed since working on this island is the effect of the sea and weather on the human psyche. The tides, phases of the moon, atmospheric pressure, wind strength and so on. Out here we cannot help but live with natural rhythms most people protect themselves from back in the cities. On this small island there is little in the way of architecture to shield us from the elements and the darkness. No monuments to remind us of who is in charge.'

Sally could see Erica was regaining her composure.

' The weather is the boss, eventually knocking down any thing we put up to protect ourselves. We look at the ever-moving sea, rising and falling with the tides and seasons. Temperatures rise and fall between day and night. There are no streetlights here; we feel the effect of the rhythms of the natural world as much as the birds and fish whether we try to deny it or not. On top of that we are women with our own cycles.'

She paused.

'Erica, you have only been here a few months, and it will take a full year for your body and psyche to readjust. When that happens, you will barely notice these mood swings; in fact, I predict you will feel better than ever shortly without the confusion of trying to manage your moods and emotions to fit male expectations.'

Erica sipped at her coffee and listened intently to what Sally was saying.

'Yes, men do get affected out here but not in the same way. After two centuries trying to control the natural world, living this close to the ocean can often prove too much for them. Uncontrollable nature can pose a big psychological problem unless we learn to live with it, live with her. I predict your father, and Dan, will have crises before they come to terms with the reality of being out here and, she softly emphasised, living with us.'

Erica was fascinated by what she was hearing. Sally's explanations made so much sense.

'I had a go at Dan and tactfully told him he was adorned with dreams but what I really wanted to tell him was he was full of shit! Why did I say that?'

'That's like most men, especially when they find themselves out of their comfort zone. Rather than go with the changes they spin an ever-stronger self-image. Spin themselves an unassailable guise to protect a fragile ego, only to find it collapse in the face of a stronger reality. When their last defence fails, they either learn from the experience and grow, or crawl away defeated. Believe me I have seen both many times out here. I have had to arrange evacuation of cocky young servicemen reduced to tears and drunkenness after failing to come to terms with this island. Those that do accept St Kilda's reality turn out to be a real asset and one or two became great friends.'

Erica felt herself calming down and tried to place her current experience in context of what Sally was saying. She also became uncomfortably aware of her period starting.

'So, what you are saying is that I am adjusting to living here. My mind and body are returning to their natural state – and Dan with his guitar playing and cliché spouting is defending himself against a natural force that in sustaining me will inevitably beat him?'

'Got it in one, Erica!'

'What about my Dad?'

'Well, he's been around considerably longer. He's also an intelligent man and, I hope, he will learn and become a great asset to us. Don't get me wrong, Erica, we need strong male energy in our lives, or we will become uncontrolled and a liability to ourselves. Ha, ha – we hens need our cock, don't we?'

Both women collapsed in a fit of giggles at Sally's joke. The serious conversation finished off with a joke had been just what Erica needed.

'There's just one thing Sally. As an expert on the human species at St Kilda, what about my Mum? Sometimes she seems a real mess and at other times a real source of strength to us.'

'That's a hard one to answer. It's hard for me to predict as there never were many middle-age women out here. I haven't been enrolled in the Grand Mother's Council yet! We can look at her motivation for coming here; didn't she give up a senior teaching position?'

'Yes, she got mugged in the school car park and lost her nerve afterwards.'

Erica explained about the carjacking and Deborah's loss of confidence in the face of Edinburgh's youth.

'At first she was dead against coming here, thought it was a crazy idea. After the mugging she just gave up and followed Dad in his dream. I thought it was a great idea to get away from all that crap and start again but Mum didn't seem to have strong feelings about it either way, she just eventually agreed to come.'

Sally thought for a moment.

'Well, I reckon that given her age we could be in for some fireworks; her menopause must be just around the corner. I remember my Mum had an affair in her late forties. It was like a final fling before her fertility ended. My Dad understood in the end and now they have both retired, ruffled feathers have settled. The rhythms of life affect us

175

strongly enough and we have plenty of time left. Deborah must feel an urgent need out here, hope Dave's up to it!'

The two women laughed again at the thought of Dave pursued by an amorous Deborah.

'Dan had better watch out too!'

Erica frowned at the thought of her mother chasing Dan.

'Yep, all nature runs to the tidal clock out here. You'd be amazed how it ticks. Fish lay their eggs at full moon, they hatch and swim away at the next; we are no exception, Erica. If you want to know more it's all in that marine ecology book over there.'

Sally pointed to the bookcase beside the window.

'Changing the subject, Sally; we haven't had many tourists recently, have we?'

'No,' Sally replied. 'I suppose it must be a sign of the times. No one's got spare cash anymore. Don must be getting worried after spending so much on that new boat of his and to be honest this can't be the most attractive place to visit given the rough sea crossing and steep ground once you get here. Last year I had a fright when one of the tourists had an angina attack halfway up Conachair. He had taken the route up from the Gap and since that incident I asked Don to advise visitors to follow the road up the hill; then at least we can get to them easily, or could have, when we had a vehicle to use.'

The short St Kilda summer season quickly passed with meagre tourist numbers tailing off with the departing seabirds at the approach of autumn. Advice to follow the road up the hill had kept Sally's first aid treatments to little more than pulled tendons and sprained ankles. Thankfully for her, most visitors kept to the relatively level ground of the village but even a few of those found themselves incapacitated following three hours of seasickness.

Don had hoped that by investing in his new twin hulled craft, the extra speed would have brought more business.

The hydrofoil *Beluga* came to be known as a vomit comet around the Leverburgh guesthouses. The reputation spread and, along with economic recession, brought no increase in paying passengers. The downturn had become a real cause for concern.

Without an upturn the following year, Don advised Josephine he was going to have to cut his losses and sell the boat. That would mean he would not be able to supply the Williams family as often as she, or they, had hoped.

9

Review

Josephine and Ian, the Islands Factor, sat down at the round table in the corner of the Western Isles Trust Office.

'It's not looking good, Josephine.'

Ian explained that funding for St Kilda was being pulled. They had always known European money for nature conservation was under threat but hadn't expected funding for archaeology to be cut too.

'I tried the Scottish Government, explained we have the country's only dual world heritage site. Do you know the response I had from the minister? I was told that there would no likelihood of state support for a rocky island out in the Atlantic that no-one could get to. Public funding would only be given to mainland national parks accessible to the majority population.'

Ian was genuinely concerned.

'We are going to have to think outside the box, Josephine. I know we have discussed this before, but I think we have to push forward the agricultural tenant idea now. We have the Williams family on the island as custodians; could you sound them out for the role? It would mean year-round occupation of the island if we were going to be able to apply for CAP funding, of course. The latest amendment to the Common Agricultural Policy was insistent on that condition. I know we are not supposed to have anyone out there permanently, but essential agricultural occupancy should swing it for us.'

'I think we ought to tap into the sustainable tourism option too, Ian.'

Josephine had done some research the day before. They could attract more funding by encouraging public access. Historic Scotland had not been keen on deliberately building up visitor numbers for fear of damaging the very resource they sought to conserve. Now Historic Scotland would no longer fund the Trust to manage the archaeology, they could surely be more entrepreneurial about managing the island. Josephine was quite keen on building an eco-tourism business at St Kilda.

'Don Macintyre rang the other day and told me that unless he had more business next year, he is going to have to sell the *Beluga*. The fuel costs are bankrupting him at present.'

'I thought he would be blasting people around the Minches at high speed in that new boat of his?'

'That's what he had hoped! More horsepower equals more speed but the boat's got a bad reputation as a vomit comet.'

'Please, Josephine, don't go there!'

Ian hadn't been to St Kilda in years having been put off by past experience of, what felt to him, a near fatal bout of seasickness. The small helicopter flight was even less appealing for very similar reasons.

Having to choose between being thrown around by the sea or by gusting winds, the senior manager tried to avoid visiting the island as much as possible.

Josephine arrived with Don on the *Beluga* as a passenger on his last scheduled trip of the season. She had convened the meeting in the Manse living room which doubled as the island conference venue now the Base was closed.

Dave had got the generator fuelled early that morning and the room was warmed by the rarely used electric storage heaters in there. Lachie brought an offering of cakes from Leverburgh, and high atmospheric pressure had kept seasickness away.

The *Beluga* had to slow down through mist hanging low across Village Bay but, after a smooth crossing, the meeting proceeded at eleven o'clock as scheduled with the sun breaking through on a perfect St Kilda autumn morning.

Josephine stood in front of the wall mounted TV screen, unused for many months. Images of happenings in the wider world had begun to feel irrelevant to the Williams' as they acclimatized to living on the island.

She began her presentation by explaining the near impossible financial position the Trust found itself in regarding St Kilda. The Williams family listened intently to what she had to say concerning their future. Sally was also present as whatever was coming up would inevitably affect her too. Don and Lachie stood at the back of the room by the picture window looking out onto the deteriorating church building.

'To put it bluntly, we cannot afford to financially support you here next year. We are a charity, and people are no longer giving. We are losing our members in droves and external funding is becoming next to impossible to find. We have even approached a few American philanthropist foundations, but we just don't seem to be able to obtain across the board funding anymore.'

Josephine explained the wider picture.

'The national government refuses to support an island, however historically important, that few will ever manage to visit and European money for conservation is non-existent now the Brussels is focussed on funding sustainable community. It's not only us, The National Trust for Scotland; Historic Scotland and Scottish Natural Heritage have lost their funding from Europe and St. Andrews House will only support projects they consider readily accessible to the general public. So as things stand we are facing a bleak prospect out here.'

She could see the Williams' shifting uncomfortably.

'However, we have looked into alternative options, and it seems we could tap into the European Social Fund on the basis of resettling an agricultural community. Supporting small farmers has always been a cherished aim since the Treaty of Rome and I am feeling sure the St Kildans, had they remained on the island, would have been highly eligible for support. There is also more recent provision for eco-tourism business support.'

Josephine looked directly at Don.

'So, what we are suggesting is that next year, if you chose to remain here, you consider yourselves, and I include you in this Sally, as small farmers rather than custodians. Don, you should be able to find extra income bringing eco-tourists out here.'

Turning to Dave and Deborah she continued enthusiastically.

'You will be free to manage the island sheep as you see fit and,' she hesitated, 'if you wish you can reinstate cultivation in the village fields; for the first time since 1930. Without funding both Historic Scotland and SNH are de-listing St Kilda. To be honest, since the 1930 evacuation and supposed protection, the island has never seen so much damaging change. The Base and radar infrastructure changed things here more since 1957 than over the previous thousand years.'

Don chose to mention the cost of running the boat service out to St Kilda regardless of European subsidy. The deciding factor would be fuel costs of the *Beluga*. It was a fast craft but that inevitably meant high fuel consumption.

He was an astute businessman and knew the storage tanks near the helipad held many thousands of gallons of military diesel fuel. The Williams' small generator and handful of oil lamps were hardly likely to exhaust the reserve in several lifetimes. He wanted to know if an arrangement could be made to refuel the *Beluga* from island supplies. It would make all the difference between viability and running at a loss for his Leverburgh based operation.

He was playing his trump card quite deliberately. Few other boat operators would make the risky crossing and without a guaranteed supply service, he knew there would be no European funding for any St Kilda eco-tourism project.

Josephine did not like being put on the spot like this but considered his argument valid.

'I doubt there will be a problem with that Don. That diesel has been a concern of mine. Without regular maintenance of the storage tanks, I am worried that one day we could have a leak and big pollution issue to deal with. What I can do is ask the MOD to empty their diesel storage tanks on pollution risk grounds. I am pretty sure they will throw their hands up and say the pumping operation would cost more than the diesel is worth to them. Using the fuel for the purpose intended; running diesel engines until it is exhausted would seem the logical solution.'

Josephine looked at the Williams'.

'So how do you feel about becoming small farmers and running an eco-tourism enterprise?'

The family, apparently thoughtful, were as enthusiastic as she was. Erica spotted a knowing wink aimed at her from Don.

He had obviously planned for this inevitability already. A far as his business acumen was concerned this was going to work.

'There is one thing I ought to warn you about, though.'

Josephine addressed the whole group and spoke measuredly.

'You are doubtless aware of the predictions for climate change. Generally speaking, the planet is warming but here in the north Atlantic things are not so clear. The arctic ice is melting and the Greenland icecap deteriorating. However, there are certain sub-arctic localities predicted to become colder. What this means is that you could find St

Kilda actually becomes colder as ice breaks away and begins to flow south carried on changing ocean currents and the now prevalent north-westerly airflow. There is also the possibility of increasing volcanic activity in Iceland which could affect St Kilda. What I am warning you about is that climatic events could make agricultural viability a bit of a challenge though, in terms of strict economics, European funding should keep you in the black. So, I will leave you all to think about it over the next few days. If you decide to call it a day and evacuate I will understand completely but if I was in your shoes I'd relish the challenge of bringing St Kilda back to life.'

10

Growing Plans

After all that Josephine had emphasised regarding not making changes to the island, her enthusiasm for doing just that came as a surprise to them all. Even Don scratched his head, bemused.

'Well, if she wants to give me free diesel to keep coming out here, I am not going to argue!'

Josephine had explained that the constraints she had insisted on were due to funding regulations from Historic Scotland and Scottish Natural Heritage.

If it been simply up to her, she would have encouraged an eco-museum approach where at least one blackhouse would have been restored and its allotted fields cultivated and grazed in a controlled manner.

The custodians would now be encouraged to live as latter-day St Kildans, she said, like before the village went into decline. She would have liked the Trust to have built a small tourist business on the back of a century and a half's preconception of sustainable island Utopia.

'But my hands were tied, you know,' she apologised.

'So, feel free to make plans for next season; can I assume you do not have any great urge to evacuate right now?'

'Deborah opened her mouth to speak but then, as the incident in the school car park flashed back in her mind, thought better of voicing her doubts.'

Dave was more than enthusiastic. 'This is what I have been waiting for all my life. Christ, what an opportunity!'

Erica and Sally were chatting excitedly at the back of the room, planning to turn their dreams of repopulating the village into reality. Agatha looked as if her mind was elsewhere than in the Manse living room at that moment, but a quiet satisfaction betrayed itself in the small smile that crossed her face. Only Dan felt left out of this display of family enthusiasm.

Dan turned to Don and asked about opportunities to leave the island during the winter months. It occurred to him that he had two choices; either go back with Don and Lachie that evening or stay on St Kilda for the next few months, maybe longer if the weather turned bad.

'The deciding factor will be sea conditions, Dan. What I intend to do is to bring out supplies to you, as much as the boat will take, during calm windows in the weather. As you must be aware by now, the island lies in the path of regular Atlantic depressions sweeping in from south Greenland. You can come back with Josephine this evening or take a chance and stay longer which may mean next winter at St Kilda, I am afraid.'

Dan felt Erica slide her arm through his.

'We are going to need a strong young man about the place from now on,' she teased.

'St Kilda failed after strapping men like you left the women and oldies to fend for themselves.'

The simple gesture swung the argument for him.

'OK, if you put it like that, Erica; how can I refuse?'

Dave was amused to see Dan decide so easily. It really was quite a commitment Dan was making as the only genuinely young man in the group.

'Thanks, Erica. It really is true that an inch of....'

'Dad! Don't you even go there,' she warned.

All the same, she felt pleased her female powers of persuasion had been acknowledged.

'But you can move mountains, dear daughter.'

Dave responded in an equally teasing manner.

Deborah moved up to Dan and put her own arm through the crook of his free arm and purposefully pulled him away from her daughter.

'So, if you are staying now, you had better pull your weight young man. Come and help me get the supper ready. Sure you can manage a can opener?'

Deborah led Dan out of the living room and down the corridor to the kitchen. Erica looked surprised as her mother led Dan to the kitchen, her intuition sensing her mother's gesture as possibly more than she would like to admit.

'If there is nothing else to discuss today, I reckon it's time I got back to Leverburgh,' commented Josephine.

Don nodded, 'Aye, the weather doesn't look good for tomorrow and I'd rather not have you decorating my cabin again, Josephine!'

He grinned at her for Josephine was well known among the local boatmen for having poor sea-legs and on the new high-speed craft she was even more susceptible to seasickness.

Josephine picked up her coat and attaché case and left with Don and Lachie to walk down to the jetty. Lachie started the dinghy's small outboard engine and took them over to the *Beluga* rolling gently at its mooring a few yards off the jetty. Don had to follow the biosecurity rules with Josephine on board.

He fired up the twin diesel engines while Lachie hoisted the dingy up over the stern. The departure marked the end of a season unusual for the number of calm crossings. Free diesel was going to make next year even better, he thought.

Agatha came outside to see them off and the *Beluga* roared away from the village, bouncing on heavier swell at the mouth of the bay. They wouldn't be seeing Josephine until next year, if at all if her job fell through.

'Do you fancy eating with us tonight, Sally? It feels appropriate considering our new venture together. Spam sarnies and Tennent's OK with you?'

Dave was in a jocular mood that evening. After towing the official line all summer, he was now encouraged to turn his dreams into reality.

'My God, Dad!' Erica was momentarily appalled.

'Sally, I can assure you we will be having neither tonight.'

'Please yourself girl, or should I say hen!' he loved to tease his eldest.

'More Tennent's for the lads, then.'

Dave was looking forward to having Dan around as another man to share the load with. The thought of being cooped up with four strong minded women for the winter was hard enough and he could do with some male support.

'I'll leave you with your Dad and go and help Debs and Dan in the kitchen.'

Sally had decided not to rise to the bait.

Deborah was already preparing an impressive evening meal. Dan was sitting at the table chopping vegetables. He had already rigged up a small extension lead from the digital TV in Erica's bedroom and a small speaker, pillaged from the Puff-Inn, was pumping out a lively reggae beat.

To her surprise Erica noticed Deborah and Dan had already opened a bottle of red wine. She realised she was witnessing a familiar domestic scene, though on this occasion Dan was occupying the subservient role formerly played by her father. They could have been back home in Edinburgh had it not been for the sound of the generator.

'Do you want any help, Mum?' she asked.

'No thanks, Erica. We're just fine, aren't we Dan?

He nodded to the beat. 'Find a glass, Erica!'

'Later, Dan, thank you. Well, if you don't need me I'll leave you to get on with it and go back to Dad and Sally.'

'We'll give you a shout when it's ready!'

Deborah called back without looking up from her preparations.

Erica observed her mother invigorated in a way she hadn't seen since they arrived on the island. Phase two of the resettlement was at least starting on a cheery note, she thought, but all the same she sensed a slight rivalry from her mother concerning Dan or, she reflected, was she just imagining it?

Dave and Sally were poring over an archaeological plan of the village.

'I know you want to get cracking with cultivation, Dave. I agree winter is the right time to prepare for Spring sowing, but let's not try to reinvent the wheel. The St Kildans kept sheep and protected their gardens behind high dry-stone walls. Here and here.....'

She pointed out the planticrubs, small garden enclosures, dotted around the planned settlement.

'You can tell the difference between the handling pens and garden enclosures by the gateways or lack of them. The livestock enclosures have gateways but not the walled gardens. The sheep and cattle would not climb over six-foot walls to get at the vegetables and there would probably have been a boy or girl tasked with keeping them out of cultivated areas within the head dyke. There would have been plenty of children to keep occupied before infantile tetanus took most of them. It is a good thing I jabbed you all when we first arrived.'

Dave agreed that it had been a sensible precaution before they began working with the potentially infected soils of the village.

The epidemic of infantile tetanus in the late nineteenth century had always been an unexplained phenomenon. The Free Church minister explained to the grieving mothers that the deaths of their newborn was the result of sinful behaviour, may be even the behaviour resulting in their pregnancies.

Dave had mentioned, before they arrived, how Reverend Mackay, the second permanent minister, had been ridiculed by the islanders over his more extreme doctrines. They should all seek penitence in ever more arduous manual work that not he, but God demanded of them.

The divine request appealed to the egos of the men folk who rose to the challenge. With God's help the magnificent stone walls of their planned village would be the envy of the Hebrides. God would be pleased, and they would prosper. The God-fearing St Kildans would certainly show a thing or two to the decadent Catholics of South Uist and Barra, boasted Reverend Mackay.

Dave had been shocked by Agatha's explanation for the infantile tetanus outbreaks. As an ecological phenomenon, tetanus was simply keeping the size of the population within numbers the island could support, nothing to do with God or such nonsense. However, she did acknowledge the human, even ecological, need for a spiritual dimension to life in such a remote environment.

'Dave.....are you still there?'

Sally noticed Dave appeared vacant, lost in a private reverie of stone wall building.

'I think we should just repair what's here already before thinking of anything grander, don't you?'

'Oh, yes. Sorry Sally, I was miles away. You're right small is beautiful, as they say. I agree, we need to trial vegetable growing first as I am sure the weather will make things very different to my allotment back in Edinburgh. I'll make sure enough of the planticrubs are in good shape by Spring, to keep the sheep off our plants.'

'It will be milder, less frost to worry about and from what I read the villagers over-fertilised their growing areas. Should be fine by now and if we can keep the salt spray off and sheep out, we should be in for bumper crops.'

Sally continued at some length.

'According to Dunvegan Castle records, St Kilda produced the best barley in the Hebrides. They had to pay rent to the MacLeod estate in kind and the barley harvest made this a wealthy village in the past. As you get to know this island better you will recognise many small, cultivated areas and just past the Factor's House you can see the remains of a small threshing barn.'

Sally continued.

'There's even a small watermill further up the street where the dry burn crosses. I know Erica wants to add solar panels and micro-hydro energy in her blackhouse project but she's basically reinventing what's already gone before. They cultivated every corner possible, leaving Glen Mór as the only large open area free for quality grazing and milk production. That was probably because it was the only easily accessible pasture. The close-cropped slopes you see on the steeper hillsides today wouldn't have existed then. Livestock was managed as they needed long heather for thatching blackhouse roofs on a regular basis.'

Dave listened intently.

'The economy of the island was dependent on maximising its natural resources. Whether it was seabird products, peat digging or cattle grazing, every possible square inch was put to good use. Plots were rotated so everyone had a fair crack of the whip, even the cliffs were rotated under run-rig. That shared way of life came to an end with the building of the new village. The bull even had his own little house in the nineteenth century; maybe the cows had to knock before going in for service? You guys were well catered for in the new village!'

Now, Dave was looking slightly confused.

'But wasn't the village enclosure system meant to bring an improvement in living standards as well as land husbandry? I thought that was the whole idea. Most of England's agriculture was improved that way, which is where the idea came from. Agreed, it wasn't universally popular with the peasants who had their centuries old common lifestyle disrupted. By parcelling up the land into

190

individual properties and allotments, the Enclosures enabled England to feed her growing industrial population; wouldn't that principal have applied here too?'

Sally explained further.

'With fields fertilised to the point of toxicity and the island young driven away by the unceasing labour demanded of them, it could hardly be considered an improvement, Dave. Then to cap it all, disturbing the ground like that allowed tetanus to run amok in the babies. You know, this community was killed off by, so called, good intentions.

'From what I read,' Sally continued.

'I got the impression the Enclosures made white slaves of England's poor. Protest and you were driven from the land that ran in your blood. I once went down to the West Country; that whole region is full of stone walls and hedge banks. They must have built by gangs of workers pressed into wage slavery by the landowners. Now you are hard pressed to find anyone working on the land at all, just the odd tractor driver. Where did all those people go?'

She didn't expect Dave to answer and continued.

'It was the same up here, maybe even worse. English landlords drove their tenants from the land to be replaced by sheep. The so called 'peasants' were considered almost sub-human and ethnically cleansed in a way Nazis would have proud of.'

As Sally continued her rant, Dave began to wish they had left the subject well alone.

'Read Neil Gunn's *Butcher's Broom* if you don't believe me. Even out in the Hebrides local landlords followed the example of English agri-barons. The difference was that our 'peasants' still accepted divine right long after the Battle of Culloden had been lost, especially out in the west, away from Edinburgh's influence. We were subjugated by Queen Victoria but still believed she was one step removed from God and likewise the puppet Lairds and Church ministers appointed beneath her.'

Dave really didn't want to listen to this but politely let Sally go on.

'St Kilda was never cleared for sheep production; probably too uneconomical to bother with. Out here, they must have heard of the Clearances and their clansmen and women sent into exile as penitents by the vengeful God imposed on them. The self-same Ministers came here and convinced the contented villagers of their sinful, immoral way of life. Ha! A way of life that had fucking sustained them since time immemorial.'

Taking a breath, she continued with her monologue.

'You know there was a nurse on the island in the late nineteenth century. She wanted to take practical measures to prevent tetanus killing the babies but, no she was told, it was God's way of punishing the sinful St Kildans. She was stopped from saving the future of the village by those stupid bastards. You know, Dave, if she had managed to stop Ministers from anointing newborn umbilical cuts with infected Fulmar oil we might have a thriving community here today. Luckily, some women had the sense and will power to get away to give birth on the mainland and bring back a few healthy babies, but not enough to keep the population viable.'

Dave was about to respond but she cut him short.

'Then, of course, with limited genetic resources the risk of inbreeding reared its ugly head. Had nature been allowed to take its course, allowing in fresh blood from visiting seamen, and even frisky tourists, we could have kept them healthy. But then the poor buggers would have been driven from the church, exiled for immoral behaviour that could actually have saved them'

'Exiled to where?' Dave managed to ask.

'I could imagine two communities on this island, the righteous here in the sunshine of village bay with sinners banished to the darkness of Glen Mór. God there is so much pain in this landscape! Those ministers really got things sewn up here, Dave – and I mean that in more ways than you probably imagine. We women were beaten down by male doctrine out here and I am telling you, it's not going to happen again!'

Dave had been tempted to challenge her extreme view of events leading to the decline of St Kilda. There was more to the story than simply patriarchal intransigence, but he could sense tonight was not the time to argue with her.

He could see Sally was close to tears and managed to steer the heavily loaded discussion back to gardening and the delicious evening meal he could smell wafting from the kitchen.

'Sorry, Dave; I rather got ranting again but you have to agree nineteenth century 'improvements' paved the road to hell with their good intentions.'

'I do think there was more to it, Sally; the tourism business for a start, but can we leave it for tonight and enjoy the meal Deborah's making for us?'

She agreed, blew her nose and smiled at him. The redness of her eyes betrayed the emotional release since she herself had been released from constraints of MOD employment.

She was glad Dave had seemed genuinely interested in the way she felt. Dave had to admit he had enjoyed listening to Sally open up in a way that Deborah rarely did.

The last time his wife dropped her professional mask she had broken down after the mugging in the school car park. Dave noticed she now appeared to be developing a new professional role as domestic matriarch and equally hard to influence.

'First and foremost, we have to remember this venture must be sustainable. We are not going to be able to sell island produce to pay our rent. We might make a bit selling odd bits and pieces – home spun socks maybe? The Kildans did it.'

Sitting round the supper table the group bounced their ideas around.

Dave had appointed himself chair of the discussion and was not impressed by female grimaces at the mention of knitting socks for tourists.

'Our income is going to come from milking the European Social Fund and eco-tourism. We are going to have to put on a good act for Don's passengers. With free diesel, I reckon he will bring out as many as he can. The Trust still owns the place so we will have to work with Josephine but at least our hands are no longer tied, that's if she keeps her job of course. So, who's coming up with the first good idea?'

Erica and Sally were first with their idea to restore one of the village blackhouses. They would make it a perfect example of twenty-first century resettlement complete with woodstove, solar panels and micro-hydro. That way the cottage would remain clean inside, which was important, they added.

There could be quite a bit of heavy work involved so extended family help would be appreciated. Dave hadn't thought much further than vegetable gardens but could see the sense in working with Erica and Sally on a joint project. Together they would restore the first St Kildan farmstead in nearly a hundred years.

Deborah said she wasn't much good with her hands outdoors but would happily provide domestic support for the rest of them. The thought of younger members of the family out working to build a future for them all appealed, and she would play her part supporting them with hot meals and home comforts at the end of the day.

'If Don doesn't use up the entire diesel supply first!'

Agatha, pragmatic as ever, thought about what she could offer. She didn't really fancy the hard labour of restoring a farmstead but suggested she could lead nature orientated guided walks.

She would liaise with Don about that. She could lead visitors down to the seal caves below the Amazon's House, show them remote seabird colonies. Don might even arrange outings to Boreray and Soay for them. She would never get to the outlying islands without his assistance and if there was money to be made so much the better. Getting away from historic constraints of the village also appealed to her.

'So, Dan, if you are going to be living with us what can you offer St Kilda's resettlement project?'

Dan was put on the spot – what could he offer? He was genuinely perplexed; he'd come out basically to have a good time with Erica, but she seemed to have changed. Still the same Erica in many respects but St Kilda had given her a new sense of purpose and having teamed up with Sally, he could see himself being pushed aside. Edinburgh values didn't seem to fit here, and it was confusing him.

It was Deborah who suggested a role for him.

'Dan, this island has an amazing spiritual heritage. It's been neglected since the 1930 evacuation. The church has hardly been used since and the outlying chapels, St. Brendan's and St. Columba's, lie in ruins. Iona makes a living from spiritual guidance based on Celtic Christianity; why don't we do the same here? I can just see you walking around with cloak and staff leading your flock around the Promised Land!'

Deborah laughed at the idea she had suggested. 'With your long hair and beard, you could be another Rasputin, the mad monk of St Kilda. How does that grab you?'

'Ra–ra, Rasputin......lover of the Kilda Queen!' sang Dave, getting in on the joke but failing to notice the colour rising beneath Deborah's open necked shirt. She turned her face away before the heat showed in her cheeks.

'Roderick the Impostor, even!' Sally mentioned the salacious tale of the renegade priest of St Kilda evicted by Church missionaries for fornication on the island.

'OK, you're on!'

The idea appealed to the showman in Dan.

'Just as long as I don't have to play a puritan Church elder!'

The rest of the group laughed at his concern.

'Perish the thought, Dan. If there's one thing we could never imagine in a million years, it's you as Puritan!'

Erica knew him a little bit too well but wasn't going to let on to the others. She didn't know her mother well enough though.

Deborah turned to Dave, 'You're going to be our great leader, no doubt. With your passion for stone walling, you are beginning to sound a bit like old Minister McKenzie. Just make sure, like him, you are not just building edifices to your own ego.'

Dave was surprised to realise his wife must have researched the history of their island as much as any of them, in spite of her expressed desire to keep to a domestic role. Reflecting on her words, he wondered if they said more about him than he cared to admit.

'To tell you the truth, Dave; this adventure feels to me like the Old Testament story of Lot and his family escaping to the wilderness from God's destruction of Sodom and Gomorrah. He had two daughters with him as well, if I remember that story correctly?'

'No turning back then, Debs, or you'll be a pillar of salt! Mind you, as you spend so much time standing on that wave-soaked jetty looking back to the Uists, it might happen anyway!'

As the scientist of the family Agatha had no idea about the biblical Lot reference, though Erica shifted uncomfortably in her chair. Agatha decided she ought to find out what her sister's embarrassment had been about. Her mother took Dan to the counter near the stove, and both brought the meal over to the table.

'For even when we were with you, this we commanded you, that if any would not work, neither should he eat,' Dave jokingly attempted to say grace.

'Come on guys, dig in!'

Deborah changed the subject quickly before conversation on religion turned to point scoring or argument. Sally, now silent after her earlier rant, considered the banter across the table. She had worked in the Western Isles as a district nurse and had heard such conversations before.

On the islands many a true word had been spoken to her in jest and she hoped the Williams were not going to prove another example of ancient memories, real or imagined, reaching through time to connect with and determine their future.

'This is lovely Deborah; how did you make the sauce?'

The pasta bake certainly had something different about it and Sally reckoned Deborah could do with some backup moving the subject away from the Scriptures.

'I found lots of unopened herbs and spices in the kitchen cupboards when we arrived, and I saved the best of them. There's Star Anise in the tomato sauce which gives it the interesting flavour.'

Deborah and Sally discussed creating interesting meals from resources the island had to offer. While the dried food and cans lasted, there would be no trouble satisfying Erica and Sally's vegetarian preferences. Don, given a little notice could bring them anything they wanted during the visitor season. Should times get tough, as Dave often joked, there were plenty of fish in the sea and sheep on the land.

'And eggs on the cliffs,' added Agatha, provocatively.

'You're the expert there, Agatha! We'll leave that highly illegal task up to you. Thinking about it, naturalists like you made the whole Kildan way of life unviable by making egg collection illegal...'

Deborah gave Dave a warning look leaving him in no doubt the conversation should be moved on.

'Well, anyway one thing's for certain; we are going to have our work cut out to get things ready for next season.'

Dave had voiced the opinion they all agreed on.

'But for tonight, let's just relax and enjoy ourselves. Thanks for the lovely meal, Deborah; anyone for more wine, seeing this bottle's finished?'

Conversation at the table was jovial with no further point scoring. As the evening drew on Erica and Dan went outside to smoke and find privacy on the shore below the Feather Store. Agatha returned to her room leaving Dave and Sally to clear the table and wash up. Deborah sat outside on the Manse step taking in the still mild evening air. For now, sea was quiet but would soon turn otherwise as the north Atlantic winter approached.

Dave soon found out that repairing the village's garden enclosures wasn't going to be as easy as he had anticipated. While Erica and Sally had taken on the more complex project of restoring a blackhouse they appeared to be making better progress.

The planticrub walls were single skinned and generally took the shape a circle or ellipse. The granite stones were also heavier than they looked, and the rough surfaces soon wore through the leather gloves he had found in the workshop.

Dave's only stone walling experience had been as a conservation volunteer while a student in Cumbria. Walls made of regular slabs of sedimentary sandstone had been straight forward to build but here irregular lumps of igneous granite needed a different and more individual approach.

It had been agreed to restore one of the cottage steadings at the far end of the village, near the burn running down from Mullach Mor. It was close to running water and Erica had plans for a hydraulic ram pump and micro-hydro electricity generator. The far end of the village was also close to the track up to the top of the hill where there was still a decent, accessible peat deposit.

The downside of that choice was the gusting wind which could come unexpectedly from any direction meaning they would have to place the solar panels with some ingenuity. South facing wasn't simply going to be enough, they would need protection from unpredictable winds.

On a positive note, the steading would be close to the beach which could be idyllic on summer evenings. It would also make the garden vulnerable to salt laden blasts in winter. Like the nearby graveyard, surrounding the garden with a continuous high stone wall was going to prove essential if they were going to grow anything worthwhile.

Dave, too, quickly realised there was no point in trying to erect straight walls with squared corners. Gusting winds would make short work of demolishing any wall standing square against it.

He drew inspiration from the elliptical cleits dotted around the island, many quite deliberately placed in the windiest spots to dry and preserve island produce. End on into the wind, the fixed dry-stone structures allowed the wind to suffuse through and use rather than block its energy.

It was a clever system, he realised. Wind energy blowing through planticrub walls maintained a frost-free environment inside, ensuring a supply of winter vegetables to keep the St Kildan population supplied with a balanced diet outside the bird nesting season.

The trick was to build up in a spiral pattern, making sure each stone was well locked into its neighbour. Dave felt an almost personal affinity with his handiwork once he had acquired the knack.

The Western Isles Trust had faithfully rebuilt several planticrubs in the village. Supervised by an archaeologist, working holiday volunteers had an endless task repairing damaged walls where Soay sheep had jumped up and over into the sheltered grazing, lush even in the depths of winter.

As he was building, it sometimes felt he was taking one step forward and two back as agile yearlings jumped up on his new built walls. He knew the villagers would have kept heavier commercial sheep around the village, Cheviots probably, which would not have jumped up like these feral Soays.

He was experiencing a new problem for St Kilda, not insurmountable, but he had to take special care to lock each stone with the next. As taught in Newton Rigg College all those years ago, he would walk around the top of the wall himself, using his own weight to check for any weakness. He began to think some of the Soays regarded his work as a challenge and were making a game of scrambling up newly restored walls to get at the sheltered grass inside.

Erica and Sally worked tirelessly restoring the blackhouse. The substantial double skinned walls had suffered less from hooves of scrambling sheep. Built end on to the wind, the low doorway and windows of the cottage faced into a small alley between the now partially restored home and the semi-ruin next door.

Archaeological plans found in the Manse office showed some interesting features they could incorporate. Blackhouse walls, twin-skinned and over a metre thick were in-filled with smaller stones and rammed earth. In many instances they contained integral cupboards and bed spaces. Both women found the idea of secluded bed alcoves, either side of the central hearth, appealing and made a point of including these in their restoration project.

200

The interior of the cottage was damp underfoot but once they had uncovered and cleared the drain in the lower end of the floor, the higher living quarters soon dried out. With the floor cleared they found stone slabs underneath on which the central hearth had stood and would soon support their wood burning stove.

The window frames were still in position and, using timber from the Base scrap wood store they replaced the originals following decayed patterns in situ. Don would bring them glass panes and there were several tins of useable putty left in the workshop. There was plenty of timber to line the walls and make a new front door. Their home would be dry and cosy.

The low wall that divided human from animal occupation was rebuilt; Erica said she was really looking forward to installing a new wood-burner and seeing the first smoke issue from the stove-pipe chimney. Standing inside the restored shell of the cottage, hardly a breath of wind entered the building. Sally then stated the, by now, obvious flaw in their planning.

'We are going to have to put a new roof on before we go any further, Erica. We will have to get Don to bring us a load of thatch. There's nothing left on the island long enough, because of the sheep grazing. Dave is right, this is another problem the St Kildans wouldn't have had to deal with.'

'God, it's going to cost a packet bringing thatch out here,'

Erica was concerned and then laughed.

'I just can't see Don letting us use the *Beluga* as a hay cart, can you?'

They made a satellite phone call to Don that evening and he said he would see what he could arrange for them. They agreed to have the phone switched on at the same time the next day and he hoped he would have come up with an answer for them. The thatch shouldn't be a problem, he had said, just getting it there would take some ingenuity.

Don rang back as arranged. He had come up with an answer, but it wasn't going to be cheap. A military vehicle enthusiast lived near Stornoway, and he had a fully restored ex-Soviet PTS-M tracked amphibious transporter. It had a ten-ton payload and was basically a barge on caterpillar tracks – were they interested?

'This'll bring as much thatch as you need, Erica. We just need calm sea conditions and no wind or there'll be nothing left on board by the time it gets to you!' he joked.

'I'll also need to come out with *Beluga* just in case. Those amphibious landing craft can be a death trap if it turns rough. The promise of free diesel swung it, and I suggested if he brought a few forty-gallon drums out, you'd fill them for him. How does that deal sound to you?'

'Apart from the diesel, what's it going to cost us Don?'

'Hard to say, Erica. If you used local water reed, local to Scotland that is, it shouldn't be too bad. Why not have a word with Josephine? She would know a good source from some loch side or other. Just get it delivered to Stornoway, and we can take it from there.'

Erica rang Josephine and a price was arranged. The Trust had a reliable source for their other properties. Reed was regularly cut to prevent many inland lochs from silting up. It was standard wetland conservation management, and they would just need to collect at loch-side, otherwise the cut reeds would be disposed of by burning.

Erica rang Don back and asked him to arrange collection of enough reed to re-thatch their blackhouse. To be on the safe side, Don reckoned that she would need enough to fill the ten-ton Russian amphibious transporter. It would never weigh that much but thatching reed was a bulky load. Best to hire a ten-ton tipper truck, they shouldn't go far wrong if they filled it right up.

'But Don, I'm out here and don't even know the first thing about hiring trucks and so on. Can you arrange all this for us?'

Erica was out of her depth wheeling and dealing with Hebridean acumen.

'That'll cost you another barrel of MOD diesel,' he teased.

'Sure, no bother Erica. It might be short notice but next period of calm weather we'll be there. Give me a ring when it looks calm out there and I'll tell you when we are on our way.'

Erica reported back to the family at their evening meal. Dan took advantage of the impending delivery to borrow the phone and ring Lachie. He had run out of dope, and it would be a few months until Mothan was in season. Even if it lived up to his expectations, which he wasn't sure about, he was most definitely going to try and smoke it. The deal was arranged and even if the *Beluga* couldn't come out just yet, Don was cool about it; business was business after all.

Due to the recession on the mainland, all parties involved jumped at the chance of supplying the St Kilda thatch order.

The Soviet PTM-S lumbered into Village Bay just two weeks later, accompanied by the *Beluga*. Don was known to be a good 'fixer' round the Hebrides and this job hadn't proved too difficult and the weather was on his side, not like the sheep he helped take off Eilean an Taighe a few weeks earlier. The wind and currents in the Minches sometimes combined to generate the 'Blue Men,' pillar like waves throwing small boats around like corks. It had been more luck than judgment they escaped the Sound of Shiant in one piece that day.

Don chatted over the VHF radio to Garry, owner of the amphibious transport vehicle. Garry had brought his son along to help unload the thatch and the strange vessel used its variable speed twin screws to manoeuvre its approach to the beach slipway.

Its arrival coincided with low tide and engaging its caterpillar tracks Garry drove the hybrid Soviet craft across the beach before climbing the concrete slipway to the helipad hard standing area. The whole Williams family, with Sally and Dan, walked over to greet the strange vehicle piled high with thatching reed tied down under a heavy waterproof tarpaulin.

Garry parked the amphibious vehicle beside the fire pond pump house as the onlookers gathered around. He stepped down from the PTM-S and shook hands with them all. Garry had been impressed by the performance of his Russian military surplus.

Don arrived a few minutes later after tying his dinghy to the jetty. The tide was too low to bring the *Beluga* alongside that morning. Bio-security measures had last been observed when he brought Josephine out several weeks earlier. As far as the conservation bodies were concerned the big fear was the arrival of rats at St Kilda which could predate on the eggs and chicks of ground nesting birds.

It had happened on many other British islands and, so far, St Kilda had been spared. The Soviet transporter, driving straight up into the village with its load of freshly cut thatching reed, would prove to be the greatest bio-security threat since the wreck of the fishing boat 'Spinningdale' in February 2008.

'So, where'd you like your thatch, folks?' Garry had offered, a door-to-door delivery service and turned to Dave, ignoring the women.

'Well, if you are offering, maybe you could take it right up to the blackhouses. You'll easily see the one my daughter has been working on.'

'Hang on a minute, Dave. There's always been a total ban on driving any kind of vehicle off road for fear of damaging the World Heritage Site. Josephine would have a fit if she heard about this!'

Sally was concerned that driving a large, tracked vehicle across the village fields would sour relations with the Trust.

'What Josephine doesn't know about won't worry her, Garry. Go for it; that's what I say!'

Don was enthusiastic to see the exotic vehicle put through its paces.

'You'll have to follow the road toward the power station, then turn left into Red Square, past the KGB offices, ha, ha!'

The irony of Soviet military hardware manoeuvring through the heart of a redundant Cold War UK military base did not escape him.

'That way you can drive on concrete most of the way.'

The Soviet vehicle, or should it be called a craft; no one could make up their minds, finally left the concrete standing at the scrap wood store and headed up the grassy slope toward the cottages.

Surprised sheep scattered as Garry revved the machine's 350 horsepower V-12 diesel engine emitting a plume of black smoke from its exhaust pipe. He was enjoying this; something very good about using a powerful machine in a wild environment. The load of thatch crossed the dry burn with ease and in spite of its bulk the tracked transporter caused little damage to the ground.

The underlying gravel soil proved surprisingly resilient to the vehicle's well spread 18-ton weight. Even so, this was the first time in memory that any type of vehicle had been driven into the old village.

Pulling up outside Erica and Sally's black house, Garry switched off the engine and stepped down with his son, Edward, to untie the tarpaulin sheet protecting the thatching reed. Agatha came up the path from House Five, the workshop, carrying four long-handled forks. Together with Dan, the three women unloaded the bundles of reed within fifteen minutes.

Unsurprisingly, to Don, once the bundles of reed had been lifted out, thirty empty oil drums could be seen stacked in the bottom of the hull. Garry was obviously going to take full advantage of free MOD diesel as part of the deal.

In their enthusiasm to get on with the task, no-one noticed the female brown rat and her three kits run out of reed bundles stacked on the ground. The rats quickly disappeared into a collapsed section of consumption wall next to the Street.

Sally went into nearby House One and returned with two six-packs of McEwan's Export, left by the last sheep research volunteers. All but Agatha celebrated the arrival of the new thatch by downing a can of beer.

'Can you show Garry where to fill up, Dave?'

Don was keen to keep his part of the bargain. Garry had a handy piece of equipment and just the job for deliveries like this, even better for moving sheep around remote islands.

Dave climbed on board the PTS-M and guided Garry and Edward to the delivery hose on the side of the power station building. With Dave out of earshot, Don took Dan to one side and gave him the large, padded envelope placed inside his waterproof jacket for safe keeping. This is from Lachie, Don. I'll leave it with you to sort things out with him later, OK?'

Hebridean deals worked on the principle of trust. If trust was ever broken, there would be no future business, especially when there was an element of illegality. A previous archaeologist had difficulty getting supplies sent out from Benbecula after failing to pay his account with the small supermarket on time.

Alongside the power station, Garry filled the fuel tank of the amphibious transporter and then filled each of the thirty oil drums he had brought with him. Considering the rapidly escalating cost of fuel this wasn't a bad deal, and he had fun playing with his big toy into the bargain.

Filling the *Beluga* was going to be little more difficult, but Don had brought an electric transfer pump to run off the boat's electrics. He would pull up alongside the moored *Beluga* and let Don pump out a couple of barrels for his return journey. They'd have to somehow get full barrels down to the jetty when the tourist season began, easier said than done without a vehicle available.

Garry was keen to get going and be away from the rocks of St Kilda as soon as possible. The amphibious vehicle behaved like a powered bathtub and would struggle against gusting winds close to the islands. The morning crossing had been smooth enough but a line of clouds on the horizon beyond Levenish indicated weather would be coming in from the south-east within a few hours. Village Bay would then be dangerous for the best of craft and skippers; Garry and his tracked barge were neither, Don thought.

The amphibious transporter trundled along the concrete road to the beach. The tide was high now and Garry's craft was in the sea within a few yards of the end of the slipway. Don winced as he heard gears grate as Garry changed the power transmission from tracks to the craft's twin propellers.

The PTS-M was immediately underway toward the moored *Beluga*. Don walked down to the jetty and set off in the small dingy to rejoin his vessel. The two craft bobbed side by side for ten minutes as diesel fuel was transferred to the *Beluga*. Don had thought to bring some large tyres to use as fenders to protect his blue and white paintwork from the olive-green steel plate of Garry's rugged vessel.

With the transfer complete the two craft separated; Garry and Edward waved back to the residents gathered on the jetty to watch their departure. The PTS-M pulled away sounding like a large heavy goods vehicle as the rising sound of *Beluga*'s engines echoed off the cliffs.

They had been very lucky with this delivery; it wouldn't always be so easy. Erica had already talked to Don about supplying a woodstove and flue pipe; he implied that should be easy to obtain on Harris and he'd bring one out with him next trip, though that might not be for a while should the winter weather deteriorate, as he would normally have expected.

The high-pressure system centred over the north of the British Isles ensured good, if somewhat cold working conditions. Dave continued repairing garden walls around the village. Sheep still jumped up but by now he had mastered the walling technique well enough to prevent collapse, so he thought.

Erica and Sally progressed well with the blackhouse. Thatching the roof caused some discussion but the plentiful supply of scrap wood in the Red Square store enabled them to fabricate rafters and sways to suit.

They found a good roll of galvanised soft wire in House Five previously used to tie down pitched roofs of the six restored whitehouses. This was perfect for wiring the sways to the rafters supporting the thatch in place. Not exactly the traditional method of using tarred string but then what was tradition nowadays anyway?

Dave agreed galvanised wire served the purpose well enough and that was all that really mattered. The original villagers used whatever they could find to make running repairs, considering the difficulty of getting building materials out to the island. They had even used stone tools well into modern times.

When they had regular access to iron and steel tools, old stone implements were recycled and used in wall repairs. The two women were lucky to find spare glazing panes in the Base workshop and after some trial and error worked out how to cut the glass to fit their window frames.

With winter upon them, they looked forward to Don to bringing pre-cut glass out in the Spring.

Using the door on the Lady Grange cleit as a pattern, they made a weather tight door to protect their entrance. Lady Grange, Rachel Chiesley, had been exiled to St Kilda in the eighteenth century following acrimonious separation from her husband. He had feared she would inform the Hanoverian government of his Jacobite sympathies. Sally often referred to this lady's plight during her many rants on the injustices perpetuated on women by male dominance at St Kilda.

The outer shell of the black house was completed just before winter weather broke on the island. Bending double to avoid being blown over by the gusting, salt laden blasts from the bay, Erica and Sally turned into the narrow alley from the Street and entered their new home.

With the roof newly thatched, nets formerly used to cover St Kilda's waste skips were weighted with stones and thrown over to keep the thatch in place. With glass in the windows and a secure new door, it felt uncannily calm inside. All that was left was to panel the interior walls.

Once again, piles of discarded pallets left behind in Red Square provided more than enough material for the job. Within a week they were ready to fit the woodstove, but the stormy weather had made it impossible for Don to bring it out. A celebration was called for all the same, so they decided to follow tradition and light an open wood fire in the centre of the floor. It seemed they had made too good a job of the thatch. The non-traditional reeds had been packed too tightly to let the tarry smoke rise through the thatch.

The two women sat around the fire with a flask of tea and home-made biscuits until they could stand it no longer. With eyes streaming, they spluttered their way outside to the Manse for a shower. Dave was in the kitchen and made

209

unappreciated comments about a pair of kippers having just entered, by the smell of it.

'Don't worry, girls. I've just been speaking to Don, and he reckons he should be able to come out with your new stove next week. High pressure is slipping southwest so the winds will turn more northerly. It will be calm for a few days before winds pick up again, so he has a window in the weather to get here.'

Life on the island slowed for the winter but Dave kept working in all weathers, determined to finish the garden walls in time for Spring planting. Once the walls had reached about five foot high the work became more bearable, providing him with shelter from cold gusts and snow flurries.

Dave noticed with some concern that the Soay sheep had discovered this too and on more than one occasion disturbed them sheltering within his newly restored planticrubs. At least his substantial stonework stayed in place as the chastised beasts scrambled back outside. The rebuilding of garden walls had become a *cause célèbre* and he began to compare his own modest efforts to the Herculean rebuilding works led by Reverend Neil McKenzie in 1834.

The woodstove and flue pipe were delivered the following week as promised. Erica and Sally took a hand cart from the Base workshop down to the jetty. Don arrived on the high tide and tied up alongside and with Lachie they made easy work of manoeuvring the second hand Jotul into the cart.

With Don and Lachie pulling and the two women pushing they hauled the cast iron stove and flue pipe up to the black house before walking it inside on its four sturdy legs. Rather than locate the stove in the middle of the floor, Erica had decided it would be far more space efficient to install it at the upper end of the house with the chimney pipe sticking up through the thatch roughly where a fireplace chimney would have been in a whitehouse. Lachie left them planning how they would seal the thatch where the flue pipe went through the roof and went to find Dan who owed him for the herbal cannabis that he had sent over with the thatching reed.

Dan hadn't been seen much during the wintry weather. He had preferred to stay inside the Feather Store 'planning,' which was how he described his periods of absence from the daily grind outside. Deborah had spent a fair amount of time in there 'advising' and her role as family matriarch occupied the rest of her time.

When Lachie went up the stone steps and opened the crude wooden door of the upper Featherstore the smell knocked him back. The smell of Dan's unwashed clothes mixed with stale red wine barely disguised the smell from the herbal cannabis he had all but finished smoking since Lachie had last supplied him. With red eyes and hoarse voice, he greeted Lachie.

'Come in, man! Good to see you, Lachie.'

He moved to hug him, but Lachie pulled back, repulsed by Dan's unwashed condition. He could have sworn there were remnant vomit particles on his jumper making a manly hug even more repulsive.

'Never mind about all that, Dan. I believe you owe me a few quid, like.'

'Hey, man. It's cool, it is really, but I just can't get to the bank here you know, and I don't suppose you take Visa, eh?'

'A cheque will do, Dan – or we can go to the boat and Don has a Visa machine on board. He'll give you the cash so we can do it that way.'

'Man, oh man! Just realised I left my card back in Edinburgh so no can do I am afraid.'

Dan was used to blagging his way out of situations like this using boyish charm back in Edinburgh but quickly realised it wasn't going to work this time.

'So, Dan, you're telling me you can't pay, maybe won't pay even?'

'Come on, Lachie. It's not like that.'

'Like fuck, it's not Dan! OK, let me make things quite clear; just remember where you are, dickhead. You're on St Kilda and you are going to need us if you ever want to get off again. So, you are going to pay up pretty damn soon or start training to be a fucking long-distance swimmer!'

Lachie walked out slamming the door behind him to rejoin Don who was arranging refuelling with Dave.

'We can use that hand cart to move barrels down to the jetty then use your transfer pump to fill the boat. How does that sound, Don?'

'OK by me, Dave. Lets' give it a go.'

Don had brought four empty plastic twenty-gallon barrels with him, and the two men carried them up to the power station with ease. They placed them up-right in the hand cart and filled them from the delivery hose. The weight of the eighty gallons of diesel was as much as the cart could carry.

Dave hadn't thought to check the tyres before they started the job. One pneumatic tyre flattened under the load, making pulling it along the level road difficult. When they came to the steep descent to the jetty, the overloaded baggage cart became near uncontrollable.

Don slipped and fell releasing his grip on the steering handle, leaving Dave to take the full weight of the cart and fuel barrels. Dave tried to hold the cart back, but it was impossible. As the cart ran out of control down the slope, the flat tyre caused it to turn violently throwing Dave to one side and tipping over. The full plastic barrels fell out and rolled down to splash heavily into the sea in front of the *Beluga*.

Don was rarely heard to swear and, despite his suspect wheeling and dealing, he considered the teachings of the

Free Church a worthwhile code to follow but this time he made an exception.

'Fuck it! Bloody, bloody fuck it!'

The only good thing he could think was that the tide was high, and the barrels hadn't ruptured falling onto rocks. He picked himself up and went over to Dave, who was lying at the bottom of the slope near the overturned hand cart. He went to help Dave to his feet but when he cried out in pain he realised Dave had been hurt.

'My back, Don, I can barely move. Christ what a balls up! Where are the barrels now?'

'They're in the water but they are okay for now. I'll send Lachie to find Sally; she will know what to do.'

Lachie had witnessed the commotion on his way back from the Feather Store and came straight down to the jetty. He ran up to the village and arrived at the restored blackhouse to find the two women still working out how to fit the woodstove.

'Sally, can you come quick! Dave's taken a bad fall on the jetty and hurt his back; we don't really know how to move him.'

'Right, let's go to the medical wing and fetch the stretcher.'

This sort of incident had been commonplace during her MOD employment. It could be a simple pulled muscle or at worst a fractured vertebra. She prayed it was simply a pulled muscle, but she couldn't take any chances. They picked up the stretcher and some blankets to roll and place on either side of the patient to stop him from turning. When they got to the jetty, Dave had managed to get himself up onto all fours but could stand no further, even with Don helping. It was a good sign, she thought. It was unlikely to be anything cracked or broken. She ran her fingers down his spine and just above his sacroiliac joint felt a small lump.

'You've got a compressed disc, Dave. A slipped disc to you. You're not going to die but it's going to be painful for a while. Let's see if we can put you on the stretcher and get you to the medical wing.'

They strapped him into the stretcher and placed rolled blankets either side of him. Supported on the stretcher, the pain was all but gone but as soon as he tried to move it came back with a vengeance. With Erica and Sally at the head of the stretcher and Don and Lachie taking the weight at the bottom they carefully carried Dave up the slippery slope and in through the deserted loading bay, up the stairs to the medical wing. They placed him, still strapped in the stretcher, on to Sally's examination couch.

'You can leave him with me now; you had all better get down to the jetty and do something about those diesel barrels bobbing about before they get burst open on the rocks.'

Don, Lachie and Erica walked quickly back to the jetty and stepped into the *Beluga*'s dinghy. Don kept a cargo net in one of the bulkhead compartments of his boat and, reaching the *Beluga*, leaped agilely on board and threw the net down to Lachie and Erica.

'Quick now! Get over there and throw the net over the barrels, then tow them back here. We can pump them out as they are, floating will be OK if we don't let them roll about too much. Keep them tight in the net.'

Don got the transfer pump set up and within a few minutes Lachie and Erica had the barrels netted and alongside. It still proved difficult to pump out barrels bobbing on the swell, but the task was achieved without further accident. The *Beluga* was refuelled and ready for the return trip.

Lachie took Erica back to the jetty then returned to the *Beluga*. He climbed back aboard and winched the dingy onto the stern. Don fired up the engines and without waving they headed off at high speed in the direction of

Harris. It had not been the best of days and now the adrenalin was wearing off Don was beginning to feel his own strained back.

'So how did you get on with that Danny boy, Lachie?'

'He never paid me, Don. I told him he'd better if he ever wants to get off St Kilda again.'

'OK, Lachie. We'll play it that way. I've seen his sort before and believe me, they all pay up in the end!'

11

Personalities

Deborah heard none of the commotion on the jetty. Listening to afternoon radio, with the regular throb of the generator in the background, she knew nothing of the re-fuelling accident. Her chores complete, she decided it was about time she paid Dan a visit.

Though he had spurned her first advances a few days earlier, he had been receptive, appreciative even, of her innuendoes but for her it hadn't been a game. Like most young men, she thought, he had run a mile rather than get involved with a real woman. For some inexplicable reason she had been feeling very real over the past couple of weeks. Perhaps she had been too hard on him; it was time to make amends, try a more subtle approach.

She tentatively knocked on the Feather Store door. The wooden lock appeared damaged where Lachie had slammed it shut earlier without fully sliding the bolt back. She heard movement inside but no sound of footsteps approaching the door. The sound she heard was Dan retreating to one of the inner bedrooms. After a minute or so she just opened the door and went in.

'Jesus Christ, Dan! What a mess in here. What on earth is the matter with you, living in squalor like this?'

Then the smell hit her. He couldn't have changed or washed since they had the row, and that had been over a week ago. Empty red wine bottles littered the room and an ashtray on the corner of the trestle table was overflowing with home rolled cigarette butts. There was another smell too, one she had recognised on the clothes of some of her more intelligent yet often lethargic students back at the High School.

Dirty crockery lay on the counter; the unwashed plates speckled with droppings where mice had feasted on scraps he had left and not cleaned up. Deborah heard a slight rustle of bedding from one of the inner rooms and opened the door to find Dan cowering on an old iron single bed beside the small window looking out onto the bay. He looked scared, even though Lachie's earlier threat had receded with the departure of the *Beluga*. On seeing Deborah, he burst into tears.

'I'm fucked Deborah. I owe Don and Lachie shitloads of money for dope, and I can't pay them. There's no way I can out here, is there? We are a bloody cashless society again,' he added ruefully.

Deborah was less than impressed with what she found.

'Dan, you are going to have to pull yourself together if you're going to stay here. We can't cope with you if you are going to fall to pieces when the going gets tough. I am sorry I gave you a hard time last week, but that is no excuse to wallow in self-pity. I'll ask Don to take you off next time he's in.'

Dan burst into uncontrollable sobs.

'That's just it, Debs, they refuse to take me until I pay for my deal. Unless they take me, I won't be able to get them the cash and I don't have cheque book or cards with me. My money is back in Edinburgh, and I have no way of getting at it.'

He looked at her, his expression that of a small boy wanting her to take responsibility for his predicament. Deborah had known a few of her students break down like this at the college and referred them to the student councillor. She was going to have to deal with this situation, however clumsily, herself.

'Oh, dear, you are in a bad way, Dan,' she teased.

'You'd better come to Mummy then.'

She sat down on the small bed next to him. The springs creaked with their combined weight as she put her arm around him. He pressed his head to her bosom, and she found his unwashed condition arousing for reasons she couldn't quite fathom and, taking a bold risk, slid her hand inside the front of his jeans. With his face nuzzling into her left she felt him stiffen at once. She gently squeezed and stroked and felt him come surprisingly quickly.

Amazed at herself for what she had just done, Deborah lifted his head from her chest and looked him straight in the eye. She felt the situation bizarre enough to continue the jocularity.

'You must have really needed that, Dan.'

She did feel genuine concern for him this time. Despite his outward bravado, he was obviously still a little boy underneath. In her albeit limited experience, most men were. Deborah wiped her fingers on Dan's shirt; it really couldn't have got much grubbier. Now visibly relaxed, he was beginning to return to an unclean version of his old self.

'Tell you what, Dan; come over to the house in a few minutes. Go and have a good shower and put on some clean clothes, if you have any. Then join us for supper. Good food and company will do you the world of good, and for now at least, please keep our little secret?'

He nodded and she left Dan to regain his usual extrovert composure. Deborah walked back over to the Manse and was surprised to see Dave moving stiffly toward her with the aid of a walking stick.

'What on earth have you done, love?'

This was getting to be one of those days, she reflected. Dave limped inside and sat down carefully on a high-backed kitchen chair and related events leading to a stupid, very stupid accident.

If only they had blown that flat tyre up before trying to move the barrels or only tried to move one at a time. But then everything was clearer in hindsight. He explained how Sally had fixed him up, given him some gentle osteopathy to get everything back in place but he would have to be careful for a few days and not lift anything heavy. No stone walling for a week or so until his inflamed lower back muscles settled down.

He certainly wasn't going to tell her about the rest of his experience in the consulting room and had no inkling of what had just occurred in the Feather Store between Deborah and Dan.

After he had been left strapped to the stretcher on Sally's examination couch, Dave expected Sally to have carefully released him, given him a thorough examination before manipulating his lower spine. A bit of massage, maybe a few chiropractic manoeuvres and he'd be up and gone. He did think she was leaving him strapped down for longer than was necessary and after a couple of cans of McEwan's with Don and Lachie earlier, he quite badly wanted a pee.

'No problem,' she said.

Instead of allowing him to get up, as he had expected, she fetched a cardboard urinal bottle, undid his zipper, pulled his penis out of his pants and held the bottle in place. He found it impossible to urinate with the partial erection that occurred despite his lower back discomfort.

'Oh, dear David, what are we going to do? Looks like I am going to have to take care of that for you, aren't I? If you can't pee normally, I am going to have to catheterise you.'

This really had been the furthest thought from Dave's mind when he was deposited in Sally's examination room for minor back injury treatment but strapped up and almost pain free he was powerless to resist. He had to reluctantly admit to himself he was enjoying the experience.

When Sally donned her white latex gloves and slid the smooth catheter into his urethra the sensation left him lost for words. All he could manage was a whimper and gasp as the tip of the tube pushed painlessly through the sphincter and entered his bladder. With his erection subsided the urine flowed freely into the bottle she placed at the other end of the tube. She gently withdrew the catheter when he had finished urinating. Having relinquished all bodily control to Sally, Dave felt she had made the first move in a game he would later find hard to resist.

'Better now, Dave?'

He felt like putty in her hands as she un-strapped him from the stretcher and carefully turned him over to begin the manipulation. Not a word more was spoken about what had just happened but both acknowledged Sally as dominant in a power exchange game. In spite of Dave's professed yearnings to lead his tribe to the Promised Land, she had skilfully led him into a world of submissive fantasy. For Sally, the self-professed radical feminist, she had taken a perverse pleasure in exerting sexual power over her male patients.

While employed by the MOD, she had occasionally left her male patients wondering over unexpected aspects of their treatment. It had been her way of putting a bit of colour into a grey male world and at the same time feeding her own fantasy.

There had been few protests; her white coat conveyed an authority her patients willingly accepted in their regimented lives. Now without MOD structures in place, social parameters were becoming blurred. For women of new St Kilda, she realised, life could and often would become experimental as they found their new roles.

St Kilda society had been as balanced as the natural world around them before the ministers arrived. If she had her way, it soon would be again. For now, she needed to exercise feminine control until that time came. Sally had tried the traditional practise of leaving a sachet of Mothan under her pillow, but dreams of a much-wanted family still eluded her.

Agatha had been out walking the cliff paths at the time of her father's mishap with the handcart. Though having no knowledge of the personal events of that afternoon she was astutely aware of energies already at play in their nascent community.

She had picked up on her mother's subtle flirtations with Dan and his weak attempts to resist and his pathetic escape attempt through alcohol and cannabis. Sally's desire to dominate had been obvious from the start. Her experience of working on the island previously was proving useful but, Agatha calculated, also made her vulnerable to the unexpected.

Her father was OK but a remarkably easy man to predict. He had brought them here to follow his dream of pioneer resettlement, albeit aided by the Trust and abandoned MOD food stores. She smiled at this; as a keen naturalist she had read the work of Henry David Thoreau, written in his cabin at Walden Pond. Like so many male authors on wilderness living he couldn't have done it without the support of women at home.

Her own mother seemed to have willingly accepted the role of the strong pioneer woman, looking after her men to ensure they were fit and strong enough to support the family. It was all so obvious; they were all working out their fantasies free from mainland constraints.

Constraints here, she thought, were the elements and rhythms of nature. Her scientific training told her there should be no other way, but the draw she felt to visit the ruins of the Amazon's House in Glen Mór on an almost daily basis was hard to understand.

The Great Skuas nesting there during the summer had come to accept her as a familiar and trusted figure in their territory. The large and usually aggressive birds accepted her presence, almost befriending Agatha as she sat for hours on end enjoying the spirit of place. While idly chewing on Mothan leaves she felt an almost tangible presence around the 'horned structures'; the ageless horseshoe shaped stone compounds visiting archaeologists found so puzzling.

Agatha would have scoffed at meditation back in Edinburgh but out here she found herself doing just that. Her mind was beginning to relax and unquestioningly accept the idea of a female deity, long trapped on the island. Agatha had read how, when sea levels were lower, St Kilda was at the tip of peninsula reaching out from Harris. St Kilda's mythical Amazon really could have ridden out to hunt across the Western Isles with her pack of hounds.

Now, as sea levels rose, Agatha sensed the deity was trapped and, like any trapped wild creature, the Amazon, Cailleach, Morrigan or whatever she was called, needed to be treated with respect. Agatha had developed the objective skill needed to reflect on her own place in the landscape. The Cailleach was embedded here, every rock and stream a portal to her energy, her life force.

It dawned on Agatha that it was no wonder there had been plane wrecks in this valley. Intrusive flying machines downed by inexplicable gusts on the clearest of days. Exiled to the cold north side of the island the Cailleach would not tolerate desecration of her home by men with their noisy polluting machines and lack of empathy for the world around them.

After chewing Mothan, she realised the Cailleach had summoned aggressive Skuas in 1960, to protect Glen Mór, after Operation Hardrock had blasted a huge chunk out of the southern slopes of Conachair. The revelation gave Agatha goose pimples, the sensation almost erotic in intensity. Suddenly, she knew why so many curious tourists had been driven back by Skua attack after venturing into the Cailleach's retreat. The Cailleach summoned Skuas from Arctic regions to protect herself and chewing another smoky Mothan leaf, Agatha knew what she had to do redress the two-hundred-year-old injustice.

Snapping out of her reverie, Agatha again noticed the muddy green material poking out of the damaged cleit at the site of the small plane crash on the day of their arrival. As far as she knew, the deer hunters had all perished bar the one shocked survivor they had met on the jetty. In fact, she was secretly pleased the remains, both mechanical and human, had tipped over the cliff to lie hidden in submarine caves beneath the island. The aging but still visible remains of the Sunderland flying boat were bad enough. Another smashed plane would further compromise the *Genius loci* she found so inspirational.

She would pull it up and throw the ugly piece of green canvas over the cliff to join the rest of the male rubbish hundreds of feet below. She pulled at the material and found it stronger than she had expected.

It seemed to be the same material used in her climbing rucksack. It was a heavy duty Cordura bag of some sort and after a struggle she pulled it out from under muddy turf and fallen stones inside the cleit. The bag was roughly five feet long and broader at one end, which seemed to be where most of the weight was located. It had a shoulder strap running from end to end and a heavy-duty zip fastener running the whole length of one side. The fastener was corroded and seized but she decided to take the long bag and its contents down to the village and free the zip in the workshop at House Five.

Walking back down the steep track the heavy shoulder bag annoyed her. Bumping against the outside of her thigh she had to change the bag from shoulder to shoulder to stay comfortable.

She continued past the Operation Hardrock quarry and Milking Stone, carefully replaced by the army sappers. It pleasantly surprised her that the military had managed to keep a modicum of respect for the spirit of this island. Turning left from the track she crossed the burn nearly losing her footing when the bag slipped from her shoulder and knocked her ankle.

Quietly cursing, she slung the bag back on her shoulder and made her way along the grass strewn Street to House Five. She entered the cottage but found the light inside too poor to see well enough to free the zip. She placed the long bag on the low wall outside and fetched a can of WD40 from the steel flammable liquids cupboard. Agatha sprayed the thin penetrating oil along the length of the corroded brass zip and waited a few minutes for the lubricant to take effect.

Erica came out of the alleyway beside her newly thatched blackhouse having waited long enough for Sally to return and help with woodstove practicalities. Looking up the Street she saw her younger sister apparently struggling to open a long green bag.

To her irritation, Agatha spotted her sister walking toward her; she had hoped to discover the contents by herself. Now Erica was going to get in on the act.

'What have you got there? Bloody hell Agatha, that looks like a gun-slip; where did you find it?'

Erica briefly had a relationship with a forester who she soon discovered to be an unstable gun enthusiast. A survivalist, he described himself; a 'Prepper' prepared for the breakdown of society, and he was preparing to defend his woman and family living in the wilds of Assynt when the collapse assuredly came. In Erica's opinion, rather than being the deep ecologist she had hoped for, her forester boyfriend revealed himself as a rabid eco-fascist and she quickly ended the relationship. She realised she had attracted a stalker who wanted to control her as much as the Highland deer population.

'Here Agatha, I'll hold the bag while you work the zip.'

Agatha worked the zip back and forward until it eventually freed, and the bag opened along its full length. She reached inside and quickly realising what the bag held' pulled out a hunting rifle. It was well wrapped in a protective and lightly oiled cloth. The telescopic sight lenses were protected by plastic caps.

'That's a Tikka T3 Lite Stainless! One of the best hunting rifles you can get. It's light as well as weather resistant.'

Erica was amazed.

' Do you remember Rory? That mad forester I went out with for a few weeks; he had one of these and took me target shooting. There was no way I was going to shoot deer, but target shooting was cool. I amazed myself, never thought I would enjoy guns, but I loved using one of these. My shoulder aches thinking about it! Hey, is there any ammo for it?'

Agatha rummaged further into the bag and discovered ten small plastic boxes each holding 20 rounds of 100 grain ammunition.

'This must have been heavy to carry, Sis. Let's try it out; the magazine holds 3 rounds. We'll soon find if it works OK.'

Erica had been given basic firearms safety instruction by Rory before he let her try out his rifle, so she knew to set up the target well away from the Base and any other buildings.

She placed a spare plywood window shutter on top of the remains of the Head Dyke, above the shore. Erica considered this to be safe for if she missed the target, the bullet would fall harmlessly into the sea. The breeze proved a problem setting up the target, so she propped it up with some large stones.

A white spot where the green topcoat had flaked off the plywood made for a suitable bullseye. Walking back, she estimated the range to be about two hundred and fifty yards and adjusted the telescopic sight to the distance, placed one round into the magazine and worked the bolt to load it into the chamber. Lying across the path, she rested the rifle on top of the low turf capped wall, took aim at the green board, breathed out, as Rory had taught her, released the safety catch and squeezed the trigger. The rifle cracked and a small, neat hole appeared in the white patch. The green board then slid to the ground after the stone propping it up dislodged. The bullet that had faultlessly punched through the target and ricocheted off a beach stone. Rather than falling harmlessly into the sea, the spinning bullet whined across the foreshore to hit the steel door of the jetty storeroom with a resounding metallic bang.

'What the fucking hell!'

Dan's nerves had already been strained to breaking point that afternoon and he had gone down to the jetty to contemplate over a well-deserved spliff. Dope psychosis was making him paranoid about the return of the *Beluga*. He was preparing himself for a beating unless he paid up, that is what would have happened in Edinburgh, but out here he was getting shot at.

'Shit!' Erica realised what had happened, put the rifle down on the gun-slip to prevent it getting damaged on the stone wall and ran down to the road. She could see Dan pacing up and down on the jetty shaking his head in disbelief.

'Dan, I am so sorry!' she shouted. 'Are you okay?'

'For God's sake, Erica!' he yelled back.

'What were you thinking of, and where the fuck did you get that gun from?'

Deborah had heard the shot from the Manse kitchen where she and Dave had been sharing a pot of tea before she prepared the evening meal. Both had been quietly contemplating the strange events of the afternoon and had been snapped into the present by the crack of the rifle, at once followed by a loud clang and angry scream from the jetty.

226

'You stay there, Dave. I'll go out and see what that was all about.'

Dave hobbled to the window to watch his wife march out toward the top of the jetty. He saw her shake her head as Erica explained what had happened.

'No one has been hurt, that is the main thing,' she assured her mother.

'You'd better bring that thing down to the Manse and we'll keep it safely under lock and key.'

Deborah thought a firearms incident was just typical of Erica, she would always be the wild child no matter what and she was certainly old enough to know better than play with guns.

She had played with men enough back in Edinburgh and when pregnant she hadn't even been able to tell Deborah who the father was. An abortion seemed the only sensible choice but when she collected Erica from Spire Murrayfield Hospital, she knew it had been a big mistake.

Had she let Erica have the baby, she would have no doubt settled into single motherhood in Edinburgh instead of playing with guns out here. Deborah would have been a grandmother had she not insisted on Erica's termination. She had wanted to do the best thing for her daughter but had looked forward to becoming an active grandmother before becoming too old to be appreciated.

Being a mother was the hardest job in the world and no matter how old, these girls would always be her babies. She also wondered if the tense relationship between her and Dave around that time made Erica promiscuous to compensate for passive aggression at home. They just hadn't been getting on while Dave was unemployed, and she was going from strength to strength in her teaching career. Now, at least, Dave seemed fulfilled and happy out at St Kilda.

Agatha joined them; she had already put the rifle back in its slip and slung it over her shoulder.

'Who's going to steal it out here, Mum?'

'OK, clever clogs, we do at least need to keep it safely away from your crazy sister before there really is an accident!'

Deborah was not amused by her younger daughter's nonchalance. The three walked back to the Manse and Deborah pulled the loft ladder down from the hatch in the hallway ceiling.

'Pass that thing to me and I'll put it up in the loft for now. If anyone has any better ideas, keep them to yourself!'

Deborah climbed up and placed the rifle in the loft storeroom on a shelf alongside unsold books and postcards. She came back down to the hallway to find Dave making his way from the kitchen to find out what was going on.

Deborah explained that Agatha had found a hunting rifle in a cleit near the plane crash site. There was also some ammunition, and their crazy eldest daughter had decided to try it out, nearly shooting Dan in the process.

Dave tried very hard to suppress a smile but in doing so spluttered into a full-throated laugh at the absurdity of the afternoon.

'Oh, Erica; you really are a piece of work sometimes.'

By this time Sally, having also heard the shot, appeared to ask if everyone was alright. Erica was by now wishing the ground would open and swallow her. Agatha was standing beside her; passive and smug as usual whenever emotional tension was in the atmosphere.

Deborah assured Sally that everyone was just fine while wishing she would simply piss off and keep her nose out of family business. This was her house, and she was going to stay in charge, especially of the two men on the island.

'OK, that gun stays up in the loft unless I say otherwise. Is that clear, girls?'

The sisters nodded acknowledging that Dave's authority left no room for argument. It suited Erica to play her father's game for the time being, at least until the embarrassing incident was forgotten. Agatha shrugged her shoulders and went to her room while Erica went outside to talk with Dan, still nervous from his afternoon experiences.

Don had been right about the deteriorating weather conditions. Atmospheric pressure was dropping rapidly to the south. As the unusually deep and intense depression span toward Skye, severe south-easterly gale force winds and an accompanying storm surge headed toward St Kilda. It was going to be a wild night.

Erica helped Dan clear up the mess in the Feather Store, never very inviting at the best of times. Rather than let him spend the evening alone in the small flat, she decided to invite Dan up to House One to share the planning of his so-called spiritual tours of the island. He readily agreed, looking forward to her company and an evening beside the only functioning wood stove in the village.

The sudden blast of wind slammed the window shutter with such force the glass cracked across two panes.

'Fuck! Shit!'

Dan's nerves were still on edge despite Erica's attempts to calm him down. She liked Dan's idea of resurrecting the island's spiritual significance rather than concentrating solely on the quantifiable archaeological and natural history aspects of St Kilda.

However, since the Western Isles Trust had pulled the plug, they were going to have to be creative to make the resettlement financially sustainable.

Shutting the wooden lock to the Feather Store door with some difficulty, they realised the wind speed was picking up rapidly. They both stood and watched the movement of the sea with amazement. The waters of Village Bay were palpably rising.

The eastern horizon, instead of being flat was visibly rippling even at a distance of several miles. The sea level, still far from rough, rose and poured over the jetty in a steady torrent before hitting the beach and rising to lap at the doors of the helipad waiting room. St Kilda's wittily named International Airport Lounge was in danger of inundation.

Sally watched from the Factor's House amazed at the storm surge pouring into the bay. Even as an old hand she had never seen the sea level rise like this.

Within moments the south-easterly gale hit the village, rattling the slates and lifting the roof light in her bedroom to fall with a crash audible throughout the house. She could feel the force of the wind shaking the house.

No wonder, she thought, that the abandoned Victorian cottages could not withstand onslaughts like this. Sally opened the porch door and struggled into the wind, forcing her way outside to the back steps up to the bedrooms. The door was almost ripped out of her hands when she opened it, and it took most of her strength to close it behind her to enter the upper level of the house. Though a tempest raged outside it was warm inside. She was relieved to find the iron framed roof lights unbroken and secured their large nineteenth century latches.

The noise of the wind blowing through the slates was incredible. How they didn't just blow off in such a wind, she would never understand. Opening the back door just enough to squeeze through and back out into the wind, she made her way down the steps with difficulty, turning the corner to be bodily thrown against her own front door.

She had just managed to get inside when, through the kitchen window, she saw Erica and Dan struggling through the wind on their way to House One. Dan's long hair was lashing out in front of him; Erica's long coat flapping wildly around her knees as the pair made their way along the uneven granite sets of the Street.

Erica almost had to drag Dan from the Featherstore. Bad weather wasn't his thing as he had kept trying to explain but she insisted they left the squalor of his apartment and begin their planning in relative comfort where flat surfaces were not covered in droppings or stained with mouse urine. There was also the woodstove to look forward to.

The effort of going out into the gale made Dan cough, his sore throat and smoker's lungs were unaccustomed to the clean air being forced into them. The wind sucked his breath away when he turned his head sideways to take in the rapidly changing sea conditions in the bay. A huge swell had begun to crash along the slopes of Dun and vortices of winds, water devils, drove spinning columns of spray up onto the seafront roadway. For once he was glad of being led by Erica toward the shelter of House One. He had enjoyed watching wild weather from the now cracked and draughty Featherstore window but being caught outside in it was another matter altogether.

Dave and Deborah had seen the storm surge enter the bay from the Manse windows. Deborah had run to the porch in time to see Agatha struggling down the slipway with her camera to photograph the drama of the sea pouring over the jetty wall.

She tried to call her daughter back, but her shouts were ineffective against the howling wind. When the first large wave exploded over the wall behind her Agatha scurried back along the jetty to safer levels at the top of the slipway. Deborah ran outside and grabbed hold of Agatha's arm and pulled her back into the house. Mother and daughter were both panting with the effort, both fighting the pull of the wind and Agatha also fighting the pull of her mother.

'What the hell are you playing at, Mum!'

Agatha was enraged that her mother should pull her like that.

'I was perfectly okay out there; I love it, and I was going to film the sea. We don't see something like this every day!'

'Agatha, you are my daughter, and you can do what you like out of my sight over in Glen Bay but I'm not going to watch you drown in front of my very eyes, right outside our front door!'

'Jesus Christ,' Mum. All I got was a little wet from a wave I didn't see coming.'

'Well, I did see it coming, my girl. Look Agatha, I am sorry if you think my reaction was over the top, but you just wait until you have children of your own. You'll think differently then. I just don't want to lose you, alright?'

The wind gusted violently and the generator in the Flare Store spluttered before picking up again. 'That's all we need, the genny packing up too!'

'Don't worry Mum, it was probably just the wind backing up the exhaust, it has done it before.'

'So now you're the expert mechanic as well as ecologist? What do you know about engines then?'

'You'd be surprised about what I know around this place, mother.' Agatha growled.

Deborah felt the colour rise to her throat; if only it wasn't so obvious, she thought to herself. How much did her deep and devious younger daughter really know?

Dave came to the hallway after hearing voices raised above the clamour of the wind. He saw his wife's flushed face, concluding it to be the result of tension between the two. Agatha turned and marched to her room leaving Deborah standing in the hallway, her flush subsiding.

'What was that all about?' He questioned.

Deborah thought she picked up an authoritarian rather than caring tone in his voice. To her embarrassment the flush rose once more.

'Our beloved youngest was only trying to drown herself to get a good photo from the jetty, Dave. Maybe, I was being overprotective but now she will drive me nuts by walking round for days with that supercilious face she puts on every time she thinks she has got one over me.'

'Got what over you?'

Dave was mildly amused but also feeling slightly anxious concerning the secret he shared with Sally.

'Never you mind, Dave; women's business - if you must know.'

Sally settled down in her front room in the Factor's House. She had reopened the old fireplace but during winds like this all sorts of debris blew down the chimney, from dried moss to desiccated mice. When she lit the peat fire for the first time in nearly a century, she had inadvertently asphyxiated several of St Kilda's oversized mice nesting in the chimney.

She had got into the habit of digging a little peat and stacking it to dry in a convenient cleit each time she went for a walk on the hill. Bringing down a rucksack full of dried peat each time had proved a worthwhile effort and setting a cheery fire on a wild evening like this made it well worth doing. Going for a walk was all very well, she had often thought, but going for a walk with a purpose so much better.

As every visitor remarked on, the island was littered with these small stone structures. There were over a thousand stone cleits, many still capped with turf roofs and ideal for keeping anything dry, including sheep and oneself when caught out in bad weather.

Sally thought the Soays little more than vermin and their incessant grazing damaged the island ecology. Western Island Trust archaeologists had been for ever trying to find a way of stopping them climbing on cleits while the Soay Sheep Project insisted they were to be treated as unmanaged wild animals.

The St Kildans would have sorted this out had they not evacuated leaving scientists to mismanage the islands. She had not been surprised to read that 100 of them had been brought over from Soay to 'maintain the grazing' and bred, well like wild sheep. Four-legged lawnmowers even able to graze cleit roofs until the turf capping disintegrated.

Aggressive Skuas occupied the flatter ground and kept the sheep away from their nests allowing the vegetation to recover but often attacked her while digging peat. She thought that Skuas could prove to be a keystone species in restoring the ecology of St Kilda. Not only did they deter human presence away from the village, but they kept the sheep on the move and predated on their lambs.

It was just a pity that the Skuas also predated on anything else they could get their beaks into, including the Puffins and Storm Petrels she loved to watch on her days off. Not even Gannets were safe. The large and graceful seabirds were picked off and harried by packs of Skuas until, exhausted and bloodied, their victim flopped into the sea to be ripped to pieces. What kind of nature conservation was this? The St Kildans would have kept the balance by driving these vicious killers away from the smaller birds that underpinned their livelihood.

She stopped there, knowing her thoughts were about to spiral down to a self-induced bad temper.

'Come on, Sal! Get that fire going and think about what you're going to eat tonight.'

She often talked to herself, a consequence of living alone, she had realised and accepted long ago. Her meal wasn't going to take too much thinking about, something out of a tin and a dried staple to go with it. Sally was looking forward to the fresh vegetables Dave had promised her for next Spring, but she thought he might have underestimated the sheep problem, somewhat.

Dan and Erica had managed to get the House One woodstove lit though the gusting wind caused back-draughts of smoke to puff out into the living area. They both thought that the smell of peat smoke wasn't that unpleasant, certainly an improvement on the smell of mouse urine in the Featherstore. There was no way to light a fire in the Featherstore as the only fireplace was in the cluttered and unliveable storeroom downstairs. Built into the slope, the damp lower storey had been used as a builder's store since the Trust repaired the building.

Erica placed two mugs of tea on the table. 'Sorry, there's no milk, Dan. I've got some dried stuff if you're desperate; otherwise, you'll have to wait till I get my house cow over here.'

They sipped at their sweet black tea and Erica decided to get the ball rolling.

'Now then, Dan; you are going to lead spiritual tours of the island, right? So, we need to do some planning. Like where to go, what to see. First, let's throw some ideas in the pot. I know you have been doing some reading, so you start then.'

Dan thought for a bit before picking up a nearby pencil and sheet of paper on the windowsill. He began to jot down ideas as they came to him, drew circles around the words the paper and began to link them with thin lines.

Mind-mapping, he had been told at University, was the way to get a plan like this off the ground. Edinburgh University seemed a long way off in time and space from where the two of them now sat but the principle remained sound.

The circles he drew on the paper held the words 'Kirk,' 'Graveyard,' 'Christchurch,' 'St, Columba,' 'St. Briannan,' 'Altars' and 'Sabbath.' The graveyard seemed central on the paper with the names of chapels and outlying altars around the edges of the sheet. The Kirk seemed to make the plan look a little asymmetrical, which he considered might not be surprising.

Built in the eighteen-twenties, the Kirk had been designed to throw almost every other spiritual aspect of the archipelago off balance. True, the new ministers had re-

235

consecrated earlier altars erected on the outlying islands of Dun, Boreray and Soay.

The Church of Scotland had considered them Pagan even though there were historical associations with the Irish missionary saints. After the Disruption of 1843, the Free Church encouraged worshippers to engage with natural elements. In trying to replace the more secular Church of Scotland, the radical Presbyterians acknowledged wilder energies as much as their semi-pagan forbears had done. Away from spiritually stifling Edinburgh, the wilder location the better to commune with God, rather than his idols.

Erica looked at Dan's mind-map and thought for a moment.

'Just one thing, Dan. Haven't you mapped out a very male spiritual landscape here? These centres of ritual; it does look like a predominantly paternal structure to me. I'd like us to include female spirituality in the tours too.'

'I'm not quite sure what you mean there, Erica.'

Dan was puzzled because he instinctively knew there was something important missing from his plan.

'I'd like to see you include places of natural reverence; I don't mean huge vistas to Boreray but maybe some small, secluded spots where flowers grow free from grazing sheep; where we can hear the seals singing to their pups and importantly where the Cailleach can be found; her cave. Even the Amazon's House could be included though I do think that story a bit of male fantasy!'

'Sorry, Erica, I hadn't thought of it from that angle.'

'No, you men rarely do; but let's not get bogged down with it now. Can you draw a plan to include the places I have just mentioned, and we'll try and work it all together?'

Dan drew his second mind-map to include the Cailleach's Cave, the Tunnel where seals sing to their pups and the Well of Virtues, the fount at the foot of Glen Mór, formerly named Tobar Brighid, Brid's Well when the

Apostle of the North banished the Spring Maiden from the island. St Brighid of Kildare had been appropriated by the Catholic Church, but the Presbyterian Free Church had banished her youthful spirit all together.

Only the elderly manifestation, the Cailleach remained, still smarting from the injustices imposed on the mindscape of St Kilda in the nineteenth century. Brighid, associated with the warm south of Village Bay had been banished by male activity to Glen Mór. The Cailleach lived on resentful in the north of the island, he told Erica.

There were just one or two places where Brighid remained, mainly in flower rich rocky burns running down from Mullach Mhor. The Soays seemed to have a natural aversion to getting wet. They sheltered in cleits from the rain and wouldn't graze at the water's edge unless there was no drier alternative. Facing south, these sunny clefts were Brighid's last refuge.

'Yeah, right! I'm with you, Erica. We need to include the Milking Stone and the Plain of Spells.'

'That's better, Dan. The new St Kilda community is going to need all these spiritual resources if we are going to survive. Hey, what about Shoney the sea goddess. You'll like this one, Dan.

The islanders used to throw a big party and go down to the sea and offer home-made beer to the sea in return for Shoney delivering seaweed as fertiliser for them. Candles would be lit and floated on the water and then it was party time. Not much likelihood of inbreeding in those days, if you get my meaning!'

'This gets better and better, Erica. You get on with your blackhouse and leave this project to me.'

The plan was hatched and consummated by Erica's production of a partly emptied bottle of single malt.

'There're a few drams left here, let's celebrate our spiritual tour business for next year. I bet Don will be all for this, it'll mean extra punters for him. You know, Dan; I really am getting quite excited about it!'

She crossed the table and hugged Dan, still seated, from behind giving the top of his head a light kiss.

'Who knows where this is going to end, Dan?'

Dan and Erica met up the following afternoon to continue planning their spiritual tours. Relative normality had returned to the Manse and while Dave took the day off to nurse his sore back, Sally and Agatha took a walk across the island, bird watching. Deborah kept busy inside the Featherstore, intending to restore order and cleanliness in there.

Dan suggested starting at the nineteenth century Kirk would be appropriate. Erica was initially hesitant but had to agree getting their visitors together under one roof would be a good way to start, especially if the weather was against them. Dan also thought perhaps an act of communion would be a good way to start.

Erica was against this until Dan explained he meant an act of communion with the island not communion with an imagined God justifying domination by the British Empire, its map still hanging on the wall of the schoolroom annex.

'Can you imagine, Erica, St Kildan children being taught about South Africa and Canada and their place in Queen Victoria's Empire ignored? That must have felt unreal considering their parents' whole world would have revolved round the Hebrides.'

'Yes,' she replied, 'and don't forget how unreal it must have been for their parents moving into a new structured settlement where equally structured religious practice bound their society in servitude to patriarchy. You must have heard Sally go on about the killing of the last Great Auk. Stoned as a witch, I tell you!'

Erica was becoming emotional.

'The last northern penguin was murdered out on Boreray where chains of so-called Christian bondage weren't quite strong enough to suppress older fears. If they hadn't had to go out to earn cash to survive, they would have waited until better weather. They thought the harmless Great Auk was conjuring up the storm to spite them.'

Dan had heard this story before but thought better than to interrupt.

'Now we must put up with the spite of Great Skuas, the Bonxies. The road to hell certainly was paved with good intentions but the change from shared run-rig to enclosed plots must have been complicated enough without the Minister trying to enclose mind and soul as well.'

Dan reached inside his jacket and produced his silver hip flask

'Well Erica, I propose a toast to the loosening of minds as well as ecclesiastical ties. I have prepared a new communion wine just for the occasion.'

Dan passed the silver flask to Erica. She unscrewed the cap and sniffed the contents. 'Okay, Dan.... what have you got in this?'

'Erica... it's OK, really it is. I picked some Mothan growing near the borehole and let the leaves steep in vodka for a few weeks. I have been taking it for a couple of days now. Hardly notice any effect other than the vodka but the herb has a magical reputation.'

'Oh yeah, are you going to enlighten me before I drink it Dan?'

'Well to start with it's anti-biotic.'

Erica looked quizzically at him.

'Go on, tell me more then.'

'OK, the leaves are slimy, right? Insects get trapped in the slime and are absorbed over several days. It's a tactic used by certain plants growing in bog conditions where it's too acid to absorb enough nutrient from the soil.'

He noticed the mouldy fly dead on the schoolroom windowsill.

'And the slime being anti-biotic keeps the insects from going mouldy. If I was an insectivorous plant, I'd want to keep my flies fresh, wouldn't you? It's the same with the tiny Sundew that grows here too.'

Dan was on his pet subject now.

'There's lots of folk lore about this plant, so I read. It was used for curdling milk and used as a poultice against infection on cattle. It was also rubbed into cows' udders to stop fairies from stealing the milk. If anyone had unnatural good fortune, they were said to have drunk milk from a cow that had eaten Mothan. The best story of all concerns women and the effects of Mothan.'

Erica frowned and waited for some chauvinistic comment, but he went ahead to tell her how Mothan was a dreaming herb. It could be put in pillows to induce pleasant dreams for the sleeper, foretelling of the man she would marry and could also be used by a woman to entrap a man.

'And just how is a woman supposed to use Mothan to entrap a man, then?'

Dan explained. 'All you must do is to chew leaves of Mothan before kissing the man you fancy. When your saliva mixes, he is trapped as completely as any insect gently landing on the Mothan leaves. In a state of blissful dreaming, he is oblivious of her ulterior motive.'

'And what might that ulterior motive be, Dan?'

'You tell me, Erica,' he laughed.

Erica cautiously put the flask to her lips. She hadn't forgotten the furore over Dan's mixing Fly Agaric mushrooms in vodka back in Edinburgh, but Mothan didn't sound too bad. She took a sip and found it hardly tasted of anything other than the spirit.

'How would you describe the taste, Dan? There's something there but I can't quite put my finger on it.'

'How about love juice?' he quipped.

240

Erica blushed; he was dead right. That was what it tasted like. Regaining her composure, she repeated his words.

'If I was to kiss a man, then he'd be mine for ever, right?'

'That's about the deal, Erica.'

Dan approached her and pursing his lips teased her to kiss him. Entering the spirit of the occasion Erica reached out taking his tousled head in both hands and pulled him to her. Not only did she kiss him but provocatively slid her tongue into his mouth to make sure he received her saliva.

'Blimey, Erica. In the house of God too! You've got me now.'

'And about time too, Dan. Now let's get on with our planning.'

She took another swig from the flask and sat down back to front on the teacher's highchair resting her chin on top of the back rest. Dan took the flask back, had another swig himself before putting it away in his pocket.

Like the good pupil Dan sat at the long school desk while Erica kept her dominant position astride the teacher's chair.

'Here's my idea, Dan. We start off here as agreed then take in the Christ Church graveyard, the Fairies House, St. Columba's Chapel site, St. Brendan's Well, Cailleach's cave, Plain of Spells, Milking Stone then into Glen Mór for the Amazon's House, Stone Circle, Well of Virtues and finish at the Tunnel. How does that sound?'

'It's a lot to take in, a full day even. They could bring packed lunches as no one is going to fancy walking back to the village for lunch then back over the hill to finish the tour. Especially if they have got to run the gauntlet of Bonxies a second time.'

'You've got a point there. I have another idea. How about restoring the Amazon's House a bit. It can't be too bad as Agatha often sleeps the night there.'

241

'Plenty of Mothan grows around there too – we could open a tea house!'

'Yeah, we'd have ourselves a right little love nest, wouldn't we? God, the tourists would be having orgies down there if we did that!'

Erica was getting back to her old flirtatious self. Whether it was the vodka or the Mothan she couldn't be sure, but something was making her feel good that afternoon.

'Tell you what, it's not a bad afternoon. Why don't we go to the top of Conachair and look out across the islands. We might get more inspiration up there drinking your New Communion wine.'

The pair made their way up through the village and past the Factor's House where they turned right and walked up the slope into An Lag. Dan was out of breath and sweating heavily by the time they reached the cliff edge. Erica was in her stride and pointed out the white peaks of Boreray and the Stacs. Even at a distance of four miles you could see thousands of Gannets swirling, rising and falling around the rocks whitened by years of guano dropping. Turning left and up the steepening path to Conachair, the island summit, Dan was lagging behind.

'Come on, slow coach. It's not that bad.'

She felt so good, so energised. Dan, by comparison, felt weak and exhausted.

'Going to have to stop smoking,' he whispered.

Barely able to speak, he followed her up the rough grass slope. Though a smoker he wasn't usually this fatigued. Erica got to the top first and stood by the small cairn looking out over the rest of the island and the wide Atlantic horizon. Behind her lay the hills of North and South Uist, some fifty miles distance. She could just make out the white statue of the Catholic Lady of the Isles standing against a backdrop of military radio masts that dotted much of the

South Uist ridgeline. Erica could never accept the virgin birth as more than another piece of male bullshit.

Dan finally made it to the summit and collapsed at the foot of the cairn. Erica was already considering the distant summits of Soay, Boreray and Dun. Levenish was too small and inaccessible, so she had no plans for that island.

Even before he had recovered from the climb, Erica was asking Dan what he thought of extended tours taking in the altars on Soay and Boreray. There probably would have been one on Dun so no problem going there either if they got Don to run them over.

'Just think, Dan. We could build Beltane fires for the Spring, Samhain fires for the Autumn Celtic New Year and ...'

Dan cut back in, 'Yeah, and a fucking great Wicker Man on the beach! Get real Erica, I am knackered getting up here so how is the average tourist going to feel. We want them to pay for a good time not to end up half dead!'

Erica felt hurt by the put down but could see his point. She was a young woman and in her prime.

'That Amazon's House idea sounded like a good one. We could make it habitable in a bunk house sort of way and, you know, it could be a winner all round. We would charge extra for accommodation down there. It would pay for itself soon enough. Don would be happy as he used to charge double price for campers when the Trust ran this place. Seats had to be paid for both ways, even empty ones.'

He continued to voice his thoughts.

'Thinking laterally, if I put extra business his way, he might even let me off the dope debt. Realistically though, we are going to have to keep our tour plan to Hirta, Erica. Do you have any more thoughts?'

As the words left his mouth a Great Skua swooped past cuffing his head with an extended webbed foot.

'Oh, fuck off, bastard shite-hawk!'

The large brown sea bird turned to make another attack run. Dan was ready for it and waved his arms as it came close. Making its staccato alarm call the Skua turned and crossed An Lag gliding its way back along the cliff edge to Oiseval.

'Cool down, Dan. It's only defending its nesting ground.'

Like Sally, Erica hated to see male aggression directed toward the island's wildlife, no matter how annoying these large birds could be. Also sensitive to the moment, Erica mentioned a discussion she had had with Agatha a few days earlier.

'You know, Agatha reckons the Bonxies were summoned here by the Cailleach to drive off insensitive men like you. What do you make of that?'

'Well, that sounds even crazier than Beltane fires on Soay. They're just large birds and bloody annoying ones too.'

Erica left it at that, not wanting to challenge him further and risk spoiling the late afternoon sunshine on Conachair. They sat down together with their backs to the cairn and looked out across the deserted radar installations on Mullach Mhor two hundred feet below them.

'Any more of your brew, Dan? I fancy bit more communion while we are up here.'

He passed her the flask from his hip pocket. The subtle flavour seemed enhanced from the warmth of his body, and she drank deeply. She passed the flask back to him and he finished the last few drops before screwing the cap tight and replacing it in his pocket. Erica snuggled up next to him happy to be there with a man she felt a growing respect for. There weren't many young men she respected but Dan was growing on her.

'Hey, what's that?' Dan had spotted a large white bird glide across the top of Glen Mór to land softly on a large cleit in the distance. As it turned its head virtually one hundred and eighty degrees to see where the human voice had come from, they could see, unmistakeably, that it was a large white owl.

'What on Earth?'

Dan, an amateur birder himself, was genuinely surprised to see this Arctic visitor. The solitary Snowy Owl had been recorded on the island for several years, but this was the first time Erica or Dan had seen it. It settled down to tear at something held in its talons.

'Probably a St Kilda mouse,' said Erica.

'Those owls usually hunt Lemmings, but our mice are just as big. Anyway, we are honoured to see it. I bet Agatha knows about it being here but has, as usual, kept it to herself.'

'So much for global warming if Snowy Owls are taking up residence in the Western Isles.'

Dan was bemused, 'I wonder what's going to turn up next, Polar Bears?'

'Hey Dan! Look out there. Can't you see the Viking long-ship rounding Boreray, and yeah, just look at those monks landing on the beach. Must be Saints Brendan and Columba if I'm not mistaken.'

'Stop taking the piss, Erica.'

Dan was interested in archaeology and knew a fair bit related to St Kilda. He loved reading old stories embedded in the landscape and, like Agatha, spent many hours dreaming life into the myths and legends around him.

He had spent many hours researching myths and legends associated with Mothan. Hebridean lore claimed it was the first plant to be trodden on by Christ so, he considered, if the Christians appropriated it, it must be a scary herb.

Mothan grows well in damp acid ground, and he thought with so much of it growing around the military borehole the unique chemistry of this herb must have percolated into the island's main water supply. It was no wonder, he thought, that the guys lost their work ethic, unknowingly taking Mothan in water drunk with subsidised whisky.

Returning by the most direct route, it didn't take long before the two were at the foot of Conachair standing on the raised glacial mounds looking across the village.

There was so much to see, even for the untrained eye, something new became clear daily. Having read so much about St Kildan domestic arrangements she could now see the Norse water mill, the threshing house, the corn drying kilns. Everything had been laid out so well by the architect of the new village.

Seeing the several small burns channelled toward the Norse mill reminded Erica she must order a micro-hydro generator for her soon to be completed blackhouse. The combination of water, wind and solar energy would make their own new settlement the envy of the Hebrides, once again, if she had anything to do with it.

Those earlier innovations were crude, but they were in sympathy with their environment and acknowledged the spirit of place, unlike the diesel fired power station standing as a monument to twentieth century social folly.

There was so much potential here, she reminded Dan. They were all going to play their part now there were women as well as men involved in the planning process. She was happy that Dan could be left to planning the spiritual tours, for after all, in most traditional societies, women had more practical things to be getting on with.

Dan had done his research on the island's folklore from the fantastic to the mundane. He thought he had been thorough, but the Cailleach myth was stretching things a bit too far; a female warrior roaming the winter landscape or an Amazon riding out across the Hebrides with her pack of hounds. But then, the Hounds of the Morrigan – he had heard of that myth, so maybe not quite so fantastical after all.

In defending Ulster, hero Cuchulainn had been helped by Morrigan, the Phantom Queen. She could shape shift into the form of an eel, a wolf or a cow, or a Bonxie, he wondered. Cuchulainn rejected her offer but not so easily dismissed, she helped by stampeding cattle onto the battlefield. Cuchulainn injured one of the cattle, a red and white heifer leading the charge which turned out to be the Phantom Queen herself. Her wounds were only healed when the hero accepted the offer of drinking milk from her teats. A classic Gaelic myth concerning masculine rejection of female aid. The wounded and angry Queen Morrigan was only healed once the hero accepted her as an equal.

Glen Mór was, according to Erica and Sally, historically the female zone where cattle were tended and, naturally, the Amazon's House was in that northern valley. It was also where all the trouble occurred, from plane wrecks to Bonxie attack. All in all, it was a very unfriendly place for any male bold enough to venture down there.

Each evening when the women returned from milking, they poured a libation on the Milking Stone, firmly within the male zone. Failure to do so brought bad luck to the southern village.

With cattle long gone from the island, the practice had been overlooked for years. Come to think of it, there had been few women here for many years either. Dan was astounded at where his thoughts were leading him.

Glen Mór, now empty of cattle was a hostile place for men as he quickly realised after being sent packing by Skua attacks. There was an angry, likely wounded, female spirit down there. Peace would only come to St Kilda once she was accepted, when male and female interests were reconciled. Instead of being trapped, miserable in a masculine landscape, she should be free to ride out with her hounds again. First, cattle should be returned to Glen Mór.

Fucking hell, he thought. The story of this island is beginning to come together, Erica's house cow would be a good start.

During his research he had also come across the tale of Roderick the Imposter, a charismatic preacher at St Kilda before the Church of Scotland took charge of the congregation.

Modelling himself on St John the Baptist, Roderick had appointed himself the spiritual leader of the islands working, generally, toward his own material gain. Dan read with interest how he offered salvation to the women of St Kilda in return for a night in his bed.

He consecrated a 'Holy' bush. Should any person's sheep eat as much as one leaf of this bush, then the owner should give up the sheep to Roderick. Apparently, the islanders built a high stone wall around this bush to prevent such an occurrence.

Looking around the village, Dan could readily see small circular stone enclosures lending credence to the story. The part of the tale that Dan really appreciated came at the end when the disgraced Roderick was sent for trial at Dunvegan on various charges ranging from immorality and sheep stealing to blasphemy.

The story told of his eating Mothan for good luck before the hearing. Roderick, though banished from St Kilda, got off with nothing more serious than a public warning to mend his ways and refrain from communion with other men's wives, especially in the name of God. Cunning or what! Dan was impressed; if it was alright with God, and a bit of Mothan was involved, you could get away with just about anything out here.

Dan had returned to his freshly cleaned and uncluttered apartment with some trepidation, but he was glad Deborah had sorted it all for him. Inspired by Erica's enthusiasm for Green Tourism he settled down for the evening making rough notes before getting down to drafting a schedule in the morning.

Erica left Dan to his planning, feeling she had sown seed in fertile ground. He was a dreamer but could get it together when the need arose. She would forgive occasional self-pity if he played his part in the resettlement project. He always landed on his feet and would make a good man to have around soon enough. For now, she had her own house plans to work on.

The blackhouse restoration was coming on well. The roof had been thatched and door and windows replaced. It really was quite snug inside the shell even though the tarry smell of burnt pallet wood still lingered from the open fire lit to celebrate the new roof.

Erica would get the woodstove fitted promptly and, with smoke piped outside the cottage, she would bring blackhouse living into the twenty-first century. On Don's advice she had taken the very sensible precaution of ordering a twin wall insulated flue pipe with high temperature rubber roof flashing. She neither wanted to set the thatch on fire nor have to deal with rainwater leaks in her beautiful new thatch roof. It seemed incongruous to make a hole in the new thatch, but a modern woodstove had to be an improvement over a smoky open hearth. Her blackhouse was not going to be black on the inside if she could help it.

Fitting the stove and flue pipe proved easier than she had expected. The insulated flue pipe was simply pushed up through the thatch with no need to cut the long reed stems. Once the high temperature rubber flashing was in place it could rain as much as it liked.

At St Kilda it usually did rain a lot, and the next part of the project was to rig up a micro-hydro generator in the burn beside the cottage. Technically a bit more challenging than the woodstove but having already consulted off-grid living suppliers before moving to the island she knew it could be done. She would just have to wait now until Don and Lachie returned to place her order.

Sally suggested it would be a good idea to employ one of the redundant radar technicians to attend to the electrical side of things. She knew of former electrician who had taken retirement when the Base closed and had often enthused over renewable energy solutions for the village. He had openly criticised the island's reliance on imported diesel fuel, all the while surrounded by inexhaustible solar and wind energy. Robert, she knew, would be happy to help and could fix up her wind generator and install solar panels while he was at it.

Dan busied himself with the finer details of the St Kilda spiritual tour. A bit of a mouthful though; maybe 'Spiritual St Kilda,' 'Magical Island Tour,' 'Holy Trails'? Whatever, he wasn't going to bother with a title just yet. Inspiration would no doubt hit him while out walking the route his pilgrims would take.

Leading his flock through the wilderness really appealed to Dan and over the next few days he spent most of his daylight hours outdoors working out the route. He became a familiar figure to the feral sheep of the island, striding the ground like the new prophet he was already imagining himself to be.

Stopping at every well and natural spring he was amazed at the luxuriance of Mothan growing in damp places wherever potable water collected. Obviously, the sheep had no taste for the herb, he mused. They didn't know what they were missing. He would make sure his followers received his specially prepared St Kilda Communion Wine before following him on the little trod path to salvation.

Erica was pleased with her newly fitted woodstove. She just couldn't understand why the St Kildans hadn't used free standing stoves before, even the army had used them in their early occupation of the island. But then this had been an island culture with idiosyncrasies only an outsider would notice. She had quickly tested the stove, burning some old papers and scraps of wood to check for smoke leaks. There were none and the interior of her blackhouse would definitely remain soot free. The next part of the project would be low energy lighting.

Without knowing much about the technicalities involved, Erica had always been attracted to off grid living and had read various magazines extolling this way of life. Now, here was the chance to turn her dream into reality.

With hindsight it was a pity none of the new settlers had much in the way of electrical skills. There was endless diesel fuel still in the storage tanks and if the small generator behaved itself the Manse would have electricity to spare.

Here at the western extremity of the village running an extension lead for half a mile wouldn't be an option. She couldn't wait and determined to contact Robert as soon as possible, sooner if an out of season yacht anchored in the bay.

This was how it had been before the military came to the island. Post was taken to the mainland by passing fishing boats. When desperate, St Kilda had a tradition of launching their very own mail-boats; small model boats holding a sealed letter container. Attached to a float, they drifted with winds and currents until reaching land anywhere between Lewis and the coast of Norway.

A bit too hit and miss; she would wait until some kind of full-size boat came in. For now, the hurricane lamps worked fine on diesel oil and the burn would still be running when her micro-hydro generator eventually turned up. The cow, of course, would not be living under the same roof. A divergence from blackhouse tradition that she accepted on hygiene grounds. The animal could be housed next door in its own disused cottage.

The St Kildans had done just that when they moved into their ill-fated new whitehouses. From occupying the lower end, the house cow was given the whole of the now redundant blackhouse next door. Erica was already there, dreaming of her clean, modernised blackhouse and the cow in the empty whitehouse next door.

With woodstove and 12-volt lighting, the cow could have occupied the lower end but the thought of dung on the floor of her new home was too much. The warm milky smell of clean cow would be wonderful though. The reality, she knew, would be the smell of shit and piss. She would make sure things moved forward in twenty-first century blackhouse living.

Rebuilding the stone wall enclosures was proving more of a task than Dave had expected. The slipped disc he suffered in the accident on the jetty had left him with a vulnerable lower back. Working with coarse stones in the damp and cold of approaching winter at St Kilda split the skin of his fingertips making each an endurance test. The stiffness of his back and pain from his cracked fingertips became, in his mind, a kind of penury for sins past. Maybe a payment required of him for those months he spent at home after losing his lectureship at the university.

He had basically lived off the earnings of his wife and now it was his turn to support the family even if it did mean breaking his back out in all weathers. The walls would get built in time for spring sowing and he could already picture orderly rows of vegetables growing strong in the sun behind sheltering stone walls on the south slopes of Conachair.

The enclosed fields of An Lag were still in good shape after conservation volunteers had spent so much time and energy rebuilding the walls for no ostensible purpose. They had actually paid to come out here and labour; Dave had

252

given that concept plenty of thought while toiling alone on the hillside behind the cottages.

He was working to rebuild these walls for a reason – to feed his family. The volunteers had to pay for the privilege of engaging with hard manual labour under open skies and in all weathers. Thankfully, he hadn't had to pay out several hundred pounds for each fortnight of toil. Maybe it was something to do with an urban need to reconnect with a lost part of oneself.

Reconnection through physically reworking an abandoned landscape. The Western Isles Trust had been canny, he had to admit. Selling people their dreams and getting a whole load of hard labour done for free in the process.

Deborah hardly left the Manse during the short winter days. Not that it was particularly cold, but the dampness and mist lowering from the hills were no incentive to venture outside. She made the occasional foray over to the Featherstore when Dan was available for her.

It was understandable, she thought, that with Dave working himself into the ground repairing stone walls he had no energy for love making. Dan certainly made up for him in that respect and, if she was honest with herself, now her physical needs were regularly satisfied, he was helping her become a better wife for Dave. Life was certainly strange and out on the island away from social constraints in Edinburgh they could, at last, be themselves. Water would find its own level as she was fond of saying when they discussed their feelings around the meal table.

Away from the pressures of teaching she was enjoying her matriarch role. Erica and Agatha would no doubt come round to accepting her authority in due course, but for now with Erica setting up home at the far end of the village and Agatha spending most of her waking hours in Glen Mór there was little challenge to her domestic authority. Agatha was the one to watch out for, she realised. Creeping around with binoculars in hand.

Deborah couldn't be sure she hadn't already been observed making her regular visits to the Featherstore. Agatha was an astute young woman and would quickly deduce what was going on. Dave was a good man, but life out here demanded more than his goodness.

She might be turning into some kind of Magdalene, Deborah realised, but she had only one demon to cast not the seven she had heard Dave refer to after bringing that old family Bible back from the church. She had to admit it would be a shame to watch the ornate leather-bound Bible deteriorate further in the cold, damp empty Kirk.

The winter weather was becoming quite an issue for all of them. It was just so damn windy. Deborah hadn't really appreciated what it would be like to spend day after day struggling against gale force winds. The noise was something else, she had never experienced such a constant roar and buffeting. Slates rattled on the roofs and the infernal clanging and banging of corrugated sheets cladding the power station would drive anyone mad.

It wouldn't take long before the wind got behind one of those sheets and sent it spinning away to join the remains of nineteenth-century zinc roofs littering sheltered spots beyond the village.

The remains of the crashed Sunderland had been blown far and wide since the original crash eighty years earlier. It had been no wonder the recent Piper wreck had been blown over the cliff.

Rain had been less of a problem than she had expected. On the rare calm days, it could feel quite warm. Sally related times when there had been water shortages on the island, hence the new, deeper borehole tapping into artesian supplies originating goodness knows where. Obviously somewhere with higher rainfall than St Kilda judging by the overflowing well-head.

Swarms of midges trapped themselves on Mothan's mucous covered leaves, sustaining the plants in the nutrient poor soil. Pretty good plant all round, Deborah considered. Then there was the bonus of its power of entrapment when it came to virile young men. Poor Dan, she really didn't think it quite fair to have used it on him. His energies might have been better suited to helping Dave rebuild garden walls rather than enslaving him to her needs.

The south easterly gales again brought the sea thundering over the jetty wall. Overnight the sandy beach disappeared, only to mysteriously reappear a few days later. The constant noise of the wind, sea and shifting boulders became normal and only noticeable by its absence.

Watching from the kitchen window, Deborah noticed the change coming. Though still troubled, the sea was no longer crashing over the jetty and the white topped swell running along the cliffs of Dun had lessened. The gales were turning to blow from the west. The ruined castle on the seaward tip of Dun gave the narrow island its name.

According to Dan, St Kilda had been a stronghold for the Fomorians before the Gaels took possession of the islands. Villagers had obviously been able to get over in the past as a few acres of ancient ridge and furrow lazy beds could still be seen on Dun when the light was low. Not so simple today though.

Deborah had spotted a large rusting chain hanging in the gap between Dun and Hirta. Sally had explained about that. It was possible to wade across the gap at extreme low tide and haul oneself up that chain to access Dun, but it had been many years since anyone had done it. Deborah certainly would want any of her family putting the rusted links to the test. More recently, one of the wardens had rigged up a bosun's chair but the cables had long since rusted and disappeared.

Though becoming calmer in Village Bay, Deborah could watch the sea raging as wild as ever through the Dun gap. The waters boiled beyond the two islands with salt spray billowing through the southerly cleft to pressure wash adjacent slopes. As the gale turned more into the west, she noticed flecks of spume blowing over the ridge between Ruiaval and Mullach Sgar. The occasional flecks became a blizzard as the wind rose, soaking the leeward slopes with sea-spray. Both Dave and Agatha had commented on the way the grass suddenly ended over there.

The turf changed to close cropped Thrift. This salt tolerant tufted plant grew where grass could not, due to the salty rain blown over the ridge by such westerly gales. During the day the wind turned into the north. Village Bay was then in the lee of the storm. Deborah had thought the hills would shelter the bay with the wind coming from the north. To an extent this was true but with the fifteen-hundred-foot peak rising vertically into the wind, Conachair created turbulent blasts that spun across the bay like Atlantic djinns.

The spinning columns of sea spray were amazing to watch, and God help, she thought, any small yacht caught by one. She had heard from Sally that no helicopter would venture near the place in conditions like this. Even on calmer days, with wind in the north, the helicopter pilot would fly close to the cliffs of Oiseval to avoid the aircraft being caught in turbulence over the bay.

Dave had been out repairing stone walls all day. If anything, the unpredictable gusts were worse for his temper than the constant gale. They could come without warning and from any direction. One minute he could be working under a calm and clearing sky and the next find himself blown off his feet. He had lost count of the times he had to retrieve his woollen hat or gloves, momentarily put down.

Deborah had seemed calm enough in the Manse lately. She must be settling in, and it pleased him that, at least in the domestic sphere, things were working out well. Erica had made a brilliant job of her blackhouse and despite troubled times in Edinburgh she really was turning out to be an asset to them all.

Her blackhouse walls were solid and the new thatch barely ruffled by the gale. According to Erica the strong winds did cause the woodstove to smoke a bit. A blackhouse should at least have some smoke stain inside, he reminded her. While out working, Dave had had time to muse on their earlier existence in Edinburgh. Existence it was and not much more; now out here they could find themselves, grow into the family he had always wanted them to be.

He would assess the stability of his restored walls by standing on top to feel if any stone dislodged. Dave had become adept at dry stone walling and generally nothing moved.

He hadn't anticipated the collapse of his last few hours work though. In hindsight, the unpredictable blasts of icy wind had sapped his concentration and when the wall fell it took him with it. The turf was soft, but he fell awkwardly and twisted his lower back.

The damaged lumbar disc prolapsed again leaving him in excruciating pain. He could do no more than lie face down in the mossy turf until the agony subsided. Then, he knew, getting to his feet and taking the weight of his upper body on his sacroiliac joint would be another story. Crying with pain and frustration, Dave remembered his namesake's plea from Psalm 22 in the old family bible he had rescued from decay in the Church.

'My God, my God, why hast thou forsaken me? Why art thou so far from helping me, and from the words of my roaring?'

He couldn't remember the whole Psalm word for word but lying there on the wet ground biblical David's self-pitying lament led to his epiphany.

He was the worm and his darling to be saved from the power of the dog, not that there were any on the island. Erica had mentioned she would like one, but he knew what the words of the psalm implied.

'But be not though far from me, O Lord: O my strength, haste thee to help me.'

After thirty minutes of lying there, Dave Williams gingerly tried to lift himself to his feet using his spade as a crutch. The pain only became unbearable if he tried to straighten up, so he kept in a stooped position and made his way laboriously down to the cottages. The spade, at least, did not let him down and once on the level street his movement, though stooped became less painful. Sally saw him pass the Factor's House and came out to offer help.

'Hey Dave! What have you done this time?'

Grimacing he replied that his back had gone again, and he was going back to the Manse to lie down for a while. He would be alright in the morning, he assured her.

'Why not come down to the medical room and I'll massage it again for you, Dave. It's what I am here for, isn't it?' Unaware of Dave's epiphany an hour earlier she wasn't prepared for what she heard him growl back at her.

'Proverbs 7: 25-27, Sally! *Let not thine heart decline to her ways, go not astray in her paths. For she hath cast down many wounded: yea, many strong men have been slain by her. Her house is the way to hell, going down to the chambers of death.'*

'Whatever, Dave. I was just offering to help, not send you to hell!'

She suddenly realised what he was referring to.

'Oh, for God's sake, Dave. That was just a bit of fun, wasn't it? You didn't seem to complain at the time. Go and lie down on your own then and, if you find you do want a purely professional massage, I'll come down to the Manse, alright? And another thing, find something better to read at night.'

Sally turned back to the shelter of the thick-walled Factor's House. Making his painful and stooped way to the Manse, Dave never raised his eyes high enough to see brash ice flowing round the Point of Col at the foot of Oiseval. Deborah watched in amazement from the kitchen window as melting sea ice flowed into Village Bay.

12

Bible Studies

Erica, while not engaging in regular Bible studies, still found the dog-eared family Bible interesting reading. Friendly banter between father and daughter extended to quoting scriptures over breakfast that morning.

'Neither did we eat any man's bread for nought; but wrought with labour and travail night and day, that we might not be chargeable to any of you. Second Epistle of Paul the Apostle to the Thessalonians (3.8)'

'Right then, Dad. You asked for it!'

'And unto Adam he said, "Because thou hast harkened unto the voice of thy wife, and hast eaten of the tree, of which I commanded thee, saying, thou shalt not eat of it: cursed is the ground for thy sake: in sorrow shalt though eat of it all the days of thy life'.' Genesis 3.17'

Briefly taken aback by Erica's unexpected knowledge of key scriptures, Dave struggled for a reply, flicking through the pages.

'Aha......*Let the woman learn in silence with all subjection. But I suffer not a woman to teach, nor to usurp authority over the man, but to be in silence.* 1 Timothy 2:11, 12.'

'Come off it, Dave, don't take things too far!'

Deborah considered this quote was going too far; quite a lot too far considering her teaching background. In her opinion Dave, with his university background, should also have known better than to rake up this outdated patriarchal stuff. Her husband continued to quote from the First Epistle of Paul the Apostle to Timothy.

'1 Timothy 2:13, 14 and 15! *For Adam was first formed, then Eve. And Adam was not deceived, but the woman being deceived was in the transgression. Notwithstanding she shall be saved in childbearing if they continue in faith and charity and holiness with sobriety.'*

'What utter bollocks, Dad!'

Agatha was less than impressed by Bible quotes.

'I'm going to my room and, if the satellite internet is not on the blink again, I am going to research the causes for sea ice around our island that is supposedly warmed by the Gulf Stream. Please don't try and tell me that's any kind of message from God!'

Philosophical writings of man (or woman) had little place in her scientific interpretation of life. Biblical reference to childbearing did, however, remind her that as a young woman she could be doing just that. Having babies, but as for saving herself – from just what, she'd like to know.

Unlike her sister she had very little sexual experience. Just brief teenage flings back in Edinburgh that had left her more frustrated than satisfied. Ecology was what turned her on, pressed her buttons and if she could meet a young man who thought the same way, childbearing could be a distinct possibility.

The only young men out here were Dan and Lachie. Dan absolutely wasn't her type. Lachie who came out with Don on the *Beluga* was good looking enough, carried some excellent genes, but with a world view limited to wheeling and dealing around the Hebrides, he wasn't going to come to much.

Agatha could sense something in the air though. Something, some energy, was stirring around her. In her ecologists' opinion, even her pre-menopausal mother was showing signs of late fertility. She of course knew, that when cooped up together, women tended to synchronise their menstruation. As if subtle signals from one woman would stimulate ovulation in the others. All fascinating stuff, but she wished she could be immune herself. Living this close to open skies and ocean tides, the phases of the moon would inevitably affect her here more than on the mainland.

Men had been out of their depth on this island. The military guys turned to drink for escape from the relentless energy washing over them. Sally had recounted how there had been more drink related accidents on nights of full moon. On summer nights, drinking would then often continue until after dawn at this temperate northern latitude. Dan was fast going the same way and as for her father; well, it seemed that rather than drink, he was turning to God!

Another angle on humans in the island's ecosystem, Agatha thought. Humans, particularly male humans, she considered, exist in an imagined dimension when faced with an environment beyond their control.

When the going got tough out here, female sheep survived, and weaker males died before Spring renewed the grazing. That's after the males had beaten each other senseless during the Autumn rut. Why the hell did they do that if not to ensure survival of the fittest? It seemed obvious to her, females were definitely fitter, better adapted for life at St Kilda. Though without male insemination, there could be no new females born to carry life, or genes forward into the next generation, she reminded herself,. It was basically a very practical matter. She would think on it next time she was in Glen Mór.

The Amazon, Morrigan, or whoever she is wouldn't have bothered with romantic twaddle before reproducing herself. She would have just seduced the bravest warrior, had her way with him then sent him on his way. When her time came, that was exactly what Agatha decided she would do. Walking to her room she felt erotically charged, thinking of seducing a hero before sending him on his way. But as for finding a hero at St Kilda? Considering the men on offer, it wasn't going to be easy.

Agatha's online research continued late into the night. Making copious notes, she would have a quote or two of her own by the morning. She first looked at the Met Office Surface Pressure charts.

Unusually, the Azores high had extended into the north-west Atlantic connecting with high pressure over Greenland. Warm moist air from the Caribbean was being drawn up the eastern seaboard of North America before circulating over the Greenland icecap and back down towards Iceland, the Faeroes and the British Isles. The moisture laden air cooled as it touched the wintry landmass of the United States generating the heaviest snow falls within living memory.

It took a lot for snow to make headlines in Iceland but winter storms flowing out from Labrador were relentless. Deflected northwards by high pressure over Greenland, the storms were picking up yet more moisture from the melting icecap. Looking further east, Agatha could see low pressure over Scandinavia and the Baltic Sea where it was relatively warmer than over the north Atlantic.

Air currents in high pressure zones circulated clockwise and in low pressure regions anticlockwise and she saw that the north of Scotland and the Western Isles were caught between these two counter rotating weather systems. Winter storms were going to be drawn down between the teeth of two great cogs in the climate machine. The isobars looked pretty close together, and moisture laden air was being drawn directly from the warming Arctic Ocean and funnelled clockwise into colder air flowing anticlockwise from Spitzbergen and the north of Siberia. No wonder it was bloody freezing, she thought.

Looking closer at the surface pressure chart, Agatha saw that St Kilda lay under the eastern edge of the extended Greenland high pressure dome. The blizzards were going to be deflected by high pressure away from the archipelago to hit the Highlands and Eilean Siar, the Western Isles, with a vengeance. On St Kilda, they were going to be cold for sure, but not snowed in.

The fast-approaching arctic tempest would further disrupt the troubled socio-economic conditions on the British mainland and in Western Europe. Out here, it looked like they were going to be on their own for a while longer, at least until either the mainland weather or the national economy improved.

Another bell rang for her. She remembered at high school having to discuss a documentary by Al Gore. *An Inconvenient Truth*, that's what it was called. She remembered the importance of the Gulf Stream, otherwise known as the Atlantic Conveyor current bringing warm water from the Caribbean to the arctic.

It warmed the north-east Atlantic and made Spitzbergen the most amazingly bio-diverse of all the northern islands. The Atlantic Conveyor depended on a temperature gradient between the Caribbean tropics and the Atlantic arctic. Cold water sinking displaced warmer nutrient rich water to the surface, feeding the phytoplankton that underpin marine food chains. The greater the temperature difference between the tropics and the arctic, the stronger flowed the Gulf Stream.

Looking at the Met Office chart it was obvious that over the north Atlantic the sea temperature gradient must be lessening, as Al Gore had predicted if humans continued pumping greenhouse gasses into the atmosphere. So, the northeast Atlantic was getting colder.

As far as she knew, seabird populations were recovering after a few disastrous years. The up welling of nutrient rich waters from the relatively warmer depths would feed the phytoplankton, small marine organisms and so on up the food-chain. She thought it interesting that distant nineteenth-century industrial emissions might have played a part in the collapse of the seabird dependent St Kildan economy. There were so many angles to this fascinating place. No wonder it was a major World Heritage Site.

The surface pressure charts forecast imminent weather conditions, but sea ice does not form overnight. There had to be more to the phenomenon. Another search engine referred her to solar cycles.

She discovered there were *grand maximum* and *grand minimum* periods for solar energy reaching Earth. The effects were all very subtle but amplified through oscillations of the Gulf Stream could have a major influence on local weather conditions, particularly in Europe and Eurasia. It seemed the twentieth century had been dominated by *grand maximum* solar activity and now, the BBC website suggested, the twenty-first century was entering into a *grand minimum* period. To put it bluntly, in the twenty-first century the British Isles were predicted to experience similar conditions to the Maunder Minimum of the late seventeenth and early eighteenth centuries known as the Little Ice Age. Paradoxically, Greenland and the Arctic regions could become a lot warmer.

The likelihood of Iceland becoming warmer led her down another route. She had heard about the Eyjafjallajökull eruption in 2010 and subsequent chaotic effects of ash clouds for air travel in Western Europe. Apparently, the website suggested, this eruption was just the start of a dramatic increase in volcanic activity.

Another article she came across suggested that in response to global warming, volcanic activity increases, spewing ash and dust particles into the atmosphere to reflect away excessive solar radiation. As a living entity, the Earth would cool herself.

Agatha had to think about it for a minute but the conclusion she drew from her research made her gasp. Everything pointed to St Kilda and the north-east Atlantic becoming much, much colder and it was happening right now. Greenland was warming and driving a persistent, moist north-west air current toward them due to the melting ice-cap. Scandinavia was warming and melting arctic pack ice was flowing toward them from the north-east. Moist air from the north-west meeting icy currents from the north-east could mean months of fog and, if that wasn't enough, increasing volcanic activity in Iceland would send ash clouds over north-west Europe in a repeat of 2010. Maybe a lot worse if predictions of the imminent eruption of Iceland's Katia caldera proved correct.

The 1783-84 eruption from, Grímsvötn, had spewed out 15 cubic kilometres of ash into the atmosphere compared to the fraction of a cubic kilometre ejected by Eyjafjallajökull in 2010. Grímsvötn had had a huge impact on the northern hemisphere, reducing temperatures by up to $3\,°C$. Catastrophic effects had travelled far beyond the shores of Iceland (where at least a fifth of the population died), with thousands of recorded deaths in Britain due to poisoning and extreme cold, and there was record low rainfall in North Africa. Sod the Bible, just wait till she told them about this!

Agatha found it hard to sleep that night. Her imagination, too, was oscillating. Thoughts ranged from erotic fantasy to volcanic eruption. It all boiled down to energy flows and as an ecologist she was fine with that. When at last she did sleep, it was deep and sound. For once she lay in and only appeared to join the others for breakfast. Still in her pyjamas, she had abandoned her usual morning routine of walking the village for sightings of migrant birds.

The heavy Bible was on the table in front of Dave as he invited those present to give thanks for their meal.

'Whether therefore ye eat, or drink, or whatsoever ye do, do all to the glory of God. 1 Corinthians 10:31.'

'Amen, Dad. But just listen to what I have found out about the ice!'

Dave thought to cut Agatha short to allow time for the meaning of his quote to sink in but genuinely interested in what she had been researching, he allowed her to continue. Agatha could barely contain herself as just for once she had her father's undivided attention.

'What we could be experiencing is a solar grand minimum. That's when solar energy reaching the planet reduces. The last time this happened was in the late eighteenth and early nineteenth centuries. That was when the Thames regularly froze over, and I bet there was sea-ice here then too. Not quite sure if it was connected but there were massive volcanic eruptions in Iceland during that period as well. Putting two and two together, the eruptions that shut down European air travel a few years ago and this sea-ice appearing would suggest to me that we are heading for challenging times.'

Agatha was in her element.

'Not so for the birds though. They flourished after the cold event and just think, the feather trade and this village might not have been possible if it hadn't been for past climate change. It looks like it's happening again, Dad.'

Deborah joined the conversation.

'Think of social conditions at that time too. All that weather related upheaval led to over a century of European expansion, colonisation and conflict. White slaves of England supported by the Black slaves of Empire; not that dissimilar to what we came here to get away from!'

Deborah was becoming interested in Agatha's hypothesis. Leaving Biblical scriptures aside, Dave too joined in the discussion, raising more on the cultural angle.

'When you come to think of it, so much of our cultural landscape comes from that period. Those Christmas cards picturing snowy Georgian houses – why are they so appealing? That period of cold must be embedded itself in the national psyche. Our old home in Edinburgh New Town, the Athens of the north, reflected cultural values recognisable throughout the western world and its former colonies.

It's like the Georgian spirit of place, for better and for worse, transfers across continents through reproduction of its architecture. With it, the mindset, as I used to tell my students. All that carefully contrived classical reproduction, what an incredible piece of social engineering. Walk around New Town and just imagine, the work of long dead architects still influencing lives and minds today – just as long dead ministers must still be doing out here too.'

Erica added to the discussion.

'Yeah, I've been here before I do realise; but late eighteenth and early nineteenth century town planners did exert a controlling effect through symbolic architecture. Keep women in their place, no Black people, slavery to pay for it all and all sorts of overseas cruelty out of sight of good townsfolk, like we used to be, Dad. Also, you had to be able to see the damn architecture and if it stood out white on a prominent hilltop the effect carried for miles.'

Erica was rising to her own challenge.

'Take Calton Hill for example. The Beltane fun there could never happen in full daylight. Remember when we had televisions? The US Whitehouse beamed its subliminal message across the airways every night through news broadcasts. The presenter boosts his or her own message by associating with the ultimate neo-classical power statement right behind them.'

She let her point sink in.

'The Soviets weren't any better and what did the Nazis do? Couldn't wait two hundred years to exert control slowly and subtly, they made concrete casts of the wretched designs and threw them up in twenty years. God help any poor sod who challenged what they were doing. Getting back to Edinburgh New Town, they fashioned stone women to support the obscenity. Jenners department store has

268

acquiescent women moulded into its façade to supporting neo-classical views of family life. Nazi women bought into the deal as well, encouraged to be not only national socialists but national mothers too. Some things just never change.'

Deborah was looking puzzled, 'What do you mean?'

Deborah explained that she used to enjoy going into Jenners. Its predictable familiarity was a pleasant and stable escape from the multi-cultural chaos outside in Princes Street.

'Look further than the end of your nose next time you are there, Mum, and you will see the female figures in stone supporting the façade. The Caryatids are supposed to represent Jenners acknowledgement that women support society. If those women sprang to life and walked away, the whole damn edifice would come crashing down.'

Erica was on her pet subject and knew her mother resented challenge when it came to social status. Despite her profession, Deborah had instinctively felt that as a middle-class mother she had social capital. Jenners department store recognised and made good use of that capital. Unlike other classes, those in the middle socio-economic bands could go either way and by shopping in Jenners, to the outside world you were not going down.

'Those stone women have been supporting Jenners patriarchy getting on for two hundred years, Mum. Been standing there all this time; mute, enslaved, colonised and subjugated. Turned to stone, frozen by the architecture of Enlightenment.

Edinburgh women have been blinkered by the desire to conform to demands of male architecture. What an irony that the only sizeable group to actually see the light and get away were the Free Church bible bashers!'

As if seeking approval from her father, Erica gave Dave a sideways glance before continuing.

269

'At the 1843 Disruption the breakaway group pointedly walked out from neo-classical St. Andrews in George Street to worship well away from the all-seeing eye on its portico. No wonder they came all the way out here to evangelise free from the constraints of malignant architecture. You know, it wasn't just buildings either. The clever bastards planted hilltop groves that look like the Acropolis, if you take a second look at them. With a bit of luck climate change will blow the fucking lot down. Too windy out here anyway, so no neo-classical columns and no trees either. No wonder the Wee Frees were so keen to come.'

Agatha added, 'I did once read an article about the Forestry Commission and that it wasn't until the nineteen-seventies that they had a woman landscape architect in charge of things. Only then did they stop planting formal regiments of conifers. She changed things to make plantations fit with the landscape and be pleasing to the eye. Apparently, the way trees are managed reflects on the society that manages them. Just think about it, when the St Kildans evacuated those able bodied were sent to work for the Forestry Commission. The plantations and the control they stood for won in the end.'

'Right, we'll be alright then. There are no fucking trees or classical porticos here so we can do what we like, eh?'

Erica winked at Agatha, though the sisterly banter was noticeably not extended to Deborah who shrugged and turned away.

'Do what you like girls, but don't come running to me when you foul up. Society has its rules for a reason and trees or no trees we are still connected to it, even if you are starting to think otherwise.'

Dave returned to the cultural angle. 'Those Georgians, for all their faults, did bring structure and order. Apart from enduring architecture they introduced accurate artillery and properly surveyed maps. Quite basically, we wouldn't be here now if it wasn't for Georgian telemetry. In the twentieth century, the military employed most of the population of South Uist to evaluate missiles on the Hebrides Range. Well, if there hadn't been a military base out here, we wouldn't have use of their left behind facilities either.'

'Georgian teleonomy more like!'

Erica was back on her pet subject.

'Without that military heritage we might have had families living here, a workable community with an equal balance of women and men. There could have been children too. Just look at this crazy place. Or should I say look back at the last unsustainable century of this crazy place. We are going to have to sort this one out, sister.'

She looked at Agatha, 'are we not, girl?'

Agatha blushed. She hadn't forgotten her previous night's fantasy. That elusive hero was ever going to be a problem, she thought. As the scientist in the family, she was an Enlightenment woman through and through, but when the sun went down, she had to acknowledge other energies were drawing her away from the scientific career path she had planned for herself.

Dave continued, 'I don't reckon it was all bad, girls. The Georgians introduced civic virtues, and yes, they did express those values through the architecture of the period. Suppose that's where the term 'Period' design comes from? Neo-classical designs represented civic freedom, emancipation from servility and dependence on others. When that architecture crumbles we get the scenario for many a horror film, do we not?'

'Yeah, emancipation from sexual desire and feminine distraction. Manly 'virtues' were not to be diluted by female influence, or by engagement with common people. A discourse of patriarchy, Dad; it was nothing less. The Nazis coined an honest term for this crap. They offered 'freedom from freedom,' freedom from freedom to engage with the fullness and diversity of human life. I used to wonder why those lonely sods hang out in the back of St Cuthbert's after dark. They were Edinburgh's 'Period' undesirables, and they knew it. The authorities still move them on if they appear in broad daylight.'

Erica's rant was silenced by a loud boom followed by several sharp cracks which brought them all back to immediate reality. The sound of ice building between the islands echoed around the bay.

Larger blocks of ice could be seen passing the Dun gap though none of significant size had yet entered Village Bay. The wind and currents were taking the ice past the entrance to the bay, which was fast becoming a refuge for the remaining winter seabirds. Gannets were diving to feed away from the moving ice pack. The far-ranging birds needed to feed in open waters and avoided frozen conditions in the far north, but now arctic ice had appeared around their home islands.

Agatha noted that even St Kilda's winter resident birds, the Meadow Pipits and Starlings seemed to have migrated this year. They must have known what was coming. Sinking colder waters favoured the fish; the plankton flush was revitalising the food chain, and the Gannets would do well in Village Bay if it remained ice free. So would the returning Puffins and everything else that relied on accessible fish stocks to feed their young in the Spring. Unusual numbers of seals were hauling out on the beach to make use of what little warmth the wintry sun offered. At the edge of the high-pressure dome, St Kilda was enjoying far more sunshine than the rest of the Western Isles, let alone the mainland.

Dave explained how the St Kildans had planned their working lives by watching the movements of birds crossing the bay. What would they have made of this event? Probably some folk memory from the eighteenth-century Little Ice Age would have been related by the female Sennachie, the Storyteller.

She gave explanations the villagers could relate to through myth and story to understand natural events unfolding around them. Under Church of Scotland and Free Church tenures, interpretation of natural events continued but the male ministers quoted from carefully selected scriptures to forewarn their congregation of spiritual rather than practical consequences should they not heed the words of God, also authorised for them by the King James' Bible of 1769.

A century later, the authorised Scriptures justified the suppression of indigenous wisdom in favour of national standards. Uncontrollable natural events, such as those appearing before their eyes that day would simply be explained as the punitive will of God.

13

Winter

The winter was exceptionally cold at St Kilda. Erica had tried to spend as much time as possible in her restored blackhouse but even with thick walls and new thatch the cold had beaten her. Retreating to the diesel-powered warmth of the Manse she concluded that having a couple of cows would be a priority before the next winter. Unhygienic as it sounded, Erica realised the earlier occupants kept their cattle indoors for human warmth as much as for the animals' shelter.

Her crib bed, built into the thick wall of the cottage, was too far away from the small woodstove to benefit from its warmth. There were times when Sally thought that collecting scrap wood and bringing it back from the old military buildings used up more precious calories than she got from burning it.

The cold had also kept Sally inside the thick-walled Factor's House. She would sit by the open hearth at the gable end of the house designed by a nineteenth century architect used to the coalfields of Lanarkshire rather than the windswept Hebrides. She had collected bagfuls of peat on her island walks and combined this with military scrap wood to keep herself warm. On the occasions she accepted her need for company, Sally would appear at the Manse door flushed and smelling of alcohol, self-medicated to drive away her feelings of isolation.

Though well insulated, the Featherstore apartment was no place for Dan to fret away the winter months worrying about how he was going to pay Don and Lachie and get off the island. Of all the re-settlers, Dan felt the most trapped.

His daily intake of alcohol, often laced with dried Mothan, simply added to his fear.

Dave's patriarchal vision was often at odds with Deborah's view of family life that winter. Both saw themselves leading their tribe in the wilderness; it was their approach that was contrary.

As a professional educator Deborah allowed intuition to be her guide, sensing when and where to focus her attention and leadership. While she sought control through personal subtlety, Dave detached himself from personal engagement to deliver guidance and inspiration through daily Bible study.

Dave had not intended to go down this route to start with, choosing to read the scriptures out of personal interest, but as winter at St Kilda became ever more challenging, the Bible became an unquestionable source of comfort and inspiration. One way or another they had needed to suspend their disbelief to get through the time of hardship.

Erica's project had intrigued Don and Lachie as much as Robert, the former MOD electrician they brought out one fine but cold day in February. The pack ice had dispersed enough to allow a relatively clear passage form Harris.

It took a lot to impress Don with his lifetime's experience of sailing Hebridean waters. He was amazed at the sheer numbers of cetaceans met on passage out to St Kilda. He was beaming as he pulled the *Beluga* alongside the jetty.

Don, Lachie and Robert set about unloading Erica's small wind turbine, micro-hydro unit and solar panels. The large ex-submarine deep cycle batteries proved troublesome to unload and proved even more troublesome to carry in wheelbarrows up the steep slipway to the Manse. Several adolescent seal pups lying on the slipway grumbled as they hauled themselves away, getting under the feet of the three men straining up the slope.

'For fuck's sake, you wee bastards!'

Don admired whales and dolphins but saw no cuteness in these animals, just potential fish thieves. Don had many income streams which included salmon farming and lobster fishing. In his opinion, seals were not good news.

Now retired, Robert was happy to tolerate most of God's creatures but drew the line at Bonxies, which were, thankfully for him, away from the island in February. By April they would return to nest on the rough moorland and plague man and beast alike. He remembered how aggressive Skuas had only appeared in the 1960s, just after military arrived at St Kilda.

The ground nesting predators would never have been tolerated by the villagers, but nature conservation and non-intervention now took precedence, even as many other protected species were being slaughtered. Robert had loved to walk over the island in his spare time but had been attacked so many times that making their legal protection seem a bad joke. Agatha, however, had spent much of her summer in their nesting territory but after few investigative forays the highly intelligent Skua packs left her alone.

Agatha too, had been amazed at the sheer numbers of whales and dolphins feeding in the ice-free bay that winter. Seals had long ceased to be a source of excitement for her but coming back from the farthest point of the island, the Cambir peninsular she claimed to have seen a group of Orcas, killer whales, hunting seals through the drift ice piling up in Glen Bay. Atlantic Seals, having difficulty escaping onto the steep rocky shore, were climbing up on to the packed ice plates and the Orcas were using their tails co-operatively to create waves and wash their intended prey back into the sea. In a matter-of-fact way Agatha related how the waters of Glen Bay had turned red with seal blood.

'Oh God, Agatha. Do you have to tell us everything you see?'

Erica, though far from squeamish, hated to hear of deliberate animal cruelty even, as in this case, the perpetrators were animals themselves.

For Agatha, winter had simply meant dressing up warmer for her regular walks around the island to observe and record seasonal progressions of the natural world. The Skuas had migrated back to sea by late Autumn and Glen Mór felt empty without their presence. The dry cold from the anticyclone over the North Atlantic had even suppressed the uncanny blasts of wind that traversed the glen at any other time of the year. Apart from the arrival of Orcas in Glen Bay all seemed quiet.

Across the narrow strait the small brown sheep on Soay kept their activity to a minimum, conserving energy by sheltering in cleits and other ruins on the uninhabited island.

It hadn't always been that way. Small bothies and the storage cleits could still be seen perilously close to the head of the recent landslip. Agatha was intrigued by an isolated structure not dissimilar to the three chambered Amazon's House in the glen. Through her binoculars, she could clearly see signs of another ancient settlement on Soay. Legend had it that this was the home of a certain Duggan who, having contravened medieval St Kilda's strict social codes, was banished to Soay for eternity.

Near to Taigh Duggan lay the remains of the WW2 Wellington bomber caught by one of the inexplicable wind blasts and thrown against the near vertical hillside. The surviving crew members had crawled from the wreckage only to find the route to help blocked by strong tidal currents surging through the deep strait between Soay and Hirta. It took an expert archaeologist to distinguish between medieval and twentieth century human remains scattered amongst the nearby rocks.

At Soay's summit, Agatha spotted the stone altar built at some indeterminable time in the islands past. There was so much still to learn about these islands, but she could well imagine anyone left on Soay would do anything to escape their open-air prison. Standing on the point of the Cambir and looking across the wild narrow strait, Agatha imagined Duggan, out of his mind from loneliness, sacrificing one of the small brown Soay lambs on the altar across the water from the Amazon's House. Maybe he prayed a small whirlwind would carry him across to the human company he craved so desperately.

Agatha watched, with satisfaction, the whales feeding in Village Bay that winter. The cold winter had not only brought sea-ice to St Kilda but also changed marine dynamics. The chilled upper layers of the sea sank to the bottom of the bay displacing warmer and nutrient rich bottom layers to the surface. With strong winter sunshine filtering down through clear waters, phytoplankton, microscopic plant life, bloomed. No wonder the fish population in the Bay was good, she thought.

Everything from small zooplankton through krill to sand eels were benefiting from the winter abundance. In calm conditions the kelp forest skirting the rocky shores grew into an underwater jungle of marine diversity. While the rest of the group struggled through the winter, Agatha's activities had remained relatively unaffected apart from her avoidance of the steep frozen slopes. She had badly bruised herself that Autumn, taking a painful tumble on the rocky slopes of Carn Mor and had no desire to repeat the experience.

Agatha enjoyed exploring the island but access to Carn Mor was always a challenge. This was no doubt the reason why thousands of Puffins nested amongst the scree each April to raise their young in safety. Even Skuas would think twice before starting a low-level attack run through such rocky terrain.

The off-grid equipment found its way to Erica's blackhouse intact, and the calm conditions should have made erecting her wind turbine a straightforward job. Four stainless steel cables were used to guy the upright pole in position. Once the pole was in the ground Robert realised it would have been much easier to have fitted the generator on the pole before placing it in its upright position.

Agatha noticed this with smug satisfaction but did acknowledge that with the heavy generator on top, the pole would have been much harder to lift. Once securely in position Robert found one of his old three section aluminium ladders in the power station building. With Don and Lachie holding everything steady he climbed up to fit the generator and its blades. With the blades in position, a sudden gust caused them to rotate violently almost knocking him from the ladder.

'Watch out, below!'

Don had been casually chatting with Lachie, joking about when they were likely to see Dan's dope money when a large wrench fell and just missed them.

'Aye, it will be hard hats you'll be needing next, lads!' Robert grinned down at them.

After years of working on the Base infrastructure, Robert had become accustomed to inexplicable wind gusts.

Erica's solar panels were more of an issue for him. With their large surface area, he reckoned she was asking for trouble. They would be likely to blow away like the nineteenth century pitched roofs and their zinc cladding. He certainly wasn't going to fit solar panels on a pole for her but advised building a frame at ground level to support the solar-voltaic panels set at forty-five degrees or thereabouts, facing south. How these would stand up against one of the south-easterly gales would be anyone's guess.

Erica's electrical self-sufficiency plan included the small hydro-electric generator to be fitted in the burn at the side of her cottage. She had rightly considered it highly unlikely there would ever be a time on St Kilda without sunshine, rain or wind to provide her energy needs.

Historically there had been a watermill in the village. Not a conventional upright water wheel common in much of lowland Britain, but a Norse mill making use of a paddle wheel set horizontal to the stream. The grindstones were driven on a vertical shaft. The difference was in the water supply. The Norse mill ran from a controlled water supply while Erica's micro-hydro generator would run fast or slow according to the amount of water flowing down the burn from Mullach Mhor.

The three men worked over the weekend to install Erica's equipment. Don had long since given up Sabbath observance at St Kilda though he kept up the semblance back home on Harris. Not to have done so could well have left him with social consequences among his less worldly neighbours.

Robert completed wiring up the control panel and regulator as light faded that Sunday afternoon. Erica had already lit the woodstove and running cables along the rafters had proved a hot and dusty job. As a recent non-drinker, Robert declined the offer of beer she produced for the three of them. No such restraint from Don and Lachie and the two seafarers were already in a jovial mood by the time Robert packed up his tools.

'Well, is it going to work then, Robert?'

Lachie could be a tease at times, especially when it came to 'old' Robert.

'There's a fair chance, my lad, aye, there's a fair chance,' he replied. 'Let's just look at the control panel now.'

Gauges indicated how the three devices were performing. The micro-hydro was showing a steady current flowing into the battery, while to be expected very little was being delivered from the solar panels so late on a winter afternoon. The wind turbine was fluctuating wildly, delivering full charge one minute and almost nothing the next. The needle of the voltmeter appeared to be vibrating too. Robert went out of the door of the blackhouse to see what was happening and was perturbed to see the wind turbine turning and spinning erratically on a calm frosty evening. He went back inside to report to the others.

'It's bloody queer but your generator seems to have a mind of its own, Erica. You'd better go outside and look.'

Erica went outside and could see her new wind turbine shaking violently at the top of its pole. Cursing she ran to the pole.

'Don't you play such fucking nonsense with me, you bloody machine. Work properly, Goddamit!'

To her surprise, the wind generator turned slowly into the correct position to take advantage of the evening breeze flowing down from the hill. Back in the blackhouse the voltmeter settled down to read a steady 12.5 volts.

'Perfect!' said Robert to Don and Lachie as Erica ducked her head through the low doorway.

'What did you do to fix it, Erica?'

'I don't really know. As you said it was shaking and turning wildly. I swore at it and the next thing it was working perfectly.'

'Well, you must have the magic touch, my girl!'

Erica forgave Robert his chauvinist comment. Don and Lachie waited for the retort, but none came. She was simply pleased to have the job done.

'Reckon we could turn the light on now, Robert?' Don was eager to see if it all worked. Robert suggested Erica should flick the switch as by his reckoning the batteries should have charged up enough to run a twelve-volt fluorescent strip light. She flicked the switch and for the first time in its two-hundred-year history, electric light filled the interior of the blackhouse. They all cheered at the success of the weekend's work.

Sally entered, having walked up from the Factor's House.

'This calls for a celebration, boys!'

Erica produced the bottle of single malt she had ordered through Don just for this occasion. Lachie put more wood in the stove and the celebrations continued late into the evening. Erica put her vegetarian principles to one side and cooked tasty lamb kebabs for the men, even indulging in some of the meat herself as the whisky took effect.

'We'll make a good carnivore of you yet, Erica,' Lachie joked.

Erica realised that by eating lamb she had crossed one of her own boundaries toward sustainable living on this island. There was certainly no shortage of the animals and cute as they looked these agile sheep were causing a lot of damage. They weren't hard to catch trapped inside the shells of empty cottages and cleits.

With Sally's help, she had recently caught and slaughtered a yearling ram. Sally reckoned they would be even easier to catch on rainy days. That, apparently, had been how the sheep researchers had done it in the past. Dave was despairing over the damage they were doing to his newly repaired stone walls, and she couldn't imagine how he could protect the vegetables in An Lag once the growing season started.

Sheep eat vegetables so she would eat sheep, simple as that. With the 12volt lights burning bright and the meat and whisky finished, Don and Lachie bade her goodnight to make their way back to the *Beluga* tied up at the jetty. Robert went with them to collect a camp bed from the Manse and with some borrowed bedding was intending to make himself comfortable in the blackhouse. In planning her own home, Erica had omitted to think of more than one crib bed built into the thick walls of her cottage.

'Can't see a bloody thing, Lachie!'

Don had lost his night vision due to Erica's new electric lighting. He nearly fell into the dry burn at the back of the derelict military buildings. Looking up at the small glow from an oil light in the Featherstore window he was reminded of the other matter they needed to sort while at St Kilda.

'Just that fucker in there to deal with now, Lachie.'

The *Beluga* left at first light heading back to Leverburgh. For the first time in many weeks, they didn't have to avoid drifting pack ice and a noticeable swell was rising as the twin hulled cabin boat headed east. Don was feeling good, pushing the throttles forward the *Beluga* scattered countless feeding Gannets off Boreray as they headed for home.

It hadn't been a totally peaceful night in Erica's blackhouse. Robert had woken with a start and rushed to open the door and small windows.

'What's up, Robert?'

Erica was sleepy from the large meal and whisky and almost fell from her crib trying to get out. Wrapping a dressing gown around her pyjamas she went over to Robert standing at the control panel.

'I am going to have to check this out for you tomorrow, Erica. The batteries are over charging. I could smell the fumes. This could be bloody dangerous if we don't sort it.'

'What should we do?'

'Well, for now I have disconnected the leads from the regulator, so the batteries won't charge any more tonight. The system is just too efficient with wind, water and solar energy so freely available. You need a dump load for occasions like this. Best would be storing the energy as hot water.

Leave it with me, Erica. I'll get an old hot water cylinder and immersion heater form the base tomorrow and there's sure to be a 240-volt inverter knocking about in the workshops. They never took the cheap stuff away when the military moved out. I'll set everything up so that, when the batteries reach capacity, the excess current will automatically flow to the immersion heater, and you'll have free hot water as well as lighting. The plumbing will be simple. We can collect water from a little higher up the burn and run it down through some blue Alkathene pipe.'

'OK, Robert. I trust in your abilities but if it's all safe for tonight I am going back to bed. See you in the morning.'

They both retired to their respective beds, though Robert could barely sleep thinking about the strange behaviour of the wind generator the previous evening. As a practical electrician, he did not like inexplicable events like that.

He was up bright and early and by the time Erica, somewhat hung over, emerged he had salvaged a copper hot water cylinder, and a roll of blue plastic water pipe was stacked outside her door. Erica rubbed her eyes looking at it, taking in the fact that a man was about to make a fairly large alteration to her living space.

'We need the cylinder higher than your sink. Could be tricky so I thought of an easier way of doing this. I'll put the cylinder outside; it's well insulated with plastic foam coating. It will be above your sink and running the pipework through the walls will be a piece of cake. I've found a nice new tap in the stores so all you will have to do is build a small cleit to protect it from the elements, and the bloody sheep. The sods will be getting next to it to keep warm if we let them so don't leave a doorway. But still, that will be your job, I am the technical man round here!'

Erica held back from giving him a mouthful. She accepted the wisdom of what he was saying and wanted the job done. The tank, plumbing and wiring was completed the same day for which she was very grateful.

'You'll just be needing a tin bath now, Erica. One big enough for two?'

Erica reached for the heather besom she had recently made.

'OK, only joking Erica, but I get the message!'

Rightly sensing that Erica might like her space to herself, Robert moved his camp bed down to the Featherstore and slept with Dan that night. Robert would be eating in the Manse and leaving the island next time the *Beluga* came in, probably in a couple of days, weather permitting.

Dan had made the Featherstore bedroom facing the sea his own. Robert moved into the room at the rear with the view to the barren hillside a hundred yards or so behind the building. Erica had paid Robert in cash for the off-grid electrical equipment and had brought her savings with her for just such an occasion.

Dan noticed him place a sizeable bundle of notes into a secure pocket of his rucksack.

'Hey, Robert – I wonder if I could ask you a favour?'

'What is it, Dan?'

'Well, you know Don and Lachie, the boat guys? I owe them fifty quid like and there's no way I can get to the bank out here. I don't have my cheque book either, I left it in Edinburgh. Could you possibly lend me some till I can get to the bank when I next get off the island?'

Robert was taken back a little at the directness of Dan's approach but could see the problem. There was no way anyone could get cash here, even if they had anywhere to spend it.

When Robert worked at St Kilda the men always ran up a bar tab and settled it with a cheque at the end of the month, when their salary reached the bank. St Kilda always had been a mostly cashless community and now, for Dan, Robert's cash was a welcome sight.

'Tell you what, Dan. Why don't I lend you a straight hundred pounds then you'll have a little to spare, next time you owe anyone anything.'

Robert had correctly guessed Dan owed more than fifty pounds but wasn't going to enquire just how much. Dan thought that making at least a down payment on his dope bill would take the pressure off and get him on the right side of the Don and Lachie.

'Thanks, Robert. You're a pal!'

Feeling more relaxed and sociable, Dan produced a bottle of Puff-Inn *Glenmorangie* from under his bed.

'Do you fancy a dram, Robert?'

'No thanks, Dan. It really doesn't agree with me nowadays.'

Just for once, Dan decided not to drink alone.

Robert hadn't really participated in Erica's blackhouse celebration, feeling uneasy at the proceedings. He had just been doing what he enjoyed most, creative electrical engineering and he'd felt a little uncomfortable working alongside a young woman with considerable feminine presence, like Erica.

It had also been hard to resist drinking with the others after months of abstinence following treatment for alcohol related health problems. He would never have been able to keep off the drink had he still been working in the Base.

Like many of the men on the remote Base he had never married or maintained more than passing relationships. A lot of them were more comfortable sharing their time with other men. Not that any of them were knowingly misogynist in any way, it just seemed easier somehow.

The few women on the island, like Sally the nurse, he considered were dark horses and goodness knows what made them tick. Men were generally straight forward and predictable. Although Robert was over twice Dan's age, he could surmise what made him tick. Dan though, hadn't reckoned on Robert's depth of perception.

Dan had been entranced listening to Robert's tales of life at St Kilda. He hadn't heard much of life on the Base, especially the Friday nights in the Puff-Inn which would commonly run on into Sunday morning, Saturdays being not much more than a hazy recollection.

In their own way the Base guys had, like Robert, been keen to observe a quiet Sabbath. Sunday morning tourists were particularly unwelcome, particularly those who hired a piper to play them ashore. After several incidences of abuse shouted from the Base accommodation block the tour operators got the message and directed the pipers away from the jetty to the far end of the village.

Apparently, the good times had come to an end after the skinny-dipping incident in 2011, when a young serviceman had fallen from the gabion seawall trying to get a closer look. Dan had this tale before but hadn't learned of the consequences. After the incident had been investigated, the then civilian management closed the bar as a punitive measure.

Shortly afterwards, a performance audit was conducted, and the workforce found to be woefully inefficient. Millions of pounds worth of military assets were tied up at St Kilda and lucrative Hebrides Missile Range activities had to be suspended until the radar technicians got their act together. No one thought to investigate the borehole in An Lag, Robert added.

Dan was looking puzzled. 'What do you mean, Robert?'

'What I mean is, because they were so hung over most of the time, their performance was shambolic. Nothing ever got done on time and when it did it was rarely right first time. We were evaluating state of the art missile technology, and it was all those prats could do to get up for work in the morning. Even mid-week when they knew they had to stay sober. It was very strange and made me wonder if there was something in the water.

Then terrorists got wind of the situation out here and we were a sitting target. The only one half capable of finding out what had happened that night was the Supervisor, and he wasn't much better himself, but he was on duty that night. It was a shame it had to end for him like that though.'

Robert related to an incredulous Dan how, during a drunken night in the bar, terrorists had struck the island laying charges that demolished the communications mast sending it crashing onto the radomes below. The damage was never repaired and the terrorists, to his knowledge, never caught. They had landed in Glen Bay, and no one knew a thing about it until it was too late.

Only poor Derek heard the explosion that night. He had driven up to the top of the hill to find a scene of chaos with the mast toppled and a tangle of steel hawsers and high voltage cables that had to be seen to be believed. It had taken months to clear up and by that time the Ministry of Defence had had enough.

'Again, it all boiled down to excessive alcohol consumption by men away from the checks and balances of a normal community.'

Dan was curious about the lack of women.

'Well, there were always one or two women here, but they tended to get together as a clique and, to be honest, I reckon they would plot mischief against us men. Things would regularly go missing; important things like a bunch of keys which would always turn up in unexpected places. Rumours would start, setting one man against another and I reckon it was all women's mischief. Men rarely have the capability for serious scheming. And as for 'Aunt' Sally, there's another story, Dan.'

'Go on, Robert. I am intrigued.'

'Well, your Sally out here has quite a history. As you know she was the main nurse which included being personal councillor and agony aunt – hence her nickname. Quite a few of the men went to her feeling anxious and complaining of feeling trapped on the island. Usually, after some tea and sympathy they went away satisfied but then our Sally began to get some strange ideas.

I only heard this from some of the other guys, but apparently one or two of them went to her to talk over some personal problem or get treated for a sore back and she'd have them on the massage couch strapped down and powerless. I am sure I can leave the rest to your imagination Dan, but it wasn't the type of massage recommended for a bad back. I can tell you. No-one ever complained though, you could say she was doing the men a social service!'

Robert chuckled at his own joke, leaving Dan wide eyed with amazement. It seemed his wilder student days were nothing compared with what had been going on out here.

'But anyway, all good things had to come to an end and management kept a tight eye on things from Range Head. It always makes me smile to see 'Our Lady of the Isles,' the Virgin Mary on her pedestal just below the hilltop control centre. Actually, you can see that from here on a clear day, Dan. Sally wouldn't have modelled for that statue!'

'Aye, she would have been the other Mary more like!'

Now it was Dan's turn to chuckle.

Manly banter was just what he had been missing on this island, once again being affected by women's scheming. He did hold back from letting Robert know about his growing affair with Deborah, even though rightly it should have been her affair with him, not the other way round.

The stories continued until both headed for their respective beds satisfied from a good evening's banter. Dan raked up a few tales of his own, especially the one about getting into trouble for supplying other students with vodka laced with Fly Agaric mushrooms. Robert had looked slightly shocked at this revelation.

'You want to be careful, Dan. There have been a few strange events on this island, and I don't mean just falling off high walls trying to look at naked women.'

In a lowered voice he recounted the one myth Dan already knew much about.

'One of the lads read about the Butterwort plant that grows in wet places here. The Gaelic name for it is Mothan and there's a lot of folklore attached to the plant. It was said to keep the faeries away from the milk, but it was also used by Hebridean women to entrap the man of their fancy. They would chew leaves of the plant before kissing their intended and that was it, he was ensnared and wrapped around their little fingers before you could say hey presto! Bet Sally kept a supply in her pharmacy! It is also supposed to be a dreaming herb so think twice before you get any funny ideas.'

Dan told Robert he'd already done some reading on that subject, so not to worry.

'Anyway, Mothan or no Mothan, I am going to sleep well tonight. See you in the morning, Dan.'

The tinned and dried food in the base kitchens, as Deborah had reminded Dave on many occasions, was not inexhaustible. The tastiest items were already getting low, and they had made serious inroads into the alcohol supply once destined for the Puff-Inn. All good things would come to an end, and it looked like that moment could come the following year.

As long as the *Beluga* kept to schedule, they would be alright, but they needed a contingency supply in case of prolonged bad weather. Islanders had run out of food in the past and sure as eggs were eggs it could happen again now there was no longer a helicopter service from the mainland. As for eggs, Deborah did not want to return to the traditional St Kildan seabird diet.

'Dave,' she asked him over their evening meal.

'How are the kale yards, you know, the gardens, coming on?'

'Well, I have repaired quite a few now. It will just be a question of digging them over, raking and sowing the seed. We should have fresh vegetables this Summer. Don is going to bring me out plenty of seed, the stuff that grows well on

Harris should be fine here. Thank God there are no rabbits. He told me he has a terrible time with them back home and has to shoot them on an almost daily basis. No amount of wire netting deters the little sods for long.'

Dave had tried fishing from the jetty when backpain stopped him from working. His catch hadn't amounted to much, but he felt he was providing something. Returning to the Manse with an armful of fresh vegetables would soon be reality, especially if he could get the rest of the family outside, working as a team to dig ridge and furrow lazy beds inside the repaired stone enclosures. Like past Hebridean agriculture, human muscle and hand tools prevailed over other methods to cultivate steep and inaccessible ground. Locally produced compost included all manner of organic waste and was used to build raised beds on steep hillsides.

Enclosure at St Kilda changed island life for ever. With their rich seabird waste compost, the crofters produced Barley crops the envy of the Western Isles. The warm and enclosed south facing fields, well-watered and cleared of stones produced heavy yields during long summer days of intense sunshine.

The level ground close to the village was perfect for agricultural production. High stone walls deflected the worst of the winds and for a while the villagers could not have improved further. Stones not used in building the high protective Head Dyke were used to build the larger nineteenth century storage cleits. These large cleits mimicked the field barns of other upland areas of Britain agriculturally, but not socially, improved by Enclosure.

Dave had read about changes to rural life brought about by lowland Enclosure. St Kilda, at the extremity of the Western isles must have changed more than most. Storms brought about inevitable failure of the agricultural project despite tourists' belief in an island Utopia.

The reality of never-ending hard work and an ageing population was overlooked or consciously ignored by the visitors. As Dave was already beginning to realise, his middle-aged body, unaccustomed to manual work on this scale, was not going to be strong enough. He needed spiritual support to see the project through to completion. Not just Dave Williams, he realised, but each one of the family needed, in their own way, to draw on God's immortal, invisible wisdom to see them through.

14

Problems

Dave was particularly proud of the six-foot-high wall he had repaired around the Glebe plot. It had been originally set aside for the Minister's vegetable garden. Digging the soil had proved surprisingly easy. Not only had nearly a century of Soay sheep grazing kept deep rooted weeds at bay but several archaeological digs in the plot had left the ground friable and easy to rework for family vegetables.

St Kilda's commercial sheep, he knew, were too heavy and well fed to bother with climbing stone walls, but free ranging Soays were another matter. They showed no respect for stone walls or cleit roofs. Nothing was ever done to mitigate their effect, for the unmanaged flocks were a unique research opportunity into the ecology of an accessible, closed population of large mammals. Zoologists considered the research opportunity unparalleled elsewhere in the world.

The population rose and fell according to natural conditions and as grazing became sparse no blade of grass was spared, nor any blade of anything edible for that matter. Dave compared them to John Muir's 'hoofed locusts' relentlessly devouring the native grasslands of North America.. Only on the steepest rock faces could plants flower and set seed where these agile brown sheep feared to tread.

The population had risen exponentially to over a thousand animals before the Williams arrived, and Dave's attempts at cultivation started. In an ordinary year the Spring grass would have sustained the Soay flock but this year, with winter lingering much longer than usual, the sheep, especially the pregnant ewes, struggled to find sustenance.

Dave had already noticed how lush the vegetation grew inside the stone walled enclosures compared to that growing out in the open. Agatha had explained to him, in ecological terms, how wind prevented plants from fully developing on this exposed island. She had described St Kildan vegetation as a plagio-climax community stunted by wind chill.

Behind protective dry-stone walls, plants could grow un-checked and reach their full potential, especially on south facing slopes. The St Kildans had been aware of this and took great pains to keep both strong winds and livestock out of their southerly orientated enclosures.

Only with the harvest over were the island's heavy Cheviot sheep allowed in to add their droppings to the rich soil of the enclosures. Since human evacuation feral Soay sheep had become accustomed to free access in the name of zoological research, but to the detriment of just about everything else.

The larger enclosures and been worked in ridge and furrow lazy bed fashion and Dave was eager to try out horticultural methods known to have succeeded in the past.

He had ridged the cultivated soil inside the Glebe garden. Not only would this increase the surface area for cultivation but would also allow drainage during the periods of heavy rainfall. He envisioned vegetables growing strong in the sun, thriving in rich soils behind restored stone walls.

The physical act of cultivating the soil and sowing heritage seeds sourced from the mainland proved inspirational and, for a while, Dave forgot his daily Bible readings. He drew solace from working with rather than against nature. It then came as a complete surprise to Deborah to hear her husband screaming abuse from inside their newly enclosed garden.

'Get out of here, you fucking bastards!'

Deborah heard the clatter of falling rocks, as three small brown sheep scrambled over the wall to get away from the hail of small stones Dave was hurling at them.

'Jesus, God almighty! What have I bloody done to deserve this?'

Dave fell to his knees beside the Church wall and beat the freshly turned soil with his fists. His carefully tended young Kale plants defoliated by the yearlings.

'Dave, calm down. They will grow again quick enough. The roots are established, and they'll just be bushier plants, that's all. Come on, all is not lost!'

Deborah tried to make light of the incident but knew her husband well enough to understand the pain he felt at finding his winter efforts undone in an unguarded moment.

'The problem is, Dave, the Kildans never had to put up with this breed of sheep. Their heavier Cheviots and Closewools were selected because they didn't do this kind of damage, didn't climb over the walls. Any that did would soon end up in the pot, I can tell you.'

Dave took himself for a walk and began searching his mind for Biblical explanations for his defeat in the face of three hungry sheep. His walk took him up into the corrie of An Lag where sturdy nineteenth century stone enclosures stood firm, years after the last crops had been harvested. With wooden gates long since rotted, contented Soays ruminated in the warm sunshine, chewing cud away from the biting wind. The walls here were taller than those around the Manse garden, maybe eight feet high. Dave quickly realised the open gateways eliminated the risk of sheep scrambling over and damaging the loosely built stonework. He remembered reading that these arable enclosures had also served as sheep fanks during the annual round up or any other time the St Kildans needed to catch their sheep.

Thinking about nineteenth century agricultural methods he continued to work his way upwards to the top of the formerly cultivated and sheltered corrie between Oiseval and the slopes of Conachair. Cresting the rise, Dave could see the dramatic peaks of Boreray and the Stacs four miles distant and his mind wandered to the 500 odd feral white sheep living on St Kilda's second largest island, descendants of the Boreray flock abandoned in 1930.

It simply hadn't been economically viable to remove them one by one down precipitous paths to be manhandled into a waiting vessel. The St Kildans, he had read, used to truss the sheep's legs before throwing them into the sea to be plucked from drowning by waiting boatmen.

Dave turned left and began to climb the steep path toward the summit of Conachair. At the highest point on the island, he stood facing northward toward the dramatic land and seascapes of Boreray, the jagged Stacs rising from the submerged volcanic rim of the archipelago. The power of the view was palpable and as he stood there, exposed to the sea and sky, with seabirds swirling around him, he heard God speak from afar.

Determined to understand he quickly made his way back down to the village to consult the old family Bible for the first time in weeks. Taking the fastest route back from the summit, he regarded the gated walls of An Lag with fresh insight. On reaching the Manse he went straight to the battered Bible and began looking for the words he needed. Almost at random he flicked the pages, looking for references to human trial and tribulation in the wilderness.

After a few minutes searching he came across exactly what he needed. Dave had noticed before, that when a problem was on his mind, the answer seemed to jump out at him when scanning the pages.

It was a skill he acquired from marking of undergraduate assignments where no matter what waffle had been written, repetition of keywords and references were all he needed to see. His keyword that afternoon was *walls* and the words of Isaiah 62: 6-12 jumped out at him.

I have set watchmen upon thy walls, O Jerusalem, which shall never hold their peace day nor night: ye that make mention of the Lord, keep not silence all the day and all the night they shall never be silent. And give him no rest until he establish, and till he make Jerusalem a praise in the earth. The Lord has sworn by his right hand and by the arm of his strength, "Surely I will no more give thy corn to be meat for thine enemies; and the sons of the stranger shalt not drink thy wine for the which thou hast laboured: But they that have gathered it shall eat it and praise the Lord, and they that have brought it together shall drink it in the courts of my holiness". Go through, go through the gates; prepare ye the way of the people; cast up, cast up the highway; gather out the stones; lift up a standard for the people.

In other words, if he returned to the ways of the Lord, he would no longer grow Kale to feed Soay sheep, now his sworn enemies. That evening Dave returned to his former habit of Bible reading before they ate.

'Don't let the food go cold, Dave!'

Deborah tolerated her husband's idiosyncrasy but wasn't going to encourage it.

As woman of the house, she had more important things to worry about. Even with, sheep willing, a potential supply of fresh vegetables in the coming year it was going to be tight feeding them all. Dave briefly paused, glanced at Agatha, before concluding his reading by quoting lines selected from Proverbs 31.

'Favour is deceitful, and beauty is vain: but a woman that feareth the Lord, shall be praised. Give her of the fruit of her hands; and let her own works praise her in the gates.'

'Whatever, Dad; can we eat now?'

Agatha was unimpressed by her father's return to Bible reading before their evening meal.

'So does that mean we all have to work in the garden

297

now?'

'Well, it wouldn't be a bad idea, Agatha. Everyone else seems to have a job round here, even Dan has his guided walks to get organised. You wander off into Glen Mór most days of the week leaving the rest of us to labour on the land; it is a wonder you don't set up home over there.

What I am going to do tomorrow is build a gate in the garden wall. That way the sheep won't need to climb over and when the ground is clear I can let them in to dung the ground - great idea, eh? Just like the old fold system. For now, I am going to follow the Lord's advice and raise a great standard over the garden, The flapping flag will scare the sheep away - and we are all going to keep a regular watch to prevent the little devils getting in again.'

It did not take Dave long to build an entrance into the garden enclosure and throw together a temporary gate made from a couple of pallets he found in the empty Base yard.. The flagpole was more of a challenge, but he remembered an old yacht mast lying behind the shingle beach. With Dan's help, the mast was dragged back to the Manse and erected in the garden.

Visiting ships had previously donated flags to adorn the walls of the old Puff-Inn and very soon a somewhat battered and nicotine-stained Royal Ensign was flying over the vegetable garden. Beyond the wall sheep watched impassively, unmoved by either the flag or any of Dave's efforts to keep them away from his vegetable patch.

At the far end of the village, Sally had joined Erica, both women sitting on the low wall outside her restored blackhouse. Sally pointed out the small brown sheep clambering on top of the garden wall beyond the Manse.

'Look at that, Erica. Those sheep just get everywhere. That flag Dave put up is useless; there's no stopping them.'

Erica looked up just in time to see one of the sheep jump high in the air and fall, legs thrashing, to the ground at the foot of the wall. Both women heard the crack of the rifle followed almost simultaneously by the thud of the hollow point slug smashing into the sheep's skull.

'What the fuck?'

Erica was incredulous. She had just witnessed a perfect head shot, better than anything her deer stalker ex-boyfriend had ever managed.

Sally knew exactly what they had just witnessed.

'Looks like your Dad's got the gun out that he wouldn't let you kids play with. Well, that's one way of dealing with them but those sheep will keep coming back. There are a lot of them and nothing much to eat right now.'

Sally and Erica quickly walked down the path toward the Manse in time to see Deborah and Agatha race out after hearing the shot. Deborah was flabbergasted.

'Dave, I thought we had all agreed, that bloody gun was staying in the loft. You are surely not getting it out again!'

Agatha was equally horrified, but more at the release of male violence against the island sheep population.

'Dad, what are you doing? Couldn't you have just shooed them off like last time?'

With the freshly cleaned and polished Tikka T3 cradled in his arms, Dave's repost came immediately.

'The Lord has sworn by his right hand and by the arm of his strength, "Surely I will no more give thy corn to be meat for thine enemies; and the sons of the stranger shalt not drink thy wine for the which thou hast laboured!'

'I said we would stand guard and that's just what I have been doing!'

The small brown ewe lay dead at their feet, a drop of pre-natal milk leaking from one teat. Already, a sharp eyed Skua circled overhead waiting to feed on the carcass. Sally stood incredulous at the scene. She considered there was no need for a family argument over one dead sheep. Erica agreed and voiced her opinion that using the rifle certainly beat her plan to trap sheep in cleits as they sheltered from driving rain or strong sunshine.

'Look guys, I don't know about you, but I reckon we should be grateful for some free mutton. Yeah, I know we are not supposed to touch these things but leaving it for the Bonxies seems a right waste to me.'

Ever the pragmatist, Erica offered to skin and butcher the ewe, a proposal Deborah was ready to accept in light of their dwindling rations. Throughout the discussion over the dead sheep, Dan had been noticeably absent. From inside the Featherstore, the survivalist scenario unfolding not one hundred metres away was too real. Dan would rather keep visceral reality distant at the best of times.

Picking up the spent cartridge case, Dave took the rifle back inside the Manse securing it in the hallway cupboard rather than back in the loft. It could, he reckoned, be needed again and at short notice.

The matter of sheep in the vegetable garden was brought up by Agatha over their evening meal. She reminded them all that before any more sheep were killed, they ought to contact the Trust for advice.

'I agree that this island cannot ecologically support all these introduced sheep and in the absence of a terrestrial predator, we could take that niche. Technically what Dad has just done is to deliberately kill a legally protected species and it is asking for trouble without at least having applied for the appropriate licence.'

Agatha was sticking to the rules; she also made it known that she didn't like the way it had been done in anger. If culling was to be conducted, which she had no practical objection to, it should be done by professionals. Not by a deranged old man with an unlicensed hunting rifle.

Deborah agreed to contact the Trust as soon as possible. Luckily the satellite internet system still worked, and she sent an email to Josephine Miller, who was still in post after her redundancy threat had been withdrawn.

The problem was explained; there were simply too

many sheep, and they hadn't a hope in hell of growing vegetables unless they were culled professionally. Deborah carefully avoided any reference to the unprofessional culling that had already taken place. Josephine's reply came quicker than she had expected.

It seemed the Trust had long been concerned over physical damage the Soay sheep were doing to St Kilda's archaeology and, by overgrazing, stunting the island's ecological potential. She quickly arranged for two deer stalkers to be sent over. The professional marksmen would be over as soon as possible, before Spring lambing made the cull ethically unacceptable.

As manager for the islands, Josephine had often remarked on the irony that, having been spared the nineteenth century Clearances, St Kilda had ended up overrun with sheep and the human population evacuated, if not forcibly evicted. She hadn't really accepted the earlier evacuation from Glen Mór after it became impossible to live and work after the appearance of the Amazon, or whatever other superstitious nonsense.

Initially thought to be one of St Kilda's wonder tales, archaeologists had recently confirmed there had been a small flock of deer on the island in the medieval period. Taking one or two animals for sustenance had been traditional for centuries. Once agriculture had been improved on the south side of the island, against the women's advice, the men of Glen Mór learned to drive deer into netted stone corrals outside their corbelled huts, catching several at a time. Screams of deer being slaughtered with stone axes echoed around the Glen at the autumn catch.

The practice ceased after hunters connected the deer's screams with the sudden and inexplicably violent gusts of wind that ripped the nets from the stone corrals. It seemed the glen would tolerate a foot hunt taking one deer at a time but not organised slaughter, however primitive, following

301

modernised agricultural practices on the island. The superstitious St Kildans heeded the warning and henceforth considered Glen Mór no place for human habitation.

The wide glen was psychologically closed by a turf dyke on the high ridge separating it from the village. Crossing the ridge daily, women of the village still tended and milked cattle grazing the glen. Men venturing amongst the cattle would find themselves blown off their feet by violent gusts of wind while the animals grazed peacefully a few yards away. The message was portentous and even the women felt compelled to make libation offerings at the Milking Stone when returning to the village. Malevolent gusts continued long after the glen was evacuated.

The downing of the Sunderland Flying Boat in the 1940s and recent crash of the twin engine Piper being the latest examples of vengeful winds and subsequent fatalities. The names of airmen perished at St Kilda being commemorated on a tarnished brass plaque in the Kirk. No woman is recorded having suffered an inexplicable death on the island.

It had been several days before sea conditions were suitable for the *Beluga* to come out from Leverburgh. The Argocat had been driven across sturdy planks from the pier onto the aft deck of the boat without too much difficulty and the two stalkers were in high spirits as Don pushed the throttle levers forward to begin their crossing to St Kilda. The small eight wheeled all-terrain vehicle had been well lashed down and stayed secure throughout the crossing. The Highland stalkers however felt increasingly uncomfortable with the motion as the boat gathered speed heading for open waters. Gavin was the first to give in to seasickness and throw up into the plastic pint glass Lachie supplied as they set off. Sean followed suit soon after and three hours later, entering the calmer waters of Village Bay, the two stalkers were decidedly the worse for the experience.

Still managing a grin, Sean cracked a joke about feeling better than this after a heavy Friday night in Braemar. Grey faced; Gavin could only silently nod his agreement.

'Here we are then lads!'

Ever cheerful, Don had explained that getting the Argocat on board at Leverburgh had been the easy bit.

Now they would have to find a way of getting it ashore as they had arrived at low tide and the *Beluga* could not pull up alongside the jetty. He would have to charge them six hours waiting time to make an easy job of it.

'Don, do you think your crane would take the Argocat? It's about one and a half tonnes deadweight.'

'Should be OK, though if it ends up sinking don't blame me!'

Don had doubts about the manufacturers claim that this eight-wheel drive 'golf buggy,' as he saw it, was fully amphibious. Don also reckoned an extra six hour's payment for sharing a dram or two with these lads sounded fair enough. Sean knew the Western Isles Trust had given them a tight budget and decided to risk the Argocat on the gentle swell of Village Bay.

Don and Sean untied the lashings holding the Argocat to the deck and fixed them to the lugs on each corner of the amphibious vehicle. Don swung the rear mounted crane around and Sean bunched the straps to the hook on the end of the stainless-steel lifting cable. Lifting the Argocat a foot off the deck, the *Beluga* immediately felt less stable. Gavin groaned but gave a feeble thumbs up as Don swung the small vehicle over the stern of the boat. The *Beluga's* bow rose up, so Don quickly lowered the Argocat into the water fearing a scene of chaos in his galley as crockery slid along shelves to crash to the floor. Neither did he want the rear of the *Beluga* getting knocked about, let alone swamped.

To his amazement, the Argocat floated perfectly, in fact

it seemed more stable than their Zodiac tender which bobbed around like a cork. Sean, now pretty well recovered, jumped down into the Argocat and started the engine. Don knew the principle but again was dubious about spinning wheels driving the vehicle through the water but the heavily treaded tyres worked like high-speed paddle wheels. Casting off the loading straps, Sean grinned as he manoeuvred the Argocat left and right, evidently beginning to enjoy himself. Lachie appeared with their various boxes of provisions, two stalking rifles and a pump-action shotgun. There were also eight jerry-cans of diesel for the machine.

They hadn't been told there were still thousands of gallons of fuel in the power station storage tanks. Lachie then dragged up four heavy boxes of ammunition before Don suggested they might be pushing their luck loading the Argocat with those as well.

'It will take a thousand pounds on water, Don.'

'Yeah, and I'll bet you a thousand pounds they meant in a test tank, not crossing Atlantic swell. You just drive that thing across to the beach and we'll bring the rest in the Zodiac.'

Don hadn't built up his charter business by taking unnecessary risks and wasn't going to start now. The small slipway on the beach had last been used by the ex-Russian Army amphibious vehicle arriving with thatch for Erica's blackhouse project. Now that had been an amphibious vehicle alright, he thought, not like this jumped-up golf cart.

In spite of his misgivings, the Argocat landed safely on the beach and Sean skidded it round a couple of times on the sand before driving it up the slipway onto the weed strewn helipad. The Zodiac was lowered from the *Beluga* and loaded with the stalkers' supplies. It took two trips to the jetty to get everything ashore. Gavin, now recovered, helped carry their provisions and equipment ashore. Sean had already driven the Argocat off the beach and onto the fields at the edge of the village. Scattering hundreds of waders, the birds protested noisily at the disturbance. A sudden gust of wind took his deerstalker hat and hurled it far out into the bay as he drove the machine along the road toward the jetty, further disturbing a young Harbour Seal snoozing above the high-water line.

Gavin was already introducing himself to the Williams when Sean arrived to load up their supplies stacked on the jetty. Manoeuvring up and down the steep slope to the jetty was no problem for the Argocat and a whole lot easier than using wheelbarrows.

'Only just bought that hat! That's a fucking good start, Gavin.'

'Don't worry, we can find you another one. We can't let our heroes go around with cold heads, can we?'

Deborah joked with the new male arrivals. A minor flirtation which didn't go unnoticed by Dave.

The Williams family had all come out to greet the stalkers. Even Dan overcame his insecurities, appearing somewhat sheepishly to hand over his outstanding debt to Lachie when the two boatmen came up the slope from the jetty.

'OK, boys; you can stay up in the cottages. Number one has a good kitchen though there's no electric now. Do you think you can cope with oil lamps and cooking on a woodstove?'

'Can't be any worse than the bothies we have to use back home. Nae bother, we'll be just fine. Just show us where these sheep are you want rid of.'

'Where are they not?' was Dave's quiet, cynical reply.

Once the stalkers had settled in, they walked along the Street toward the sound of poorly played fiddle music. Erica had long fancied herself as a traditional musician and, with a poor-quality instrument she found in a storeroom behind the Puff-Inn bar, she was practicing when she thought no-one else was around. She stopped abruptly when Gavin and Sean entered her blackhouse.

'Jesus fucking wept! Where did you boys come from?'

Erica felt outraged at the unexpected and uninvited intrusion into her private space.

'We came to see a man about culling a few sheep for you, hen.'

'OK, right you must be the stalkers Dad was talking about; but you could have knocked before bursting in like that!'

'Guilty conscience, have we?' Sean winked at Gavin.

'Right den of iniquity out here so I was told back at Braemar. Sex, drugs and rock n' roll is what we heard, eh, Gavin.'

'Reckon that was before the military left, Sean. Just some frustrated women now and a sharpshooter with religious mania.'

Erica thought the stalkers had a pretty astute first impression but didn't like the way they made it seem so obvious. Where Dan fitted into their picture wasn't entirely clear. She decided to make a friendly gesture and invite them for a cup of tea while they were in her house. The men gladly accepted and listened to Erica talk enthusiastically about how she had renovated the blackhouse. Even installed a wood stove so the house couldn't technically be called black anymore.

'Yeah, there's plenty of old blackhouse ruins in the Highlands too,' said Gavin.

'The Clearances did for them. My granddad told me that the thatched roofs were lucky to last two years once the fires went out. Seemed the smoke kept the insects away but once they got in birds pulled the thatch to pieces to get at them.'

Looking up at the pristine thatched ceiling he added, 'maybe you will be needing to spray a bit of DDT up there just in case, Erica? That'd sort out the birds too, I reckon,

Sean.'

The poor jest was interrupted by a scurrying in the thatch and for a brief moment a naked rodent tail could be seen twitching through the reeds and a few hardened black droppings fell onto the table below.

'St Kilda mouse!' Erica described the island's endemic and oversized field mice to the two unconvinced stalkers.

'Fucking rat more like! Deer, sheep, rats, whatever. We'll clear the lot as long as you pay us. Reckon we could be here for a while.'

15

Stalkers

It had been Deborah's idea to throw a party to honour the stalkers arrival. Both daughters raised their eyebrows at the unexpected gesture. Edinburgh parties were remembered as if from another planet, but the women agreed it would make a welcome break from hard work and Dave's fundamentalism.

Dan perked up at the prospect of the first party St Kilda had seen for a long time. House One had seen plenty of parties in the past, but none recently. It had been the social venue for visiting conservation groups and Christmas get-togethers for military staff away from their austere quarters. The open ditch of the nearby dry burn had caught out many inebriated revellers returning to their accommodation block after a good night in House One.

Dave predictably disapproved as Deborah began preparations for the party. The wood stove was still functional in spite of a patina of rust from the damp atmosphere. Sally had used it after they first arrived at St Kilda but hadn't been in there much lately. Lighting that stove again would be the best thing for it. The warmth would benefit not just the cast iron of the stove but, she hoped, thaw out the coldness in her husband.

Erica joined in to help Agatha fastidiously wiping dust from the kitchen surfaces. As the afternoon began to fade, Deborah automatically flicked the switch near the door which, before the military evacuation, would have turned on the fluorescent ceiling lights.

'Shit! I had forgotten about that.'

Sally paid little attention to the party preparations. She had seen plenty of parties in House One and had first-hand experience of the medical consequences. Perhaps it had been the remoteness, or being away from constraints of Hebridean family life, but many men and quite a few of the women had indulged in behaviour which could be recalled to impress or embarrass in equal measure.

One thing there was no shortage of was drink. The two stalkers had brought a case of Speyside malt with them, and added to the contents of the old Puff-Inn storeroom would go a long way toward a good evening or two. The lack of electricity was an inconvenience but not one to stop the party happening. Kerosene lamps filled with diesel fuel gave passable illumination and the flickering light from the glass fronted wood stove would add to the ambience of the evening. They all mucked in to prepare food in the Manse and carry it up to the Cottage.

'Just keep it out of reach of the mice,' warned Erica.

'Rats don't you mean,' quipped Gavin.

Erica reminded the stalkers that there were no rats at St Kilda, the Trust having enforced stringent bio-security measures to prevent vermin of any sort coming ashore.

Landing craft had always been a weak point in the defence. The island warden would watch continuously for signs of rats when these vessels offloaded on the beach, but none had ever been seen. The Russian amphibious vehicle bringing Erica's thatching straw had been the first craft to land unsupervised in many years. The *Beluga,* now tied up at the jetty would have had to moor in the bay previously, for even the cleanest of vessels could not be guaranteed rat free.

Agatha had explained many times how ground nesting seabirds would be decimated by rats taking their eggs and chicks. Not even the nests of fearsome Great Skuas would be exempt from rodent predation although the adults would make short work of consuming any rat they managed to catch. Agatha had heard of Greater Black-backed Gulls catching rabbits on the island of Lundy so for the larger Great Skua, catching a rat or two would not be a problem.

As for Don and Lachie, they joked that no sea-rats would be coming to the party. They were tired after a long day bringing the stalkers over. They had also been hard at it preparing the boat two hours before Sean and Gavin turned up. If it was alright with everyone, they would have an early night, sleeping on board.

Deborah and Erica worked hard to get everything ready for the party. By the time evening had fallen, the diesel fuelled Hurricane lamps had been lit and the woodstove was burning cheerily in the hearth. Candles had been arranged on the trestle tables and a few old Christmas tinsel decorations had been brought down from a box found in the cottage loft.

Sally remarked that apart from the subtle smell of diesel it was just like the old days of conservation work parties. By the time the rest of the family and the two stalkers arrived two large pots simmered on the woodstove. It had been Dave's suggestion to put the freshly shot Soay to good use and the mutton stew smelt delicious. Sean had professionally skinned and butchered the carcass, putting his deer larder skills to good use on this considerably smaller beast. He thought it a pity there was no dog around to take care of the offal. If he lived there, a good dog would be priority number one.

Approaching the cottages, Dave savoured the smell of wood smoke in the air. Just seeing the blue-grey smoke issuing from the chimney gave the village a sign of life, a promise for the future. Ducking his head as he entered the cottage, he was struck how homely it appeared. The women had made a real effort. Erica was in a good mood and welcomed her father.

'Hi, Dad! Your Soay proved useful in the end. May it be the first of many to end up in the pot, eh?'

'Well, if Job had fourteen thousand sheep to contend with, I am sure I can manage the thousand odd plaguing these islands. Just think, Job 42:12, he considered himself blessed to have that huge flock. I would consider myself cursed.'

Winking at his daughters he continued,

'Perhaps I should let them have free reign to reproduce and also claim my six thousand camels, one thousand oxen and a thousand she asses – not just the paltry few I see before me!'

'Moving swiftly on, Dave...... '

Deborah was pleased to see that despite biblical referencing, her increasingly dour husband seemed to be getting into party mood. Music was going to be a problem though. An old Sony ghetto-blaster still stood on a corner shelf where it had been abandoned by its previous owner.

Heavy items often got left behind, considered more trouble than they were worth to pack into limited rucksack space. Rummaging in nearby drawers produced a treasure trove of assorted batteries. Many were useless, well past their expiry date but as luck would have it, eight useable size 'D' batteries were put into service and the old Sony came to life. CDs were going to be a problem, but Dan came to the rescue. He spent much of his time on the island in a world of his own. Through his earphones, digital music stored on his phone created a filter through which the realities of life could be moderated. Dan offered to connect his phone to the Sony auxiliary socket in return for taking charge of the play list.

Dave sat by the woodstove occupying himself with keeping the room warm and stirring the mutton stew. Across the room Deborah and Erica finalised the food preparations. Sally entered the cottage and produced an unopened bottle of Botanical Gin produced by a small Hebridean distillery, so she claimed.

'I've been waiting for an occasion to get this bottle out. Why don't you join me, Dave?'

Sitting down next to him she produced a couple of shot glasses from her bag and offered one to him. Dave studied her warily.

'*And be not drunk with wine, wherein is excess; but be filled with the Spirit*, Sally (Ephesians 5: 18)'

'Dave – I am sure a little of my spirit would do you the world of good. Might even make you see this island in a lighter vein rather than a source of torment for you!'

With a little trepidation Dave accepted a shot of gin and Sally passed two more filled glasses to Deborah and Erica.

'Cheers, all – here's to a new and better life for us all out here, *Slàinte mhath!*'

'*Dheagh slàinte!* We have arrived at the right time, I see.'

Sally spun round to see Sean and Gavin ducking through the doorway, both carrying bottles of Speyside Malt. Agatha came in with them and, if Sally's medical observation was correct, she appeared slightly tipsy already.

Dan looked up from his phone where he was putting the final additions to the party playlist.

'Agatha? Do not tell me you have become human at last!'

'Don't worry, she took some water with it.'

Gavin assured the others that Agatha was fine and had been explaining the layout of the island to them before they set off in the morning.

Agatha collapsed in a fit of giggles, sitting down heavily on the trestle bench beside the table. Brushing her thick but loose hair back away from her face she retorted straight away.

'Well, if Jesus could turn water to wine, that's just fine by me...'

No more giggles this time but a glance at her father cautioned him against any rebuke. Dave recognized the challenge but decided not to rise to it, considering he was beginning to enjoy the effect of botanical gin himself.

'Ecclesiastes 9: 7 – *Go thy way, eat thy bread with joy, and drink thy wine with a merry heart; for God now accepteth thy works.*'

'Amen, Dad. Now can we get on with the party?'

Erica considered Dave's biblical justification sealed the matter and tonight they were going to enjoy themselves.

'Better put a jug of water on the table too considering all the booze we seem to have acquired tonight.'

Erica took a jug over to the tap above the sink and turned it on. Water gushed out into the jug only for the flow to suddenly slow to a trickle as small pieces of skin and fur, followed by a mouse thigh bone, dropped into the container.

'Yuk! That is really gross. Hey, Agatha! Be an angel and take this jug out to the well and get us some clean water, please.'

Agatha took the jug outside and walked to the well a short distance behind the cottages. There was just enough light to see if she took full advantage of her peripheral vision. Looking straight in front was not the best strategy in such low light, she remembered that from Outward Bound training as a teenager and took pride in rarely using a flashlight unless it was pitch black.

Approaching the well, she slipped and fell heavily among Mothan plants growing around the stone rim. Luckily, the catering grade glass jug survived the impact with the mossy ground, but Agatha was not so lucky and would have a serious bruise on her thigh to show where she fell against protruding granite stonework. Wincing, she lowered the jug into the overflowing well. Carrying the heavy, filled water jug back to the cottage she took great care not to slip again and was feeling slightly nauseous from shock by the time she was back inside the warm kitchen.

Deborah noticed how pale Agatha was looking.

'Goodness, girl. You look like you have seen a ghost. Whatever happened out there?'

Crushed small purple flowers stuck to the right leg of her jeans as Agatha rubbed her bruise.

'Leave it alone, Mum. I just slipped and fell heavily. I am OK, honest.'

'Well, if you say so.'

Agatha had taken several falls lately because of her insistence on exploring the more inaccessible parts of the island. She had taken care not to let anyone see the bruises or how she treated them.

The two stalkers accepted a glass of Sally's gin and took places offered at the long table. Erica and Agatha joined Sally on the bench against the wall, sitting opposite the stalkers. Dan finished setting up the playlist and his musical choice contributed to the atmosphere as Dave placed the two large pans of stew and rice on the table.

'Fresh vegetables are in short supply I'm afraid but if these two gentlemen do their job properly, we should be in luck next year.'

There was no wine at the meal but gin and well water made a palatable alternative. GNT Sally called it.

'Gin and non-tonic water! I see we have Water of Life, *Uisge Beatha* for later.'

Sally's taste for alcohol was no secret that night. With the meal consumed, plates and pans were put to one side as Sean produced his malt. Gavin had brought a second bottle, from another small distillery, and Dan joined in the occasion by producing a flask of his 'special brew' concocted weeks earlier for 'communion' purposes. He had thought the evening an apt moment to evaluate its efficacy.

The fumes from the diesel fuelled oil lamps were not adding to the occasion so Sean suggested they might prefer

314

a better smell in the cottage. From the inside pocket of his wax jacket, he produced a plastic bag.

'Best grass in the Hebrides, so Dan and Lachie tell me. I got it off them on the way over. They swear by it as a preventative against sea-sickness – and they should know. Strong stuff, mind, Gavin.'

It became clear that Gavin's queasiness on landing at St Kilda had been more than straight forward seasickness.

'You don't mind, do you?' Sean enquired.

Dave held his hands up in supplication, he was already feeling mellow from Sally's gin. Sharing a spliff and a dram of malt would not make him worse in the eyes of God or anyone else for that matter and it was reputed to be good for back troubles, which he certainly knew a lot about now.

'Bring it on, boys.'

Deborah was not sure what to make of Dave's sudden return to student party mode, but it would be a damn sight easier to cope with his hangovers than his evangelizing. Erica was relaxing into the evening taking long tokes on the spliff as it passed round the table. Only Agatha abstained, explaining that having to walk over the hill most days of the week, she needed to keep her lungs in good order. She would stick with whisky and water. Dan had never seen the Williams let their hair down like this and was interested to see how the evening would pan out.

The spliff was passed round the table a couple of more times, laughter increasing as it went. Months of tension were being released that evening. They should have visitors like this more often, thought Deborah when sudden piercing bleeps startled them back to reality.

'What on earth... ?'

Dan's musical ambience was shattered by the shriek of a battery powered smoke detector.

'Jesus fucking Christ, let me get the battery out of that thing!'

Dan rose unsteadily to his feet to stand on a chair before unscrewing the cover of the smoke detector. It was stiff and when the cover finally shifted Dan fell from the chair and struck his head on the corner of the table, upsetting the glasses and ashtrays. Luckily, Agatha was sober enough to catch the whisky bottle as it rolled towards her.

'You have saved the day, girl. Well caught!'

Sean had sobered enough to show his appreciation though Gavin was getting pretty stoned and could only grunt his thanks for saving the bottle. Dan dragged himself painfully to his feet and sat down again. Shards of glass littered the floor where the glasses had smashed. The cover of the smoke detector lay among the debris and, as if to make a point, the ceiling alarm emitted another loud bleep.

'I'll deal with that, being as you lot are so incapable.'

Agatha set the chair back upright and stood on it to remove the battery. There was a fair bruise building on Dan's left temple.

Deborah turned to Sally.

'Could you have a look at that for Dan, Sally?'

'Sorry, Debs, but I can't see too clearly at the moment. Bit too much self –medication tonight and I would not want to make a mistake.'

Sally at least had the professionalism to admit she was in no fit state to treat anyone that night, so Deborah decided she needed to take charge of the situation.

'Agatha – I have watched you treating the bruises on your arm where you fell. Seemed to have healed quickly. Could you give me some of the ointment and I will deal with Dan.'

Agatha was annoyed that her mother had noticed the homemade poultice she used on her bruises. There was not much either woman did not notice about each other.

'OK, I'll be back in a few minutes.'

316

Agatha returned shortly afterwards with a small plastic soap bag containing raw sheep wool soaked in the mix she had prepared to treat her own bruises. Deborah dabbed the poultice of lanolin and Mothan onto Dan's temples. He began to snivel like a small boy.

'Come on Dan, I am,' she hissed with emphasis, 'not your bloody mother!'

Dan clung to Deborah for a moment before she extricated herself, silently scorning his weakness.

'Now can we have some livelier music, Dan.... and let's get on with the party.'

Dave had noticed the way Dan had clung to Deborah. It had not seemed appropriate. After all Dan had only banged his head, it was not that much of a big deal.

Sally and Erica were relaxing again. They had found some fresh glasses and Sean poured the two women another dram. Gavin cleared up the broken glass and spilt ashtrays and the party atmosphere returned. Dave sat quietly next to the wood stove, lost in thought after seeing Dan's pathetic behaviour with his wife. What was going on? His train of thought was interrupted by Agatha reminding him the fire had nearly gone out. Focusing on the imminent matter of the woodstove, he forgot about the Dan incident and placed more broken pallet wood in the stove and waited for it to catch.

The fire in the stove quickly flared again and with lively music from the old Sony, Erica suggested they got up and danced. Dan groaned but with encouragement from Agatha, agreed to join in. Tables and chairs were pushed to one side to make space for dancing.

'This sounds interesting Erica, what had you I mind?'

Deborah was intrigued. Dave excused himself citing his bad back as an excuse not to dance.

'Back in Edinburgh, I was taught the Black-House Reel. A bit like set dancing but it is just one tight set in a close star formation. It's great fun, I'll teach you!'

So, with Dave sitting by the wood stove watching the proceedings, Erica led the dance. The five women and three men turned eight steps to the right, eight steps to the left turning and whirling till they were all giddy with laughter. Deborah was practically carrying Dan through the dance and Agatha could not help but notice how close Sean and Gavin held Erica and Sally when the music stopped. Being the odd number, Agatha sat down beside her father to wait out the next dance, some kind of techno folk on Dan's phone issued through the old Sony.

'Yeah, let's get down to it...' there was no mistaking Erica's uninhibited intention toward Sean. Sally meanwhile was leading Gavin to the far side of the room, hanging onto his shoulder and audibly whispering into his ear.

'No need for either of us to be alone tonight, is there?'

Though embarrassed, Gavin had to agree that a night with Sally, however drunk they both were, was a better prospect than listening to Sean snoring from the next bed in the dormitory next door.

Sean and Erica were going through some serious grooves while Deborah clapped encouragement to the beat of the music. As a mother she was more than pleased to see her family enjoying themselves like this for the first time since they had left Edinburgh.

As a woman, seeing Erica flirting outrageously with Sean and Sally practically devouring Gavin, she was beginning to feel very jealous. There was no way she could let on there had been anything between her and Dan in present company, though Dan did not look like he would be capable of anything tonight, stoned out of his skull with a lump on his forehead the size of a hen's egg. As for her husband, she just was not interested.

Agatha felt empathy for her father. He had come through so much only to have his dreams dashed by a bad back and hungry sheep. His attempts to feed his family

318

from the land should have supported them, but it didn't look like it was going to happen. Lost in thought and rubbing her bruised leg she was unprepared for her father's outburst.

'1 Corinthians 7:9,10 *Know ye not that the unrighteous shall not inherit the kingdom of God? Be not deceived: neither fornicators, nor idolaters, nor adulterers, nor effeminate, nor abusers of themselves with mankind,*

Nor thieves, nor covetous, nor drunkards, nor revilers, nor extortioners, shall inherit the kingdom of God!'

'Dave, for God's sake that's enough. If you don't like this party, then go home. We'll speak about this tomorrow when you are sober!'

Deborah's temper was up. She was simply not prepared to let her husband's religious mania ruin what had been, until that moment, a surprisingly good evening. Dave instantly felt ashamed of his words but, through his inebriation, also recognized the internal battle taking place for his soul. He had tried to relax and enjoy the evening, but the combination of alcohol and cannabis had unleashed conflicting demons in him once again. Knowing the best thing for all would be for him to leave, he made his way back to the Manse and his bed alternately trying to dispel and accept his drunkenness.

Back in the cottage, Deborah apologized for her husband's outburst.

'Don't worry, let him be. He'll be full of apologies after he's slept it off.'

Sally was pragmatic; she had witnessed alcohol induced outbursts many times before. She began recounting tales of St Kilda under military occupation. Great times when the Puff-Inn would serve until dawn on summer nights, and sometimes beyond. With such short summer nights, the parties would easily run over into the following day.

After privatization, the ex-military drinking culture at St Kilda was less condoned, and the early morning swimming accident had rung the changes. With hindsight she admitted, the accident could have initiated the process leading to military evacuation of the island.

It was shortly after the new borehole had been dug in An Lag that the accident to the young serviceman had happened. A few of the men had blamed the young student girls swimming naked for luring him to the edge; he had been lucky to have survived the fall. Multiple injuries had made it unlikely he would work again, certainly not at St Kilda.

'Alcohol was investigated as the possible cause of the accident but when his blood sample was analysed, it was found to contain high levels of Phenylpropanoid glycosides.'

The listeners had no idea of the medical implication, so Sally continued the modern St Kilda tale.

'His blood contained high levels of a plant derived, water soluble bactericide. He certainly wouldn't have become infected from his wounds, that was for certain. It was a real mystery, but I came to realize I had treated no-one for bacterial infections since that new borehole had been dug. So, I went up to An Lag to have a look and see if there was anything unusual going on.'

She paused, as if for effect.

'With the old well lower down the slope, there was always the risk of dead sheep or their remains getting into the water supply. Now, it seemed, the water was dosed with a naturally occurring antibiotic, but from where? It was a while before the penny dropped; all around the new borehole, the natural depression was covered in blooming Butterwort, the Gaelic Mothan plant used for all manner of Hebridean cures and has a mild psychotropic effect.'

Everyone was now listening.

'It transpires the active glycoside ingredient is readily absorbed by alcohol. Drinking St Kilda water with your whisky would prevent all manner of bacterial disease as well as reducing the effect of hangover. So, when a couple of girls go skinny-dipping and a voyeur gets so excited that he walks off the top of a wall, I was curious. He had even taken his shoes off, just stepped out into thin air above the beach, expecting to walk on water I suppose! He must have been hallucinating. The mystery is the reaction between anti-biotic Butterwort and alcohol. The glycoside mixes readily but does it enhance or reduce the effect of alcohol, or *vice versa*?'

At this point, Dan who had been listening intently, offered his opinion.

'Based on my experience of such things, the effects of alcohol on the human mind are much enhanced by a Mothan mixer. You could be right that it is the other way round though. Try a swig of this and you will understand!'

Dan passed round his hip flask containing vodka infused with fresh leaves of Mothan.

'Picked myself just a couple of days ago from the very spot Sally was talking about.'

'So, what you're saying is that if we drink some of your hooch, it's going to blow our minds then Dan!'

Sean laughed and took a swig from the flask.

'Here, try some of this Gavin. It will make a man of you, my boy.'

Gavin declined, saying he had plenty enough whisky already, on top of the smoke. Spinning beds later was not his idea of fun anymore. Especially as at the end of the evening he felt it was quite likely he would be in Sally's bed and did not want to embarrass himself more than was inevitable under the circumstances.

'Ach well. Even more for us then, Danny boy.'

Dan was not too keen on the boy epithet but grinned sheepishly at the attention he was pleased to receive from the stalkers. Dan was not the only one at the table pleased to receive attention from Sean and Gavin. Deborah had positioned herself on the bench close to Sean and across from Dan. It was as if she wanted Dan to play with the idea that she thought Sean was more of a man than he ever could be. Nothing was said but the body language was fully understood and did nothing to help Dan's feelings of low self-esteem. Sean, however, seemed to have fixed his attention on Erica who, having declined the Mothan laced vodka, was now sitting stoned in the corner at the far side of the woodstove.

'You know something, Erica? You would be quite passable with a bit of makeup, not too much mind. Not like my missus who slaps it on with a trowel!'

Erica collected her thoughts before responding.

'Does it ever occur to you to ask yourself why she slaps it on with a trowel, Sean? Could it be that living with you is just a little bit too much? Could it be that she slaps makeup on, with a trowel, to avoid facing up to the mistake of having married a prat like you?'

Erica's words were measured to hit home. Though stoned, her caustic response was drawn from experience dealing with sexist remarks while working in the bars of Edinburgh. Not visibly chastened,

. Hitting back, Sean remarked on the primitive facilities of her cherished blackhouse.

'Jesus, Erica. How can you live in that place? Even this cottage is better than that blackhouse. It has a decent roof for a start, a proper kitchen and fridge even, if the electricity worked, I would admit. Ha, you will never get a man if he doesn't have a fridge to keep his beer in, eh Gavin?'

Gavin squirmed uncomfortably at being dragged into this conversation which he could sense was straying beyond banter and into the danger zone.

'Don't know Sean, mate. Why don't we change the subject?'

'No, why should I? Our Erica here thinks she's lady muck in her little place up the end of the village. In fact, she is putting the clock back, blocking progress is what I say. If she had her way, we would all go back to run-rig. She has even got rats in there, disgusting!'

Erica looked puzzled at the remark, but Agatha enlightened the group around the table.

'We are not talking about a Skye rock band, Erica. Run-rig was a feudal system of highland agriculture, a system of living really. Each family would be allocated a patch of land to husband for three years before moving onto another patch. That way the good land was shared with the bad. Three years you would have good land while your neighbour farmed a rough patch. Then you would all move on to the next plot. Same thing happened here at St Kilda where run-rig included the bird cliffs. It was a way the landlord made sure his tenants had an equal share of the land and produce.'

'Sounds like musical chairs. When the piper stops you move to a different field or something like that?'

Gavin joined in the banter, but stayed away from sexist comments he could tell the four women around the table were beginning to resent. Not so Sean.

'Run- rig should be brought up to date, I reckon. Out here at St Kilda, it is just what we need. Don't think Dave's up to it. Not tonight anyway and Dan, I don't reckon you are either with the amount of weed you've smoked.'

'Come to the point, Sean.'

Deborah could sense something provocative was coming and wanted to tease it out of him rather than let Sean claim all the credit for risqué entertainment that evening.

'As I see it, there are two functional men in this room and four of you ladies in need of a bit of husbanding. It wouldn't be fair not to share our affections while we are here, would it Gavin? We should reinstate run-rig while we are here and husband you four one night at a time. Not a bad idea if you ask me?'

Deborah could not suppress her smirk but dared not show it in front of her daughters.

'So, it's St Kilda for swingers now, is it?'

Sally saw the funny side but when Sean said he would start by sleeping with Erica that night, Erica exploded.

'Just who the fucking hell do you think you are, coming here with your guns and arrogance. Thought you get an easy shag did you, well think again. Why don't you just get on that Argocat of yours and piss off back where you came from!'

Erica got up and stomped out of the cottage and back to her blackhouse where she locked the door and lay on her futon crib crying tears of anger. Outside the night was calm but wind rose and swirled around her home, making its presence known by blowing back down the stove pipe, reigniting embers, and sending puffs of smoke into the open space of her blackhouse.

'Oh, to hell with this. Sorry if I caused offence but think I need to get out for some fresh air. Must be that bloody Mothan vodka of Dan's.'

Sean went outside and a few minutes later, those remaining at the table heard the engine of the Argocat start up and head away from the village. Sally knew the only route he could take was up the hill toward the top of the island. She said the steep hairpin bends were no place for a drunk driver. It had not been that long ago, after the terrorist attack, when a fatal Land Rover accident claimed the life of the heavy drinking Base Supervisor.

Gavin was also concerned about Sean taking the Argocat out so late.

'What was that about a fatal accident, Sally?'

324

'Well, about a year before the military left, we had a terrorist attack. Yes, even here at St Kilda we were not immune from world events. A bunch of jihadists from the mainland thought, quite rightly, our radar installations were an easy target, though in strategic terms it was nothing more than a nuisance attack.

They chose a Saturday night when everyone would be in the Puff-Inn and they landed in Glen Bay, walked up to the top of the hill, laid their charges, and before you could say *Allah hu Akbar* all our radar and comms equipment was lying in a tangled heap. No one was hurt but as far as the MOD was concerned it was the last straw. They would invest no more money at St Kilda if we were so lax about our own security. There was one later casualty of the attack though.

The Base Supervisor heard the explosions from his room. Though having consumed the best part of a bottle of whisky that evening, he was on duty and felt he ought to find out what was going on. He drove up the hill, saw the carnage and drove down, forgetting to put the Land Rover back into low ratio. He lost control at the bend just above the quarry and rolled it over the edge. He was found in the morning and the Bonxies had already started on him. His face was not a pretty sight when he was lifted from the overturned vehicle.'

'Well, all I can say is Sean is the best off-road driver I have worked with yet. Fingers crossed he will be OK.'

'Amen to that,' said Deborah, concern having replaced her earlier ill-disguised lust for him.

'Moving away from terrorism, one thing that does concern me is the way these sheep are allowed to overpopulate and then die off without any management.'

Gavin was a part-time sheep farmer. His wife looked after their small flock while he was away, but they would never be allowed to starve as these Soays were. If he could not feed his sheep for whatever reason, they would be

325

slaughtered and put in the freezer. As far as he was concerned it was the only right thing to do.

Agatha, who up to that point had been thinking of calling it a night, looked as incensed as her sister had been over sexist remarks from Sean.

'You don't know what you are talking about, Gavin. Let me fill you in so you get the facts straight!'

Gavin did not expect criticism from Agatha after her gregariousness earlier.

'Firstly, the Soays here are wild animals. They are not livestock and the only time we intervene is if we see one seriously injured and put it down. The sheep are part of the island ecosystem, and the carcasses are a valuable nutrient source for scavenging sea birds, the St Kilda Field Mouse, and a host of detritivores. The situation here is unique in the world – where else could students come and study a totally closed flock like we have here? They are not farm animals, Gavin. They are a wild population and a valuable scientific study resource. Secondly, overriding any criticism received, we have a Government license to use these wild sheep for research and education purposes. Is that enough for you?'

Gavin considered his reply.

'That is all very well, Agatha, but don't you feel any concern when you see them dying before your eyes when they run out of winter grazing? There isn't a predator here for God's sake. A wolf or two would at least bring them a quick death rather than drawn-out suffering for the old and sick ones.'

'But Gavin, can't you understand? The pathogens and parasites are predators, even the island weather systems. When the winter gales blow, it is another form of predation.'

'Agatha, all I can say is that whether scientific study objects or farm animals, these sheep are sentient beings and need to be treated with respect.'

'Hmmph! So, you treat the Red deer in the Cairngorms with respect, do you? Drive them from the shelter of the forest into the open snow where you shoot them down. Even allow wealthy gun-nuts to make a botch of the job too, so I heard from Sean.'

Gavin realized that with Agatha, he was not going to make a convincing argument. He had to accept they were both right and they were both wrong and was relieved to hear the Argocat coming back. The sound of the Kohler diesel motor could be heard approaching down the street, technically off-road. Agatha was preparing to give Sean a piece of her mind about ground damage to the fragile island soil ecology but changed her mind when she saw the colour of his face.

Deborah had known better than to intervene when Agatha was lecturing Gavin on the Soay sheep but looked as surprised as Gavin when Sean entered. Sally was sleepy and was quietly waiting for the evening to come to a natural close, but the women were all startled by Sean's appearance when he came through the door.

'Sean, what has happened? Is everything all right?'

Deborah was genuinely concerned. His face the colour of ash, Sean turned to Gavin.

'I have never been so scared, Gavin. You know, I went for a blast on the Cat to clear my head. There is something about this place. It is doing my head in. I gunned it up to the top of the hill, stayed on the road all the way, then switched the motor off and just listened to the silence. Not a gust of wind anywhere. I could hear the munching of sheep from a hundred yards, it was that quiet. I had a smoke before deciding to come back and not be such a party pooper. I was on the way down when it happened.

The hairpins are awesome on that road, bloody awesome. Thankfully, there are crash barriers, or I would not be here now. I am not kidding you but as I approached the first hairpin, a huge white owl flew up out of the rocks and then a blast of wind hit me out of nowhere and if it had not been for the barriers I would have gone over the edge. I tell you, there was not a breath of wind up there. The owl must have known what was coming. That crash barrier is battered, man. I am certainly not the first one to have been blown against it, that's for sure.'

Sally spoke for the first time after listening to Agatha rebuking Gavin.

'Sean, that spot on Mullach Geal is infamous. If you had been there in the daylight, you would have seen the deep wheel ruts in the moor where even the heaviest of vehicles have been forced off road. We had a mobile crane up there to help clear up the mess from the terrorist attack. Fourteen tons it weighed, and even that machine was nearly blown over on the way back down. It took a large tractor and a bulldozer to pull it back onto the road. It was a close thing; I can tell you. You probably heard about the light plane crash recently? That was hit by a blast of wind over the saddle at Mullach Geal.'

Sally recounted some history and myth regarding the flat peat bog above Glen Mór.

'As I expect you know, St Kildans were a superstitious lot and while nominally Christian, like many Hebridean communities, they held to pagan practices where it suited them. The winds at the top of Glen Mór are infamous and they built a small temple to appease whatever deity it was that manifested through these inexplicable blasts of wind.'

Sally hadn't mentioned this aspect of island history before.

'When the Army built the road in the late nineteen-fifties, they just bulldozed the small temple out of the way without realizing its significance. As you come down the hill just below the quarry there is a large rock known as the Milking Stone. The women of St Kilda would tend the cattle in Glen Mór as the menfolk had too many bad experiences down there. The old settlement near the foot of the glen is known as the Amazon's House. Named after a mythical female warrior who would ride out with her hounds across the Hebrides, a Phantom Queen, so the story goes. It has to a very ancient tale as there has not been a land bridge between St Kilda and the Long Island, the Uists, since the last ice-age, ten thousand years ago.'

Sean wasn't particularly interested in a history lesson from Sally.

'Yes, but what's that got to do with me nearly being blown off the road and all the dents in the crash barrier?'

'The dents are where the mobile crane got pushed into the barrier. Must have been some wind to blow fourteen tons off the road. When it is light tomorrow, you two will be out planning the cull but while you are up there, take a look at the southern side of Glen Mór, it is like a scrap yard in places. That is where a Sunderland Flying Boat came down on a training flight in WW2..

Sean let her continue, albeit reluctantly.

'They were on a low flying training mission when the lumbering aircraft came up the glen and was suddenly slammed into the ground. The crew were all killed. It was a queer thing, but you can still see any number of spent machine gun cartridges lying in a rough line along the burn running down the glen. It makes you think the rear gunner was firing at something as they flew by.'

'Probably culling the bloody sheep, I expect!'

Sean had managed to retrieve his boyish grin and sat down to the large malt Gavin poured for him.

'There really was no explanation for that plane crash, or the other two out here that we know about,'

Sally continued to explain about the mysterious plane wrecks at St Kilda. During the war, a Bristol Beaufighter had hit the slopes of Conachair. Just its propellers remained, stuck in the moor as a reminder of the awful event. The main body of the aircraft disappeared over the cliff to lie submerged beneath the highest sea cliff in the

329

British Isles. The third crash was thought to be of a Wellington Bomber on the slopes of Soay, opposite the mouth of Glen Bay and just a stone's throw, or a wind blast, from the Amazon's House.

'I say thought to be a Wellington because it is so mangled no-one really knows. You can see parts of an airframe and a propeller near Taigh Duggan, itself a haunted enough spot on the island of Soay. Nobody has done any in-depth research, but a Wellington did go missing on a training flight around that time. The land is slipping just below the wreckage, and it will not be long before that too is under the waters of the Atlantic.'

Sally recounted that after the accident, the MOD tried to break up and bury the Sunderland to prevent sight-seeing planes coming to the same fate. The military took the threat from these inexplicable gusts of wind very seriously. They did not want any more servicemen lost that way.

'But the wreckage is still in the Glen though?'

'Yes, Sean but it is being gradually blown piece by piece down toward Glen Bay and heavier bits washed down by the burn in spate. Eventually, it will all be out of sight beneath the water and no trace of servicemen left in Glen Mór.'

Agatha was interested in the light plane crash just as they arrived at St Kilda.

'Yes Agatha, that crash fits the picture too. A group of men in a hunting party flying low up the glen when the wind knocked their plane into the ground. Just one survivor and the small aircraft quickly blown over the cliff. Creepy really, how these accidents fit a similar pattern. Male casualties and their machines blown into the sea or soon after.'

'One last question, Sally.'

Deborah was curious about the reference to Taigh Duggan, near the site of the Wellington bomber crash.

330

'It is another St Kilda story from the medieval period. Two robbers were caught thieving from the village after setting the Church on fire with most of the population sheltering inside. One was named Duggan and the other Stallar and as punishment the pair were banished to the outlying islands. Their simple bothies remain to this day. Taigh Duggan on Soay and Taigh Stallar on Boreray. They were exiled from friends and family and would have slowly gone mad from loneliness in clear sight of their former homes.'

'So, the Amazon's House would be Taigh Amazon?'

Agatha was curious about anything to do with Glen Mór, feeling more at home there than anywhere else on the island.

'No, I don't think so.'

Sally thought about the question.

'Amazon's House' is a name imposed by Victorian tourists on an obviously ancient site. The dwellings down there are from a much earlier period than even the medieval blackhouses above this village. If it is to be properly named, I would call it Taigh Cailleach, the home of the Gaelic female deity who ages with the seasons to be reborn each Spring. She symbolizes annual renewal and decay. It is interesting that the one survivor of the Church fire was female and had hidden in the Cailleach's Cave below Ruiaval when the trouble started.'

Sally had a light-bulb moment.

'At least they had minds of their own and survived, but of course, the Temple of the Seasons used to stand at the top of Glen Mór before the army demolished it to make their road. That must have been built there in reverence to the Cailleach. No wonder she is angry with men and their infernal machines! There is another possibility concerning the Phantom Queen myth. Ever heard of The Hounds of the Morrigan?'

'What, Kate Bush?' Deborah had always liked that song.

'No, Deborah. There is a mythical Gaelic female warrior Morrigan who could take the shape of a cow, a wolf, or an eel. A Hebridean Valkyrie by all accounts.'

'Oh, come now, Sally. You will be giving us all nightmares. Let us just be thankful Sean was not hurt tonight and bring the evening to an end. Don't know about you, but I need my bed.'

Deborah was tired and took responsibility for drawing the party to a close. She said she would tidy up in the morning and got up to close the wood stove down for the night. Dan was snoring lightly in the chair beside it.

'Come on sleepy head, time for bed.'

Dan woke blearily before staggering to his feet to walk back to the Featherstore.

'It's in a straight line, he'll be OK,' quipped Agatha.

Sean and Gavin made their way next door to House Two, the dormitory used by conservation volunteers in the past. Deborah and Agatha blew out the oil lamps, closed the door behind them and made their way back to the Manse. Sally followed close behind glancing back toward the dormitory. She would sleep alone as usual that night. She wished the other two goodnight as they passed the Factor's House.

'That Sally can sure tell a yarn, can't she?'

Deborah turned to her youngest daughter.

'Yes, she certainly can, Mom.'

The following morning, Sean and Gavin were up early to begin their recce of the island. They needed to watch the habits of the sheep before deciding on the safest areas to use as killing ground. They wanted to make sure that when the shooting began, there would be no stray bullet or ricochet endangering the village.

Deborah looked out from the kitchen window across the bay toward Ruiaval. The morning light highlighted not only the old lazy bed cultivation lines on Dun but also picked out relief on the headland of Ruiaval. It came as a surprise to her to see the outline of a reclining old woman gazing out to sea. Gazing out to the south, the Cailleach of Ruiaval appeared to be waiting for Spring to return and invigorate her youth. Deborah wondered why she had never noticed the figure in the landscape before, it was certainly big enough.

There was no sign of Dan, nor would there likely to be until early afternoon. He was never an early riser and after a heavy night any appearance before mid-afternoon would be surprising. Agatha had taken herself off with binoculars and notebook as usual and smoke could be seen coming from Erica's blackhouse stovepipe. Sally would no doubt be busying herself in the Factor's House, she always had something to do when Deborah wanted a woman-to-woman conversation about some personal matter. Dave was the worry that morning. He had been fast asleep in bed when Deborah returned after the party but now was nowhere to be seen. She had not even noticed him get up, being so sound asleep herself.

Dave had got up early, still full of remorse for his outburst the previous evening and walked up to the Gap to watch the sun rise over Boreray. He had not exactly got a hangover, he had made sure of drinking plenty of fresh water before going to sleep, but everything around him felt detached, as if he were not there.

Though he knew Boreray was four miles away to the east, the Gannets swirling around the Stacs looked almost close enough to touch. Angels he thought, like Angels, and he reached out toward them.

It was the imperious bleating of a lamb summoning its unconcerned mother that stopped his vision before it could fully develop. The ripples of his hallucination dissipated on the jagged rocks, three hundred feet below him. Dave quickly stepped back from the cliff edge and retched. Had he really been thinking of walking over to join Angels on the Stacs of Boreray?

He remembered reading of the nine men and boys marooned there on a fowling expedition. They had encountered the last Great Auk in the British Isles, possibly the world. Convinced that the penguin sized bird was a witch they had stoned her to death.

'What is wrong with this place? Why such morbid visions, is it heaven or hell I see around me?'

He hadn't noticed Deborah walking up behind him.

'Dave! There you are. I have been looking for you everywhere.'

Deborah had been concerned enough to start looking for her husband. Luckily, she had not got much further than the Factor's House when, through her binoculars, she could see him standing at the Gap.

Standing on the cliff edge above An Lag, she thought him reminiscent of Casper David Friedrich's painting of the *Monk by the Sea*. Dave looked so small in comparison to the environment around him, a lonely figure, standing diminutive before the power of nature. She quickly made her way up to join him.

'Come on, Mr. Monk. Time for breakfast!'

Linking her arm through his, she felt a tender warmth toward him. Something neither had expressed for each other for many weeks. A few minutes later they were back in the village.

Erica and Sally stood chatting over a cup of coffee outside the Factor's House, discussing the previous evening's events.

'Did you just hear the sexist remarks, Sally? It is a wonder I stayed in that room as long as I did.'

'I did, Erica, and that was not the end of it. Agatha had a spat with Gavin over the sheep project later. They really had their horns locked if you would pardon the pun. Animal welfare versus ecology. Gavin reckoned it was a kindness to shoot them when the grazing got low while Agatha was adamant they should be left to die and rot in the interests of the mice and beetles.'

'Well, I guess there will be a lot dying over the next few days, so they'll all be happy, including the mice and beetles.'

'Not me, Sally. I will not be happy till those sexist bastards leave our island.'

Gavin, Erica stated, was as much a sexist as Sean despite his protesting animal welfare. They were two male imposters come to disrupt their renascent island community. Her father was alright, if getting more eccentric by the day and Dan really did not count. He would be off at the earliest opportunity, back to Edinburgh where his bullshit would see him through. There was, she added, simply no more room for male bullshit at St Kilda.

Dave, who had until that moment been lost in his thoughts, commented on what he had just heard.

'Don't be too harsh on them, Erica. You know it's really hard to resist the landscape. Hard to buck patterns and values laid down by those who have gone before you.'

'What do you mean, Dad?'

'If you remember, back in our former lives, I was a Geography lecturer. Landscape was my thing, and you must have heard of the spirit of place, *genius loci* or whatever you want to call it. Think about it, those two stalkers spend all their lives working and living in a nineteenth century field sports landscape. The landscape rubs off on you, there is no escaping its effect.'

The women tolerated the unasked-for lecture.

'Yes, you can rebel but then even rebellion gets appropriated. You might win a protest, but it will always be a pyrrhic victory. They really would find it next to impossible to give up their way of life, it is all encompassing for them. Hunting, shooting, fishing, to quote a cliché, their landscape was made for such predominantly male

335

occupations. Once they become servants of that landscape, disciples if you like, there really is no escape. You brand them as trigger happy sexists which reinforces their self-image, reinforces their landscape. Why don't you try and imagine them as kind, caring intelligent human beings who could support our way of life?'

'Fucking hell, Dad. You really ask too much this time.'

'Then I am sorry, Erica, but that makes you as much a bigot as them in my eyes. You are as much a subject of Utopian feminist landscaping as the stalkers subjects of Highland patriarchy. Surely you can all find some common ground on this sheep problem?'

Deborah was getting hungry and could sense a long-drawn-out argument over gender pros and cons of sheep culling.

'Here endeth the lesson folks! Don't know about you, Dave, but I need my breakfast. Let's go!'

Thinking about what had just been said, Dave spoke the truth about their own situation over breakfast.

'You know Debs, the longer we stay here, the more we will become a part of what is embedded in the St Kilda landscape. No wonder the military guys only stayed here a month at a time and while they were here recreated through alcohol and that huge flat screen TV on the wall of the Puff-Inn. Few had any desire to participate in the landscape beyond the familiar Base.'

Deborah thought of what Sally had said about the water supply. The additional factor of Mothan influencing how they perceived their surroundings. Working as hard as he did, Dave drank copiously from the island's tainted water supply. Was it any wonder he was becoming eccentric?

'You know, Dave. I don't really buy into this landscape stuff where you say our surroundings rub off on us, sounds like some kind of remote social control. I feel a free agent and can wander here mistress of my own destiny. Maybe it is you men who need a structured existence? I would not want to be a pawn in some historical power game.'

She tried to be sympathetic.

' I know the Bible has become important to you, but at the end of the day it was written by men and gives a primarily male perspective on the human condition, doesn't it? What was it, not even two-per cent of biblical tales are narrated by women? Your faith does seem a little too blind at times. Do you ever think how we women feel about being out here? Male dominance is no longer prevalent, and St Kilda is rebalancing away from structured, dare I say proscribed ways of thinking that dominated the nineteenth and twentieth centuries.'

Deborah tried to keep her challenge kind.

'There will be an initial upheaval, but water will find its own level. I am feeling quite at home here now, I didn't think I would. But I came out to support you and the girls. Not much option considering our dire prospects back in Edinburgh. You are becoming a strange man, Dave. Working your body into the ground while you escape changing family reality by disappearing into your private head world. How can I give you courage to come through this change we have embarked on without recourse to scriptures?'

Dave was silent, unresponsive, but his mind was racing looking for a way to answer Deborah's well-meant challenge.

Reaching inside his jacket, Dave produced his pocket Bible.

'I will have to look this up as I cannot remember it off by heart yet – ah, here we are. 2 Corinthians, 5 verses 6 -9 *Therefore we are always confident, knowing that, whilst we are at home in the body, we are absent from the Lord. For we walk by faith, not by sight: We are confident, I say, and willing rather to be absent from the body, and to be present with the Lord. Wherefore we labour, that, whether present or absent, we may be accepted of him.'*

'I am sorry Dave, but you are being evasive as ever. I want you to live among us, not among the lives of ancient misogynists! Get real if you want to be accepted here!'

Deborah's scorn left Dave feeling distanced from his wife. She just did not understand, and he was tired of trying to get her to follow the words of the Lord that would carry them through challenges yet to be faced.

'As I am unable to get through to my dear husband, I will go and check on a man who, after last night's indulgences might actually need, or at least appreciate my help!'

Deborah walked out of the Manse kitchen, slamming the doors behind her, and headed for the Featherstore.

16

Tremors

Sean and Gavin had their Argocat fuelled and loaded up first thing. After breakfast, hey sat together in House One cleaning and checking their rifles before the day's preliminary cull began.

The leftovers from the previous evening still littered the room and residual warmth lingered from the woodstove. In spite of the whisky and smoking the night before, both had relatively clear heads having drunk plenty of water during the night. Gavin did remark on the sense of unreality he felt when he woke that morning.

Lying in bed in House Two, he had heard scurrying of mice through the background sounds of sea and birdlife. Most of the smaller seabirds were leaving the island to migrate out to sea, now the business of raising chicks was done with. The small balls of fluff matured at an amazing rate, fed from rich pickings around the North Atlantic islands. Young Puffins and Petrels left in their thousands when the moon was full.

They always left at night to escape predation, especially from Great Skuas. Agatha made sure to remind Sean and Gavin to extinguish all lights before they retired for the night. Should the moon be hidden by clouds or fog, the inexperienced young birds would head for the nearest light and find themselves in great danger when dawn broke.

Should a Skua attack at sea they instinctively dived to safety. On land this was not possible. Agatha had picked up many a fledgling and kept it safe until dusk when it could be released hungry but eager to resume its life journey on the open sea. So much marine activity was associated with phases of the moon.

'A bit like we females,' she quipped.

'Our energies flow with the tides too, especially out here surrounded by the ocean. We could use the Tide table for family planning, I reckon!'

They engaged in a bit of mutual banter before setting off.

Agatha had walked up to House One to ask the stalkers if they would mind her seeing how they planned and executed the cull.

'That's fine by us, Agatha. But there are a couple of practical issues to consider. Firstly, and foremost, we are using high powered rifles fitted with sound moderators, so we need you to keep well out of the way. You really ought to wear a high visibility jacket, but on second thoughts forget that, as it could spook the sheep. You should just keep well away so as not to distract the sheep while we drive them into killing ground. I do wish we had a couple of dogs; it would make life so much easier.'

'The sheep have never known dogs and would probably just scatter anyway. You need to quietly encourage them to go where you want them.'

Agatha had experience of managing these feral Soays and knew what she was talking about. If you wanted to catch one, then you had to encourage it into a confined space such as a derelict cottage or a cleit. There were over a thousand of these simple stone storage structures on the island, she informed them. Practically one for each sheep.

'Tell you what boys. I'll hide in a cleit then I can watch what is going on through the ventilation gaps and the sheep won't see me. Then if you make a bad shot and the bullet comes my way, I'll be safe inside the stone walls.'

'That's it then, sorted! Get your lunch and jump on the Argocat with us, Agatha. Don't waste your tidal energies walking up the hill now.'

Sean joked with her. He was starting to warm to Dave's youngest daughter after the hostile run in with Erica the night before.

Dave made no attempt to follow Deborah to the Featherstore. He felt past caring. After a few months at St Kilda, his wife was no longer the woman he knew and loved back in Edinburgh.

She had changed in this very different place. He was no fool and considered how the neoclassical landscape of Edinburgh, had quite likely, held their family together.

Out here, in this abandoned place, fragmented cultural remains of the past influenced their lives, not always in a positive way. He had his Bible to guide him through the turmoil, but these women didn't take him seriously. How could he guide them if they increasingly refused to listen?

If Erica was to be believed, they didn't need guidance in rebuilding a balanced community on the island. They needed families and children, and she hoped that when the new tourist season began, they could convince a few able-bodied men to stay with them and help in the procreative process.

'Genesis, neo-Genesis, that's it!'

Dave spoke out loud feeling an arousing mix of emotional pain and pleasure at the thought of his daughters conceiving the new St Kilda. Thank goodness, he thought, Deborah was past all that now with her fiftieth birthday coming up.

It would be good to have a look at the Book of Genesis, to throw a bit of light into the darkness he was feeling since his wife stormed out earlier that morning.

He went into the Kirk and opened the large English language Bible. He had put it back there after realising the rest of the family were not taking his Bible reading seriously enough. Dave had always been attracted to the story of Joseph and his coat of many colours. As a child it had fascinated him. He quickly found the relevant passages in Genesis 37 but then noticed a seemingly more lascivious text in the next chapter which rekindled his bitter-sweet

341

arousal concerning Erica's fecund ambition.

Genesis 38: 2-10, it all seemed to be about the pleasures of sexual infidelity and subsequent angst. Just for good measure the Lord slew you for it afterwards!

The tension inherent in the passages he had just read triggered a lower back spasm forcing him to lie on the Kirk floor in front of the Pulpit. Staring up at the damp-stained ceiling, patterns of light flickered through the south facing window. It was interesting, he thought, that this Kirk was laid out lengthways south to north, but then Dave remembered that was the orientation of all the older buildings and cleits of the village. They had been built at a time when the population respected and lived with the forces of nature, not God quite so much.

No builder in their right mind would have orientated the Kirk east to west as was the usual Christian tradition. Destructive gales blew in from the south-east, through the open mouth of the bay, and all but the modern buildings respected their energy.

Robert Stephenson, of light-house fame had built this Kirk taking the power of nature into account, giving it more credence than the light of God in his design. The Kirk had withstood the elements for over two hundred years while the military complex was crumbling after just fifty. He turned over to get more comfortable, reaching for a kneeling cushion from an adjacent pew to put under his chest.

'Dave! What are you doing on the floor, man?'

Sally stood in the Kirk doorway looking down at the prostrate man in front of her.

'It's my back again, Sal. It just went on me and I'm better lying down for a few minutes until things click back into place.'

'Tell you what, Dave. I think you should come back to the Factor's House with me, and I'll give you a cup of tea and a massage in which ever order you prefer – just like last

342

time, if you like.'

He turned and looked at her, grateful for a gesture of kindness after Deborah's tantrum earlier. Sally's enigmatic smile took his thoughts back to what he had just read about Onan and his brother's wife.

Dave carefully got to his feet. Sally reached down for him and replaced the kneeling cushion on the back of the pew. She linked her arm through his and led him out of the Kirk, closing the heavy black door behind them.

'Better keep the Lamb of God out of the House of God, Dave!'

The pair made their way slowly across the rough pasture toward the Street and the Factor's House. Going inside, Sally sat Dave down at the kitchen table while she set up her massage bench in the living room, across the hallway. She then went back to the kitchen to make them both a cup of tea. The mains water supply still functioned but she wouldn't use it for drinking. Going to the old well near the Kirk would be no fun though the water there was still untainted with nothing but grass growing around it.

'So, Dave. Tell me about it, what happened this morning. When I came into the Kirk you had a face like a ruptured crab.'

Dave managed a grin despite the combination of lower back pain and anxiety.

'It's Deborah, we had a blazing row this morning and she stormed off on me. I think we should follow the words of the Lord, to get us through our time in the wilderness, but she just doesn't understand. He speaks to me, gives me advice. I have worked so hard, rebuilding walls, tilling the land till my back is breaking, literally it seems today.'

He was glad of Sally to confide in that morning.

'She used to support me, bring me food when I was hungry, water when I was thirsty. We would sit and share a glass of water together while I rested from my labours. We'd talk about rebuilding a community here. Not for us,

343

being somewhat past it, but my eldest daughter was talking about encouraging young men to the island to get something going. Talk about having a couple of Sirens on board!'

Sally was expert at teasing out the anxieties of her patients but listening to Dave it wasn't easy to keep a professional distance. As the island nurse, on this trip as on all others, she had tried to keep an objective distance so that anyone could feel safe confiding in her if they so wished. It wasn't always easy; she had her own feelings and needs to consider too. Tea and sympathy were often all they needed as most of the problems she met stemmed from personal relationships. The situation here was no different.

She went outside with her kettle, heading for the water butt. Dave was curious as to why she didn't fill her kettle from the kitchen taps. When she came back, he asked her why.

'It's the water here Dave, I am not keen on drinking it. You'll see black staining in your kettle no doubt. The water supply is rich in some mineral or other, I'm no expert, and it's very soft, acidic water even. I always collect rainwater while I'm out here. I think it is much healthier than water from the ground, however much it is treated. Anyway, what makes you think you are past it, Dave? How old are you, actually?'

Sally knew of course. Dave was fifty-two and his wife forty-eight. They should have been in their prime at St Kilda, away from the stress of struggling to make a living in Edinburgh, but once again she was having to treat psychological problems on the island.

Their alcohol drinking was very modest, compared to the old days when she had to scrape men up off the Puff-Inn floor on occasions. When she had first met Deborah, she seemed a broken woman after losing her senior teaching position. Now after a few months out here she was looking revitalised. Many a forty-eight-year-old on the mainland would give their right arm to look as vibrant as Deborah. It was not surprising she was becoming frustrated with her husband's Bible obsession.

However, it was not for her to become personally involved in the Williams family affairs; she would just be a good councillor and listen without criticising either way. But the thought of Erica seducing young men hit her in the stomach.

Deborah approached the Featherstore and noticed waves lapping gently at the turf above the low cliff edge at the front of the building. It had been New Moon the night before and it hadn't been easy finding her way back to the Manse in the darkness. This Spring tide was the highest she had ever seen, or maybe she had just never noticed how close it reached to the Featherstore, perilously close to Dan's upper storey accommodation.

His flat had probably the best sea views in the Village but was also in the most precarious position when southeast gales blew. Surely, it wouldn't be long before storm driven waves undermined the building to bring an end to the late eighteenth century warehouse. The upper floor flat was a recent conversion to help accommodating increasing numbers of visiting researchers and writers, happy to rough it with the mice.

Banging on the backdoor, Deborah heard Dan's footsteps approaching more confidently now he had paid his debt to Don and Lachie. He was surprisingly buoyant considering the state his head should have been in after the party. Still, plenty of water was always the panacea at such times, and he had known many.

'Hi Debs, what brings you here so early?'

Dan invited her in and to her surprise, the flat seemed in reasonable order. There was an odour of cannabis as usual, but to her surprise had to admit she now quite liked the smell.

'Are you going to make a girl a coffee then, Dan?'

Dan made them both a cup of coffee and they sat in the low armchairs by the window looking out across the bay. Deborah was fascinated by the unusually gentle waves lapping almost to the lower front door of the building. She felt restless and kept shifting her position in the armchair in front of him.

'What's the matter, Debs? Got ants in your pants or something?'

'Yeah, something like that – oh, put that coffee down and come here.'

Dan got up from his old battered, but comfy armchair and went over to Deborah. The coffee Dan had made for her was strong and without milk she needed a glass of water with it.

'Before you sit with me, could I have a glass of water?'

'Sure – how do you take it?'

'In a glass, smart-arse!'

Dan returned with water in a somewhat dull glass. He had yet to learn to wash glasses before greasy plates.

Deborah patted the tattered cushion beside her on the old two seat settee and he sat down beside her. In spite of making efforts to tidy the flat, he hadn't gone as far as a shower that morning. Showers were in reality a stand-up wash and Dan would go outside and wash, pouring water over himself from a large plastic bowl. The lack of hot water meant it didn't happen very often. Once Deborah would have been repulsed by the scent of an unwashed male body but was again surprised that she found it, not to put a too fine word on it, quite arousing.

Sat on the small two seat settee, their thighs pressed together as he sat down next to her. Dan thought, mischievously, that she would be uncomfortable feeling him so close. But he liked the thought that she had come to see him, rarely had anyone else taken the trouble since he had been there. Away from the centre of activity, the Featherstore was out on a limb, as far as social activity was concerned. House One had been where it all happened, until now. He wriggled his hips against Deborah's.

'Come on, budge up, my lady!'

He expected her to at least try to move, even get up and cross to the other chair, but she made no attempt to pull away from him. Instead, she rested her head on his shoulder. He could feel her warmth and instinctively kissed the parting in her thick hair, which she had let down while he got her the glass of water. To his surprise, he could see tears welling in her eyes.

'Sorry about this, Dan. But I need someone to talk to right now.'

'Don't know if I'm really the right person for this – wouldn't Sally be better?'

Deborah was emphatic that he was the one she needed right then.

'No Dan! Sally is not who I need right now. I am absolutely sick and tired of being the wife and mother who holds everything together for the family. What about me and my needs?'

Dan had no experience of this situation. He had known plenty of women, girls really, who would match him at his own games but now, faced with an older woman telling him her problems, he realised he was well out of his depth.

'I have just had a blazing row with Dave. Can't stand his quoting the Bible on just about everything we do and talk about. The Bible is so male orientated, one sided. Worst of all he avoids our own reality by disappearing into the world of Moses and the Promised Land or some other such fucking nonsense. I didn't come to St Kilda to be ignored, Dan.'

Not knowing quite what to do he put his arm around her, prompting sobbing and more tears.

'Just let me get this out, Dan. I need to cry, and I'll be OK in a minute, honest.'

She looked him in the eyes, and he found Deborah's

warmth and emotional release aroused him too.

'Dan, it's been so long. I really would like some closeness; is there anywhere we could lie down?'

'Well, you are straight to the point, Debs! I'll say that for you.'

Outside the high water lapped at the steps of the Featherstore. The Moon was at its closest point to the earth for centuries. Had they known, this perigee brought the Moon to just 330,000 kilometres from the Earth and being so close, the gravitational effects were bound to influence more than tidal ranges.

In the Factor's House, Sally led Dave into the living room and was helping him get undressed for the massage. The last thing he wanted was to have another back spasm while trying to take his socks off. She very professionally stripped him down to his underpants and helped him climb up onto the massage bench.

'That's it, Dave. Lie face down and get comfy. Then I can get to work on you. Are you warm enough?'

Dave nodded and then shivered from the chill of the room. Sally noticed and pulled a spread off her fireside chair and put it over him.

'Just a minute, I'll get the fire going. That will warm us up.'

She put a match to the split pallet wood in the grate which caught at once. Putting a fire guard in front of the spitting blaze she went to the wall cupboard for her massage oil.

'Think I had better warm my hands a little before we get going!'

Sally laughed and in spite of shivering, Dave laughed too.

'That's better, Dave. When was the last time you had a really good laugh? Bet you haven't laughed in months. It's no wonder you're so tense.'

Rubbing her hands together in front of the spitting fire, it wasn't long before the room warmed up. Standing outside her blackhouse, Erica noticed the smoke from the Factor's House chimney and put two and two together after watching Sally helping Dave into her home. Erica hoped the massage would help her troubled father. Sally's massages were the best at St Kilda, she smirked to herself, remembering her own experience on Sally's massage bench.

Although her hands were warm, the fragrant oil took a bit of getting used to. For a brief moment the coldness made his skin pucker as Sally's hands took over, smoothing and caressing his cares away. Dave began to cry, inaudibly at first, then in wracking sobs.

'I am so sorry, Sally. I can't help myself.'

'Dave, that's fine. Just let it out, you'll be all the better for it. Let go, relax. It's what I am here for. You're not the first and you certainly won't be the last one of your family I will be seeing on this bench.'

Dave never thought to ask who the first one was, and Sally wasn't going to tell him. The massage lasted for some ten minutes by which time Dave was relaxed as he was ever going to be. He climbed off the massage bench unaided with Sally beaming at him.

'There, that's you set up for the day. Here put your T-shirt back on before you freeze. The brief flare from the pallet wood had all but died away and the room would soon chill. In his T-shirt and pants, Dave walked over to Sally and hugged her. She could feel his erection pressing against her belly. This she tolerated, it was a common enough reaction from male massage patients, but when he tried to kiss her, she pushed him away.

'Dave, stop that, please! We are friends, but I don't want to encourage anything further. Get dressed now and we'll forget about this.'

Dave turned, his erection still visible and quickly dressed himself. Boundaries had been crossed, that he did realise, but why did this woman reject him?

'Sally, who was the first member of my family to lie on your massage bench?'

'Well, if you must know, it was Erica. She came to me complaining of tension last week and we had a good girl to girl chat before I offered her a massage. She was tense and concerned as to where your family is heading. She was afraid for what the future holds, especially for you Dave unless you drop this, how else can I say it, religious mania.'

Dave was thunderstruck. These women were discussing him behind his back, after all he had done for them. Did all his hard work and sacrifice mean nothing? The effect of the soothing massage was lost in an instant.

'Jezebels! Jezebels the lot of you. Plotting against me, ridiculing me in the eyes of the Lord and now you say you massaged Erica too.. You make me feel sick!'

'Dave, for God's sake!'

'How dare you blaspheme in my presence, Sally?'

Dave spoke words of condemnation about his daughter's massage. That Dave thought she was lesbian frightened Sally in a way she could not have expected. She ran from the Factor's House toward sanctuary with Erica in the blackhouse at the end of the village.

In the Featherstore, Dan was enjoying entertaining Deborah. Having finished her coffee, they shared a glass of his Mothan laced vodka. Not exactly drunk she remembered Sally's comments from the night before, but she certainly felt slightly intoxicated. Whether it was the freedom to express herself as a woman or the effects of the drink, one way or the other she didn't care. She would release herself from the shackles of male dominance and Dave could go hang. She would take what Dan had to offer. She hadn't made love with her husband more than a couple of times since arriving at St Kilda and last time he took her like he owned her. Make love? It was more like he was claiming her, and it had done nothing but make her resentful.

She followed Dan into the small bedroom overlooking the sea. The waves lapped the steps below. By this time Dan had noticed how high the tide was.

'I hope this doesn't happen too often or my house is going to get very damp.'

She considered making a double entendre relating to her own dampness but thought better of it.

'Let's not worry about that Dan. The tide will fall soon enough.'

They sat down on his single bed and Deborah pulled Dan down to lie beside her and in spite of his accepting the likelihood of the two of them getting into bed together earlier, she could read his concern.

'Debs, I am not sure about this. What if Dave finds... '

She smothered his words with an enthusiastic kiss, her tongue quickly seeking and finding his. Her hand was already on his strong erection and working to make it stronger.

'I haven't even got a condom, Debs. This is madness.'

His voice was a husky whisper even though the bedroom was a good two hundred yards from the Manse.

'Dave won't ever know, Dan, and I don't really care. I just want you, now!'

She was strong woman and heavier built than the youthful bodied Dan. He didn't object as she took control by pulling down his jeans and underpants. Quickly stepping out of her own jeans and knickers she left her own upper garments on, the warm jumper a protection against the chill from the sea below. She returned to the bed and straddled him. Seeing Deborah naked from the waist down, Dan knew as had Dave a few hundred yards away, that boundaries were being crossed and it scared him. There

351

could be no going back, and they were both running with wetness as she lowered herself on to him.

'Be careful Deborah. Remember I have no condom. I don't want to come.'

She looked down to him and smiled.

'Don't you worry, just relax and let me do the work. Anyway, I am forty-eight, you're not going to make me pregnant.'

Deborah began to ride him, gently at first. His hands resting on her buttocks following rather than guiding her movements. She felt him stiffen and swell as he neared climax. Taking his arms from her buttocks she held them down against the bed cover and sat down on him hard, all the way. Dan could feel her rhythmic grip holding him inside her. He was powerless to stop what was happening. He wanted to pull out and put an end to this madness, but she was heavier and stronger than him, and she was in control. He had never known an orgasm like it. The spasms seemed to go on for ever but when he finally subsided, she lay down beside him, her wetness against his thigh. She pulled the bed cover over them both and snuggled up to him.

'My man, my man....'

Deborah murmured something about finding her man at last before closing her eyes and letting out a short snore. Dave took his chance and quickly got off the bed and pulled his jeans and pants from around his ankles. He was soaking wet and worryingly he noticed his groin area was not only wet but coloured by Deborah's light menstruation. She was still fertile in spite of her suggesting otherwise.

'Bloody hell, Deborah! You've used me, you wanted to get pregnant didn't you. What am I, just a sperm bank?'

She woke contented and looked him square in the eyes.

'Something like that my love, something like that. Don't worry about it, consider it an honour that I chose you. You have just fathered the first child to be born on St Kilda in a

352

hundred years.'

A slight tremor went through the building, rattling Dan's crockery and empty bottles. Outside the calm waters of the Village Bay shivered. A few loose rocks clattered down from the scree above as Agatha lowered her binoculars, which she had trained on the Featherstore window. She had seen it all from the Hidey-Hole in the rocks beneath Mullach Sgar. Agatha was intrigued to see the tide retreating quickly and further than normal exposing the rocks below the Featherstore faster than the Turnstones could follow in their quest for food pickings.

The volcanic archipelago of St Kilda sits at the very edge of the European continental shelf and, off the west coast of Soay, nearly a million tons of seabed had detached and slid into the abyss. Just half a mile from the foot of Glen Bay the sea is 900 feet deep and, as Agatha had commented before, was a prime setting for earthquake and tsunami. This perigee super-moon was having a tectonic effect, pulling at continental plates as well as the ocean and those that dwelled near it.

Dave asked Sally directly if she was lesbian and corrupting his daughter behind his back. Erica had only just suggested the idea of recruiting young men to help rebuild the community, and she didn't mean just wall building.

Was this female intrigue to make fools of men? He needed advice and resorted once more to the large Bible in the Kirk.

He found Leviticus 18 advised on sexual mores. In particular should there be male homosexuality or female bestiality the land would be defiled, and in Verse 25, he read *the land itself vomiteth out her inhabitants*. In Genesis 19, there was condemnation of male homosexuality in the cities of Sodom and Gomorrah and in 1 Corinthians 6: 9 condemnations of male effeminacy and self-abuse. Despite searching the scripts, it was hard to find advice about female homosexuality.

Deborah's earlier scolding sunk in, but he was determined to find advice for women somewhere in the Bible. The advice of Paul the Apostle to the Romans cleared things up for him. In Romans 1: 22-32 he read that those who saw God in nature, served creatures rather than their Creator which led to homosexuality in both sexes.

Abandoned and lustful behaviour would become acceptable norms, even murder could be acceptable in the service of nature.

If they only worshipped the Lord, he would protect them. Erica and Sally were breaking God's divine rules if, as he now suspected they were lying with each other.

Agatha, in the service of nature rather than God was unforgiveable and 'worthy of death'! It was, he felt sure, only a matter of time before this island vomited out its vile inhabitants. The Bible said so.

The sudden pain in his lower back made him cry out and grip the pulpit for support. In his pain, Dave saw the cold, damp and the empty Kirk for what it was. Simply a tourist attraction, the collection boxes funding nature conservation, rather than God's work. It seemed that at St Kilda the Lord had left, washed his hands of them all.

Nature conservation had turned the island, their new home, into a Godless void. He had seen Angels circling around the Stacs. The Lord was still to be found across the water at Boreray and was waiting to welcome Dave Williams, his faithful servant.

Erica burst into Sally's blackhouse, startling her as she sat by her stove with a mug of tea.

'Sally, whatever is up with you?'

Erica was concerned, she had never seen Sally lose her composure like this. Normally a very private woman, this time it was Sally who needed to talk.

'It's your Dad, Erica. I know it's not a professional thing

to say, but I think he's losing it. He was as jealous as hell when I told him I'd given you a massage last week. He's got it into his head there's something going on between us.'

Erica managed tried to suppress the hint of a blush by pulling up her collar, but not before Sally noticed her reaction. She quickly dismissed Erica's blush but had to admit to herself that massaging Erica had been far more pleasing than soothing her father.

'I found him in the Kirk, poring over that old Bible again. His back is in a terrible state, he's working himself into the ground and becoming embittered at his physical limitations. You know, when I had finished the massage, he even made a pass at me. I ask you... ?'

Erica couldn't suppress her laughter at the thought. Sally looked perplexed.

'My Dad, making a pass at you? I don't believe it! What about Mum?'

'From what I am picking up, I don't things have been too good between them lately. Not since Dave started his Bible-bashing.'

Erica poured Sally a coffee which was gratefully received. She dragged over the old milking stool Erica had found in the old workshop and sat down near her friend. Feeling better, she apologized for bursting in.

'Sorry about rushing in without knocking, Erica. I know you don't like it, but I was scared. Dave had such a look in his eyes, he looked like a man prepared to kill me. I have picked up the pieces after many a bar brawl out here, but never seen a look like his before. If I had seen such a thing in the old days, I would have recommended removal from the island as a matter of urgency.'

'Well Don and Lachie are leaving tonight – do you think he would go with them?'

Erica doubted her father would leave the island. It was his dream project, and he would not and probably could not, she thought, walk away from it now.

Dave had found a broom behind the Kirk door and used it as a makeshift crutch to ease the pressure on his lower back. He carefully limped back to the Manse where he thought he had some anti-inflammatory pain killers left. Slowly crossing in front of the derelict Base he noticed Deborah in conversation with Don and Lachie at the top of the old slipway leading down to the jetty.

'I've been talking with Dan, and he'd like to get off the island when you leave. Is there some way we can arrange this between us.'

Dan was desperate to leave after his experience with Deborah that morning. He didn't trust Deborah not to tell Dave about it in a fit of anger, even as a calculated snub to her husband. Quite simply he did not want to be around when Dave found out.

Neither Dan nor Deborah could guess the informant would be Agatha who had been watching the pair from the Hidey-Hole hundreds of yards away. The deep trench in the scree had secreted St Kildans in the seventeenth and eighteenth centuries when North African slavers roamed as far as Iceland. Deborah would also be glad to have Dan out of the way now he had fulfilled what she needed from him. She felt certain she had conceived as the tide turned that morning.

'Tell you what, Debs. We'll take him back for £100 and we'll even give him a lift to Stornoway and put him on the ferry to the mainland. How about that?'

Dan was a businessman, but he would always help out where he could. We are not in a rush, so I don't mind tying up here another night. Then we can set off in the morning. If anyone else wants to leave I can take them too. The stalkers reckon a week to complete the cull, so we won't be gone for long. Any fresh supplies you need, just let us know before we sail, and we'll bring them when we come back.

'We don't want you back, you pair of sodomites!'

Dave limped across to join the three of them chatting at

the slipway.

'Excuse me, Dave. What are you on about?'

Lachie wasn't quite sure if Dave was joking or not, but he sounded serious enough.

'You two, didn't want to come to the party, didn't want to sleep in the cottages but wanted to sleep together in that boat of yours, didn't you? Leviticus 18: 22 *Though shalt not lie with mankind, as with womankind: it is an abomination.*'

'Dave, I hope your joking because if not you had better explain yourself!'

Dan had begun to realise that Dave was being deadly serious. He thought that because they slept together in bunks on board, they must be homosexual.

'Dave, I carry and will carry all sorts on my boat be they gay, straight, pink, black or white or any combination of the same. Money needs no categorisation. What I don't and will not carry is bigotry. Now I am a Sabbatarian and a follower of the Free Church and don't work on Sundays, if I can avoid it. That's as far as it goes. So, I do respect the words of the Lord, and I'll pretend I didn't hear the words you just spoke. For the record Lachie, with all his good youthful looks, reserves himself for the girls of Stornoway, not middle-aged men like you and me.'

Don reached out and put his arm around Dave's shoulder.

'Come on Dave, lighten up. It's not easy being out here and you have done better than most would have under the circumstances.'

Dave slowly and deliberately removed Don's arm from his shoulder to see Erica approaching. She was walking toward him, and it was obvious she wanted to speak to him in private.

'Dad, can you come over here a minute? I have something to talk about in private with you.'

The relationship between Erica and her father had

always been one of mutual respect and if anyone could convince him to take a break from the island, she could.

'Dad, Sally came to me and told me what happened. We both care about you and think your religion is getting the better of you. We know you mean well but wouldn't it be better if you left the island for a short while. Just a week until Dan and Lachie come back for the stalkers. It will help you get things in perspective, and we'll all be a lot better for it. Right now, you frighten us.'

'What, leave the island so you can get on with your Godless nature conservation and debauchery without me?'

'Well, Dad, debauchery would be a fine thing. But we will get on with nature conservation by culling the sheep while you rest up in Stornoway. You'll come back a new man with a manageable flock. Best of all you will be able to work your garden in peace.'

'Romans 1: 30-32 *Backbiters, haters of God, despiteful, proud, boasters, inventors of evil things, disobedient to parents.* That's what my family have come to. To think I brought you here to save you from, what can I say? Hell, yes, the hell that is now Edinburgh. There are Angels here if you would only see them. Open your eyes before it is too late. Remember what Luke said about the prodigal son, Erica. Return to the ways of the Lord and you will be forgiven.'

Deborah had heard the end of the conversation with Erica and hissed at Dave.

'Always the Lord, the sons, isn't it? Why not tell us a story about the Lady, the daughters instead of being so fucking androcentric. We don't need you anymore. Just get on that boat with Dan in the morning. Do us all a favour and fuck off, why don't you!'

'Mum, you are not helping. What's got into you?'

'I'll tell you what's got into me, Erica. I have had enough of my life being dominated by men. At the school I worked for a man who fired me and out here I work for a man who doesn't give a damn about anything except his precious Lord. Men are only any good for one thing in my opinion, the rest we women can do for ourselves!'

Deborah pushed Dave away from her and he slipped at the top of the uneven stone path and fell heavily. The improvised crutch snapping under his weight. Deborah turned away from him, not offering to help.

'You make me sick, Dave. Bloody, fucking sick!'

Don and Lachie stood appalled at the domestic violence.. Don went to help Dave to his feet.

'Best keep away from her for a while, I reckon, Dave. Come and join us on the boat until Dan sorts himself out and we'll put you in the Featherstore while Debs cools off. Don't know what on Earth has made her like this.'

Don and Lachie helped Dave down to the *Beluga*. The tide was falling fast, and it was with some difficulty that they got him down the iron ladder onto the boat. The three men went inside the well apportioned cabin interior. Dave was at once fascinated by the high-tech navigation equipment and frankly amazed at how comfortable it was on board.

The hardships of St Kilda were going to be left behind for a few hours. Don and Lachie had forgiven Dave for his earlier outburst, they weren't one to hold grudges except when it came to unpaid debts, as Dan had found out. As soon as the debt was paid the grudge was forgotten. They were like that.

It was warm inside the *Beluga* and Dave felt at home with a mug of tea in his hands. Biscuits were passed around and the radio played softly in the background. Some kind of Gaelic country and western by the sound of it. He couldn't understand a word, but the music was good after the hostile silences he had endured in the Manse lately. Lachie produced a bottle of whisky usually reserved as a treat for the passengers. It wasn't for nothing they won awards for their Hebridean hospitality.

'We've got bottled water here if you want it, all the way from the Co-op. You don't want to be spoiling your whisky with tainted water from the island!'

Agatha had also been watching the goings on at the top of the jetty slipway. She had seen her mother push her father and the subsequent fall. Now he was on board with Don and Lachie he would be alright for a while. Unlike Erica, she didn't wear her heart on her sleeve, but when it came to their father, but she didn't like to see him hurt and humiliated like this. Now it was time she joined Sean and Gavin for a ride up the hill in the Argocat and get the sheep cull underway.

17

The Cull

With Gavin and Agatha aboard, Sean drove the loaded Argocat uphill to the T-junction on the ridge above the village. Beyond, the ground dropped steeply into Glen Mór. The sea was as calm as the air that morning, there was barely a breath of wind, and it looked like it was going to be one of the rare St Kilda days when midges would be a nuisance. Sean selected the lower gear ratios and manoeuvred the machine across two hundred yards of moor before coming to the worn-down turf dyke delineating extent of the former grazing area. He switched the engine off and all three stood for a moment taking in the view and the silence.

Beyond Glen Bay, they could see the cliffs of Soay, beneath which they heard seals calling. On such a day as this sound would carry for miles. About two thirds down the glen, to the left and slightly raised in the moorland they could see the lochan at Arigh Mohr.

This small body of water was the only natural freshwater pool on the island and, in recent years, completely taken over by Great Skuas for bathing and socialising. Those who worked on the island had nick-named it the Bonxie Pond. Woe betide any other seabird with the audacity to alight on this pool.

The burn running down the centre of glen was littered with broken aluminium wreckage from the WW2 Sunderland flying. The trail of spent cartridges had mostly disappeared into the boggy ground alongside the stream, though from time to time a few would wash up after a wet spell. To their right, Gavin could see a line of cleits abruptly ending before the ground dropped into the glen. He was curious and asked Agatha about them.

'Cleits were generally built by the men of the island. They didn't want to build any further, but if you look further down into the glen you can see remains of older structures.'

Agatha pointed out the enigmatic dwellings that even the archaeologists couldn't really explain. They described these ruins as horned structures. Three stone beehive cells in a triskel layout enclosed within a horseshoe shaped wall. The horns of the wall extended out from the two outer beehive cells with a narrow entrance way where they almost met. Effectively a gated enclosure around the small dwellings.

Sean reckoned he had seen similar structures before while he was in the army serving in central Africa.

'No, Sean. They are unique to St Kilda, it's one of the reasons we were designated a World Heritage Site.'

Agatha was adamant but Sean was unconvinced.

'Ah, but you haven't been where I have. We were trying, somewhat unsuccessfully, to control Islamist insurgents in the north of Cameroon, near the Chad border and we raided compounds just like these. The villagers knew trouble was coming and while they lay hidden in the small conical huts their sheep and goats were corralled inside the horseshoe shaped walls. Just a narrow gateway between the horns of the wall, as you can see here.'

'Well, I won't argue with you, Sean. I've never been there myself, so I'll take your word for it.'

Gavin had been studying the glen below them through his binoculars.

'Agatha, there's one of those horned structures, as you call them, that looks in pretty good condition. Pretty much as Sean just described he had seen in Cameroon. Why is that?'

'That will be the Amazon's House. It is the only one of these structures that has been restored. Even the turf roof is in good condition. Seems the sheep know better than to get up and wreck that roof.'

Agatha knew there was something special about that building, not because it had been restored but by the way the sheep behaved around it. If she hadn't been scientifically trained she would say they were showing deference. They trashed every other turf roof they could climb onto.

'That's interesting, it looks like the tide has come way up over there. Much higher than at Village Bay.'

Agatha had noticed a strand line on the turf at the foot of the glen.

'The tide must have risen 30 foot yesterday, blimey! Hey, it must have been a tsunami. I thought there had been a small earthquake when I was up in the scree and rocks started falling. There must have been an underwater landslip, and a section of seabed shifted and tipped over the continental shelf. That would account for a tsunami alright.'

She omitted to tell the two men what she had been observing from the Hidey-Hole. The ground had certainly shifted in the Featherstore that morning, she thought.

'Enough, enough, let's get to work.'

Sean was impatient to start the business of the day. While the other two discussed archaeology and the tsunami, he had been studying the ground beneath them.

The Glen was a U-shaped glaciated valley so if they fired from the centre the ground rose in front of them in three directions. If they shot toward the sea, the bullets would fall harmlessly enough. They would have to conceal themselves though. He thought the horned structures would be pretty good places to shoot from. The sheep wouldn't know what hit them and, with sound moderators on their rifles, they wouldn't hear much either.

The three of them got back onto the Argocat and Sean carefully drove through an opening in the Turf Dyke eroded by years of sheep hooves. They had to hang on as the eight-wheeled vehicle negotiated the steep concave slope into the glen. Just as the ground levelled out a white Snowy Owl flew up from a ruined cleit, one of the few built from stone found beside the burn.

'That's the bugger that put the shite up me last night!'

'Language, Sean, please!'

Agatha was serious, but Sean thought she was just teasing him.

'We're not in church, you know!'

No, not in church she thought but in this place he could at least show some respect for Her.

'I reckon that one will do, Sean.'

Gavin pointed out one of the horned structures with its corral walls virtually intact. They could shoot safely in any direction, as long as no one came walking through the glen, which was highly unlikely.

Sean gave Agatha a large shiny whistle which he used when refereeing Youth Club football matches back home.

'You hide yourself over there in that other compound and if you see anyone coming, give a good blast on the whistle and we'll know to stop firing, OK?'

Agatha was OK, and quite looking forward to seeing how the sheep reacted. They never showed any interest when one of their own died from natural causes, just continued grazing around the body.

'We've never shot sheep before, so we don't know how the flock will react. Just have to see how it goes.'

The Soays had scattered as the Argocat came down the glen. They had never seen a vehicle of any type driven off road before but were settling down to graze again on the north side of the valley. That was good, Gavin had said. The sheep would be well lit by the sunshine from the south and clearly visible. Shooting into the sun was next to impossible with telescopic sights.

Agatha walked over to the adjacent compound and

settled herself in. No problem with wind or rain but there were the Skuas to contend with. They were getting interested in what was going on in their nesting territory. Due to Bonxie attack men rarely ventured into the glen and never on their own. She waved back to the Sean and Gavin, indicating that she was safely in her watching place, and they could begin the cull.

The rifles were unpacked from their slips and magazines loaded. The sound moderators had been left on as the stalkers had not wanted to recalibrate the sights each time they used the rifles. They would just have to consider range and windage. As there was no wind to contend with at all, it should be an easy job. They had their sights set for around 100 yards as they didn't want to shoot beyond that range and risk not getting a clean kill; through the heart or better still a head shot.

Resting his rifle on the compound wall, Gavin was preparing to take aim on a brown ewe with a creamy belly about fifty yards in front of him. A sudden rush of air passed his head as the crosshairs settled just behind her shoulder. A heart shot was preferable to a head shot, less chance of missing but not so good if you wanted to butcher the carcase afterwards. The Skua twisted and turned above him and came in for a second pass. This time it put its feet out and gave the stalker a hefty slap on the head.

'For fuck's sake!'

Gavin stood up cursing and reached for his cap, folded up in his jacket pocket. The incident caused Sean some merriment until exactly the same happened to him. The sheep grazed unconcerned.

'Hey Agatha, can you do something about these fuckers? They are really pissing us off!'

Agatha called back, explaining that that was what Bonxies did. Nothing she could do about it. They were at St Kilda now, so they would have to get used to it.

Grumbling the two stalkers tried again, settling down

in the compound after taking Agatha's advice to extend a walking pole fully above their heads. The Skuas were wary of careering into the poles and kept their distance but were still making aggressive passes over the heads of the two stalkers.

'OK, pal, let's try again, shall we?'

Sean wanted to make a good job of this cull. Making a botch of culling sheep wouldn't look too good on his record. Taking aim on a three-year-old tup, he made absolutely sure of a clean head shot at no more than 50 yards. There was absolutely no wind to consider and as the cross hairs came down onto the unsuspecting rams head, focussed just in front of the ears. Sean held his breath and squeezed the trigger.

The sound of the bullet hitting the ram's head was louder than the report of the silenced rifle, but to Sean's horror he saw the animal run away, gouts of blood pouring from where its nostrils should have been. Even as close as 50 yards, all he had managed to do was badly injure the beast. He ran out from behind the compound wall to follow and finish off the ram but was knocked to the ground by a sudden blast of wind. Before he got back to his feet a second bullet hit the ram behind its left shoulder and the animal dropped. Gavin had seen the botched shot and while Sean was safely on the ground he put an end to the ram's suffering.

'Christ! I thought you two were professionals. Even my dad is a better shot than you, Sean!'

'It's the bloody wind out here, it came from nowhere. There are no trees; you can't see the leaves moving to warn you.'

'Well, I am not hanging around to see you two make a botch of this. Either shoot them cleanly or not at all. You are going to have to do better than this if you're going to cull the flock around the village.'

Agatha was incensed and stormed off, heading back up

the glen toward the village. She turned right at the Turf Dyke and followed its line until she took cover among cleits near the Lover's Stone. The rock overhanging the southern cliffs of the island was a favourite haunt of hers and from this position she could look down unseen onto whatever Sean and Gavin would do next.

The shooting of the tup had made a group of ewes and lambs uneasy, and they herded themselves through the narrow entrance of the Amazon's House corral. It was if they were seeking sanctuary but the reason, so Sea and Gavin thought was to shelter from the gusting winds that could certainly now be felt if not seen blowing around the foot of Glen Mór. The stalkers looked at each other.

'You thinking what I'm thinking, Gavin?'

'Yep, let's get it over with.'

They started the engine of the Argocat and very gently drove it across the rough turf and blocked the entrance to the restored Amazon's House compound. Once again they picked up their rifles and rested them on the Argocat body and aimed them into the compound. For the restless sheep there was no way out over these high restored walls. They instinctively resisted escaping into the unknown darkness of the stone chambers which might have saved them.

The Skuas retuned with a vengeance. They had teamed up, as they always did when faced with a determined intruder and rained one blow after another on the heads of the stalkers who had left their walking poles in the ruined compound across the glen.

'Fuck this for a lark!'

Sean had had enough and reached into the rifle box of the Argocat. He pulled out the pump action 12 bore shotgun and fitted its ready loaded 14 round magazine.

Firing at the circling Bonxies, one after the other fell injured or dead around the Amazon's House walls. The sound of repeated shotgun firing echoed around the glen and only when the fourteenth shell was fired did the echoes of gunfire die away.

Agatha watched the slaughter of Skuas with horror. Not only for the violent deaths of so many protected birds but also in the knowledge of the tragedy that would inevitably follow.

The remaining Skuas retreated to watch from safety on the higher slopes of Mullach Bi. They were intelligent birds and knew that their attacks would be no match for the Sean's shotgun. They also went to ground like this before high winds made flight impossible.

When Sean began firing at the Skuas, the trapped sheep panicked and all but one escaped from the enclosure. One last elderly ewe lay on the ground, panting with fear. She expired as Gavin walked over to her.

'Well, that was bloody clever Sean. Now they have all escaped. Gone round the corner toward the promontory below Mullach Mhor where you had your fright last night.'

Gavin was not impressed at the unprofessional way Sean had managed things so far but sought a way to save face for both of them.

'Tell you what, Sean, why don't you load that blunderbuss of yours with buckshot, we have plenty in the ammo box. I'll drive the Argo, and we can try and herd them into a corner. They are bound to run now so rifles won't be much good but with oo-SG buckshot you should be able to bring them down without making too much of a mess of it.

Running toward the promontory of Gob na h-Àirde, the sheep would arrive on a relatively level and open acreage of rough pasture. They would have 360-degree vision but on the narrow headland they could also be trapped.

Gavin knew that and zig-zagged the Argocat like a sheep dog working its flock. The sheep huddled together at the end of the level ground, beyond which lay the path to the Tunnel, a sea cave open at both ends which ran beneath them.

The Tunnel was home to hundreds of seals and countless nesting Guillemots whose raucous chatter gave the cave a prehistoric atmosphere during breeding season. As they came within 25 yards of the huddled flock Gavin gave Sean the signal to begin firing.

From her vantage point near the Lover's Stone, Agatha could not see what was happening on the promontory but again the sound of repeated firing horrified her. The air in the glen was clear and still, yet she sensed movement among the rocks off the path to the Cambir, the other headland across from Glen Bay.

The sound of firing ceased for a few seconds while Sean reloaded his magazine. Then it began again. Whether it was the toughness of these feral sheep or their wool that absorbed kinetic energy from the buckshot, many sheep were being injured rather than killed outright. Agatha saw one older ewe limping badly and coughing painfully as she attempted to lead younger and more inexperienced sheep to safety.

She watched as the Argocat come round the corner of the hill and saw Sean blasting the group with his pump action shotgun. They staggered and fell but through her binoculars, Agatha could see that many of the sheep were left lying badly injured. She ran toward the slaughter in a vain attempt to try and stop it. Gavin and Sean were enjoying this now, roaring round in their off-road vehicle shooting at anything that moved. A blood lust had taken them over, as Agatha was to recount later.

The whirlwind, a djinn, as the Islamic saboteurs would have called it, blew down from the Cambir and headed across Glen Bay to where the cull was taking place. Agatha had no idea of the size or power of the spinning wind until it crossed the bay. The column of water must have been one hundred and fifty feet high, at least twenty feet across and it was heading straight for the Argocat, now at the neck of the headland.

At the last moment Gavin saw it coming and tried to outrun the wind as it made landfall. Approaching the edge of the cliff above the northern end of the Tunnel, like the sheep they had been shooting, he had no room to manoeuvre.

'For fucks sake, Gavin! What are you doing?'

Sean had dropped his shotgun and was hanging onto the Argocat for his life as Gavin raced the machine across the rough ground along the cliff edge. Left and right he drove but the spinning vortex matched his every move before suddenly hurling its energy onto the vehicle and its occupants.

The machine was picked up and thrown high into the air. Gavin fell from the driver's seat while Sean hug on grimly to the anti-roll bar as the Argocat smashed into the cliff below Conachair. Agatha had stopped and stood both amazed and terrified at what she was witnessing.

No-one would ever descend the 1200-foot cliff to retrieve either Sean or the machine that lay smashed on top of him. She could see Gavin's body lying on the turf at the edge of the promontory. There was a chance he had survived the fall, but she had to see to the sheep first.

Many sheep lay dead on the rough pasture, some with terrible wounds. Some were still alive but with shattered limbs and blood-stained fleeces. As she surveyed the awful scene, the spinning column of water returned, noticeably smaller with much of its energy spent. It circled around her before turning right along the cliff path to a small stone walled enclosure built by St Kildans centuries previously. The vortex shrank further before disappearing with a hiss into a rocky cleft within the improvised enclosure. Agatha heard the wind dissipate into hidden caves beneath her and apart from the breathing of the Atlantic, all was still and quiet once more.

When she found a sheep injured but alive she lifted its head and, with her razor-sharp pocketknife, deftly slit its throat. The sheep died quickly and humanely as she had been trained when working as a volunteer shepherd. When she came to Gavin he was lying in an unnatural position. Even though he was still breathing, his spine was obviously broken. Gavin was barely conscious as Agatha lifted his head and slit his throat.

Gavin's blood poured onto the turf to mingle with that of the slaughtered sheep. He died just as quickly and humanely, she considered.

Rather than have to explain the circumstances of Gavin's death as any different to Sean's, Agatha dragged his lifeless body to the cliff edge and tipped it over. They worked together and they died together, that would be her story. The trail of blood to the cliff edge would soon be washed away by rain and salt spray. As his body hit the water two hundred feet below a great sigh, almost thankful Agatha thought, came from the crevice in the rock where she had seen the misty vortex disappear.

Agatha walked back along the strip of coastal pasture, took a drink at the Well of Virtues, Brighid's Well as it used to be known, then continued until she came to the burn of Glen Mór. There she squatted to wash the blood off her hands and pocketknife. She spotted a suitable stone at the stream's edge and honed the blade to its previous sharpness.

When it came to dispatching injured sheep, she wanted death to be as quick and painless as possible. With traces of blood removed she began the long climb out of the glen toward the ridge road. Agatha did not follow the tracks of the Argocat, where the three of them had driven down earlier. She felt an instinctive resistance to following in the tracks of a machine complicit in the morning's slaughter. As the ground began to rise in front of her she bore left, heading for the point where the line of cleits from Mullach Geal terminated. From experience she knew it was the least exhausting route out. Once in the glen there was no easy

371

way back to the village.

There was no urgency to for her to return. The stalkers were gone and the sheep grazing peacefully again. It always surprised her how quickly they got over traumatic events. The right attitude, she thought.

Looking back, she could see the remaining Skuas had settled back on the small lochan, bathing contentedly. There still being no wind, she decided to return via the summit of Conachair. The views across to Boreray would be impressive that day and with the sea so calm there was good chance of seeing whales too.

At the S-bends she saw the dents in the crash barrier. Heavy dents where large machinery had hit it, and she saw the olive-green scuff marks where the small Argocat had scraped along the steel guard rail the night before. The Snowy Owl was often seen near this place, but she doubted it would return for several days after the commotion in the glen earlier. The owl had probably sought refuge on Soay, though it would return once it got hungry. The oversized St Kilda Field Mice were a satisfactory substitute for the owl's normal diet of arctic Lemmings.

Continuing along the road toward the defunct radar station at Mullach Mhor, it was the silence that struck her the most. Up here at around 1000 feet above sea level there was always a slight breeze, it was never totally still at the top of the hill and in the past there been the sound of wind in the wires to guide walkers in the mist. Now the mast and its supporting wire cables lay in a tangled heap to the right of the buildings.

In a way, she thought, it was lucky the mast hadn't fallen down into the glen. The wind must have blown uphill and sent it crashing toward the Base. Turning right toward the short slope to the summit, Agatha crossed the last worked peat beds on the island. It was easy to imagine why the community here failed in the end.

She didn't count the military community as such, with ten men for every woman at best, it couldn't be considered anything more than a male colony.

She imagined the hardship of trying to keep warm and be able to cook meals dependant on walking to the top of a 1000-foot hill to carry peats back down again. The fuel was dried in the line of cleits along the ridge before being carried down in creels to the village.

Once soldiers arrived here during the First World War, the young St Kildans heard of an easier life and began to question the hardships of their island life. It had been a Spartan existence and one in which only the fittest survived. Charles Darwin had been right.

It would be like that again when the new community was established, they would follow the islands rules and only the fit would survive. It was good that, historically, more girl babies survived tetanus than boys. Only the fittest would survive into manhood to fulfil their limited purpose.

The Bonxies of Mullach Mhor watched her as she climbed the slope to the summit. This tribe of Skuas had not been involved in the mayhem below. They had their own territory to defend and would fight off the invader when a member from another group entered their nesting ground. They were known to be cannibal when the opportunity presented itself, and if it hadn't been for the bounty of newly dead sheep to feast on, the Glen Mór Skuas would have dined on their fallen comrades.

Standing at the summit, the light breeze from the west rustled her thick dark hair. Looking across at Boreray and the Stacs, the whiteness of the gannet colony shone out, millions of white birds and their droppings reflecting the mid-day sunshine. Such whiteness and purity compared strikingly with the rusting tangle of metal, broken glass and concrete lying on the moor behind her.

It had been hot work climbing to the summit and she took a drink from her water-bottle, filled in the Manse earlier that morning. The day was barely half-way through, yet so much had happened.

Gannets swirled around Boreray as usual, some breaking off to fly in tight lines toward their distant feeding grounds, tired stragglers being picked off by Bonxies. Survival of the fittest again she thought. Agatha's gaze followed the line of the cliff path down to the Gap and was surprised to see her father standing at the edge and like her appeared to be gazing out toward Boreray. Patches of white flowered heather lined the path as she made her way down the steep slope toward him.

'Hi Dad, what brings you up here? Your back must be a lot easier today.'

'Hello Agatha, I could ask the same of you. Aren't you supposed to be over in the glen helping with the cull? I heard all the shooting, but it stopped a while ago. Did it go alright?'

'Yes, Dad. There are a lot of dead sheep down there.'

Agatha decided not to give her father any more detail about what had actually occurred in Glen Mór that morning and asked him about the night before.

'I had a great time with Don and Lachie. I slept on their boat; I mean really slept for the first time in weeks. Just being off the island by a few feet made such a difference. To be honest I was glad to get away from your mother for a night too. I think it does us all good to have a break sometimes. They are such a good pair, those two and to think I got so wound up about them.'

He had forgotten she had not been present at the altercation at the top of the slipway when Deborah had pushed him, but Agatha knew exactly what he was talking about.

'I believe Dan is leaving with them tonight. Then the Featherstore will be free, and I think I'll move myself in there and leave the Manse to you girls, eh? We prophets need time to ourselves, don't you think?'

Dave was making a small joke at his own expense and Agatha appreciated that. He had been a good father to her but now had the good sense to voluntarily stand aside. Smiling at him, she thought it was good he jumped before he had to be pushed.

'Erica suggested I went off with Dan, but I feel so much better now.

I'll stay and do my bit, whatever I can until my back recovers properly.'

Gazing out toward Boreray they both marvelled at the whiteness of the Stacs that afternoon.

'There are Angels there, Agatha. That's where we need to be, not on this god forsaken island, if you'll pardon the expression.'

'Yes, Dad. I do believe you're right!'

Agatha linked arms with her father and the pair made their way back to the village. At the bottom of An Lag, Agatha told her father she'd leave him to make his own way back from there as she needed to go and speak to Erica.

Knocking on the door of Erica's blackhouse, she entered to join her sister at the table.

'Sit down, Agatha. All over in the glen for today, is it?'

'Yes, that's what I wanted to talk to you about.'

There would be no mention of her slaughtering Gavin but obviously something had to be done. If she had her way she would have let things be. Nature had taken its course and the fittest survived. She began to relate what had happened and when she told Erica how Sean had blasted the Skuas as they tried to defend their territory, her sister's face noticeably darkened. Then chasing the sheep in the Argocat and making a complete hash of culling them and how she had to intervene to put so many out of their suffering.

'Where are they now, Agatha?'

Erica was intending to have them off the island that very evening regardless of what Dave or anybody else thought. Murdering male bastards had no place on their island and she told her sister exactly what she thought.

'I agree, Erica. They are gone now and won't come back.'

'What do you mean, now?'

Agatha related the outcome of the cull as she wanted it understood. In their bloodlust the two stalkers had driven too close to the cliff edge at the back of the Tunnel. There had been one of those inexplicable gusts of wind which had picked up the Argocat and thrown it against the rock face. Both men and their machine were now at the bottom of the sea.'

'Where the crabs can feast on them for all I care!'

Erica was outraged but realised the men would be missed at the end of the day when they failed to return.

'We'd better let Mum know about this; she'll have to let that Josephine woman, back at the Trust, know what's happened.'

The sisters walked through the village to give Deborah the news. They had agreed not to let Dave know first, as they were unsure of his reaction. The last thing either wanted was a Biblical rant doubtless connected to lambs of God and divine wrath. Deborah was the level-headed parent at the moment. Agatha again remained silent on what she knew about her mother's seduction of Dan.

Erica and Agatha walked into the Manse and found Deborah in a surprisingly jovial mood.

'You'd better sit down, Mum. There's been an accident.'

Deborah knew it couldn't be Dave. He was outside showing a renewed interest in the walled garden. Agatha explained what had happened near the Tunnel. It was a long and hard walk there and back and Deborah had only been there once just shortly after the family arrived on the island. Her knowledge of the topography was sketchy.

'You are saying the Argocat was blown off the cliff edge. Agatha, are you sure they are dead?'

376

'Absolutely Mum. They stood no chance and retrieving them will be next to impossible. It wouldn't surprise me if the currents down there have taken them over the edge of the continental shelf. They could be lying under 1000 feet of water by now.'

'I'll go and have a word with Don and Lachie and see if they have any ideas on what to do.'

The sisters followed her down to the jetty where she found Don checking the fuel filters of *Beluga's* twin diesel engines. We have just helped ourselves to some diesel and there might be a bit of water in it after all these months. We don't want to break down on the way back.

'Don, we need your help. There's been an accident, and we think the stalkers are probably dead. The Argocat was blown over the cliff above the Tunnel and there's no sign of either them or the machine. Do you think you could take us round there in the boat to see if we can do anything?'

Don let out his breath in a hiss and looked pale. He called Lachie up from inside the boat.

'We are going to have to go around to the Tunnel, Sean and Gavin have gone over the cliff.'

'Bloody hell, do you think they are alright?'

'I doubt it, they are probably dead by now. There is a problem Deborah. The currents off that headland are treacherous and I don't want to risk damaging the boat on the rocks. The tide races through the tunnel and if the charts are to be believed a channel has been scoured all the way to the continental shelf. Anything or anyone falling in there would be swept into the abyss well before we had time to get round there.'

This was just what Agatha wanted to hear. Erica didn't show undue concern either.

'What we need to do now is go out beyond the mouth of Village Bay and call the Coastguard and let them deal with it. I can't call from here because the VHF signal is blocked by the Oiseval hill."

Dan with years of local experience knew they had to sail out from the bay to be able to call out. He invited the three women to come with him, Agatha in particular would have to give an eyewitness account of what had happened.

Lachie issued the women with life jackets and untied the mooring ropes. Don reversed the *Beluga* out from the jetty before turning and heading out toward the small island of Levenish at the mouth of the bay.

'Got to be careful with shallow rocks round here, we don't want to be joining the stalker boys just yet, do we?'

Don's graveyard humour didn't seem out of place. Hebridean boatmen faced death every working day, if their passengers only knew. So many uncharted rocks around the islands and ferocious tidal races to contend with. In some conditions a malevolent wind blew against the tides in shallow seas creating columns of angry water that since time immemorial had been known as the Blue Men, waiting to drown unwary sailors.

Don didn't think that after several hours the accident constituted an emergency so called the newly reopened Stornoway coastguard office on their working VHF Channel 67.

'Stornoway Coastguard, Stornoway Coastguard. This MV *Beluga*.'

The call was sent twice and once he had finished his tea, the duty operator answered the routine transmission.

'MV *Beluga*, MV *Beluga*. Stornoway Coastguard, how can we be of assistance Don.'

'Ah, yes Andy. We have an incident at St Kilda to report. I'll pass you over to the young lady here who can tell you all about it.'

Agatha winced at the condescension but took the handset from Don and proceeded to tell Andy, the duty coastguard operator what had happened. Andy knew the waters as well as Don and agreed the stalkers would have stood no chance. There was no point in sending the helicopter out from Aberdeen as there would be no-one to pick up dead or alive.

He would pass the matter on to the Police and all he could suggest was that the Health and Safety Executive might want to visit, as it was technically a workplace accident. Don shook his head, it was highly unlikely HSE would come out so far to investigate what was obviously just a tragic accident, no more.

Agatha's statement should suffice and considering the currents, Sean and Gavin would be listed as lost, presumed dead at sea. It would be up to the Western Isles Trust to inform their families and look into their own safe systems of work should stalkers be employed at St Kilda in the future.

Once the call to the coastguard was finished, Don turned the *Beluga* around and headed back to the jetty. They tied up and Agatha was asked to remind Dan to be down at the jetty with everything he wanted to take no later than 0800. As before, Don and Lachie opted to stay on board rather than brave the still frosty atmosphere in the Manse.

Sitting round the table that evening the family discussed the traumatic events of the day. Dave had returned from the Gap, still convinced of the existence of Angels on Boreray, but opted not to share this belief with Deborah who was still visibly shaken by the accident.

'One moment they are here, those young guys, and the next they are gone.'

'But Mum, they got it all wrong. It was complete mayhem down there. Something got into them, bloodlust maybe, but they were driving round like lunatics on that machine firing at anything that moved. I'm glad they told me to keep well out of the way. There were so many injured sheep that I had to dispatch afterwards.'

Agatha explained most of what happened in a clinical, dispassionate way.

379

Erica was less restrained.

'The bastards, if I had seen them firing buckshot willy-nilly like that I would have taken our own rifle and put a stop to it. A pity you didn't dispatch them as well, Agatha.'

'Now then girls, *Vengeance is mine said the Lord.* I agree it was a botched cull so what we will have to do in the future is somehow keep them out of the village area. Up on the hill and over in the glen, they are a good food resource for us. Just not in the vegetable gardens I'm planning.'

Dave was trying to remain pragmatic over the incident.

'You could try just asking them to keep out?'

Agatha was being sarcastic but thought to herself that when the time was right she would go down to the glen and ask for the sheep to be kept out of the vegetable gardens.

'So, what's Dan up to tonight, then?'

Dave had been aware that Dan was planning to leave in the morning. Erica said she had seen him sweeping dust out of the Featherstore and having a general clean up. Although he was planning to move in there himself he hadn't been aware Deborah had been thinking the same.

As far as she was concerned, their marriage was over and she didn't want Dave sleeping under the same roof, let alone in the same bed as her. She would tolerate his presence for just one more night. Erica knew from the earlier conversation with Sally that all was not well between her parents but tactfully kept the knowledge to herself that evening. She suggested they should invite Dan over for a last drink before he set off in the morning.

'I don't think that's a very good idea, Erica. He'll want to get himself sorted out and if he gets drinking he won't be able to get his act together in the morning.'

The last thing Deborah wanted was for Dan to mess up her plans now. Agatha remained   impassive, now was not the right time to let on what she had seen from the Hidey-Hole.

'Well, if it is all right with you miserable lot, I'll go over to the Featherstore later and be sociable with him.'

Erica knew nothing of Deborah's seduction and simply expected Dan would be glad of some company for his final night on the island. After the meal was cleared away, Erica went back to her blackhouse, lit the woodstove then walked back to the Featherstore to find Dan. When she got there, she was amazed how spotlessly clean the apartment was. Dan was still scrubbing at some stubborn dirt in the corner of the sea-facing bedroom.

'Blimey, Dan! What's come over you? You'll lose your credibility as the island slob if you keep this up.'

Dan looked up.

'Just a minute, Erica. Let me finish this corner then I'll be with you.'

'I just wondered if you'd like to come over to the blackhouse for a drink. Hey, have you eaten tonight?'

'Er, no, not yet. Actually, I would like to come over to yours, Erica. There's just been too much stuff going on around here today. I need somewhere to chill for a bit.'

'Come on then, put the dusters away and I'll make you some supper.'

The two of them walked along the weed strewn seafront road to the fire pond and followed the burn up to the end of the Street and Erica's blackhouse. Standing outside for a moment, Dan took a long glace across the bay toward the *Beluga* tied up alongside the jetty. This was his last night on the island.

Last night on this island of crazy women, he thought to himself. But still Erica was alright, the least crazy of the lot of them. He followed Erica inside and sat down beside the warm woodstove. What a luxury after the cold Featherstore. It would still be appalling in there next winter and apart from damp and cold, he badly needed to get away from Deborah.

'Aye. I'll be off with Dan and Lachie tomorrow. I heard all the shooting, did the start of the cull go well? Mutton for you lot and I'm going to miss it!'

It never occurred to Erica that, being so busy cleaning the Featherstore before he left, Dan might not have heard about the accident.

'Oh God, Dan. Don't suppose anyone's let you know. There was an accident down in the glen. Sean and Gavin were lost.'

'Lost? What do you mean, Erica?'

'I didn't see it myself, so I only have Agatha's word for it. She was down there with them. In the frenzy of chasing sheep, the Argocat went over the cliff. Don and Lachie reckon they have been swept out and over the edge of the continental shelf. We won't even find their bodies.'

Dan was dumbstruck. All he had been thinking about was his being used by Deborah and then dumped. These men, great guys in his opinion, had been killed and he had been the last to know. Didn't anyone here even think to tell him, was he so insignificant here.

In the grand scale of things, his being shagged by Deborah was insignificant compared with this accident, he knew that but still couldn't bring himself to engage with much more than his own hurt.

'Isn't there anything we can do?'

'It's been done, Dan. Agatha was the only eyewitness, and she spoke to the coastguard from the *Beluga*. They had to go to the mouth of the bay to make the call, you might have seen them go out for a short while.

'Yeah, I thought maybe they had gone fishing or something.'

'Apparently the coastguard reckons there's nothing can be done either, other than fill in reports when the time comes. The Trust will no doubt have some serious paperwork to do but as far as we are concerned it was a tragic accident, like all the others in Glen Mór.'

Erica spared him her hope that the crabs would have a good feed over the next few days, passed him a can of

Tennent's and went to make them a sandwich.

'Afraid, I am still on mutton from the sheep that dad shot. When I get round to it, I'll make a smoker. Then I can cure the odd leg of mutton and hang it up, really ethnic or what?'

Dan was a little surprised at Erica's levity following the accident but accepted that there was nothing any of them could have done. If anyone should be upset, it should be Agatha. Having witnessed the event, she seemed the coolest of all. Of all the women on the island, she was the most unfathomable, he concluded.

'Is your sister OK? I mean she must have seen everything.'

'Oh, don't you worry about her. It's just another ecological event as far as she's concerned. Men, guns and machines; testosterone mixed with sudden releases of kinetic and fossil energy as far as Agatha is concerned. She will be fine, like water off a duck's back to her. She'll be more concerned about the Skuas they killed at the start of the carnage.'

Dan had to admit to Erica that he thought killing Skuas might not have been such a bad thing. They always attacked him each time he tried to go into the glen to plan his, now abandoned, guided walks program. He had given up any desire to venture further than the line of cleits on the northern side of Glen Mór.

'Think I'd better forget you said that Dan, before we fall out over it. The plan, as I understand it, is find a way of keeping the sheep out of the vegetable gardens while using them as a meat resource. Agatha thinks she knows a way to do it but isn't really letting on. She thinks she can draw on some kind of divine support. Fuck! She sound's as crazy as Dad sometimes. What is this family all about?'

What indeed? Dan thought and, thank fuck, he would be away from them all in the morning.

There was a knock on the door and Sally stepped into

the open blackhouse. While listening to Dan, talking as he ate his sandwich, Erica had lit a couple of hurricane lamps placed in alcoves she had built into the wall. In spite of the low energy LED lights, she preferred the ambience from the oil lamps.

'My, what a cosy scene I see before me, got room for a *ménage à trois* or is this a private party?'

'Don't you bloody start, Sally! Anyway, to what do we owe this dubious pleasure?'

'*Du Vin, du Pain, du Boursin* my girl. Can I join the party?'

Erica looked at her vaguely, not recognising the reference to an old television advert for a popular French cheese.

'Sit yourself down but keep your hands off Dan, he's mine tonight. Poor bloke didn't know about the accident till just now. Bit of a shock to lose a couple of mates like that.'

Dan was shocked, but also at the flippant way they dealt with the deaths of Sean and Gavin. A couple of men die, oh well there'll be more along soon. It was scary that life out here in the North Atlantic, well male life at least, seemed cheap to these women. Erica produced three more cans of date expired lager, and they sat down to chat.

'How are you feeling now, Sal? After Dad's little *faux pas* this morning?'

'Oh, I'm OK now. Just a bit worrying at the time.'

Dan was looking puzzled, so Erica thought to explain another event he had missed that morning.

'Dan, you are off tomorrow but I must ask you to keep this to yourself, alright?'

Dad nodded his agreement. Whatever was about to be revealed would go no further than the three of them.

'Well, as you know Dave is struggling with lower back pain and Sally gave him a massage to ease things for him.'

She looked at Sally in a conspiratorial way before proceeding.

'So, after Dave had his massage, he gets up nimble as you like and makes a grab for Sally dressed in no more than his underpants.'

Here she couldn't contain her giggle.

'And apparently, he had an erection like a flagpole!'

The two women fell about collapsing in giggles at the thought of the ever so pious Dave damn near erupting out of his boxers. Even Dan had to laugh with them, it was so preposterous.

'Come on Dan, your turn now. Tell us a joke!'

Sally was in a good mood and wanted to forget about the unpleasant events of the day as soon as possible. Dan decided against telling jokes, most of his once large repertoire long forgotten since arriving at St Kilda. There hadn't been much, if anything, to joke about lately, as far he was concerned.

'Well ladies, there is one thing........'

'Yes..... ? Come on Dan you can tell us, can't he Erica!'

'Actually, Dave isn't the only one who's been making passes where they shouldn't have been made.'

Dan was getting into his element with the two women waiting for him to divulge his juicy secret. He paused for effect before telling them about his morning with Deborah.

'You're telling me that after making Dave's life a misery, she went over to the Featherstore and shagged the living daylights out of you! You are kidding us, not Deborah as well?'

'Yes, there was no stopping her. I didn't have a say in the matter, she just took me.'

'Dear, oh dear young man. What's up with that family, what are they like! A couple of latent swingers by the sound of it. They ought to lighten up a bit with all this free love going on. So, who's Agatha shagging when she goes off down Glen Mór for the day, ha, ha?'

Sally and Dan were having fun recounting their wayward adventures with Dave and Deborah Williams, but

Erica was failing to see the funny side.

'Hang on a minute, you two. It's my parents you're having a laugh about. Okay, it may be a bit ludicrous to think of Dad losing the plot in his underpants but Mum, making a lot more than just a pass at you Dan, is downright revolting.'

Erica got up and began pacing the room thumping her fists on any available surface.

'It's just not funny, Dan. How do think it makes me feel to think of my mother and .... you! You are a man, like it or not, and you could have said no. Just say no! We were all taught that at school, and you let her make a complete fool of herself. Why didn't you say no, Dan?'

'It wasn't like that, please believe me. It wasn't something I wanted, she made me do it.'

'Oh, yeah, right! Blame my mother now, why don't you. Christ, you are such a pathetic weakling Dan! Go on, just fuck off out of my house and make sure you're on that boat in the morning and don't come back!'

Sally tried to sooth things in the blackhouse by speaking to Erica as Dan got up to leave.

'Hey you two, that's enough. It's hard enough out here without falling out with each other. Erica, at the end of the day they were two consenting adults. I didn't consent to what your father had in mind, it's me who should be up in arms not you.'

'Well, if you'll excuse me I'll get my sorry male head out of here and leave you to argue amongst yourselves. Jesus, I have had enough of this place. Two great guys got killed this morning, I don't give a toss who's shagging who and neither should you. Good night!'

Dan had had enough and mild natured as he was, his temper was close to snapping. Getting away from the island and its crazy inhabitants would be the best move he could make.

Erica had had enough too.

'Sally, if you don't mind, could you just go as well, please? I've really had enough for one day. It's really nothing you've done or said, I just need some space tonight, alright?'

Sally finished her beer and got up to leave.

'See you tomorrow, Erica? Sleep well.'

With Dan back in the Featherstore and Sally in the Factor's House, Erica collected her thoughts on the day's events. She could smirk at her father's behaviour, but not her mother's. Dan was kind of, well, her friend if not her actual lover. Now that could never happen and after he was gone, the only man left on the island would be her father. She did like Sally and sensed things could develop with her, but it wasn't what she wanted. She decided a smoke would calm her nerves and rolled a spliff from grass she had bought from Lachie. Taking it outside, she sat on the low windbreak wall in front of her rounded cottage and lit up.

It was peaceful in Village Bay that evening. Just a slow gentle swell breaking quietly on the beach. The distant call of seals could be heard coming from the Dun gap. A bit like dogs she thought, but their howls were nowhere near as lonely sounding. The grass was doing her good, apart from the dryness in her throat.

She fetched a glass of water from the bucket she had filled at the well where Agatha had tripped over. Normally she would have drunk rainwater but had run out until the weather broke. They had had surprisingly little rain so far that year.

She couldn't be quite sure when she first noticed it but there seemed to be some commotion in the Dun gap. Erica could hear the song of the seals turn into disgruntled barking and growling as they were sprayed with cold seawater while dozing on the flat rocks.

A vortex, a column of water was spinning between Dun and Hirta and edging into Village Bay. Slowly exhaling, she watched as the waterspout appeared to try and cause as

387

little disturbance as possible to the dozing seals. The light was fading but it was still possible to see the animals look up, grumble and settle down again.

The spray spun across the bay before hesitating in front of the Featherstore. It then curled around the end of the jetty and Erica saw Don quickly go to the aft of the *Beluga* and lash down his inflatable tender. As if satisfied with the men's preparations to leave the island, the spinning water-devil followed the curve of the beach before disappearing into the half-submerged Cailleach's Cave below Ruiaval.

Erica rubbed her eyes and pinched out her joint to save it for another time. She really felt dry and finished off her glass of well-water before drinking another straight off. Had she really seen a water-devil on such a quiet night? When strong winds blew down from the hill they could be expected or in Glen Bay at almost any time, but here on a tranquil evening in Village Bay, she must be imagining things. It was time to hit the sack and start afresh in the morning.

Dan had his belongings down on the jetty before Don and Lachie had barely surfaced.

'You're keen, alright. Anyone would think you'd had enough of this island!'

Inscrutable as ever, Don didn't miss much, and he had long sensed Dan's wish to get away from the island. He had factored this into the leverage regarding the unpaid debt earlier. Now he was pretty eager to get away himself. The business of the two stalkers was unsettling.

There was really nothing any of them could have done after such an accident, which was the hard part about it for him. To simply write off two men's lives could never be easy, though he thought it strange that Agatha, who had witnessed the event, seemed totally unmoved. She was very matter of fact about it. These women were an odd bunch, no wonder Dan was eager to get away.

Dan was invited on-board for coffee and waited while

the other two ate their breakfast. He felt hungry watching them eat bacon sandwiches and asked if he could make himself one. He hadn't wanted to make breakfast in the Featherstore after spending so much time cleaning the kitchen area. He had been determined to leave a good impression when he left but had no idea that Dave would be living there after he left.

While the *Beluga* was readied to sail back to Leverburgh, Don left Lachie in charge and walked up to the Manse to say goodbye and arrange a time for their next visit to St Kilda. Knocking on the door, he went in without waiting and found a frosty atmosphere between Dave and Deborah. They both looked up and Dave was the first to speak.

'Ah, good morning, Don. So, you are off then?'

'Aye, yes. I wanted to arrange a date to come back with you before we leave. Dan's on-board already so we can get off promptly. So, when would you like us back?'

Deborah spoke this time.

'Dan I think if you came back next week sometime that would suit us.'

'Next week! Isn't that a bit soon?'

Dave couldn't see the urgency. He had no idea of his wife's plans to send him away. Deborah had made her mind up that, apart from their struggling marriage, he would be better away from the island for his own, and their daughters' sanity.

'Yes, Dan. Come back in a week's time. I'll email you if there is any change of plan.'

'OK then, good job you can still crank up that generator. You ought to get yourself another satellite handset in case one day it doesn't start. I could get you one and bring it over next week, if you like.'

Having no practical knowledge of things mechanical, Deborah agreed it would be a good idea. As much as she respected her daughters' practical abilities, she didn't think they extended to fixing the generator. It would be better to have some way of contacting the outside world if push came to shove.

'I'll let you know how much you owe me when I come back, okay?'

Don was eager to get back to the boat and set off so said his goodbyes to Dave and Deborah, then left the Manse for the jetty. Lachie had already warmed up the engines which ticked over, burbling, waiting for him to take charge and open the throttles for the trip back. Don untied the mooring ropes and stepped on board to take the controls from Lachie.

Though more than capable, Lachie handed control of the boat to Don who, as well as being his personal friend, owned the boat and paid his wages. Twin propellers reversed, churning the water and pulled the *Beluga* away from the jetty before Don pushed both throttle levers forward, turned the boat and headed out toward the mouth of the bay. With a change in the weather coming, the boat left the relative calm of Village Bay and began to rise and fall on the increasing swell.

'Sea's running from the north-west, Dan. Hope you are a good sailor!'

Lachie was joking with Dan who was already failing to see the funny side of the boat's rolling motion as it crossed the swell.

'You'll live, man. They all reckon it's worse on the way out to St Kilda.'

18

Revelation

With Dan out of the way, Dave thought Deborah was blooming. He hadn't seen her so bright and positive for a long time. The atmosphere in the Manse had improved beyond recognition and he had begun to think that all would be well with their venture to resettle the island. He still kept up his Bible readings which appeared to be tolerated by the women around him, even appreciated by his youngest daughter.

It never occurred to him that, apart from Agatha, they were being considered a harmless irrelevance. Dave was using biblical scriptures to underpin his position as island patriarch. Agatha had other ideas.

The *Beluga* had been gone two days when Agatha chose her moment. It came as the family sat down for their evening meal. Dave had finished his short reading and started a more general conversation about the day of the stalkers' accident.

'That day even started oddly, we were bickering with each other, and I had a murderous bad back.'

'And you made a fool of yourself with Sally, so I heard!'

Deborah had heard the gossip and thought it a good moment to embarrass Dave in front of his daughters.

Dave's feelings of optimism evaporated in an instant. He felt the ground shift beneath him as his wife made his foolish pass at Sally known to all. What Deborah hadn't allowed for was that his daughters already knew and while not condoning his behaviour, though it understandable given the circumstances.

'Mum, Dad had a terrible bad back and went to seek help from Sally while you were occupied in the Featherstore. Isn't that right?'

Agatha met her mother's surprised expression with calculated full eye contact.

'You've told us about Dad, now are you going to tell us what you were up to with Dan that extraordinary morning?'

Deborah was on the defensive. No-one was eating, waiting for her to answer. She looked at Erica and at once understood her eldest daughter already knew what had been happening in the Featherstore.

'But.... how did you know?'

She was genuinely shocked that the whole family seemed to know about her affair with Dan. All except Dave who looked thunderstruck as the implication behind his wife's obvious discomfort wormed inside him.'

'How did we know what! What has been going on behind my back, Deborah?'

'While you were having your back seen to, Dad, she was busy shagging the daylights out of Dan!'

Erica could barely disguise the disgust she felt for her mother. As far as Erica was concerned, her father was a special, if damaged, man and worthy of at least some respect from his wife. She had seen enough family breakdown in Edinburgh, now it was happening here. Agatha sat back, a small smile quivering around her mouth. It was going just as she had planned.

'I think your God might have forsaken you somewhat, Dad. What does the Bible say about unfaithful wives, then?'

Dave was put on the spot in front of the women. It seemed his daughters held some grudging support for him in his predicament and it would be good if he could remain magnanimous, however hard that might be.

'Dan was a foolish young man to allow himself to be used like that. Proverbs 7 describes a *young man void of understanding who was forced by the flattering of her lips*

392

to go to her as an ox goeth to the slaughter, or as a fool to the correction of the stocks.'

'Yes,' Agatha continued.

'I have been reading that bit too, Dad. It also says, *for she hath cast down many wounded; yea, many strong men have been slain by her. Her house is the way to hell, going down to the chambers of death.'*

Erica was as surprised as her father at her sister's knowledge of the scriptures. In an attempt to diffuse the situation, she tried to introduce some levity.

'As a fool to the correction of the stocks. It sounds like the fool was the one who went to Sally's massage parlour if you ask me!'

Erica thought carefully before continuing.

'But, Mum, why did you do it? Why risk our family for a few hours of pleasure with that, what can I say, *young man void of understanding.'*

She had wanted to say with that complete prat but thought to humour her father if possible.

Dave remained silent for a while waiting for his own moment. A decision had to be made, he knew, but one that did not make him look any more foolish than he already felt. Deborah was waiting for the outburst of rage she felt must surely follow but it appeared Dave was expressing empathy with Dan.

'I'll refer to Proverbs again. Chapter 6, verse 32, *But whoso committeth adultery with a woman lacketh understanding: he that doeth it destroyeth his own soul.'*

It was Deborah who exploded.

'Damn the lot of you, you're all on his side. Dave, we have hardly made love since we got here and now it's all my fault!'

Looking at her daughters.

'Christ, he has sympathy with Dan who at least managed to treat me like a man should! And you Agatha, why have you been reading that patriarchal garbage?'

'I hope the blasphemy made you feel better, Deborah. I am glad that Agatha has chosen to read and gain some understanding from the scriptures. Erica, I feel would make a good Quaker but you Deborah could do no better than pick up the Bible yourself.'

'Jesus, if I pick that book up at all, it will be to throw it into the cess pit where it belongs.'

Deborah was past caring, it seemed they were all against her but at least she had known, if not exactly love, she had known physical affection not just pie in the sky twaddle about Gods and Goddesses.

Dave had come to a partial decision and explained that he would go and stay in the Featherstore for a few days and think things through in peace. Erica had her blackhouse retreat and that would just leave Deborah and Agatha to share hostility in the Manse. The meal was hastily finished, they still needed to eat, before arrangements for separate accommodation were finalised.

Agatha went to her bedroom early, giving the appearance of wanting to keep away from her mother. In reality, she couldn't have cared less about what was going through her mother's mind that evening.

Dave was grateful that Dan had left the Featherstore apartment in a clean and tidy condition before he left. If anything, he was relieved to be on his own where he could dream unchallenged.

Deborah knew, instinctively, that it would be a waste of time trying to talk anything through with Agatha. Was she really her own daughter behaving like, well like some kind of family psychopath when it came to things emotional?

Talking to Erica would be a waste of time for much simpler reasons. Her eldest daughter had branded her with shame. Tearfully she realised the only woman she could talk to was Sally and made her way over to the Factor's House.

'Don't beat yourself up too much over it, Deborah. This island has a strange effect on women at the best of times. I've seen it before when the young lasses used to come out on conservation holidays. Away from the social constraints of the mainland there was no stopping them and the guys working here weren't going to say no were they?'

Sally explained powerful effects of the ocean, the moon and tides had on everyone, especially women visiting the island for the first time. Their bodies had to acclimatize to a raw power of nature rarely met in modern life.

'It's your age too, Debs. You're approaching the end of your fertility, and it is quite common for women of your age to go off the rails a bit and have one last fling. Think yourself lucky you are married to Dave. A lot of divorces happen in middle age due to lack of male understanding of what their wives are biologically experiencing. From what you have told me, it sounds like he is more concerned about the effect you had on Dan. Bloody loved every minute, if I know young men!'

They both laughed at this, though Deborah knew that for Dan it was a little more complicated.

'Well, it's too late for the morning-after pill but I ought to give you a pregnancy test sooner rather than later.'

'You think that's a possibility, Sally?'

Sally reiterated the power of the natural elements around them, and this reminded Deborah that she did unexpectedly 'come-on' just before making love with Dan. It could be possible.

'Bring me a urine sample as soon as you can, and I can give you an answer in a few minutes. I've had to do a few of these tests in my time.'

Sally gave Deborah a knowing wink which put her at ease.

'If I bump into Dave, I'll have a quiet word with him, but from what I am picking up I don't think any lasting damage has been done.'

That evening Dave lay on the single bed in the Featherstore overlooking the sea. He was deep in thought, not so much about the revelation of Deborah's unfaithfulness with Dan but more on his own situation at St Kilda. It been his great opportunity to make something of himself, restore the island community that had fell apart in 1930 to be replaced by a military community, recently evacuated due to what seemed mainly alcohol related problems.

There had been a security lapse which allowed a terrorist attack but that should have been more of a wakeup call rather than a cause for evacuation.

It was odd that the men rarely ventured into Glen Mór. It did feel an eerie place after the plane crash on the day of their arrival. The hunting party never stood a chance, and it was an accident that shouldn't have happened. A bit like Sean and Gavin, both experienced stalkers. It should never have happened to them either.

He knew he wouldn't be going over the hill to the glen anytime soon. His back wouldn't let him climb any further than the Gap and further stone walling was out of the question for the time being. A brief adrenaline rush hit him when he remembered Deborah and Dan, probably copulating on the very same bed he was lying on now, but he quickly dismissed the thought, put it in a box and sealed the lid as tightly as he could.

What had happened, had happened and he was being tested by God. Abraham was expected to slaughter his beloved son to prove his faith. Forgiving an errant wife should be easy, compared with that.

'Thank you, Lord. You've let me off lightly this time.'

His words echoed in the empty room as he poured himself a glass of water from the jug Agatha had filled for him earlier. As he drank the fresh well water, his thoughts returned to the Angels he had seen beckoning him from Boreray.

Deborah walked up to the Factor's House carrying a small plastic container under her jacket. She had just passed her ovulation date and needed to be tested now, but she didn't want it to look too obvious what her second recent visit to Sally might imply. Once inside she passed the container to Sally who placed it on the kitchen counter.

'Just a minute and I'll go and get the testing kit. It hasn't been used for a few years but there's nothing there to go off. We'll soon know the outcome.'

The testing kit consisted of a box of individually wrapped EPT sticks. Sally unwrapped one and dipped the end in Deborah's urine sample.

'Got to hold this in here for twenty seconds, then wait two minutes, OK.'

Sally replaced the cap over the moist end of the stick, and they waited for two minutes. To Deborah they were the longest two minutes ever, but as Sally suspected, a blue line appeared in a small aperture on the side of the testing stick indicating that, indeed, Deborah was pregnant.

'Well Deborah, you are going to have to consider your options and sooner rather than later. First of all, think of yourself, do you want to have a child, at your age? There'll doubtless be grandchildren coming along soon. I can't give you a termination out here, but I can arrange for the procedure to be done in Stornoway, but it has to be your decision, no-one else's.

There's Dave to consider too, assuming you are going to stay together. How would he feel about bringing up Dan's child? It's not every man who could be happy with that and the last thing a child wants is to be resented by one of its parents. I am not going anywhere near the guilt thing, but repercussions could be long lasting.

I suppose we have to think of Dan too. If you carry the child he would probably go either of two ways. He could want nothing to do with the child or live a life of angst trying to be a good father and I assume that is not a scenario you are seriously thinking of?'

'Er, definitely not, I am afraid, Sally.'

Dan had served his purpose and there was no way Deborah wanted him back on the scene.

'As for the child, he or she would need a loving family, even if that family was just you, or a foster family until adoption could be sorted out. Due to your age, you should also consider amniocentesis. Testing for Down's Syndrome'

It was becoming clear to both women that in her moment of passion, Deborah's maturity had played no part when it came to considering the consequences.

'There is one other thing you should seriously think about too. There have been no babies born at St Kilda since the 1920s. I must emphasise this to you, Deborah. This island has a tragic history of infantile tetanus, the 'eight-day sickness.' There was nothing wrong with the fecundity of the population but between 70-80% of newborn infants died of tetanus within the first two weeks of life. Most succumbed within eight days hence the local name for the disease.'

Sally gave Deborah a moment to let the disease risk sink in.

'At its height, the population reached two hundred souls, never anymore and way before birth-control was ever thought about. The 'Eight-Day Sickness' was considered God's way of keeping the population at a level the island could support. You've seen the way the sheep breed until they starve. Out here, infant mortality has always prevented the human population going the same way.'

Things did change, she added.

'By the end of the nineteenth century, it was known for St Kilda women to leave the island to give birth. That way they avoided, not divine retribution for their carnal sins, but avoided nature's way of conserving the meagre resources available to all species out here. They could have overpopulated the island, Agatha would say. For land animals, humans included, it really is life on the edge here. So, whatever you decide, Deborah, I must strongly advise you to leave the island. If you opt for a termination, then you need to leave the island as soon as possible. You probably need to have a heart-to-heart talk with Dave, too.'

'It puzzles me, Sally, why Dave shows so little interest in all this. It's as if he doesn't really care about my affair with Dan. I wish I could make him out, I really do.'

'Talk to him Deborah, that really is the only way if your marriage is going to survive.'

A few days later, Deborah decided to bite the bullet and walked over to the Featherstore to speak with Dave. It felt odd knocking on the door to speak with her own husband. Having a serious talk with her husband didn't feel too daunting, especially as her knock was acknowledged by a cheery response from inside.

'Come on in!'

Entering, she saw Dave sitting in the worn armchair by the window. An oil lamp illuminated the large Bible he had taken with him and had been avidly reading.

'Hi, Debs! I wondered when you'd be over to see me. Think I have had enough of my own company for a while. Mind you it has been great sleeping in here with the sound of the waves and the seabirds right on my doorstep. I haven't really missed the Manse with its generator and mod-cons. You know, Dan left this place really clean and tidy.'

'Yes, I gathered that. To tell you the truth, Dave. I wanted to have a talk with you about Dan and what went on, and why. I am taking a risk, but you seem so relaxed about what happened, I am hoping we can talk about it?'

Deborah walked over to her husband and rather than tower over him, she drew up another chair and sat down beside him.

'Don't worry, Debs. As they say, the Lord moves in mysterious ways. He is testing me through this situation. By accepting without recrimination, I hope I am becoming a better man in the Lord's eyes. At the end of the day, I still have my Faith and there are plenty of references in the Bible about forgiveness for fallen women. Consider Mary Magdalen, how she cared for Christ in his hour of need.'

'It's not forgiveness I am here to talk about, Dave. There are some practical issues we need to discuss. I am pregnant and not by you.'

If Dave was shocked by Deborah's revelation, he barely showed it but began turning the pages as if looking for the appropriate scripture. Deborah was quicker than her husband.

'I know what you are looking for Dave, it's in Luke, right at the beginning, if I remember rightly. Elizabeth the wife of Zaharias became an older mother and gave birth to John the Baptist.'

Deborah had rehearsed this moment in her mind before walking to the Featherstore. She knew her husband would seek Biblical explanation for the situation. Dave quickly found Luke 1 and scanned the verses.

'Well, Debs, you are spot on. Elizabeth was favoured by God and a close friend of the Blessed Mary, Mother of Christ. This was meant to happen! Though something similar happened with Abraham and Sarah, didn't it?'

'If you say so, Dave.'

Deborah had not researched further than Elizabeth and John the Baptist.

'Now, Dave. I'd better tell you the options Sally gave me, or should I say us? We have to take this seriously for our own benefit and for, er... wee John's sake too. Let me finish what I have to say before you give your opinion, okay?'

Deborah went ahead to tell Dave the options. She could have an abortion as soon as possible and the problem, if that is what it was, would be over. She would be left with an emotional stain but no further consequences. She could go ahead and have the baby which could lead to Dan wanting to be involved. The baby could be at risk of Down's Syndrome due to her age, but she could be tested for that. She ought to have the baby off island due to the statistically high risk of infantile tetanus.

Apparently the St Kildans considered infant mortality an act of God, natural population control. There was the child to consider, he or she had to grow up in a loving family, either their own or with adoptive parents. Whatever the outcome she would have to leave the island for a while, either for an abortion or to give birth inside a hospital safely away from the scourge of tetanus.

Dave took only a moment to consider.

'You must stay and have the child on the island. The St Kildans were right, it will be God's will whether the child, who we will call John, lives or dies. Just think, he will be the first child to be born here for a hundred years!'

Dave was excited at the prospect of not only a child for the island but also for the direct intervention of God. Deborah had other thoughts.

'You are wrong, Dave. Firstly, the child could easily be a girl and I'm not taking the risk of him or her dying of tetanus. I have thought long and hard about it and have decided I do want to go through with this pregnancy. Let's be honest, it has nothing to do with you. No, it was not an immaculate conception, before you get any funny ideas, but the child is mine and I intend to have it away from here. Sally will arrange things for me.'

'Ephesians 5:22-23 *Wives, submit yourselves unto your own husbands, as unto the Lord. For the husband is the head of the wife, even as Christ is the head of the church: and he is the saviour of the body.*'

'In your dreams, Dave! I will have this child, who I hope will be a girl, and I will have her in a hygienic hospital on

401

the mainland. If that is your final opinion, I'll bid you goodnight!'

Deborah stormed out of the Featherstore slamming the door behind her as Dave searched for further scriptures. He needed to support his insistence that Deborah stayed and subjected her pregnancy and delivery to God's will. Returning to Hebrews 11, he read more about Sarah, wife of Abraham who gave birth to his son Isaac at a late age.

'Of course, that's it!' Dave interpreted what he had just read to fit the situation.

Sarah gave birth to Isaac and Abraham was tested by the Lord. He had to be prepared to slaughter his son as sacrifice to God. It came right at the last minute, but God spoke and allowed Abraham to spare his son.

God wouldn't really allow Deborah to leave the island, taking his son away.

God would throw up a great storm to prevent Don's boat arriving or some other such thing to prevent her leaving.

All he had to do was go along with her plans to leave until God spoke and all would be well.

Dave was satisfied and closed the Bible. He poured himself a glass of water from the jug, filled at the well that morning.

Back in the Manse, Deborah was fuming.

'OK, Agatha. You seem to know all about it. I am pregnant! Sally confirmed it for me this morning and of all the options, one thing is for certain. I am going to have to leave for a while. I might even decide to stay away for good as I will have a child to look after in a few months' time. Your father, of course, wants me to stay here and give birth on the island. He couldn't give a monkey whose child it is, but he is certain it will be a boy, and it will be God's will whether he catches infantile tetanus or not. Over my dead body, Agatha, over my dead body!'

'So, when are you off then, Mum?'

Agatha seemed almost as unconcerned about it all as her father. What was the matter with this crazy family? There was going to be a new baby, and nobody gave a toss that it was the result of an affair she had had with Dan.

Well, that wasn't strictly true. Erica resented her for it though she reckoned that was more female jealousy than anything else. She had to smile at the idea that as a middle-aged woman she had beaten her nubile daughters to the bed of the only young man on the island. What she hadn't realised was that the poison of female rivalry ran deeper than she could imagine.

Agatha was only too delighted that her mother would soon be out of the way, for she had been reading the Bible too. In fact, Agatha had decided it was high time she spent more time with her father to read the Bible together rather than study independently. It was all part of her plan.

'Sorry Mum, I was a bit blunt then, we don't really want to lose you. I know you and Erica don't see eye to eye at the moment so if you want someone to talk to, go ahead.'

'Thanks, Agatha. I have just had about enough. My emotions have been going wild just lately. One minute I am as horny as hell and the next I am a man hater. What's going on?'

Agatha thought for a moment before replying. It was actually a bit close to the way she had been feeling too. Her mother was obviously going to be tearful, she hoped it wouldn't set her off as well.

'Sit down, Mum. It's going to be alright. It would be easy to say it's an age thing with the menopause just around the corner. As a scientist that's what I would say, but as a woman I think there is more going on out here than we realise.'

Agatha explained how she herself had felt at the last spring tide. She had a huge period and was alternately horny and tearful afterwards. The small tsunami seemed to add to the effect the big tide had on her. She had kept out

403

of the way to avoid getting into unnecessary arguments and had been spotting birds in the bay from the Hidey-Hole. That's when she had also spotted her mother with Dan, but tactfully thought not to mention it again.

'The movement of the tides affects us, Mum. More than we can imagine. Back in town the same thing happens but there are so many other distractions. Out here we get it full on, is it any wonder we go a bit crazy. Sally says you get used to it eventually and settle back to normal. I wonder, if there were more people here would we be affected so strongly? Maybe it is one of nature's ways to get us to repopulate this island.'

'Oh well, that's alright then. Lots of women use the excuse of things happening to them beyond their control!'

They both had to laugh at Deborah's implication. She thought of a past conversation with Sally.

'Sally once said there was something in the water out here that makes people go a bit crazy, maybe she is right? She reckoned the military guys out here were doing relatively fine until that new borehole was commissioned. Doesn't it look pretty with all the Butterwort growing around it? It will die down soon, and dry autumn leaves will probably fall in the well. Could it be that's what she meant?'

Agatha thought for a moment before replying.

'No, I don't think so, the Butterwort, or Mothan as it's called round here, contains a powerful anti-biotic. Probably do us the world of good! It was used as a cure-all by the St Kildans in the past. Supposed to bring us good luck if we chew it, so we had better start munching, I have been doing it for ages, Mum.'

Deborah had read the tales of Roderick the Imposter, a rogue minister who modelled himself on John the Baptist. After his carnal method of saving female souls was rumbled he had summoned to Dunvegan Castle for trial. On the way, so the story went, he chewed copious amounts of Mothan and got let off with not much more than a slapped wrist and told to behave himself in future. She had remembered this tale after coming up with the John the Baptist ruse to placate her husband.

'So, what am I to do, Agatha? My maternal instincts tell me to have the child, yet my common sense warns me it might be born with Down's syndrome. By the time I can have the amniocentesis test, it will be too late for a termination. Then shouldn't Dan have a say in this decision?'

'Dan's a prat. You can leave him out of the picture, Mum! He won't want to know; I'll tell you that much.'

'Your father wants me to stay and have the baby here and whatever happens will be God's will. He started citing the biblical story of Abraham, Sarah and Isaac. Think he could relate better to that old patriarch than to the related tale of Elizabeth and Mary I told him about to start with.'

'You are bit cunning yourself, Mum. Clever stuff to use the Bible to justify your actions to Dad.'

'But anyway, Agatha, the upshot is that I feel I want to have this child, and I need to get off the island rather than put my baby at 70-80% risk of infantile tetanus to test the will of God. So, when am I going? As soon as Don brings the *Beluga* back here, which I believe is next week sometime.'

'Yes, Erica was talking about that. He's bringing her a small house cow. She's really looking forward to it.'

Over the following few days Deborah busied herself with preparations to go. Dave kept himself out of the way and showed no obvious concern over his wife planning to leave the island. He seemed wrapped up in a world of his own and took long walks over Conachair, stopping often, to gaze northward toward Boreray.

He spoke with his wife over superficial domestic arrangements and there was no discernible bitterness displayed over the coming separation. As far as he was concerned, it was God's will. They seemed to have acquired what they both wanted. Deborah was carrying her late conceived child, and Dave had never felt so connected with God.

Erica and Sally would still meet at the far end of the village for coffee and chat in the blackhouse while Agatha returned to her habit of spending long hours walking around the far side of the island, usually in Glen Mór. The family rarely saw each other, taking separate ways and the island remained peaceful while they waited for the *Beluga* to return.

19

Jacob's Ladder

The *Beluga* arrived the following Wednesday. Don had never been able to predict exactly when they would arrive unless there was a prolonged period of calm weather. Dave was away, up at the Gap, but as soon as they heard the twin diesel engines slowdown in the bay, Erica and Sally ran to the jetty to meet the boat.

The arrival of the first cow on the island since 1930 was a cause for celebration as far as Erica was concerned. She had left the choosing of the cow to Don.

Like most Hebrideans he had a working knowledge of livestock husbandry. He knew that heavy commercial beasts would be a handful on the island, not least for their size. They would need shelter in harsh conditions and the derelict Bull's House would not hold a modern breed. Don had chosen a Dexter, the small breed from Ireland thought to have been bred by the Celts.

He had thought getting the beast off the boat and onto the jetty would be a problem, but the cow proved nimble and, glad to see firm ground after the three-hour sea crossing, jumped easily ashore. The animal paced the jetty taking in its new surroundings. When Erica approached, the cow was at first nervous and wouldn't let her take the halter. It had been thoughtfully left on by the previous owner, a crofter from Luskentyre.

Erica and the cow faced each other along the jetty. Luckily the railings erected to prevent tourists from falling off the edge deterred the cow from jumping. Don and Lachie grinned as Erica tried to coax the animal toward her. Only after a gently swirling breeze lifted strands of dry seaweed off the jetty did the cow relax and let Erica take the halter. The bond had been made and Erica led the Dexter up to graze in front of the empty Base.

'You can let her go, Erica. She trusts you now and, if I was you, I would bucket train her. Douglas raised her to the bucket so she will know what to do. She must be hungry now, didn't like the crossing much.'

Lachie hadn't liked clearing the mess after she had scoured on the crossing either, some coarse grass inside her would soon sort that out. The island Soay sheep were curious. None had ever seen another grazing animal but soon accepted her.

'There's just one thing you need to watch out for, Erica. She wasn't raised here so there is a possibility she could pick up something she has not been vaccinated against. I was going to warn against Red-water Fever but as there are no ticks on the island, that's unlikely. From what I know, I don't think the St Kildan cattle suffered any more or less than any others from bovine diseases. She's three years old, so worms shouldn't be a problem. Her last calf was only a month ago so she'll milk fine for a while, but you will need to have her artificially inseminated or get yourself a bull in a few months' time. Let me know what you decide, and I'll arrange it for you. Just remember to choose semen from another Dexter or another small breed to avoid problems when she comes to calve.'

Don was happy to advise Erica on anything she needed to know about keeping the island's first house cow for nearly a century. Right now, Erica was entranced and desperately wanted to give the cow a name. The small beast looked at her and lowed.

'That's it you midget. Bridgit the Midget!'

'Queen of the Blues!'

Sally remarked, unable to contain her own admiration for the animal.

'There was an old pop song about Bridgit the Midget, wasn't there? Don't suppose that's a very nice thing to call her but Bridgit is an apt name for the Hebrides. She is the patron saint of boatmen and cattle amongst many other things, so I reckon Bridgit is a good name for her.'

'Bridgit she is then, Sally!'

Erica had fallen instantly in love with the small cow, now earnestly grazing nearby. She announced that after she had been milked she could shelter inside the blackhouse when the weather was bad and no, she wasn't going to build another pallet bed for Bridgit when Lachie teased her about molly-coddling the beast.

Deborah had got everything packed that she needed to take. In the unlikely event she would want to return with her child to St Kilda, the rest of her belongings could stay.

Dave had seen the cow being unloaded on the jetty and made his way down through An Lag, passing the sheep fanks and thought what a good place it would be for a few small cattle, like that Dexter. South facing and out of the wind and salt spray, the grazing would be sweet. If he could keep the sheep out, he was sure a few Dexters could be raised in those stone walled enclosures.

When he reached the slipway he saw Deborah passing her large rucksack and wheeled holdall onto the *Beluga*. It looked like she really was leaving him. Engaging his thoughts on livestock farming had briefly taken him out of his religious bubble, but the reality of watching his wife readying to leave hit him hard. Tears ran down his cheeks as he walked up to her on the jetty. Putting his arms around her he tried to give Deborah a hug, but she froze before shrugging him off.

'Bit late for that, Dave. Perhaps, if you had shown me some emotion earlier I might have stayed. Come on Dave, you have your God now. He's probably more use to you out here than I ever will be. I'll be in touch and let you know how we get on, the child and me. I'm not promising but I might consider coming back after I have had the baby. We'll just have to see how things work out. Look, dry your tears

Dave and I'll give you a hug before I get on board.'

She held him close, acknowledging her own fierce determination to move on. This man in her arms felt like a small boy to her now. Lost in a boys' own fantasy world, justified by an imagined God. It felt good to be leaving, bringing up a child out here might have been alright for a younger woman, but not for her. She released Dave from the embrace and saw that he had already emotionally disengaged from her.

'God is testing me, Debs. He is testing me, and I will not be found wanting. Go in peace and let me know how you get on. You will be warmly welcomed when you come back. I don't think the Prodigal.....'

'Prodigal daughter I think you meant to say. Thanks, Dave. It is good to know there will always be a place for me here if I need it. Now it's time to be off.'

'1 Corinthians 7:12-15 I will not *put you away* and you are *not under bondage* to me, Deborah.'

She kissed her husband lightly on his heavily stubbled cheek and stepped down lightly onto the deck of the *Beluga*. Don had already started the engines which ticked over as Lachie released the mooring ropes from the iron bollards on the jetty. The boat gently reversed out over the kelp which seemed to be growing thicker than ever in the clean and sheltered waters of Village Bay.

As the boat disappeared around the Point of Col heading back toward Harris, Dave allowed himself a few wracking sobs before switching off from the situation.

Apart from his God, he was now the only man on the island. He had listened to the Lord and led his family away from the mess of mainland life. Now like Lot, his wife had turned back, and he was left alone with his daughters, and Sally the paramedic nurse.

Before the boat left, Don had spoken with Dave to tell him they couldn't come out the following week because there were missile trials taking place on the Hebrides

Range and shipping had to avoid the sea area east of St Kilda while live firing was happening. The weather forecast was good, so he hoped the Range would get it all over with quickly but, he had added, given past form the lads at Rangehead, they usually made a meal of things.

With Deborah gone, a vacuum needed filling, and the scriptures were the obvious source for advice. He had found solace in Timothy on more than one occasion. Timothy understood and he turned to him again.

1 Timothy 3:5 *For if a man know not how to rule his own house, how shall he take care of the church of God?*

He hadn't done too well in ruling his house so far but there was still time. He could see no reason not to take a second wife.

Thinking of Abraham, as he often did, he knew of Abraham's two wives not to mention his concubines. There should be no problem, and he might even have a divine right to another wife while Deborah was away. After all, it had been she who had committed adultery.

There was only one available woman on the island, and he decided to chance his luck with her once more. This time, however, he would be more of a gentleman. For the time being he stayed in the Featherstore, leaving the Manse to Agatha who was only too pleased with the arrangement. That evening he walked up to the Factor's House and knocked on Sally's door.

Proverbs 18:22, he thought. If I find myself another wife, *it will be a good thing,* and I will return to *the favour of the Lord.*

'Hello Dave, what can I do for you so late?'

It had taken Sally a while to answer the door. Had he known, he might have been surprised at the number of empty Gin bottles Sally had been stashing at the back of her bathroom. It was cold in there now that the power-station stood lifeless but the back boiler in her fireplace still produced enough hot water for the occasional luxurious soak.

'Well, first I'd like to apologise for my behaviour the other day. I don't know what came over me like that. To be honest, I suppose I was feeling pretty desperate for affection after months of coldness from Deborah.'

'That's okay, Dave. Perfectly understandable given the circumstances, but I am afraid you were barking completely up the wrong tree.'

'What's that supposed to mean, Sal?'

'Oh God, I didn't want to have to explain but now Deborah has left, I suppose I must. I don't tell many people this, but I used to be married and lived on a croft near Tarbert. My husband and all his family were staunch members of the Free Church. Don't get me wrong, they have some excellent values when it comes to family life but when I needed help the Free Church proved inflexible and unforgiving. I was banished and considered an abomination, just because I had an affair, with a woman.'

Dave was taken aback; he hadn't expected this. He was now a single man, and he wanted to begin courting a single woman. In his eyes it should have been simple.

'I have four children who they managed to turn against me. We haven't been in contact for years. My husband divorced me on the grounds of adultery, he couldn't bring himself to admit his wife was if not actually lesbian, had proved to be bisexual. Not only was I banished but after our divorce, he was given custody of the kids. Apparently I was considered too deviant to be trusted with their upbringing. Can you imagine what that was like? To lose my husband, my children and wider family network simply for following a perfectly natural inclination that could have harmed no-one. It turned me against men and their precious Church, I can tell you. I will never understand what was so wrong that I would be considered an outcast. Come with me... '

Sally led Dave into the bathroom and opened the cupboard behind the door. The shelves were stacked with

Gin bottles, mostly empty.

'Those are my friends, my lovers now. The only thing I can rely on now is alcohol and when it's finished I don't know what I'll do. I am medically trained so I know what the stuff does to you. I am physically dependent as were so many of the guys who worked out here. Yes, I know I cover it up well and I'd appreciate it if you didn't spread it around. Erica knows of course but no-one else does. She has been a real pal to me as I am sure you are aware and no, we are not a pair of lezzies before you start worrying about it, just good close friends. There is a difference, you know.'

Dave did not know what to say. The wind had been taken completely out of his sails. A slap in the face he could have understood but here was Sally showing herself to be a far more complex human being than he had ever imagined.

'Sally, I am so glad you told me this. It explains a lot I didn't understand or failed to see before. You have been open with me so I will admit that it had been on my mind to ask you to marry me when I came up here?'

'What, Dave? I thought I was the crazy one!'

'The thing is that from what I have been reading in the Scriptures, without a wife I am a less of a man in the eyes of God.'

'That's complete and utter bollocks and you know it, Dave! So, you thought that by marrying me everything would come right for you. Marrying me would be the worst thing you could ever do. Could you afford my gin bill? Because I can't!'

'Sally, Abraham had two wives, and it did not displease the Lord.'

'Did you hear what I said, Dave. A thousand times no, I am not going to marry you. Not now, not ever. Christ I need a drink.'

Sally reached into the cupboard and pulled out the half-emptied bottle she secreted when Dave unexpectedly knocked on her door. Putting the bottle to her lips she took

413

a large gulp.

'You are welcome to join me if you bring a bottle to share but I expect you'll want to go home and think about your situation. You know, I reckon everybody who worked at St Kilda had something to hide, to run away from. What was your real reason for coming here?'

Sally opened the door for him, and Dave walked back to the Featherstore, his head spinning from Sally's revelation. Part of what she said had been spot on, but he couldn't imagine what he was running from. To the contrary he was trying to build a better life. This was just another test, and he quickly dismissed his doubts as he had done when Deborah left earlier in the day. The Bible remained where he had left it on the table in the Featherstore and he sat down with water rather than alcohol to seek solace in the Scriptures.

He could hardly imagine a time when he had felt lonelier. In just one day, his wife had left him and again he had made a complete ass of himself over Sally. It should have been straight forward, but it wasn't.

Here he was on an Atlantic island that should have been the key to an idyllic future. The trouble was other people ruined his dream by not sharing it with him. His two daughters thought like him, he was sure. Erica was a hands-on young woman who any man could be proud of and even his enigmatic Agatha had shown an interest in the Bible lately. There was a chance this would work out in the end, but it would depend on his daughters. He would invite them round and together they could make plans. At the end of the day, he was their father, and his opinion should be respected.

Sally walked over to Erica's blackhouse to discuss Dave's latest attempt to win her over.

'It's really getting too much, Erica. I hope he understands now why his paternal ideas are so crazy. That sort of thing just doesn't apply out here. It never did. If he

414

tries it on with me one more time I am going to have to leave, I can't take it anymore.'

'Yeah, he is becoming a bit of a worry. A horny old man with a bad back, perhaps you should invite him back and give him the treatment, Sal?'

'What! You mean just like in the old days out here?'

'Yes, he is a kinky old sod, he'd love it – and I did pick up somewhere that he had enjoyed a previous session with you. Instant cure for his bad back or something like that.'

Sally was thoughtful and considered the wisdom of Erica's suggestion for a moment. Her treatments had been much appreciated by the men from the Base in the past and no trouble had come of it.

'Well, why not? The only thing Erica, is I'd like you to bring him along so I appear professional, on the surface at least.'

Erica grinned and couldn't suppress a giggle at her father's expense.

'Okay, I'll go and get him. You can get things ready in the Factor's House. Don't forget to light the fire for him!'

The two women walked along the street together planning how they would take Dave's mind off things and with a bit of luck, after the evening was over, he would stop bothering Sally. Sally popped into the Factor's House while Erica continued the length of the street to the Featherstore. Knocking on the door, she went inside without waiting to be invited. Dave was poring over pages of Genesis and looked up, surprised to see her standing there.

'Dad, Sally and I have put our heads together and come up with an idea you might like the sound of. She is offering to give you another treatment for your back, and by treatment I think she could be meaning something more than a simple massage. She used to do this for the men of the base sometimes, when she was employed here.'

Dave was intrigued and wanted to know more.

'Men had problems out here, as you already know.

415

Young and not so young men away from their wives and girlfriends for a month, sometimes longer, needed to have an outlet for their, shall we say, energies. We reckon this is what has been getting you down and I doubt any amount of Bible study would substitute for female hands in the right place.'

'Erica, are you saying what I think you are saying?'

'Yes, Dad. It will all be very clinical, nothing to get concerned about. Trust us, we have only your best interests at heart.'

Dave thought it quite a coincidence. Here was his first-born daughter suggesting some kind of sexual service just after he had been reading about Lot in Genesis 19.

The similarities were striking. Lot's wife had turned back from the wilderness and been turned to a pillar of salt leaving only two daughters to continue his line, which they had apparently done willingly, so he had read. He felt aroused at the thought of such a thing manifesting itself right here and right now. Was Agatha going to be involved too, he asked.

'No, Dad. Just me and Sally. She was a bit embarrassed after what she said to you earlier and wanted me to ask you to come along. That alright with you?'

'Fine Erica, do I need to do anything?'

'Just put that Bible away, Dad. You won't need it again tonight.'

And, with a bit of luck, never again ever she thought but tactfully kept it to herself. Her Dad was alright, but bloody hard work at times. He needed a woman's touch that was all.

By the time Erica led her father to Sally, she had a fire blazing in the hearth and the massage table was ready in the warm living room.

'Take a seat both of you. Do you want to stay and help me, Erica?'

Dave sat down in the armchair and, to his surprise,

Sally poured him a large glass of gin.

'There you are old man. Just so you know, I didn't mean to upset you earlier. It's not every day a girl gets asked to marry, is it?'

It had actually happened quite a lot in the past during drunken evenings in the Puff-Inn, just another hazard of being a divorced woman working alongside heavy drinking and lonely men. She passed Erica a glass of gin too, and the three chatted amiably, enjoying the warmth of the fire.

'I'm feeling quite relaxed now, don't want to put you to the trouble of a massage. I'm okay, really.'

'Dave, last time you had a terrible lower back. That was business, tonight it's going to be pleasure if you get my meaning.'

Erica couldn't resist a giggle and snorted into her gin which was certainly having the desired effect.

'Oh, come on Dad, loosen up. She is offering you, for free, the kind of massage businessmen pay a lot of money for back in the Edinburgh. You must have heard of the goings on at the Bad Moral Hotel!'

He had heard of alleged goings on at the Balmoral Hotel and Dave blushed slightly at the implication, but secretly was beginning to look forward to what the two of them had in mind for him.

'Just get undressed down to your underpants, Dave. You can put this dressing gown on if you feel chilly or a bit exposed. Don't know why you should though, we both seen it all before, eh Sal? When you're ready just climb up on the bench and lie on your back this time.'

The bench was close to the hearth and Dave felt quite warm so close to the fire but encouraged by his daughter he had done what Sally asked and now lay on the bench staring up at the slightly smoke-stained ceiling. There had been many a back draught down the chimney on windy nights, of which there were plenty.

'One more thing Dave, to ensure you get the most out

of this, I am going to ask Erica to strap your wrists and ankles to the bench. That way you won't be able to suddenly change your mind.'

Sally winked at Dave, and Erica gently took his wrists and strapped them to the sides of the bench, then moved to his feet and strapped his ankles. Erica did think it looked slightly ridiculous, her father being strapped down to the bench in just his underpants and had to work hard to stifle a laugh. It was in the best interest of all of them that they broke his religious mania and so far he didn't seem to be protesting. For his part, Dave began to shiver in anticipation of what was coming. If God thought it was OK for Lot, then it was alright for him. He was disappointed when Erica got up to leave.

'Right then, Sally. I'll leave him with you, and you can tell me how you got on in the morning.'

Sally walked over to the wall cupboard at the opposite side of the room and put on the white medical coat she kept hanging up there. It was surprisingly clean considering it had been in store for a long time. From the top shelf, she took down a box of latex gloves and put a pair on in front of Dave, who by this time had stopped his nervous shivering.

'Just what are you intending to do with those Sally?'

'Wait and see Dave, just wait and see. First of all, we need to remove these pants, don't we?'

From her pocket she produced a pair of surgical steel scissors and began to cut the material between the right leg of his boxers and the elastic waist band. Gently she lifted the material over to his left side, nearest the hearth. He looked in better condition in that department than a lot of others she had seen in the past. No flabby beer gut to get in the way for sure. This man was as well toned as he could be for his age. Hard physical work did have some benefit for him. Perhaps, she thought, if his back hadn't gone, he could have worked out this religious nonsense in some kind of constructive way.

'Just have to check under here first, Dave.'

Sally slid a well lubricated latex gloved finger into his anus.

'Jesus Christ, what are you doing?'

Dave struggled to rise from the bench, but the straps held his wrists and ankles firm. All he could do was arch himself upwards as Sally's finger explored inside him.

'Man of your age, Dave. He might have prostate trouble, just checking for you.'

She kept her finger inside him until he had no choice but to relax. She slowly pushed her finger as far inside him as she could reach and began to slide it back out. She noticed the moisture on the end of his foreskin. I spite of the initial protest; it was going to work. She kept one finger in his anus and brought the other hand over to his penis and began to massage it. Strapped to the bench, naked and vulnerable, Dave became tearful as his erection rose.

'There, there Dave. It's alright and you'll be so much the better for this when I am finished.'

Sally really was doing this for free. In the past she at least had been given a bottle of gin or whisky for her services. Never mind, if it cures the old sod of his mania, that's all that matters.

'Now let's make a good sinner of you, Dave.'

Skilfully she manipulated Dave, powerless in her hands, until he ejaculated copiously. Semen splashing across his stomach.

'Wow, Dave. I reckon you needed that. It's been a long time since you came, that's for sure.'

To her surprise, rather than letting out a satisfied sigh as had most of her earlier clients, Dave let out a howl of anguish and she withdrew her finger from his anus. Shaking and shuddering on the bench he began to froth at the lips.

'Fuck....don't go having a fit on me, Dave. I'll get the straps off you.'

As the seizure took hold, Sally was unable to get him off the massage bench in time and with one wrist still attached he fell to the floor pulling the bench over with him. He looked a pathetic sight crumple naked on the floor, semen dripping from his now limp penis and one wrist still strapped to the bench lying across him. To make matters even worse, he appeared to have defecated as he fell. Quickly Sally undid the remaining strap and helped him get up. Thankfully it hadn't been an epileptic seizure but an extreme reaction to emotional turmoil he was experiencing.

'Look, you had better clean yourself up Dave. Here put on the dressing gown and you can use my bathroom to clean yourself.'

Bewildered, Dave put on the gown and went to the bathroom. Luckily the blazing fire had heated up the water and by the time he emerged he looked presentable, if still in Sally's dressing gown. Sally had thrown the soiled latex gloves on the fire and hung up her white coat. The massage bench was folded up back in the closet.

'Oh dear. Are you alright Dave? I wasn't expecting anything like that to happen.'

'I'll be a lot better when I've got my clothes back on and another gin would be nice, Sally.'

'Phew, there's me thinking you'd be really mad at me for controlling you like that. A lot of men like it, but just a few don't. I thought you'd be one of those, when you screamed out. At least you look relaxed now, that's the main thing.'

'You've certainly relaxed me; I'll say that Sally. But the Bible says it should have been my firstborn daughter to take my seed. Tonight, it all went to waste.'

Sally was perplexed, maybe nothing had changed for him. Had she simply reinforced his perverse convictions?

'Dave, nothing went to waste tonight. You came in here a tormented soul lost, dare I say trapped, in the world of

420

the Old Testament. Now you are back with us, in the here and now, at St Kilda in the twenty-first century.'

Discarding his cut boxers, Dave dressed himself and Sally poured him another large gin. She had already topped her own up. They sat opposite each other staring at the fire rapidly dying away before Dave placed an armful of scrap pallet wood on the embers. The fire soon blazed again.

'Tell me Dave, I'm intrigued about why you thought it should have been Erica who took your seed. Whatever made you think of such a thing, to put it bluntly wouldn't that be incest?'

There was a knock on the front door which interrupted their conversation. Sally got up to see who was there.

'Oh, Hi Agatha. What can I do for you?'

Agatha had slipped while walking down the slope from Conachair, just above the village. The scree slopes were good areas for finding unusual plants and she had been out botanising that evening. The slopes were inherently unstable and, even as the most agile member of the family, she had taken a tumble. Agatha was holding her left arm with her right hand as she came into Sally's living room. She was surprised to see her father sitting there in the room with an intriguing aroma of wood-smoke and the medical disinfectant Sally used to clean up the mess left by Dave's loss of bodily control shortly before.

'I've hurt my elbow, Sally. Could you take a look at it?'

'OK, take your jacket off and roll up your left sleeve for me.'

Agatha's elbow was grazed and visibly red and swollen. Sally slowly moved the limb feeling the movement of the tendons and elbow joint.

'I think you have just badly bruised yourself, Agatha. It all feels fine in there, but you'll probably be black and blue by the morning. I'll give you a tubular bandage to support your elbow for a day or two, but there's no serious damage. Just take more care next time, this is an unforgiving place,

421

and it could be your head you bruise next time. Might knock some sense into you!'

Agatha narrowed her eyes at Sally's joke but was curious as to what she and her father were up to.

'We were just discussing the Bible, Agatha. Your father reckons it is quite alright by God to commit incest. Why don't you stay and join us for a drink, we might both learn a thing or two from this Bible of his.'

Dave was put on the spot with both women eager to understand his argument. He could direct them straight to the right scripture and he asked Sally if she had a Bible he could borrow.

'Well, it's not on my reading list, for sure, but I think there is an old Gideon's Bible in the spare bedroom upstairs. I'll go and get it.'

When she came back, Agatha was sitting on the arm rest of her father's chair sipping a small glass of gin herself.

'Here's the Bible, Dave. I must say I find it hard to believe the Bible says incest is okay though.'

Dave turned to Genesis 19 verses 30-38.

'Tell you what, I'll let Agatha read it out to you. Then you'll know I am not making it up! It's about Lot and his two daughters Pheiné and Thamma after Edith, his wife, had been turned into a pillar of salt for looking back toward God's destruction of Sodom and Gomorrah.'

Agatha took the book and began to read out loud.

'And Lot went up out of Zoar, and dwelt in the mountain, and his two daughters with him; for he feared to dwell in Zoar: and he dwelt in a cave, he and his two daughters.

And the firstborn said unto the younger, our father is old, and there is not a man in the earth to come into us after the manner of all the earth:

Come, let us make our father drink wine, and we will lie with him, that we may preserve seed of our father.

And they made their father drink wine that night: and

the firstborn went in and lay with her father; and he perceived not when she lay down, nor when she arose.

And it came to pass on the morrow, that the firstborn said unto the younger, behold, I lay yesternight with my father: let us make him drink wine this night also; and go thou in, and lie with him, that we may preserve seed of our father.

And they made their father drink wine that night also; and the younger arose and lay with him; and he perceived not when she lay down, nor when she arose.

Thus, were both the daughters of Lot with child by their father.

And the firstborn bare a son and called his name Moab: the same is the father of the Moabites unto this day.

And the younger, she also bare a son and called his name Benammi; the same is the father of the children of Ammon unto this day.'

'Dave that is pure filth! Whoever wrote that must have been the first recorded pervert in history. Okay, I like the biblical justification for getting pissed but for an old man to be shagged by his daughters; that really is too much.'

As a mother herself, Sally was shocked, but Agatha carefully considered the scripture she had just read out. It wasn't quite so clear cut for her, and she explained her scientist's reasoning.

'I'm not so sure, Sally. Erica probably wouldn't agree with me but livestock breeders sometimes mate father and daughter to get pure offspring. Take the sheep for example, we have the purest Soays in the world out here and genetic testing has shown inbreeding is common amongst them. Any malformed lamb would quickly die leaving healthy stock to continue the line. From a woman's point of view if there was no other man available, wouldn't it be preferable to us becoming withered old crones before our time?'

The wind blew down the chimney sending smoke and ash into the room.

'Oh, bugger! I've only just cleaned up. What's up with the weather tonight?'

Sally was not totally surprised at Agatha's comments regarding Lot and his daughters.

'All I can say, Dave, is don't get any more funny ideas. Remember it will be three against one if you try it on!'

'Didn't you listen to the reading, Sal? It was the two daughters who tried it on. No one else came into the story.'

To add emphasis to the jibe, Agatha, still seated on the armrest of his chair stroked her father's hair.

'What are you lot like, I give up! Anyway, I reckon it's time for my beauty sleep. Time to chuck you out.'

Sally had had enough of being social for one night and didn't want to share her dwindling supply of gin any further.

Agatha and Dave walked back along the street arm in arm. Stopping outside the Manse, Agatha asked her father if he would like to come back inside the Manse. She was pretty lonely on her own in there and it would be great if her father came home again. They ought to invite Erica over for a meal the following evening; Sally could come too if she wanted. After the dramas of the past few days, they should all start afresh.

Erica had been preoccupied with welcoming Bridgit to the blackhouse and surrounding pasture. The fields around the village were still lush due to over-manuring in the nineteenth century. The grass kept pace with the sheep in the longer growing season, now climate change made the island winters milder. Agatha had remarked on this to Erica before and warned that the climate could easily tip the other way. The frozen winter they had just experienced might not be a one-off event if the Gulf Stream was shifting its course.

In spite of earlier declaring she wouldn't do it, Erica brought Bridgit into the blackhouse each evening and, following tradition, the cow was stalled in the lower side of the cottage where her dung built up surprisingly quickly. Ash from the wood stove was mixed with the dung though Erica drew the line at adding her own excrement to the compost. She was engrossed in her increasingly self-sufficient lifestyle and began to see less of her sister and father. Sally was virtually off the radar now the cow had arrived.

Erica would spend most evenings indoors content with bovine company. Dan had introduced her to his Mothan laced spirit and Erica continued steeping the plentiful herb in whatever drink was available. Not being much of an alcohol drinker, she had experimented with making Mothan tea and even considered smoking it. Leaves of the plant hung on strings near the woodstove to dry out. The herb in whatever form it was consumed helped her suspend her disbelief concerning they situation they all found themselves in. Deborah and Dan had already left and, if she was honest, her father was becoming a liability to them all. It wasn't meant to be like this and only she had managed to make a decent go at resettling St Kilda.

There had already been two deaths, her mother had left and her father almost invalid due to back troubles. He sought solace in the Bible and now increasingly in the company of Sally, who seemed to exert some kind of hold on him. As for her sister, she seemed implacable and inscrutable as ever. It was a shame Dan had had to leave but, after the business with her mother, inevitable under the circumstances. Erica was deep in thought over a mug of steaming Mothan tea when Agatha knocked on her door.

'Agatha! What brings you here?'

'I thought I'd let you know Dad has moved back into the Manse and we are hoping to have a family meal and try and start afresh after the dramas of the last few days. Will you come and join us?'

'What about Sally, is she going to be there?'

'No, I asked her, but she declined saying she would

rather stay out of our personal business. There was bound to be family stuff to discuss, and she thought it would be easier for us without her being there.'

'Yes, I would agree with that. She seems to have some kind of hold over Dad at the moment. Did you know she had her children taken away from her following a lesbian affair? Just shows you how intolerant the Western Isles can be when it comes to Free Church dogma. Then poor Dad, effectively impotent since his back went, has to rely on female strength to get through his days out here. What a turnaround, Agatha.'

'Hold on, Erica. You can't blame the church for everything. It's down to individual interpretation in the end. I have actually been reading the Bible a bit with Dad and some of it makes a lot of sense.'

'Not you too, Agatha! Well, you won't get me organising my life around that drivel. Anyway, when's this meal going to take place? I could do with a change of scenery and by the way, what are we eating?'

'I thought you'd ask that so, as the best shot here, could you cull one of the old barren ewes and we can have mutton stew. Dad said he could do the butchering but thought it would be good to involve you by doing the killing. I took the liberty of bringing the Tikka and some ammo with me. It's just outside the door waiting for you.'

Erica went outside and saw the rifle in its heavy-duty slip propped against the blackhouse wall. She brought the weapon inside and leant it up in the corner of the room.

'Thanks, Agatha. That will be no problem. Quick and clean with one head shot, not like those barbaric lunatics with their shotgun. In fact, I might as well do it now, there's one old ewe been hanging around the end of the street this time of the morning for quite a while.'

As Erica predicted, the old ewe was grazing slightly away from the hefted group of younger ewes and lambs at the west end of the village. She was grazing at the top edge of the burn with rising ground behind her.

'Perfect, pass me the rifle, Agatha.'

Agatha unzipped the rifle from its slip and passed it to Erica who worked the action a couple of times. Her father had obviously oiled the mechanism when he put it away after he shot that sheep in his vegetable garden. Erica took one cartridge from the pocket of the gun-slip and slipped it into the breech. No need to bother with the magazine on this occasion. She put her elbow through the sling and leaned her forearm against a protruding stone on the blackhouse wall. Erica took aim and as she slowly exhaled, squeezed the trigger.

The crack of the rifle echoed around Village Bay. The other sheep looked up briefly before returning to their grazing. One shot aroused curiosity, anymore would have generated alarm and scattered the flock. The old ewe was nowhere to be seen having leapt into the air to fall lifeless beside the burn.

'Well shot, Erica! Now can I borrow your wheelbarrow, please?'

Agatha took her sisters wheelbarrow over to the burn and dragged the ewe up from the waterside. It was lucky the ewe hadn't fallen in the stream; with a wet fleece she would have been far heavier to drag up the bank. With the ewe in the barrow, Agatha called out goodbye to her sister and headed off toward her father waiting in the Manse.

'So, tomorrow night then, Erica. You might as well keep the rifle up here for now. You can pick up the rest of the ammo tomorrow.'

The following day passed quick enough for the three of them. Sally had taken herself for a long walk to the far side of the island, intending to keep well out of the way. Her obsession, as she realised it was fast becoming, for wanting to control Dave needed thinking through. She was no fool and needed to consider whether her desire to control stemmed from having had so much taken away following

427

her divorce.

It wasn't too bad when the Base guys were there. Her controlling urge was diluted among them, but now with just one man she would have to watch herself. It wasn't his fault she had lost her children, but it was the fault of another God-fearing man, her ex-husband.

Dave was far happier back in the Manse with Agatha. He hadn't needed much encouragement to return to the family home now Deborah had left. In fact, he thought it better in almost every respect living with Agatha. Her chirpiness and obvious contentment such a contrast to the last days with Deborah.

He had skinned and butchered the ewe, and everything was ready for their evening dinner. Just a pity there were no fresh vegetables, rather than tinned ones fetched from the old Base storeroom. Next year, he thought. Next year things would be very different.

They worked together to clear and lay the kitchen table. Agatha had managed to find some un-grazed wildflowers amongst the rocks and placed them in a clean jam-jar at the centre of the table. She even added a sprig of Mothan picked from around the well. A couple of candle sticks were borrowed from House One and a several bottles of wine retrieved from the Base. It was going down, but the old Puff-Inn cellar would keep them supplied a bit longer. All in all, Agatha had to admit, the Manse was beginning to feel very homely. If what she had in mind came to pass, next year the Manse would be homelier still.

When Erica arrived after first settling Bridgit into her stall, the light was fading. There was always so much to do, and she had to make use of the available daylight. She knocked as was customary before entering the Manse.

Dave and Agatha were already seated at the table, both had a glass of red wine poured already. The mutton stew was simmering on the electric cooker, a gentle hum from outside indicating the generator was not running under a heavy load.

'Come in and sit yourself down, Erica. Welcome home firstborn!'

Dave was in a jovial mood. In his opinion it had been bliss working with Agatha to get everything ready for the evening. The wine she poured him had helped too. He poured Erica a glass and Agatha got up to serve the stew. Three bowls of mutton and vegetables were soon steaming on the table, and it was Agatha's suggestion that they said Grace before starting their meal. The three of them held hands and, in deference to Erica, she thanked their gender-neutral Maker rather than God for the food on their table.

'Right then, tuck in folks.'

Agatha served her sister and father with as much as they could eat and importantly kept their glasses topped up, especially her father's. With the meal finished, the three of them retired to the living room at the back of the Manse. The generator briefly laboured as Agatha switched on the electric heater, feeling a late evening chill in the room barely used since Deborah had left, taking her own chilliness with her. The long defunct flat screen television on the wall remained blank but Agatha suggested a Bible reading to entertain them before turning in. She rather hoped Erica would stay the night with them.

Dave, in spite of consuming the best part of a bottle and a half of Merlot, was eager to read to his daughters.

'Tell me Agatha, which passages would you like?'

'Genesis Chapter 19, of course Dad.'

Agatha used Biblical justification to convince her father but, even knowing the past closeness between them, she wasn't sure of Erica.

'You know, the story of Sodom and Gomorrah with Lot and his daughters. It's the best bit in the Bible!'

Dave had to laugh at Agatha's impropriety.

'Hey, Aggie!.... can that be you?'

Erica had heard of Sodom and Gomorrah but beyond

429

Lot's wife being turned to a pillar of salt had no idea of what was coming. Dave had brought the large family Bible from the Featherstore when he moved back in. In spite of his obvious drunken state, he composed himself before reading Genesis 19 to his daughters.

Agatha responded first.

'Isn't that great, Erica. It means we can sleep with Dad and it's okay with God. You'd think we'd be sent to Hell but apparently not. I am so exited Erica. I made up the double bed for you and Dad and I'll be in there with him tomorrow night. Next year, we won't just have vegetables, Dad, we'll have babies! St Kilda will live again.'

'Christ, Agatha! That is the sickest thing I have ever heard. Are you behind this, Dad?'

'No Erica, it wasn't my idea, but I think it's a great one! Come on then girls, I believe you as my firstborn should be first, Erica.'

'In your fucking dreams! You are crazy to even imagine I could go along with this. Agatha you have been plotting this for days, haven't you?'

'But Erica, we need children to rebuild St Kilda. We can't do it on our own and there is no other man available. It's alright, it really is. The Bible says so, isn't that right father?'

'I am out of here, right now and if there was a chance I'd be off the island tonight and away from you perverted lunatics. Agatha, think what you are doing. You are the ecologist; you know the risks.'

Agatha smiled as Erica left, slamming the door behind her. She heard the porch door slam a moment later as Erica stormed off into the night.

'Don't worry Dad, she will be alright in the morning. So, it looks like it's going to be me first, doesn't it?'

Dave was dumfounded. Drunk as he was it would be a very major step to go along with this and sleep with his daughters, even if sanctioned by the scriptures under their present circumstance. Agatha could sense his slight resistance and snuggled closer to him on the settee.

'Come on Dad, or should I just say Dave. You won't regret this. How long has it been for you? I can barely remember the last time I had a man, never I would say, as back in Edinburgh Dan was just a boy then.'

Agatha had never slept with Dan, but she knew her father saw him as a rival and would want to expunge the memory, even if it been Deborah making all the moves in their affair. Dave had had a lot to drink, and his voice was slightly slurred as he rose unsteadily to his feet.

'I need to go to bed, Agatha. This is all a bit much to take in.'

'Let me help you, I've made the bed for us.'

Agatha, who had hardly touched her wine, gently led her father into the double bedroom and sat him on the bed.

'I'll just go outside and switch off the generator and be with you in a moment. Here's a candle from the table. Be careful you don't knock it over.'

Agatha went outside and switched off the generator. The stars were bright that night as the rising wind had blown clouds away from the island to stream out over the Atlantic. Everything was clear and open; it was beautiful with only an occasional sleepy seal call to disturb the night. What a night this was going to be, what a fateful night, she thought.

Agatha went back into the warmth of the Manse, the electric heater clinked as it cooled down and she went into the double bedroom to find her father had undressed himself and was now fast asleep and snoring in bed. She undressed herself and climbed in to join him. She would let him sleep for a while and curled around him, spooning she had heard it called. Dave awoke in the early hours to feel Agatha pressed against him. Her young breasts pushed into his back and her pubic hair warm and soft against his buttocks. This was meant to happen he convinced himself.

431

Agatha awoke from her own light sleep and nibbled at the back of his neck. He turned and they kissed, passion rising in both of them. He put his arms around her, and she responded fiercely by clinging to him, her breasts pressed against his chest this time. She pushed him gently until he was on his back and lifting the duvet, she kneeled over him, her nipples brushing the greying hair on his chest.

'Just lie there and let me do this, Dad.'

His erection was stiffening as she guided him inside her and lowered her buttocks on to his thighs. He moaned as he handed control to his daughter. In the darkness she was smiling but Dave had closed his eyes and did not see her delight. As she gently rose and fell she could feel him swelling inside her until with a shuddering gasp she felt his warm semen ejaculate. His purpose at St Kilda was finished but she wouldn't spoil the night for him just now. He was asleep again by the time he had subsided, and she lifted herself carefully away to lay beside him. She had used her father for his seed alone, but even so she loved him and settled down to sleep beside him. Agatha held her hand tight between her legs, she didn't want any of her father's seed going to waste as a damp patch on the sheet.

Dave awoke to find Agatha dressed and standing beside him offering a mug of hot tea.

'Morning, Dad. Here's a cup of tea for you. How's the old head this morning?'

Slowly, Dave sat up in bed. Agatha rearranged the pillow behind him. Realising his nakedness and semi-dried stickiness in his groin he made sure to pull the duvet up around himself. Agatha didn't appear to be embarrassed in the slightest to see him there, but he was confused about the night's events. He knew Agatha had made love to him, yes it did feel like love. Was it wrong or was it right? I didn't feel wrong when he thought of it as a man and woman making love, but as father and daughter. Wasn't that the old joke about isolated highland and island communities?

The reality might not be so funny. Genesis 19 had said it was okay, but he would have to check further passages on this subject when he got up.

'Breakfast will soon be ready, Dad. No bacon and eggs I'm afraid but we can stretch to beans on toast. Erica made some bread yesterday and left a loaf with us before she went home.'

Erica, Dave remembered, had left under exceedingly strained circumstances. Would she even speak to him again after last night? What was happening to him? He needed the Bible. Dave quickly got dressed and ate the beans on toast Agatha had made, then began scouring the book, still where he left it on the kitchen table. There were plenty of injunctions about sex with in-laws but nothing specific to sex with daughters. It was either condoned or so totally wrong it was beyond redemption. He just couldn't tell. Agatha seemed very happy this morning, no sign that anything was wrong at all. She was not confused, so why should he be? In fact, Agatha seemed happier and more relaxed than ever that morning. She came and joined him at the table, and he thought it was time to ask.

'Agatha, about last night. Why did we let it happen?'

'Because I wanted to, Dad. I am a grown woman now and I have been so excited about resettling this island, starting our own new community. I am sorry if you feel I used you a bit, suppose I did really. It won't happen again as I am sure I conceived last night; I know I did.'

'You mean you took me for my seed, an available sperm donor and that's it?'

Dave was incredulous that his daughter could be so scheming. Resettling St Kilda had been his dream, with him at the head of the family. Not a sperm donor to be discarded once the deed had been done. He felt sick when he realised how Agatha had manipulated him to get her way, quoting Genesis 19 as justification. At least Erica had had the good sense not to go along with her scheming, but where was Erica now?

Smoke was coming from the blackhouse flue pipe, so it was likely she was at home. He left Agatha clearing up in the Manse and walked the length of the street to speak with her. It was odd that Bridgit hadn't been put out that morning. He knocked on the blackhouse door and waited for an answer.

'Who's there?'

He could hear Erica coming to the door cautiously and waited for her to let him in. She stood in the doorway, blocking his entrance. Her eyes were red from crying.

'Dad, what have you done, what have you done?'

'But Erica, I was taken advantage of. I couldn't have imagined just how scheming your sister has become.'

Erica viciously cut him short.

'Dad, that is just typical. Blame the woman when all you had to do was say no. You knew how wrong it was, but you just let her use you. Yes, you heard me. You have been used by your own daughter. God help all of us and as far as I am concerned, I never want to see you again. What you did was unforgiveable, not just in my eyes but in the eyes of your precious God too, I expect. Please just go and leave me to get on with my life in peace.

Dave turned away dejected. His wife had left him, one daughter had used him and the other rejected him. There was only one person left he could talk to, and he made his way to the Factor's House. When he got there, Sally was waiting outside for him on the porch step.

'I'm sorry Dave, but I don't think I can see you today. I'm too mixed up. I shouldn't have been playing games with you. I need to sort my own head out before I try and help you again.'

The ground twisted and shifted beneath him as Dave walked back toward the Manse, but he knew he didn't want to go back inside with Agatha there. He turned and went into the Kirk and picked up one of the pocket bibles in the schoolroom. He read from Genesis 28, he would go again to his father's house in peace and the Lord would again be his God.

Like Jacob, he must have been dreaming all this. He took the short walk up through An Lag to the Gap, three hundred feet above the ocean. He saw Angels ascending and descending the ladder reaching four miles to the island of Boreray. Without hesitation, Dave stepped off the edge of the cliff and onto the foot of the ladder to join them.

20

Finality

The atmosphere in Rangehead was tense. The success of multi-national sea-trials, led by the US Atlantic Fleet, were vital to the future of the Hebrides Rocket Range and by extension the future of the Hebridean economy in general. The fact that the control room had lost contact with one of several sea-skimming Banshee target drones was more than embarrassing considering the recent debacle at St Kilda.

The British developed Banshee had been in service since the 1980s when various navies found themselves vulnerable to attack from sea-skimming missiles. The Banshee 300 had developed a malfunction in its control receiver and was now racing toward St Kilda, skimming the Atlantic swell to mimic an enemy attack from beyond the horizon. It should have been skimming the sea toward a US cruiser out to the west, in the direction of Rockall.

The Banshee would float if knocked down by a 'hitile' such as the British Rapier missile. The Rapier, fast as it was, needed to hit its target to explode. With dummy warheads used for training purposes Rapiers simply punched target drones out of the air and damaged Banshees would be retrieved from the sea and patched up to fly again. There was no real danger from an out-of-control fibreglass drone, it would eventually run out of fuel and fall to the sea, where the small, bright orange unmanned aerial vehicle would float and be easily retrieved to fly another day.

This Banshee, however, was being tracked toward St Kilda and if, as Rangehead suspected, the guidance mechanism had locked the drone would be likely to enter Village Bay within the next few minutes and crash ignominiously into the old Base. An incident which would rub salt into the still open sore following the removal of MOD employees from the now decommissioned St Kilda tracking station.

Very reluctantly, Rangehead asked for help from the US Atlantic Fleet. The exercises were being monitored from a *Nimitz*-class aircraft carrier and when the request from Rangehead was received, it came as no real surprise. With one thing and another, the American military had come to expect overstretched British defence systems to prove unreliable. Knocking down one of their Banshee drones from beyond the horizon would be a useful training exercise for the carrier's MK 29 Sea-Sparrow launch team.

Erica's house cow was grazing near the old diesel power station when she glanced seaward, hearing the buzz of the approaching Banshee. A few accompanying Soay sheep briefly looked up before resuming the morning's grazing with their new flock leader. None of the sheep had ever seen a cow before and now followed Bridgit as the alpha female. Ovine business would no doubt return to normal when the rutting season started. That was Agatha's advice to Erica who had expressed some surprise at Bridgit's woolly following.

The sound of the approaching drone became clearly audible to the sisters as they discussed their father's tragic accident. They went outside Erica's blackhouse in time to see the bright orange drone pass Levenish, apparently heading straight for them.

'For fuck's sake! What's that coming toward us?'

Erica looked at Agatha, who for once seemed lost for an answer.

As the Banshee entered the mouth of the bay, a blast of wind roared down from the hill and a water-devil spun out into the bay. The spinning column of water intercepted the Banshee just as it passed the end of the jetty, within metres of the old power station. The water-devil tossed the

Banshee away to career wildly into the basalt cliff below Ruiaval just as the Sea Sparrow flashed through the Dun Gap.

The U.S. navy fire team were enjoying this one and wanted to show off their control skills to the embarrassed Brits. One minute the Banshee was there on their screens, the next it was gone, smashed into a thousand pieces and sinking to the sea floor. This Banshee was not going to be retrieved.

The Sea Sparrow, deprived of its target, screeched across the bay to smash through rusted curtain doors on the seaward side of the power station. The explosion inside sent shards of shrapnel spraying out toward the grazing animals. Internal diesel tanks ruptured instantly, and fires broke out, rapidly growing in intensity.

Erica screamed and ran toward the scene.

'Bridgit! Bastards! Bastards! Fucking bastards!'

It took Agatha a moment to catch up with her sister now kneeling by the head of her injured cow. One of the animal's hind legs was clearly broken and lying on the ground she lowed in pain as the black smoke from the burning power station drifted over them. Agatha reached for the knife attached to her belt.

'Agatha, what are you doing?'

Erica's voice was as menacing as it was questioning.

'I'm going to put her out of her misery, Erica. I've done it many times to the sheep. A grazing animal with a broken leg will suffer for days and never be able to eat properly. If infection doesn't kill her, starvation will and out here the Bonxies will soon have her eyes out. Let me slit her throat, it really is the kindest thing to do.'

Tine went to cut Brigit's throat when a heavy punch from her sister knocked her sideways.

'If she needs putting down, I'll do it!'

There really was no argument that euthanasia was the only choice for the cow lying on the ground surrounded by

438

rusty metal and broken concrete. Agatha let her sister run to the blackhouse and fetch the Tikka rifle. Agatha quickly slit the throats of several injured sheep lying nearby. Erica walked back slowly with tears running down her smoke blackened cheeks.

'Stand aside Agatha, I don't want any more accidents.'

Erica loaded the rifle with a single hollow-point round. With the safety catch on, she lay the gun on the ground and kneeled to kiss Bridgit gently on the forehead exactly where she would place the muzzle of the rifle. At such close quarters the telescopic sights would be useless, and it had to be a final painless end for the animal. She released the safety catch, placed the muzzle on the still moist patch on Bridgit's forehead and fired. The hollow point bullet expanded inside the animal's brain and the deformed lead slug span down through the cow's body to exit her abdomen. Through the gaping exit wound the intestines could be seen still heaving against the shock of the impact. With a heavy sigh, Bridgit died and with her died Erica's hopes for resettlement at St Kilda.

The carrier reported back to Rangehead that the Banshee had been destroyed. The problem was solved and now perhaps they could all get on with their exercise. It was only when the fire spread to the Base that the smoke could be seen from Rangehead.

From the observation post above the 'Lady of the Isles' monument a large fire could clearly be seen burning on the horizon. Clouds of black smoke billowed from the west and as evening fell the smoke was underlit by the glow of flames beneath. There was nothing to be done that evening and Range Control certainly did not want any more American intervention on their patch.

A phone call to Don secured the *Beluga* to take an inspection crew out at first light. Reluctantly it was agreed that they needed to inform the Americans that the *Beluga*

439

was going out and would they please refrain from firing on the boat, it was not a training target.

Range Control tried to remain as discreet as possible, and Don was asked to pick up the inspection team by dingy from the beach below Rangehead before crossing to St Kilda. Once aboard, Don, grateful for the extra business, set off for the islands.

Agatha had dragged the dead sheep to the low cliff edge in front of the power station and tipped them into the sea the previous evening. She had wanted to do the same with Bridgit but even had she been strong enough, Erica was firmly against her sister disposing of the cow that way.

There was no obvious answer, and Erica had stayed with her all night to keep early morning Skuas away from the carcass. Something had to be done with the body, she even thought of butchering the dead animal but there was no way of storing such a large amount of meat with things as they were.

What would the St Kildans have done? Probably divided up the meat amongst the island families so that each would have a manageable amount to deal with. Today, it was impossible with just Agatha, Sally and herself left. Erica was still sobbing when some two hours after leaving South Uist at full throttle, the *Beluga* roared into the bay.

The devastation in the aftermath of the fire was clear to see. While most of the sturdy power station building still stood, blackened by diesel smoke, the flimsily built Base buildings were destroyed by the fire which had quickly spread and made the adjoining Manse uninhabitable. Agatha had temporarily moved into the Factor's House with Sally, neither of whom wanted it to be a permanent arrangement.

Agatha had thought to leave Erica to grieve over Bridgit, not realising her tears were as much of frustration at the failure to even begin to rekindle a sustainable community at St Kilda. Agatha fetched them both fresh water from the well. As they drank, Erica's swore that, once again, men had caused everything to go wrong on the island and now here they were, back again, to gloat over the success of their missile strike.

Erica rubbed her sleep deprived eyes and stood up. That was it! The men had fired a missile at them to deliberately prevent her rebuilding the community. They didn't want women here at all, it was so fucking obvious! Well, they had three women here to deal with and they meant business. Erica picked herself up and ran back to the blackhouse to pick up her rifle and this time collected several clips of ammunition. They were not coming ashore, no way!

Don had spotted Erica running toward her blackhouse.

'There's Erica, at least she's alright. I wonder where the others are.'

The *Beluga* headed toward the jetty. Don was intending to disembark the inspection team so they could send back a preliminary report as to what had happened. There was an element of *schaden freude* that the Americans had fouled up on shooting down the Banshee.

That was the obvious first conclusion, but the Trust would have to be informed too. After all, it was their island in spite of a sizeable chunk still leased out to the British military. The lease required removal of all military buildings on termination of the lease and the Americans would certainly have to contribute to the astronomical cost of demolition now they had already started the job with their botched missile strike.

By the time the *Beluga* was alongside ready to be tied up Erica was standing on top of the decrepit gabion sea defence wall shouting at the men to clear off. She was waving the rifle in one hand and pointing at the boat to emphasise her anger at their presence.

'You bastards! Do you think you could get rid of us so easily? I don't give a shit about the buildings but why did you have to go and kill Brigit?'

Don heard the last words of her rant aimed at them and decided to step ashore and find out what had happened. He was as concerned as Erica if something had happened to the cow.

'Get back, Don! Get back or so help me, I'll shoot you.'

Erica levelled the Tikka at Don as he stepped onto the jetty. He raised his hands and stepped back on board.

'Well gentlemen it seems we have a problem. Apparently, we are not welcome. She's a friend of mine, so I recommend we leave it for now and come back another day when things have calmed down.'

'Not likely, Don!'

The senior member of the inspection team from Rangehead expressed his concern that after paying Don around £200 a head for the return trip, the guys were going ashore and that was that. The inspection team gathered together at the top of the steps waiting for instructions. Erica still had them covered and the team found it more than disconcerting to be faced with an armed stand-off. It should have been a leisurely day assessing the damage caused by the US Navy's Sea Sparrow.

Mike, the team supervisor looked up at Erica with a mixture of pity and frustration.

'Come on, girl. Put that thing away and we can get on with our work. Then we'll go and leave you folks in piece.'

Mike had walked barely a couple of steps when the shot rang out. The bullet hit the concrete close to his feet and ricocheted noisily out across the bay.

'Now fuck off, the lot of you! Come any further and you're dead.'

Mike made the quick and correct decision to retreat, ordering the men back on board.

'Jesus Christ, Don! That woman's mad.'

'Aye, and she's a crack shot too. She meant to miss just then. I don't want to be around if she aims to hit us.'

Don reversed the *Beluga* away from the jetty, before turning the bow eastwards back toward the Uists. The swell was building, and the boat lurched unsettlingly toward the mouth of the bay. Whether from nervous tension or seasickness, Mike suddenly threw up.

As usual, Lachie helped Don with domestic arrangements at sea and he should have spotted the signs and passed Ian a sick bag, conveniently contained in a plastic beer glass. This time he groaned and reached into the cupboard beneath the cockpit to retrieve a mop and bucket. He took a backward glance to the island and saw Erica had run along the shore to watch them from the 1918 naval gun emplacement.

'She's still watching us, Don. Thank fuck that old cannon's just held together by rust or she'd be thinking about blowing us out of the water, I reckon.'

Mike, who by now had been given a fresh sick bag, asked to use the VHF radio to call Rangehead. Don passed the handset to him.

'We had to abort the inspection. You won't believe it, but we were shot at by a lunatic woman with a hunting rifle. Can you inform the Police and let them deal with this. We can go out another time when she's off the island.'

'There's no need to involve the Police, Mike. She'll be fine in a day or two. That island gets to you, and I have taken quite a few off suffering from depression, usually after a heavy night or two. You don't know what she's been on, and the killing of her cow must have tipped her over the edge. Just leave her be for now and I'll talk to her before the team go ashore next time.'

'No way, man. She's a danger to herself as much as us. I am going to let the Police deal with it. Crack shot or not, I doubt she's got a licence for that thing so it shouldn't be a problem to get her put away for a while.'

When the duty officer in Tarbert received the complaint, he could barely believe his ears. This simply did not happen in the Hebrides. There was no armed response unit in the isles and even if there was, how were they going to get to St Kilda? He would have to contact the mainland.

It appeared the nearest armed response unit was based in Glasgow and trained in anti-terrorism and gang related firearm incidents. Urban firearm situations were their forte and he could imagine the collective groan at being sent to deal with not only a rural incident but one on the outermost of the Hebridean islands. The firearms unit would have to be helicoptered out and it would cost the Glasgow council taxpayers a small fortune; St Kilda was such a bloody expensive place to get to. Don's passenger business pretty well kept the Tarbert economy afloat, but it would take too long to get the Glasgow boys out there on the *Beluga*.

Erica walked back to her blackhouse, satisfied for the time being that the Rangehead team had gone. She had run up to the Gap to make sure they weren't going to land in Glen Bay and sneak back to the village, over the hill. Agatha and Sally had seen and heard the commotion and were waiting outside the door for her.

'Come here, Erica. You need a good hug, a bloody good one.'

Sally held Erica close and let the emotion inside her pour out. Erica was sobbing again as Agatha took the rifle from her and put it away indoors. The three women went inside to talk about what to do next. Sally and Agatha were silent for a while, not knowing what to say.

Erica's well controlled shot had taken them over a threshold. Things could not be the same again and Erica knew that as much as any of them.

Sally spoke first.

'The Police are bound to be involved, Erica. I know Mike and he doesn't let go of things like this. Don would have been alright about it, but I am afraid we will be visited

444

again in the morning. There's no way they'll get themselves together to come out today, but they will be here in the morning. Whatever you do keep that gun hidden and let me do the talking. I am a qualified nurse, and you are having a bad bout of clinical depression, OK? We should be able to have you placed under medical supervision for a few weeks and then get back to normal. One thing I would say is that I think it is time you called it a day out here. We tried to resettle St Kilda but its led to deaths and chaos. Time to admit defeat, don't you think, girls?'

Agatha didn't say a word. What could she add? She could hardly admit to the thrill she felt at imminently having the island to herself and her child to be. Sally was sure to go off island with Erica when gun toting Police arrived in the morning.

'You are probably right, Sally. But I can't leave, not after we have tried so hard.'

Erica felt sick with tension knowing the challenges the morning would bring. At that very moment she was torn between making a stand against the undoubtedly male Police officers who would come to arrest her or leaving quietly, accepting Sally's diplomatic diagnosis of severe depression. She was intelligent enough to allow herself the rest of the day and night to think things through before making her decision.

'It's your call, Erica but we'll be in the Factor's House while you think about it.'

Being separate from the Base, unlike the Manse which abutted the military buildings, the Factor's House had escaped the fire started by the American missile. Agatha and Sally walked back to the two bedroomed house where Agatha had salvaged what she could of her belongings and moved into the spare room.

Sally was uneasy about the arrangement but for the time being there seemed no other choice for Agatha. They would all be leaving in a day or two and the island could be left for the sheep and birds.

The Police helicopter had refuelled at Stornoway before making the crossing to St Kilda. The intelligence had been good. Somehow, the officers had known about Erica's feminist leanings and wisely thought to send out a couple of female police firearms officers. They would hopefully be perceived as less provocation than their male colleagues.

The two markswomen were landed at Glen Bay before the helicopter circled the island to approach from Village Bay. The Police pilot approached cautiously, hovering over Dun and keeping out of accurate range of Erica's rifle. Agatha saw thousands of distressed seabirds leave their nests in panic as the machine hovered over their breeding grounds. The Puffins would never return to their burrows after such a disturbance and countless chicks would be abandoned. Incensed, she ran to the blackhouse and screamed at Erica.

'This is all your fault, Erica. Look what they are doing, they're ruining the breeding site. They are only supposed to approach the helipad well away from the breeding grounds, down the middle of the bay, don't they know that rule applies to all helicopters. It is up to you, Erica. Do something about it!'

Erica had hardly slept that night and in her tiredness and confusion, her mind was made up. She would make a stand. Picking up the rifle and placing an unopened box of ammunition in her daysack she made her way to the Hidey-Holes in the scree slope below Mullach Sgar.

It took about five minutes to get there, and the police had already spotted her picking her way across the boggy ground, then up to the scree before disappearing from sight. They radioed the two armed policewomen making their way up Glen Mór toward the ridge.

'Suspect last seen on the scree slope above the beach in Village Bay. You should be able to look down on her when

446

you cross the ridge. Meanwhile we will try to land at the helipad and let's keep our fingers crossed she has had time to see sense since yesterday.'

The two policewomen made their way up Glen Mór under the watchful eye of hundreds of Great Skuas. The Bonxies did not attack as they would have done had male police officers approached, but they were wary. Rising beyond the Well of Virtues, the pair laboured uphill passing the Amazon's House on their left.

In spite of their police physical training the two armed women struggled up the steeply sloping glen. Urban training scenarios were no preparation for action on a volcanic island in the North Atlantic.

They were both shaken by the unexpected blast of wind that lifted them off their feet to fall back toward Glen Bay. Picking themselves up and re-slinging their sniper rifles the two policewomen made it to the turf dyke boundary at the top of the glen. Exhausted they sat down on the remains of a peat drying cleit to recover. They were about to comment on the incredible view out to Soay when the radio message came through. Their suspect was last seen on the scree slope below them on the Village Bay side of the hill. They got up and walked the short distance to the military roadway, cracked and weed-strewn since the last MOD vehicle had left months before.

Village Bay lay before them and the ruins of the Base clear for all to behold. To the left still lay heaps of rusting steel and broken radomes following the opportunist terrorist attack on the radar station at Mullach Mhor. Scree sloped away towards the village and the bay.

'How on earth are we going to find her in all this lot?'

The other policewoman shrugged and spoke on her radio to the officer commanding in the still hovering helicopter.

'OK, just stay in position until we spot her. We'll know soon enough.'

447

The pilot cautiously flew the Strathclyde Police Eurocopter slowly past the Dun gap and followed the cliff edge of Ruiaval to cross above the scree slopes intending to descend safely to the helipad above the beach. It was, he reckoned, foolish to risk flying in straight across the open bay with an armed and unstable suspect watching their every move, from wherever she happened to be at that moment.

The pilot swore audibly as Erica's first shot entered the belly of the helicopter. Fear gripped the two unarmed officers on board and all three quickly smelled the leaking aviation fuel.

'We are going to land, now!'

The pilot yelled at them to brace as he took the machine in a rapid controlled descent to the helipad. The sudden blast of wind coming down from the hill took the pilot unawares and the helicopter lurched sideways across the beach. In trying to turn, the main rotor contacted the shingle bank heaped up by winter storms.

The Police Eurocopter, its rotor blades mangled, spun to crash on its side on the grey sand where the freshwater stream of the west burn, Abhainn Mhor, reached the sea. Securely strapped in their seats, the occupants of the helicopter, bruised and shaken, knew they had to get away from the machine and its leaking fuel tank.

Erica watched as the three men ran for cover behind the earth bund sheltering the power station fuel tanks. She didn't want to kill anyone, but the two police markswomen weren't to know that.

Sitting on the ridge at Mullach Geal the two policewomen saw the cautious progression of the helicopter above the scree, heard a rifle shot and saw the machine suddenly veer off to be hit by a gust of wind and crash land on the beach. They spotted their colleagues run for cover behind the earth bund surrounding the main diesel storage tanks.

Eileen Macarthy whispered to her colleague Liz Stobart.

'She must be down there. The guys in the chopper must have spotted her before they veered off. Pity they smashed the chopper but at least they look okay. She will be watching them and not expecting us to come down from above her.'

Sally had seen the crash and come running from the Factor's House with her medical bag. In the past she had been stationed at the helipad on flight days just in case such a thing happened. At least she had seen the guys get up and run away, they couldn't be hurt much which was a blessing. Panting, she arrived at the diesel tanks.

'Get down!'

The pilot hissed at her to keep out of sight of the scree slopes. He explained how the chopper had been shot at, piercing the fuel tank and then a gust of wind had hit them at a crucial moment as he tried to land. At least they had made it to cover here among the tanks.

Sally was pleased there were no serious injuries to deal with and, getting her breath back, she retorted.

'If she had wanted to kill you, she would have done so. Erica is a crack shot, and she is letting you live so don't get any ideas about taking her on. Leave her to me now and I'll talk her out of making any more mistakes with that wretched rifle of hers.'

Erica watched Sally leave the cover of the earth bund and make her way, out in the open moorland, toward the foot of the scree slope. The path was now hard to see but in MOD times there had been a famous cross country run that took in the cleft in the hillside. Runners would be reduced to their hands and knees by the ascent. She knew that Erica would be in the Hidey-Hole near the foot of the cleft. She also prayed Erica would not open fire on her as she would be totally exposed as she climbed the slope toward her friend.

'Erica, it's me, Sally. Don't shoot!'

When she dropped into the hidden trench beside Erica, she took in her friend's tear-stained face.

'I didn't mean for the chopper to crash, Sally. Just wanted to warn them off, I thought they would fly off and leave us in peace. Those bastards, did you see what they did to the birds? Broke every rule in the book, flying in like that. It was no wonder they got caught in that down draft.'

A dull explosion distracted both women and they turned from each other to see the damaged helicopter burst into flames on the beach.

'Thank God, those men got out in time Erica, or you could be facing a murder charge.'

'I don't want to kill anyone, Sally. Why can't they just leave us alone?'

Erica collapsed into Sally's arms sobbing uncontrollably for the second time in as many days. A large stone came clattering down from the scree above them as the two police markswomen took position.

'Shit! Now she knows we are here.'

Liz was never one to mince words.

'It's no wonder we are dealing with nutters in a place like this. Eileen, can you take her now and get this thing over with?'

Having Erica in their sights, their police firearms training kicked in. Having already downed the helicopter with her first shot, the policewomen were taking no chances. This was a terrorist situation as far as they were concerned, and it was shoot to kill, before anything else happened.

Eileen had the crosshairs of her telescopic sight squarely on Erica's head as she peered out of the trench down toward the beach and burning helicopter.

'Damn it Liz, there's two of them now but I don't think the second one is armed.'

'I had better shout a warning then or we'll be in deep shit when we get back.'

Liz bellowed down to Erica and Sally.

'Armed Police! Put down your weapons and come out where we can see you. There will be no further warning!'

Erica and Sally ducked back in the Hidey-Hole out of the line of sight of the policewomen. No one moved for several minutes.

'You stay here, Eileen. Take her if you can and I'll move over there to get a second shot from the ledge if needs be.'

Erica watched as Liz made her way to the ledge at the side of the cleft dividing the hillside. She could have picked her off easily but made no attempt to do so.

Agatha was waiting behind a rock at the vantage point and cracked Liz's skull with one blow from a large stone. Liz tumbled silently to fall crumpled at the foot of the slope, her body battered and, as Agatha had intended, the damage to her skull would be indistinguishable from multiple injuries caused by her fall.

The impact of the falling body alerted a pair of Arctic Skuas nesting near the foot of the slope. Every other predatory bird on the island new to keep a safe distance from Arctic Skuas. Even the large black Ravens of St Kilda would divert their flight away from the Arctic's nesting ground.

Eileen screamed in pain as the impact of the female bird's attack burst her right eyeball. She stood up, dropping her rifle as the male Arctic Skua hit her hard on the back of the head. Erica spun round and looked up the slope above her to see the police markswoman holding her face in her hands, blood running through her fingers. Agatha was above her, higher on the scree watching through binoculars as the pair of Arctic Skuas returned to their nest site, satisfied they had warned off the intruder.

Sally scrambled out of the Hidey-Hole and climbed the scree to aid the injured policewoman. She also noticed the crumpled figure in black police waterproofs lying far below at the foot of the cleft. The figure must surely be dead down there, but her concern was with the living right now. She tried to lift Eileen's hand from her face, the one covering the burst eye, but with the other the policewoman pushed her away hard. Sally tumbled backward but luckily fell on soft turf at the edge of the scree. She quickly picked herself up spoke quietly, yet assertively to the injured officer.

'I am a trained nurse; you must let me see your eye. I might be able to help and at least I can bandage it for you.'

When Eileen finally agreed to let Sally look at the injury, it was obvious that the right eye was damaged beyond hope of recovery. The impact of birds tearing beak had shredded the tissue of her eyeball. Eileen would never shoot again and would have precious little chance of staying in the Police service after this incident. While Sally bandaged up Eileen's bloody eye socket as best she could from her field first aid box, Agatha slipped away quietly to join her sister in the trench below.

The smell of trampled Mothan growing in the damp floor of the Hidey-Hole was strong as Agatha climbed down to join her sister. Erica looked vacant, bewildered by everything that had happened around her that morning.

'It's alright, Erica. It's over now. I couldn't let them shoot you, they would have too. They are trained killers, and I was watching them, could imagine what they were saying. It would have been so much easier to take you out with a sniper rifle than go through the bother of trying to arrest you. Once you had fired at the helicopter, they had full authority to kill you. You are lucky she let me call the Arctics.'

Erica looked more puzzled than ever.

'I really have no idea what you are talking about Agatha. But thank you for saving my life. I just wish we didn't have yet another death on our hands.'

452

'She slipped and fell, Erica, just slipped and fell. This scree slope is treacherous, and those city cops were way out of their depth here. They should have kept off the scree, and well away from the Arctic's nest. It's not our fault, just a pity they didn't speak to us first rather than sneak up from Glen Bay.

Had they been male police officers, the Bonxies would have seen them off for sure, but it took the Arctics to recognise the maleness of their intention. Women acting out male roles, we will have to be watchful for that from now on.'

'Agatha, this is the end. There won't be anything to watch out for from now on. I'll be arrested and taken away. Look the other police are walking up here now.'

The pilot and three policemen had left the cover of the diesel tanks bund having deduced the danger was over up on the scree. They scrambled and slipped as they made their way to join the women. The senior officer swore quietly as he saw the crumpled body at the foot of the cleft but was pleased to see Eileen receiving competent medical attention as the men struggled to the Hidey-Hole.

The sound of high-powered marine diesel engines made all on the slope turn around to watch the *Beluga* roar into the bay.

'What the fuck? Didn't that man get the message or what?

Erica once again picked up the Tikka and took aim only to have Agatha at once pull the rifle away from her.

'No Erica, no. We are going to need these guns – and we are going to need Don and the *Beluga* next year. We can't do this on our own and Don's alright, he's on our side. Now give me the rifle.'

There was a small cave on the hillside known to very few except the student sheep researchers who had come to the island in previous years to test out hypotheses regarding the genetics of Soay Sheep.

You had to wriggle through the small muddy entrance but once inside you could sit, almost stand in relative dryness. An ideal place for secret parties as the remains of candles and empty whisky bottles bore witness. Agatha placed the Tikka and two police issue Heckler and Koch G3s with full magazines in the driest spot she could find in there. When she returned to her sister, the front of her waterproof jacket and trousers were plastered in mud.

'Quick Erica, do as I say!'

They both picked up the two largest stones from the scree that they could manage and screamed as they hurled them over the cliff to fall with spectacular splashes into the deep water at the front of the Cailleach's Cave. The screaming drew the attention of the policemen, just as Agatha had intended.

'Now what on earth is going on with you women?'

The senior policeman had had just about enough and was really pleased that Don had turned up. Tourism to St Kilda underpinned Don's business, he must have seen the fire on the horizon and come out to check what had happened. Now they would at least get back to the Uists tonight, away from this god forsaken rock in the North Atlantic.

This time it was Erica's time to speak. Her future liberty might depend on what she did and said now and she thought Agatha's plan sounded workable given their present circumstance.

'We've thrown those fucking guns in the sea. I've had enough of shooting and death here. Just look at our home down there, can't you see the ruin your missile caused us. Enough is enough, I can't take anymore.'

Erica sobbed uncontrollably in front of Sally and the grouped police officers. Sally left the injured Eileen in the care of her male colleagues and went to comfort Erica. She whispered as she put her arms around her friend.

'Good ruse, Erica. Even I can't decide between genuine depression and what you're making up now. Let's keep to the story that you are severely depressed; the police won't be bothered for now. They just want to get away from this place and when I write my report and copy it to them, you'll be just fine if you accept appropriate treatment for clinical depression. After all, you didn't kill anyone, just put the fear of God into a few.'

Sally squeezed Erica's hand to secretly emphasise her tacit support for what she had been going through. Agatha was another matter and if anyone should be locked away, in her professional opinion, it should be the younger sister.

Sally supported Erica as she climbed out of the Hidey-Hole, her face streaked with mud and tears. The senior policeman muttered something about wilful destruction of police property, meaning the rifles he believed had been thrown in the sea. For now, he had the more important matter of getting himself and his officers away from St Kilda as soon as humanly possible.

When the group reached the foot of the slope, they met Don at the helipad. He had asked Lachie to stay on board and sail for help should he not return in a reasonable time. He fully understood the inherent danger of an armed, depressed woman facing trigger happy Glasgow police in such a remote location.

Pity about the chopper, Don thought.

Such an eyesore lying there on the beach and not likely to add anything to the green tourist business he had just been discussing with Agatha for next year. Agatha had slipped away as the injured parties comforted each other and briefly proposed her idea as she walked with Don toward the helipad.

So much had happened since they arrived on the island, it was obvious that Dave's idea of a nuclear family resettling St Kilda wasn't going to work. Now it was down to women to rebuild the community. Women would need men, of course, but on their terms. Agatha was wise enough to accept she couldn't do it all on her own but with Erica's help it could be possible.

'So, gentlemen and ladies, I expect you'll be wanting a lift back to the real world, will Leverburgh do you? When we get closer in I'll give them a call and I reckon the 'Moorings' will be more than happy to feed you and put you up for the night. You can get the bus to Stornoway in the morning and then, if the plane hasn't broken down again, you can get the mid-day flight back to Glasgow, all at taxpayers' expense.'

Sally gave Don a warning glance.

'I'm just going to the Factor's House for the inflatable stretcher. We have another casualty, Don. This one won't be walking off the island I am afraid. Now will you please take care of Erica while I go and get it. Two of you will need to remain here and carry the casualty when I get back, okay?'

By the time the stretcher was placed beside Liz, *Rigor mortis* was beginning to affect her body.

'Quick as you can, boys. Straighten her legs before she gets too stiff.'

The two police officers wiped their hands on the grass after straightening out Liz's broken legs. Her trousers were soaked in urine, released as she fell dying from Agatha's clubbing. Liz's arms were placed by her sides with some difficulty and only prevented from springing up again by tightening the straps of the stretcher.

'Don't worry boys, she can't feel anything now.'

Sally placed her own woolly Beanie hat over Liz's blood matted hair, and she looked to all intents and purposes as respectable as a corpse could be under the circumstances.

'Righto, let's get her down to the boat.'

The policemen carrying Liz's body were shattered by the morning's events. They had been looking forward to the scenic flight from Glasgow and what should have been a relatively straight forward arrest of a depressed female suspect.

They had lost one officer, another badly injured, and a multi-million-pound helicopter was a total write off. There was also MOD property left a smouldering ruin but that wasn't their problem.

The stretcher bearers had to put Liz's body down several times to rest, before nearly dropping her as they passed the stretcher to Lachie waiting on the *Beluga*. The stretcher was attached to the small crane they used to lift their inflatable Zodiac tender on board and the body was stowed at the rear of the open deck. Lachie was well aware that Don wouldn't take kindly to a leaking corpse inside his pristine saloon.

The rest of the group were already aboard the *Beluga* by the time the stretcher was loaded. All agreed that Sally should take charge of Erica and get her into some kind of safe accommodation for the night before local police could interview her in the morning.

It would have to be done, there was no doubting that, but Sally was well respected in Leverburgh, and her mother's croft would be a good a place as any. According to Sally, Erica was clinically depressed but genuine or not, it would be up to Erica to keep up the act for a few days yet. The authorities would soon agree for her to resume normal life once it became clear what they had all been through out at St Kilda.

Eileen had been given strong pain killers and Don joked as usual that passengers rarely felt seasick on the return journey to Harris. They were about to depart from the historic jetty, leaving the wrecked helicopter and ruins of the Base and Manse still smouldering behind them when Erica asked the obvious question.

'Where's Agatha?'

Agatha had last been seen near the helipad after walking up from the jetty with Don. It was Erica who

457

spotted her as she took a last glance toward her lovingly restored blackhouse. The home she would now have to leave, for a while at least.

It was hard to understand why it had all gone so terribly wrong for them. The Williams family had such high hopes of a new life, away from the liveable stress of twenty-first century Edinburgh, but the stress of living at St Kilda had proved unbearable.

According to Sally, the environment had changed, it was becoming milder and wetter. Ideal growing conditions and the weaker sheep were now surviving winters when previously they would have succumbed. Everything was growing so well she had more than once remarked. Just look at the Mothan, she had pointed out by way of example. The damper areas were awash with purple flowers. Milder conditions also meant more midges so the increased insectivorous Mothan plants could hardly be surprising. Arguably, just a problem when rotted leaves got into the water supply.

Agatha came out of Erica's blackhouse at the end of the village and stood gazing across the bay toward a small pod of dolphins playing along the edge of Dun. The deeper waters on that side of the bay were teeming with fish and the dolphins knew the right places to feed, as did the resident seal population.

'If you don't mind waiting for a moment, I think Erica and I should go and find out what Agatha plans to do.'

Sally needed to find out, to let Josephine at the Western Isles Trust know, if Agatha was planning to stay.

'If she is coming with us, then she needs to get a move on.'

Don, Lachie and the police team were getting impatient to leave. The Police in particular didn't want to spend another minute on the island. An unexpected hiss of air from Eileen's corpse, still trussed in the stretcher on the deck, emphasised the point.

Sally and Erica walked briskly over the fields to the restored blackhouse where Agatha greeted them. Sally came straight to the point.

'We need to leave now Agatha. So, are you coming or not?'

Agatha seemed distant, lost in thought.

'Sorry, what was that? Leave here, why?'

Erica explained, 'You'll be on your own Agatha, and I won't be back for long while, maybe not at all if I get banged up in a psychiatric hospital or something.'

Erica really did sound depressed, negativity was so unlike her, thought Sally. But, if Agatha wanted to stay then so be it. The island was unrestricted, had been ever since the 2003 Land Reform Act opened up much of Scotland for the public to enjoy without fear of gamekeepers and stalkers giving them a hard time.

'Okay, Agatha, that's fine by me but just one thing. Take good care of my cottage, please. I put my soul into making that ruin a home and as we all know, once empty, when the living fire is extinguished, it will quickly become a ruin once again.'

'Don't worry, dear sister. This place will be ideal for us.'

Erica detected a hint of sarcasm in Agatha's reply, but let it go when in the past she would have made appoint of winkling out what she meant.

'Erica, you will be back and sooner than you expect. Stop fretting and go and get your, err, treatment. I'll have the fire lit when you return. Just please don't bring that friend of yours back with you.'

'You mean, Dan? You must mean him and I very much doubt if he'd ever come back but who knows. Maybe even Mum.'

'No way, she's a liability now and I couldn't ever imagine her and Dan on the same island, could you?'

The sisters both laughed briefly at the thought of their mother's fling with Dan.

'Poor boy, he wouldn't have known what hit him, until it was too late.'

'It was such a shame Dad finally lost it though, Agatha. The affair must have tipped him over the edge, literally. This is no place for the depressed which is why I need to go and get my head sorted. Yeah, maybe see you sooner than you think. A fresh start here would be a good thing to look forward to.'

Agatha explained her earlier discussion with Don about bringing paying visitors to St Kilda to help rebuild the community. There should be families out here but families living in harmony with the island and its environment, not trying to brutally wrest their living from it as had been done over the past 150 years.

'Don't worry, I'll be just fine. And I will take good care of your cottage, Erica. In fact, I look forward to restoring a few more with you when you get back.'

Agatha gave Erica a warm hug to send her on her way. Sally extended her hand only. She couldn't trust Agatha further than she could throw her and suspected her involvement in the tragic accidents that happened over the past few weeks.

The stalkers, Dave's apparent suicide and the death of the policewoman now lying on the deck of the *Beluga*. With her affinity with the wildlife on the island, could she have instigated the Skua attack which appeared to have left one policewoman dead the other part blinded? No, that was a crazy thought!

'Right then, time to say goodbye. I doubt I'll be here any time soon, but no doubt you'll see Erica back in a few months. So better luck next time, Agatha. Don't get too fat eating all the food we are leaving behind. Don will bring you more out when you need it.'

'We will be just fine, Sally. Don't worry about us. Don't worry about us at all.'

Agatha was becoming distant again and Sally found her use of 'we' irritating. Who did she think she was, Queen of St Kilda?

Sally linked her arm through Erica's and the two women made their way back to the boat.

'She's a queer fish, your sister. There's no mistaking that. What's with the 'we' business? She will be on her own and no doubt loving it.'

Erica laughed at the thought, and they were both in better spirits as they approached the boat. Sally cautioned Erica to appear stressed before they stepped on board.

'Thank God for that! Can we just go now before Liz out there decides to get up and stay too?'

The senior police officer let out an audible sigh of relief as Don started the engines. Lachie untied the mooring ropes, and they were on their way. Three hours to get back to the relative sanity of Leverburgh, he thought. And a stiff drink in the 'Moorings' before anything else happened.

Agatha made no attempt to go to the jetty to see the group off but did wave to her sister as the *Beluga* began to bounce over the swell at the mouth of Village Bay. She ignored the ruins of the Base and chose to avoid the area as much as possible after salvaging what she could from the relatively intact kitchen area.

There were plenty of fish and birds' eggs to collect. Down in Glen Mór, after Agatha had been chewing Mothan, Morrigan had said it was okay to go back to harvesting eggs as long as she didn't over pick any one area. Just a friendly warning, but she would send the Bonxies if Agatha took too many.

The Arctic Skuas were her elite guards, Agatha thought. The Bonxies her foot soldiers.

Maybe one day that policewoman, Eileen, would come to know what it was all about and why she had to lose her eye.

The guns were safely hidden, and Agatha would have no immediate use for them, but it would be good to keep them oiled and ready as you never knew who could come sailing into the bay. Historically it had been Vikings, Barbary slavers and German 'U' Boats.So goodness knows who by the mid twenty-first century. As long as Morrigan was respected she would help them rebuild the island community, it was going to be good. As if to confirm this a sudden gust of wind ripped several more slates from the already fire damaged roof of the Kirk.

It had been over a month since her last period and Agatha was sure she was pregnant with her father's child. She went inside and sat at Erica's table.

The large Bible was still there, and she re-read the account of Lot and his daughters. It gave her satisfaction to realise that as devious and violent as she had become, her life here was preordained. It was all written down there in the Bible, God's words had borne fruit in her womb. Agatha rested her hands on her yet barely swollen belly. After taking another sip from her mug of Mothan tea she quietly spoke.

'You are a boy, and I will name you Benammi.......'

Epilogue

I hardly noticed to start with, my periods had stopped but that was the only sign of how my life would soon change. The fire had spoiled much of the Base food supply, but I fed myself well. Fishing from the jetty, collecting seabirds and their eggs; books in House One gave me all the tips I needed. Never a shortage of water and of course a near inexhaustible supply of mutton; I would try and corner my prey in a cleit rather than expend precious ammunition, better saved for what would come later.

Morning sickness was never much of a problem, a cup of Mothan tea would always settle my stomach and any soreness of my breasts was soon eased by a poultice of the same. Naturally I took care not to fall on my excursions across the island. I was still recording the bird migrations as before and Erica's off-grid electricity never failed me. No internet now the Manse had been wrecked but I saved my data to a memory stick and would upload my records when I could, probably when Don next came out.

I wasn't keen on entering what was left of the Base, too many bad memories lingered there. I followed in Sally's footsteps and collected a little peat to dry each time I went to the top of the hill. It was good exercise, and I am sure little Benammi, growing in my womb, benefited from the clean air I breathed in as I wound up the steep road to the ridge above Glen Mór.

Erica and Sally were concerned I would be lonely on my own here, but hardly a night passed without my dreaming of Morrigan, the Phantom Queen. She gave me so much good advice. We should rebuild in keeping with the environment and grow a strong community at Village Bay, unlike the inflexible nineteenth century mission and military occupation lying ruined beside us.

As Sally thought, it wasn't long before Erica came back;

I made sure her blackhouse was clean and tidy when I saw the *Beluga* on the horizon. I was actually quite pleased that Sally had come back with her; the thought of delivering Ben on my own scared me.

Sally had convinced the authorities that Erica was no danger to the public, just a young woman having suffered an unsurprising post-traumatic stress episode after the missile strike which killed her cow. Sally would vouch for Erica and effectively be her probation officer at St Kilda. Erica did receive a suspended prison sentence for possession of an unlicensed firearm, which the authorities believed was now lying irretrievable at the bottom of the Atlantic ocean.

It would take more than three enthusiastic women and a baby to rebuild the Village, but Josephine was intrigued by our plan to rebuild. She didn't like the idea of cannibalising the world heritage archaeology, but we were welcome to draw building material from the consumption walls. As for labour, we could source our own helpers, and she was sure working holiday volunteers could be put at our disposal.

As for the military mess, Josephine would have to get the MOD to deal with it, if they ever would. But in the meantime, we were still welcome to make use of what we could.

Equipment at the top of the hill had been spared the fire and, with the right volunteers and a knowledgeable leader, work parties could restore communications to the outside world. In fact, Josephine considered that a priority rather than have to rely on Don and the Beluga to get messages in and out.

Sally's medical room was badly damaged by the fire, but along with what she brought out, we had enough supplies for her to set up in the Factor's House. A real cottage hospital which would be kept busy as we worked to rebuild St Kilda.

I would be the first of the New St Kildans to have my baby delivered there. My labour was easy, being so fit and I hardly felt a thing. Maybe my pain had been numbed by Mothan, but Sally suspected the herb may have had an effect on Bennami's development. Born on twenty-fourth of June, his unworldly high-pitched crying kept on for many months, which kept me away from my responsibilities as organiser and leader of our project.

The male helpers were very useful. Their physical strength pulled us through many a difficult situation. Even so, we women were always on guard for signs of inappropriate behaviour.

Like before, out here away from mainland constraints, behaviours were not always compatible with our own, my, expectations. Not only the men; a few female volunteers behaved badly, upsetting the careful dynamic we endeavoured to maintain. Morrigan was everywhere, immortal, invincible and wise. No longer banished to the north side of the island, here on the sunny south she relaxed but was vigilant for any sign of injustice.

The so-called Druids who came out soon packed up and left when they found out what was really happening here. We were starting to rebalance nature, but their idea of planting an Oak grove was a non-starter from the word go.

Another stupid male fantasy taking no account of ecological reality. It wasn't Soay sheep grazing that was the problem. The reintroduction of White-tailed Sea Eagles had sorted that problem out by then. When we brought in new sheep they were too heavy for the Eagles to take and, thankfully, were not interested in climbing on our walls and new turf roofs.

We did make use of the old shrines and alters around the islands; it didn't feel right to ignore what felt instinctively right when it came to worship. With cattle returned to Glen Mór, the pressure was off and even the Bonxies calmed down. To be honest, there was little need for their belligerence now she was in the south. The cows do take care not to trample Bonxie nests, it was if they knew. But as before, both Bonxies and cattle were wary of men entering the Glen.

My growing up in Edinburgh might have been on another planet, many lifetimes ago. My late father is still an inspiration for me, and he would be proud of what we are achieving in his memory. As for my Mother, if she can face her past and come back, her little boy John would make a great playmate for Bennami. With guidance they could go on to great things out here.

So, all that remains is to ask you to think kindly of us out here at the Edge of the World, our *Ultima Thule*. With the help of Don and Josephine our eco-business will soon be up and running. In the meantime, if you arrive by yacht, kayak or whatever other sustainable means of transport you are welcome to come and share a cup of Mothan tea with us.

Blessed be.

Agatha.